I0699623

6-6-06

A NOVEL

ADAM CAGLEY

It wasn't a phase, *Mom!*

FAIR WARNING

Some of this stuff really screws with me, so I'd feel like a complete dick not at least giving you a heads up. If you couldn't tell from the cover, there's spiders in this book. Not literally! Oh, Jesus, sorry! I mean in the story. There's a whole bunch of spiders in the story! There's also a bit of bullying, some family drama shit, buckets of gore and a few neked people. So, you know, do with that what you will. At its core, this book is about looking back. The dual sides of the nostalgia coin. If that's a grim prospect for you, then I hope it's met with the same stupid, reckless courage we had at thirteen.

Alright, let's get to it.

CONTENTS

HEADFIRST FOR HALOS
JUNE 1, 2006

On my last day of eighth grade, before the big plunge into the murky depths of high school, the thoughtful and caring students of Buena Vista Junior High left a special gift tucked into the outside pocket of my backpack. I was used to it, of course, being the most popular boy in my grade. With my spiky dark hair, perky B-cup man-tits, baggy black shorts covered in unnecessary zippers and straps that did nothing, and my collection of graphic tees blazed with art from movies and bands only I was cool enough to correctly identify, what kid didn't want to be friends with the great Grady Burton? Why wouldn't my classmates want to do something special to thank me for all the memories? Just a little something to say, "Hey, man, looking forward to the next four years with you!" It was only natural.

The school year was unnecessarily complicated. I think it was a test to see which parents were actually paying attention and who couldn't be bothered. Our attendance records were more a reflection on them than us, after all. Achievements they could compare at PTA meetings or over the tops of aisles at the grocery store.

"Dylan only missed two days the whole last year!"

"Oh yeah? Well, *my Stephanie* didn't even miss a day when she had mono!"

Go ahead. Ask me how Stephanie got mono in the first place. And no, it wasn't me. But a guy in my assigned lunch period used to tell the story in all its sordid, salivary detail every chance he got.

6-6-06

Spring Break was an uncomfortable two and a half days off, bringing us back halfway through the Monday after Easter. Fall started the day before Thanksgiving and ended the following Tuesday for some reason. Winter Break was the week of Christmas to January 2nd. Every third Wednesday was a quarter day until you graduated from BV Junior to the big bad Buena Vista High, where it became a fully-fledged day off. Summer started for everyone, regardless of grade, on June 1st and ended July 5th. Looking back, I still have no idea why it was like that. Maybe they just liked to make sure I spent my August birthday in a classroom every year. Is June 1st even technically considered summer? Who else was gonna question it? The Super Intendant was the same guy who managed our one grocery store, for fuck's sake.

Buena Vista Junior High didn't even have proper halls, not like its big brother two blocks down the street. It was a collection of trailers dubbed "Mobile Classrooms." Even though they never moved an inch. The actual school *was* coming. Or so we had been told. Same as our parents before us and their parents before them. All they needed was the proper funding, but of course there were always more important matters that needed tending to first. The sunbaked prison on the edge of town needed a new wing. Three randomly selected intersections needed roundabouts. The high school needed a fresh mural of all three of the local Buena Vista folk heroes and fresh imported sod for the football field. But a new Junior High? Ain't nobody got money for that!

So, it sat for as long as anybody had known it, on the edge of a dirt lot that maybe one day might become something more substantial. A dozen rickety, splintery wooden rectangles with scorching metal ramps leading to steel doors hot enough to cook flesh medium-rare when the sun hit just right. Even the principal's office, sitting far enough from the others to not be bothered by them, was nothing more than a double-wide with aspirations. All surrounding the only actual "built" parts of the school, a brick-and-mortar cafeteria and a field of dying grass, complete with soccer goals that had no nets and those football goalpost things made out of cheap plywood.

All that to say: no one gave two shits what we did on the last day of school.

On any other regular day, the expanse between the trailers, cafeteria, the grass, and the dirt, at two in the afternoon, would've been dead quiet. Everyone would've been locked in their respective boxes, waiting with bated breath for the last bell to sound, half paying attention to whatever was being said at the head of the class. On the last day though, the entire lot buzzed with pubescent excitement. Kids too busy coming into their hormones to care about much else bounced and zipped from one end to the other. Hunting down last-minute phone numbers, collecting yearbook signatures, and making plans for the next few weeks of freedom.

The entire hundred-plus student body crackled with hyper anticipation, converging into their cliques. Under a tree, the Preppy Kids made battle plans to raid the mall twenty minutes outside of town. Whose mom would drive, where'd they'd go first, which part of the food court they'd hold up in. The Sporty Boys hung around the field, plotting their totally sick muscle growth in the weeks to come. Which, of course, would involve looting the new supplement store at that mall. Gotta get big to make the JV teams! Or whatever the fuck they were actually saying. Skate Dudes listed out every trick they wanted to learn and every piece of public property they wanted to do them on. Mostly the mall parking lot and its adjoining, defective fountain. The Weirdly Awkward Couples plotted out which movies were playing at the mall's recently renovated eight-screen Cinemark, on which days, and which times were best for sloppy make-out sessions. The Giant Fucking Nerds with their perfect grade point averages talked over the summer reading list. Which was entirely voluntary. Nobody would ever know if they read from the suggested list or not. They just needed a good excuse to go to—you guessed it—the mall. I very clearly remember toward the end of that school year, one of the Sporty Boys delivering an oral report entitled THE MALL: THE PLACE TO BE SEEN. I've never struggled more to hold in a laugh.

Even the handful of teachers, the interchangeable depression masks assigned to at least one grade, had big plans. Part-time jobs, mostly. Teaching services always felt like kind of a volunteer gig. Something the less-than-lucid adults rotated through until they couldn't take it anymore and bowed out. Eighth grade was Ms. Rainer. Her hair was always stuck in a crusted ponytail, sprayed and moussed until it was practically plastic. The majority of a pack of gum crammed into her mouth to cover what was really in her coffee thermos. She hid the scent well, but there was nothing she could do for her perpetually burgundy teeth and matching bloodshot eyes. Sitting at her desk in Trailer Three, under the grayed dry erase board, barely awake and making no plans at all, she definitely didn't care what we did anymore. While the rest of the annoying masses filled their social calendars, we had bigger matters at hand.

Mostly our Gameboys.

The wobbly wooden desks with their hollows for books, papers, and contraband sat in neat rows around us. Light poured in from the strangely barred windows in the back of the trailer, which we stayed away from at all costs. The sweet stink of freon from the wall unit mingled with the indestructible whiff of sweat that, by then, had soaked into the fibers of the grimy carpet under us. Rainer stared out the window next to us but paid no attention. As far as she was concerned, we weren't even there. And for the rest of the class, we might as well not have been. Our presence outside wasn't one they missed or needed. They made us aware of that every chance they got.

Any other day, we wouldn't have been allowed to sit anywhere near each other. Rainer kept an iron grip on her seating chart. We tried not to take it personally when the four of us were seated in opposite corners of the room. But at thirteen, it would've been impossible to interpret it any other way. Last Day was a free-for-all, though. When we came in that morning, knowing she wouldn't give a shit, we camped out in the far back corner. Two in back, two in front. Clothed in so much black, we actually managed to make the corner darker than it already was. Flickering tube lights be damned, we were creatures of the night. A series of see-through gray cables ran between us for the better part of the day, hovering above the floor and draped over chairs and desks.

The first cable, the first link in the chain, connected Ruben and Alex. Alexandra, if you're nasty. Or her parents. Who also had a huge fucking issue with her makeup and the streak of neon green in her hair, forcing her to apply her heavy eyeliner and clip in the Hot Topic faux-extension in the cafeteria bathroom every morning. Same with Ruben and his Sharpie-black nails. It's bad enough that their respective parents thought dragging them to Saint Andrew's at the asscrack of dawn every Sunday would somehow dampen their rising levels of angst, and not just stoke it. Girl with a boy's name and raccoon eyes. Whose only real fault, her most cardinal of sins, was having not seen *Mean Girls*. The irony wasn't lost on her. And a dude who wore a heavy black hoodie, no matter the weather, pulled up around his face to conceal the ridges and hills of acne already having its way with him. Of course they had no summer plans.

Alex served as the central hub. I mean, they were her link cables. She had enough for all of us, but only ever needed one more. It branched off and connected them to Jordan. A guy who, in all honesty, looked like our hired security with the way he was built. Taller than us, leaner than us, he was held back first in third grade and again in fifth. Eventually, his parents just stopped giving a shit. It was his older brother who made sure he came every day. Which is also where he got the black denim battle vest covered in patches for bands with names nobody could read. His long, greasy hair hung down into his eyes, ready to be cut whenever he felt like it, or his dad finally made good on the threats to do it in his sleep.

No cable linked me to them. Pokèmon, man. Hard pass. While their obsession followed them from the elementary years and showed no signs of slowing, I just couldn't do it anymore. Yeah, I played the first generation of games. Red, Blue, Green, Yellow. What child of the 90s didn't? Shit changes though, and anime creeped me out from the age of twelve onward. No idea why. Something about it and the people who obsessed over it made me feel like I needed a shower. Luckily, that's where they drew the line, my people. My chosen three. When we could talk my parents or Jordan's brother into making the pilgrimage to the mall with us, and we'd scurry into the musty sanctity of Hot Topic, they had no interest in the merch adorned with demon cat guys or glowing muscle bros. Thank God.

Instead, I rotated through the roster of other games in my black hardshell travel case that I knew we all had, trying to tantalize them into joining me in *Street Fighter* or *Tekken*. Their focus was fixed though, and their company was enough. A lone earbud dangled from each of our heads, threaded down our shirts, and connected to our legs. The iPod shuffle in Alex's pocket, the Zune in Ruben's, the off-brand SportPlayer Pro in Jordan's, and the black and red Special Edition in mine. No clue who U2 was at the time, but their iPod was cool as shit.

The hunt for creatures I didn't recognize called to them too strongly, so for the better part of the last three hours before the break to higher education, I honed my *Pro Skater* skills. Since I couldn't work on their real-life equivalent. Too top-heavy! Made the real thing real hard to do! Mom always said I'd grow into it but as the big 1-4 drew closer, I started to have some serious doubts. I tried to join the Skate Dude ranks at one point, before the four of us latched on to each other like symbiotes. Bam Margera was so seismically, effortlessly cool that I felt like all I needed was the right deck and shoes. But I was never gonna be him, no matter the gear. I was laughed out of the Walmart parking lot where the skaters gathered when I tried to ollie over a curb, ate shit and sent my board flying into an old man on a power scooter. Even if they had accepted me, Dad chucked the whole thing into the barbecue that very night.

We could see it, even then. The writing was clear on the walls. Lines were being drawn in the literal sand of the field and the dirt lots surrounding it. The clans forming now would carry over, continue, grow, and become even more exclusive. And none of them wanted us in the first place. Ruben knew Tolkien, but not enough to pass muster with the Giant Fucking Nerds. Jordan could've played football if he had any interest in organized sports. Alex gave zero shits about Paris Hilton and the cavalcade of pop stars. She tried to go out for softball once, but girls playing sports only got met with a host of unkind names and accusations. And if you told any of us we needed to like something, we immediately hated it. Birds of a weird-ass feather.

We had been in classes together on and off since kindergarten. Is that how it goes everywhere? You meet the kids you're gonna be stuck with until college while you're still trying to master not shitting your pants? I have no frame of reference. On the very first day of school, our parents told us all independently, "You're gonna meet the friends you'll have for the rest of your life today." The unofficial motto of Buena Vista schooling. For them, it was true. The adults who never left town or left and came back for some god forsaken reason. Dad poured glue on Mom's head in kindergarten, and they were married as soon as they had diplomas in their hands.

The four of us were no different. Alex puked on her desk in second grade after she ate a bad egg sandwich. I can still smell it. Ruben drank an entire bottle of hand soap on a dare. None of us knew what Poison Control was when the teachers had to call on his behalf. Jordan just kept bouncing back our way until we landed in a grade with the kid a full foot taller than us. I'd see them, they'd see me, but we didn't come together until The Changes in sixth grade. Up until then we had been wildly different kids. Our clothes actually had color! It was like one by one we were all bitten by a radioactive Gerard Way and one by one we all transformed, coming together like a pack of stray werewolves waiting for the moon to fill out. Our things were our things, and no one else could have them.

Except for my backpack, apparently.

The bell scared the everliving hell out of us, even with our lone earbuds turned up as loud as they were. Reclaimed from a firehouse after they . . . got . . . a better one? I don't know. I'm not really sure how that came to be. But every period end, every day's beginning and finale, was heralded by the same rolling, ear-shattering *CLAAAAAAAAANG!*

Alex nearly dropped her Gameboy.

"God damn it!" she hissed under her breath.

"Oh shit!" Jordan ducked like he was being shot at.

"Come on!" Ruben winced, tucking into himself as the bell threatened to cleave his skull in half.

I let the sound roll up my spine, rattling my nerves as badly as my fillings as I scowled at the ceiling. You'd think after three years, we would've been used to it. The only kids who actually looked forward to it were the ones who saw it like a starter's pistol. A call to freedom. We'd been conditioned otherwise. The bell meant more than the passage of time. It meant the return of everyone else.

The door to Trailer Three burst open. Rainer stood, holding on to her desk like she was afraid letting go would mean shooting up through the ceiling. The groups outside splintered to their assigned trailers, descending on them like a horde of locusts. They filled the classroom, attacking their desks with ravenous delight. Yearbooks were stowed. Backpacks were snatched up. Binders were clutched.

"Alright," Rainer said through a burp. "Have a good summer, enjoy your new school." She grabbed the giant tote bag she used as a purse, dropping what had to be a mostly empty thermos inside it. "You've all been great."

She was the first out the door. Let the piranha pick the meat from the cow's carcass. Why should she care? Next year she'd have a whole new group of little shits to babysit, and if our introductory day to her class was any indication, she was gonna have them put the room back together.

Some of the more excitable students practically chased her out, hitting the dirt at a sprint to the parental cars on the other side of the cafeteria or their walking routes home. Jordan and Ruben popped their link cables out.

"All the *Nightmares*?" I suggested without looking up, continuing a debate we'd been having all week.

We had plans to lock down, same as the other kids. Ours were just critically more important and infinitely cooler.

"Nah." Ruben shook his head as he tucked his Gameboy away. "Two sucks. All the Jasons?"

"Too many bad ones," Alex grimaced as she rolled the cables neatly and strapped them together with a rubber band. "The old black and whites?"

"What are we, ninety?" Jordan scoffed. "*Hellraiser!*"

We all nodded to ourselves. *Hellraiser* was an option. An appropriate one at that. The Unholy Holy Day was marked on our respective calendars. We didn't know whose house we'd assemble at yet, but the movies we chose to usher in 6-6-06 could only be picked once in our lifetimes. They had to be done so carefully, perfectly.

I killed my Gameboy, throwing the screen straight to black and stashed it away in my case.

"What about . . ." I started, staring at the floor like it had burst into flames around me.

Last I saw it, my backpack was on the floor directly under my desk. When I needed to stow my games and paraphernalia like my friends were doing, it was halfway out the door.

"Dude!" Alex cried, pointing behind me.

I turned just in time to see a couple of the Sporty Boys disappear with it.

"Oh, hell no!" Jordan was up and across the room before me.

I grabbed my game case, stashing it into the pocket of my baggy, jangly shorts as I followed him out.

"Hey!" I yelled after them like I thought it would help.

Alex and Ruben slung up their own packs and ran after us. The sun slapped me in the face like a wet towel, leaving me with an instant sheen of sweat. My eyes settled from the blinding glare onto Georgie Booker, sprinting straight to the heart of the field with my backpack dangling from his meaty hands. Georgie, that great big lump of a boy. Heavier than I was, but forgivable since he was a tackleback or defensive end or whatever the hell his contribution to the football team actually was. His stupid flattop, high-n-tight wannabe Marine haircut was a carbon copy of his dad's. Who, to my knowledge, was just a real big fan of *Full Metal Jacket.* His acne was worse than Ruben's, speckling his face in angry red mounds. Alex once suggested we spread a rumor that he was on steroids, and looking back, I absolutely agree. We fucking should've. Douchebag.

He had a good lead on Jordan, but couldn't match his easy, powerful strides. As he reached the center of the field, his lackeys converged. Filing in from all sides, a dozen Sporty Boys descended. As Jordan closed the gap, Georgie passed the ball. My pack flew from one dickhead, future domestic violence case to the next in a game of hot potato we weren't invited to. Already huffing and puffing, I joined the fray.

"Give it back, man, come on." Jordan tried to approach it diplomatically.

"Not yet!" Georgie cackled like we were supposed to be in on the joke.

I lunged from one asshole to the next, those guys that perpetually wore workout gear, regardless of whether they had practice that day or not. They just wanted everyone to know they were ath-e-letes. And, of course, I was way too slow. By the time I reached one, my pack was already over my head, soaring to the next person. Jordan had the reach, but they were too damn coordinated. Surprising, considering how heavy that pack was. Had to be twenty pounds of books, at least. Felt like it anyway. It tumbled over Jordan's head, sailed past his ribs, and blurred by me at every intersection.

Jordan kept his cool, but I could already feel it bubbling up inside me. The horrible, burning need to kick every single one of those braying hyenas in their underdeveloped nuts. They puffed out their cheeks, pointing and laughing at the sweaty tubby boy.

"We're gonna burn those tits off!" Georgie shouted at me.

"You first!" I fired back from the hip.

And the game came crashing to a halt as Alex and Ruben cautiously approached. Georgie's sadistic glee melted like ice in a microwave. My pack disappeared into the masses and a cold hush fell over them. They enclosed us, forming in around Jordan and I like a snare.

"Give it back," he pressed, his last warning.

"Or what, dumbass?" Georgie squared up with him. "You gonna get me held back too?"

"That's not how that works," Alex rolled her eyes from the edge of the scuffle.

"Who asked you, bitch?" he spat back venomously.

"Your mother!" I couldn't help it. I really couldn't.

"What'd you say to me?" Georgie snapped. The other meatheads egging him on with a chorus of Oh's and Ah's.

Jordan stepped up, glaring down at Georgie.

"You got the next four years to fuck with us," I appealed half-heartedly. "Pace yourself, spread it out a little."

"Please!" Ruben added earnestly from the back.

Thanks, dude.

Georgie glared around me to him. Ruben dropped his head and pulled his hoodie up around his face like an invisibility cloak.

"You think I'm gonna let you talk about my momma like that?" he growled at me. That most egregious of crimes.

"Do you even know who she is?" Alex dumped gas on the fire.

Rumor was, he didn't.

"I'll kick your ass too, you little slut!" Georgie bellowed over me.

He had no basis for calling her that. No one ever did. They just couldn't think of anything better, and she had heard it so many times since puberty struck that it lost all meaning.

"We just wanna go home." Jordan's fists slowly curled into mallet heads, the thick chain of his empty wallet dangling next to them.

I noticed. Georgie noticed. His whole crew noticed. They could take him if they all banded together, but who wants to start summer break with a black eye or a busted lip? Who wants to get the parents involved that quickly?

Alex and Ruben held their breath the same as me. The look in Jordan's eye said he'd eat every single last one of them alive, cross trainers and all. When in reality, I'm sure he was actually wondering if he had Hot Cheetos at home. Jordan looked like he knew his way around an ass kicking, but had never thrown a punch in his life. Didn't stop him for a second. He stood rock steady, as Georgie tried to will himself tougher, to be the badass he thought he was.

My guess is somewhere around here is when they snuck in my farewell gift, because I had no idea where my backpack had ended up. Until that flattopped toad grew the most devious smile and said:

"Alright! Fuck it. Where's his shit?"

Georgie turned to his nervous backup, waiting for my pack to produce itself. A kid in head-to-toe Reebok pulled it from behind his back and stepped forward with a grin matching our instigator's. Like the passing of an Olympic torch, he graciously accepted it and held it over his head.

"Tell you what, fatboy," Georgie gloated, jowls jiggling. "If you can catch me, you can have it! How 'bout that?"

"Seriously?" My eyebrow cocked.

"You need the exercise," he stabbed back.

On paper, I probably could've done it. But Georgie was used to running in bulk, for long stretches at a time, and I was not. If I didn't catch him in the first thirty seconds or so, he'd disappear with all my shit. I'd have to explain to Mom what happened to it, and she, inevitably, would want to talk to the principal, Rainer, and the parents of everyone involved. Giving everyone involved a massive headache in the process.

Jordan's hand darted in a flash, ripping the strap from Georgie's before he could do a damn thing about it. He held it tight, not yet handing it to me. Georgie staggered back a half step, unsure how to proceed with this latest offense. Jordan didn't break his eye line, even as Georgie's bounced from me to him, to my pack, to the ground, and back to start the cycle all over again.

"Whatever, *stupid,*" he finally sneered at Jordan, the best he could do before turning his attention back to me.

I watched his mind reel and flip, searching and scouring for some vaguely threatening parting message. He was coming up dry though, so instead, he kicked my backpack full of books as hard as he could. Like he was going for the touchgoal. As much as that had to sting, hitting all of my old textbooks, notebooks, and the couple of just-for-fun-books I had in there, I can guarantee it hurt me more. The pack slung up in Jordan's grip, flying back and straight into my balls. All the air shot from my lungs, and a searing throb spread up my stomach like I had been stabbed with a branding iron. I dropped to my knees, tears brimming around my eyes. Alex and Ruben ran in as Georgie and his friends flocked away, laughing so hard I thought they might piss themselves.

"You okay?" Ruben fretted.

"Not really," I groaned, trying to catch my breath.

"Where'd it hit?" Alex checked.

"Where do you think?" Ruben poked back at her.

Jordan dropped my pack and took a step after them.

"No," I coughed. "It's cool, dude."

"You sure?" He stopped.

"Yep." Slowly, I rose to my feet, grunting through the pain. "I'll live."

"We can go after them!" Jordan pushed hopefully.

"And do what?" Alex quizzed.

Jordan shrugged. He hadn't thought that far ahead yet.

"Let's just get out of here," I winced as I picked up my pack and slid my Gameboy case inside. "Before they decide to come back."

"Yes!" Ruben agreed. "That!"

At no point was it clear if I was going to vomit or full on shit my pants, but I slung my backpack over my shoulder and headed back across the field. Jordan racked in next to me, with Alex on my other side and Ruben attached to her hip.

"Thanks." I smacked Jordan on the shoulder.

"Got your back, man," he beamed proudly.

We fixed our respective earbuds, turned up our individual playlists, and stepped away from Junior High. The throbbing in my gut began to dull. MCR helped. They always did. The equal measures of pain and manic rage in Gerard's voice told me that he totally understood. He promised that he, too, was not okay. Dude had been through worse, after all. Everyone knew the story about how a certain terrorist attack changed his life perspective and set him on the course to achieving godhood. Everyone in my circle, at least. I never had to ask to know what they were listening to. If it wasn't the exact same, it was at least a band on a similar tree. Whatever we needed to score our first steps into the larger, meaner world Georgie felt so inclined to welcome us to.

We passed the classrooms and made our way toward the cafeteria. On the other side of it, beyond the dirt lot full of cars fighting each other to get out, the neighborhoods began. Like an oasis, small one-story houses surrounded by trees in a life-to-death gradient emerged. On the far side of the lot, dirt gave way to pavement and sidewalks. Short, squat chainlink fences enclosed the houses and their lawns that were either dried brown or on their way to it. Dogs barked every few houses, their muzzles pressed through the gaps in the fences, defending against our imagined threat. Ruben walked on the outside of us, practically in the gutter, for that exact reason. Alex kept her head forward, ignoring it. Jordan smiled at them like he was hoping to make friends. I just hoped the bigger ones wouldn't figure out they could jump the fence with enough motivation.

"*Evil Dead*?" Ruben picked up our debate, newly inspired.

"The first two are exactly the same," Alex protested.

"So?" Jordan and I questioned at the same time.

"*Army of Darkness*!" I argued.

"That movie rules!" he added.

"Practical effects," Ruben pointed out as Alex shook her head like she was dealing with a rabble of barely trained chimps.

We threaded our way through the (there's honestly no better way to put this) poorer side of Buena Vista. The neighborhoods that my parents always complained were "eye sores". Past them, on the other side of one of the town's three major intersections, across a small shopping plaza housing the Albertsons with its perpetually sticky floor and the McDonald's that served as the unofficial town square, were the "nicer" neighborhoods. Only a step up, really. We're not talking mansions here. Buena Vista maxed out at middle class, intermingling with lower middle class. The difference was in house height. Some of them grew —two stories, same square footage—while others stayed low to the ground. The lawns became a little more lively. Light green to stiff yellow. Chainlink was replaced with heavy rod iron with sharp barbs on their ends, like they were preparing to fend off the zombified end of days. Block walls peppered with illegible graffiti sealed the whole thing in.

We rounded the corner off of the main drag, wedging us between a row of cinder blocks and yet another fucking dirt lot. That one was special, though. Mostly out of convenience. Centrally located between us all, the abandoned forest green power box on the lot's edge was the practical equivalent of Alex's Gameboy. A hub for us. Once planned as a new tract of houses, that idea was thrown away before the ground had even been graded. It was where I caught lizards in my even younger years. Where Jordan's brother told him he could occasionally find discarded porno mags. Where Ruben went to look for scorpions. And where Alex hid when her dad told her that good girls don't play sports. Where we met to walk to school, and where we separated to go home. Jordan was the first to peel off as the sizzling metal cube drew closer.

"See you guys?" He always threw on a question mark like there was a chance we'd say no.

"Yeah," Ruben nodded.

"See you," Alex seconded.

"Thanks again, dude," I waved.

He threw a hand up over his shoulder as he waded into the thicket of dried brush and dug out hills, meant for jumping dirt bikes but seldom ever used. A block wall on the far side of the lot, an opening for a drainage ditch that was never properly installed, led into his one-story, dead lawn side of the equation. We never thought about it then, but looking back, its pretty damn clear that if it wasn't for his brother and the two jobs he worked, Jordan never would've been able to stay there. His parents were too fucking strung out to keep them from the clutches of the chainlink side of town on their own. One of life's great mysteries to a thirteen-year-old, though.

Alex, Ruben, and I continued along the cracked, uneven sidewalk to the entrance of our own neighborhood. A short walk in past a stop sign, the road split in two directions. To the left was a cul-de-sac, mostly two-story houses, mostly green lawns. To the right, the houses shrank until a left-hand turn banked away into the cluster beyond. Alex and Ruben waved as they turned away from me, following the other side of the neighborhood to the right.

"Later!" Alex chimed, the end in sight.

"You gonna be online?" Ruben asked.

"Almost always," I shrugged back.

"Sweet."

And we parted. The two of them walked together as I hung left. Alex was a few houses before the turn, but Ruben would have to follow it down another two blocks. I crossed to the other side and pressed on to the cul-de-sac's rounded end. A tag on the bulky neighborhood mailbox oozed black paint down its rusted side. From behind one of the houses, someone splashed into an above-ground pool. Garage doors hung open for absolutely no reason other than showing off their clutter and the few that had been converted into places to loudly, obnoxiously, *drunkenly*, watch football. Or whatever other sport our neighbors had to be furious at.

A tall fire hydrant sat centered of the curve, flanked by two nearly identical houses. One was garishly painted with a bright pink trim that pissed Dad off nearly every time he saw it.

"Who the hell paints a house that color?" he'd grumble like he had forgotten or hoped it might magically change.

A Raider Nation flag hung from the mounted pole near its front door. Its lawn was overgrown, full of crabgrass and dandelions. A van sat on flat tires next to its garage. Christmas lights hung from its roof year-round. The other house stood in direct opposition to it. The trim was a neat and tasteful hazel. The lawn was manicured with microscopic precision, spreading out like a sea of emerald from the bright rose bushes under its front bay window. Its sole car was parked in the garage, where I knew for a fact the Christmas lights were stored.

I cut up the lawn, a softer incline than the driveway. A fake rock to the right of the door held the only key I ever needed. The deadbolt was easy, but the handle gripped it for dear life, refusing to let go. There was a jiggle and a shake, a specific pattern required to get it out. After a beat, the key pulled free, and I returned it to its hiding place, peering over my shoulder to make sure no one was watching like I was trained to do. Why one key opened both locks, I will never know or understand. As a kid, it didn't matter, but now it just feels wildly unsafe. It had been that way for as long as I had lived in that house, though; for as long as I could remember.

A blast of AC swept the sweat from my face as I opened the door. The tiled entryway fed into the family room on the right, resting in the light of the bay window. Pristine white couches filled it. The ones nobody was allowed to sit on except for special occasions. Behind it was the small dining space where Mom stored the long wooden table she received as a wedding gift, that only saw action on important holidays. Easter, Thanksgiving, and Christmas. Nothing else carried the same weight.

Directly ahead, behind a small dividing wall, was the kitchen. Where the overwhelming majority of our meals were eaten. Its white countertops and matching cabinets constantly shined, never dull or dirty a day in their lives thanks to Mom's borderline OCD. To my left were the stairs, carpeted in blue and flanked by a lacquered wooden rail on one side. Beyond them, toward the back of the house, I could hear her voice. On the phone. Always on the phone.

"I think he just walked in, I gotta let you go."

I crossed into the living room and the couches I was actually allowed to sit on. The exact same color as the carpet, one sat against the wall while the other floated freely in a perfect L-shape in front of the two-ton big screen Dad brought home when I was still small enough to fit inside it. I think I spent the better part of a week pretending the box it came in was everything from the Batcave to the Millennium Falcon. Some jittery Daytime talking heads ranted wordlessly on the screen, muted and ignored.

"Alright, I will. Love you too," she added to the phone.

The clunky, cordless phone beeped as Mom hung up. She pushed herself up from the floating couch, not that it made much difference. When my growth spurt started the year before, I threatened to become taller than her. It was only a matter of time before I'd be looking down at the June Cleaver haircut she insisted on keeping.

"Mee-Moo?" I asked, pointing to the phone.

"Who else?" she chuckled.

Mom's mom called anywhere between five and seven thousand times per day. Usually with such interesting developments as a different mailman or a trash can left out on her street.

"How was the last day?" she asked excitedly as she came over to the kitchen counter and the phone's charging cradle.

"Fine," I grunted, my balls still aching a little.

"Any summer reading?"

I knew a list existed, just not what it contained. It was crumpled at the bottom of my pack somewhere. There was no way they'd make us read anything cool like King, or even Lemony Snicket, so I had zero reason to give a shit. Mom saw differently. When I didn't answer immediately, she knew I was holding out. Her eyebrow curled knowingly.

"I got it somewhere," I admitted to my shoes.

"That's what I thought," she smiled, victorious. "Well, drop everything in the cabinet. We'll get going on the reading list on Monday."

"*Alriiiiiight*," I whined as I made for the door directly next to the TV.

Throwing my shoulder into it, I told that stupid hunk of wood exactly how I felt about the summer reading list. It clunked dully into the washing machine waiting on the other side. I shuffled past, less than a yard, to the heavier door separating the house from the garage. Perfect darkness waited beyond it. For only a moment though, before the motion light in the ceiling kicked on and filled the garage with dull yellow.

Dad's cherry red Pontiac Aztek waited inches from the door. Bought new back in '01, its plastic shell was already fading to a worn gray from sun exposure. Towers and walls of boxes surrounded it, stacked neatly and according to a system and process I was oblivious to, labeled in Sharpie to designate CHRISTMAS, EASTER, HALLOWEEN, or OLD STUFF. Next to the door was a tall, beige metal cabinet. Once meant to hold tools or auto parts or something, I'm sure Dad had plans when he brought it home, beyond storing old school shit. My first day of first grade, though, Mom called dibs.

I shuffled carefully past the car. The plastic latch on the cabinet clicked and I gingerly opened the squealing door, careful not to hit the Aztek's front bumper. Inside, literally everything I'd ever needed to complete a grade sat in tenuous stacks from the floor up. A hook at the top waited for my backpack, along with the few others I'd had through the years. Buzz and Woody. Luke Skywalker. One that suggested I actually went to Hogwarts. The plain pumpkin orange I had been carrying the last three years waited to join them.

Next year, I promised myself, *I'm asking for straight black.*

I rested the soon-to-be-retired pack on the stacks of old books, binders and folders full of loose papers. Unzipping the big main pocket, I pulled the textbooks out first and surgically added them to the stack like a game of Useless Information Jenga. I stuffed my game case into my pocket and wedged my for-fun books under my arm. A paperback copy of Johnen Vasquez's *Johnny the Homicidal Maniac* that Mom didn't know I had, a hardcover of *'Salem's Lot* Jordan's brother let me borrow, and the fifth Harry Potter.

With the books secured awkwardly under my arm, I went to work sifting through the papers at the bottom of the pack. Folded haphazardly and squashed into oblivion was what I knew was the damned dreaded reading list. It went into a different pocket than my Gameboy, too unholy to touch the sacred case. The rest were pulled out, stretched flat against the cabinet door and stuffed into folders.

The small outside pocket never held much. Pencils, calculators, things I'd probably need new versions of next year anyway. They, too, needed to be stowed. I unzipped the pocket, ready to dump it all out by the handful, and there it was. My gift from Georgie Booker and his friends, on behalf of the kids I'd be stuck with for another four years. Crusted, flaking, dried out like it had never known moisture.

A perfectly cylindrical hunk of dog shit.

THE TASTE OF INK
JUNE 1, 2006

The house shook as I slammed the garage door, struggling to juggle the stack of books under my arm. Didn't mean to slam it, in all fairness, but I didn't really have a choice either. It could've been worse, I guess. It could've been fresh. But that's not really the point, is it?

They're only gonna get shittier, I spiraled.

The worst-case scenarios fluttered through my head, rolling out like a runaway film reel in the time it took me to walk back to the kitchen. Images of cliched locker stuffings, hallway ass kickings, even more backpack theft, threats, taunts, and general abuse simply because they could. Football. If Georgie and his boys joined the high school teams the way they constantly bragged they would, not a single solitary teacher would give the first flying fuck what they did to me or my friends. The last time Mom had to intervene, our old gargoyle of a principal indifferently croaked, "Well, has Grady tried being more like them?" All she could produce in response was an exasperated sigh. No, he hadn't. And he had no interest in doing so.

"What was that?" Mom asked from inside the kitchen as she started her dinner prep, snapping me out of my spiral.

"Georgie Booker!" I shouted like I was challenging him to a duel at high noon.

"Oh god," she groaned. "What'd he do this time?"

"The last bell!" I landed at the counter, dropping my books to punctuate my rage. "He stole my backpack and crammed a dog shit in it!"

"Language!" she snapped automatically.

"Sorry! A dog poop! He crammed a dog poop in the front pocket!"

Mom rubbed her eyes and sighed, already shifting into Problem Solving Mode.

"Alright, well, we were gonna have to get you a new bag next year anyway."

"Yeah . . ."

"I'll call his dad."

She was already heading for the phone, a tiger baring her fangs and flashing her claws.

"No!" I cut her off.

Technically speaking, I knew it wasn't Georgie who put it in there. He was too busy trying to pick a fight. His fault, regardless. A dull ache coiled below my bellybutton like it was trying to make a point. Literal insult to injury.

"He needs to know what his son did," she scolded.

"No, Mom, seriously! It's not gonna help."

Mom read the terror in my eyes as easily as one of her old Danielle Steele books. It registered immediately and she let off the throttle a little.

"Where was Ms. Rainer?" she quizzed.

Ms. Rainer, who lived in perpetual fear of my mother's wrath. The first and only time we were graded on a curve, she threatened to go all the way to the Super Intendant when the Georgie's of the world dragged me down from an A to a B-.

"She was already gone," I griped.

"She didn't see you all off?" Her eyes were wide with shock.

"No, she grabbed her thermos and ran!"

"Oh yeah, her *coffee*." Mom knew what was up.

"He'll just say he didn't do it, Mom," I pleaded. "Nobody saw it but us and them."

"Alex and all them?"

"Yeah," I looked away.

Mom shook her head as she stepped around me and went back to her work.

"She used to be such a sweet girl."

"I know." I had heard this all a billion times, from before I even knew Alex, war stories from the Elementary School PTA meetings.

"Do you remember that play she was in back in third grade? That one about the owl and the farm girl?"

"Yes," I seethed.

"Such a sweet girl," Mom tsked. "I wonder what happened there."

She traded pigtails and Disney dresses for colored streaks and eyeliner, that's what happened there.

"Alright," I conceded, grabbing my shit and heading for the stairs.

"Are you okay?" she called after me.

"I guess!"

I stomped up the stairs to really drive home my displeasure at the whole situation. My head low, watching my feet boom down on the blue carpet, I climbed. With the books back under my arm, I worked my Gameboy free from its pocket as I hit the top. Straight off the stairs was my bathroom, painted in bright yellow sunflowers, one of Mom's more recent projects. Off to the right was the sealed door to my room, neighboring her and Dad's. Fittingly, no light filled that side of the house. Yet the sun beat through the upstairs hall, shining defiantly through the door to Dad's office on the left.

His desk chair rolled back into the open door, his already-white mustache twitching inquisitively. The only hair on his head, the rest packed up and shipped off years before I was even born. Dad wasn't old. Well, he wasn't *that* old. He was just stressed 110 percent of the time. Like the adult world held nothing but problems that he alone had to solve, at the cost of every last strand he had. It made for a super appealing look at what was waiting for me if I ever had the nerve to grow up.

"What's with all the stomping?" he questioned.

"Georgie Booker's an asshole," I growled as I banked toward my door.

"Hey!"

"Sorry, Georgie Booker's a butthole."

"Thank you! What'd he do this time?"

"Put a dog poop in my backpack," I grunted as I fought with my doorknob.

"Little asshole," Dad muttered under his breath. "Well, you needed a new one anyway!"

With that, he slid back out of sight to his desk, back to his never-shrinking stack of customer invoices and billing statements, the matter settled.

I managed to work the door open with two fingers and kicked it in to my private little cave. My crypt, if I ever had my way. The walls were bright blue. Brighter than the carpet even. Buried under my collection of Hot Topic and comic book posters, a mural of generic sports people fought to remain relevant. Leftovers, holdouts from my pre-tween room renovation. I didn't have the heart to tell Mom I didn't want sports shit. She was too excited, and I was too agreeable. That went right out the window the second hormones started flowing and Amy Lee started giving me funny feelings. Every time I asked if I could redo my room in black over the last couple of years or so, Mom had the exact same response.

"No! Absolutely not!"

Part of me wondered if I'd be looking at Kinda Shaquille O'Neal dunking over Not Tony Hawk and Maybe Mark Maguire until college. The posters were a statement. Gerard, Ville Vallo, Shinoda and Chester, Krueger, Batman, Vader, Edward Scissorhands. They were my wallpaper.

No, Mom. This is me now.

The bed was even the same, for fuck's sake! Mostly. A bunk at one point, the top was gone now. I was the only one occupying it, why did I need the other half? Was there a sibling inbound that nobody knew or bothered telling me about? The baseball bat-shaped posts remained.

Directly over it, in a place of honor, perpetually on guard duty, Big Red himself was tacked to the wall. Ron Perlman's half-demon monster hunter, Hellboy. Over-sized Samaritan revolver dangling from his trench-coated hands, both burdened and unbothered as he brooded over his shoulder. The silver fist and sword emblem of the Bureau for Paranormal Research and Defense blazed brightly behind him. His edges were curled and worn, tack holes stretched and wide. My patron saint of monsters and demons. Mom hated that poster above all others. The rest she could pretend to ignore or dismiss as a phase, like Bionicle or my incredibly brief stint with a pogo stick, but something with such a sinful name took days of convincing before she'd let it into the house. It was the rosary hanging from his wrist that finally allowed him to pass.

Across from him, next to my closet door and under my window overlooking the backyard, sat a small box TV on a stand Dad bought off of a client. Complete with a DVD/VCR combo, my PS2, and the N64 I couldn't bring myself to get rid of. Stacks of movies, games, and books littered the floor around it. Almost all of which would've been approved of as little as Red if they had ever been inspected any closer than a passing glance following the weekly order to "clean up that pigsty."

A small desk was added at the start of sixth grade, tucked between my bed and the door, intended for homework and projects and the like. I used it primarily as a place to display action figures, the cheap iPod dock I snagged at a garage sale and the laptop Dad willed to me when he upgraded to a desktop. Who's lap it was meant to top, I still have no idea. The damn thing weighed fifteen pounds at least and its battery heated up like a nuclear reactor in mid-meltdown. And that was before I fired up any of the pirating sites I liked that made the hard drive work for its money. Mom kept a firm enough hand on the cable parental controls, but she wasn't hip to the internet quite yet. If I wanted blood and boobs and music I didn't need a credit card or a parent present to buy, there was only one way.

Everything in that room, everything that was my own and not lent to me or forced into the space, I bought myself. The toys, the posters, the books, most of the movies, a good amount of the games, I couldn't rightfully ask for them. For starters, my birthday and Christmas took too long, and Mom and Dad rarely had any clue what I was talking about for the most part. Some of the bigger, more expensive seasonal requests, I could give them pictures of and they did their best to accommodate. Everything else was on me, especially the things they wouldn't have been particularly stoked about. Summers going back the previous three or four years had been primarily used to teach me responsibility. Dad really wanted me to get a head start on the Real World he was so excited about. I'd go to work with him during the day, handing him tools as he serviced sinks and toilets, and everything after 4pm was mine. At the end of every week, he'd hand me two crisp twenties. Which I spent no sooner than they could make their way into my pocket.

'06 was the only exception.

I tossed my Gameboy onto the bed, bouncing the case toward the wall. My iPod took some finicking, but eventually I got it into the dock with a wedge of cardboard behind it to get the connection just right. My playlist took over the room, blanketing the walls in crackly, not quite clear sound. Distorted guitars and vocals aside, it was kind of a piece of shit. But hey! That's why it was twelve bucks and not a couple hundred.

"Turn it down!" Dad howled from the other end of the hall like a reflex.

The volume buttons stuck, but I tapped down as many times as I felt was reasonable.

Twice.

I pushed it twice.

"More!"

Two more.

"Keep going!"

I pounded the button down two more times. An acceptable level if I had super-powered hearing.

"Thank you!"

Up one.

I eased myself down in the creaky desk chair Mom and Dad gave me, and fired up my Three Mile Island laptop. The black screen woke up and turned blue. No Sleep Mode to speak of, it needed to reboot every time I opened it. The thin black remote for my TV sat right where I left it, next to my pillow on the bed. While I waited for the laptop to drag itself back to life, I spun around in the chair and clicked it on. The music would keep going, of course, I just needed something to look at other than the slowly dotting progress bar on the laptop's screen.

A list of important channel numbers was taped to the back of the remote, but I didn't need it. Most of it was committed to memory by now. MTV was too mainstream, too preppy. They only played the cool shit periodically, when the TRL crowd had gone to sleep. That early in the evening, my eyeballs would be assaulted, retinas burned to a crisp by bright colors and dudes with giant diamond chains. Cartoon Network was always a safe choice, if the old people cartoons were done for the day and the anime had fucked off. Still too early for that. If I clicked over to it, I'd more than likely be greeted by some voice actor screaming at the top of their lungs about their chi or whatever. G4 it was then. They almost always had something on that I could care about, or at least use for filler, so that's exactly where I went. Morgan Webb, the queen of cool, snarky gamer girls, was going over the pros of some new PlayStation title that I never got around to buying or asking for when the Windows chimes echoed behind me.

I spun back around as my desktop slowly emerged from its slumber. The clutter of icons and thumbnails made sense to me and me alone. Just like my walls, the bright mountain landscape background was littered with a shotgun blast of more important things. Even more games and entire folders of stolen media. I waited for the crawling infant Wi-Fi to connect while I dumped everything with the SCHOOL label on it straight into the trash. No point in keeping what Mom had a cabinet full of physical copies of. Each folder and file got a whispered "fuck you" as I dragged and dropped, sending them off to the digital abyss with a CLUNK. Good riddance.

With that dealt with and the little bars telling me I was connected, I got down to the real meat of the matter. Alex had AOL and Jordan used the internet at the library, but Ruben and I shared MSN Messenger. You know, like the cool kids did. I clicked it open, logged in, and set my status to Online. I didn't have to look very hard, didn't have to scroll far for the contact I needed. There was only one. Outside of the girl I met in a chat room who may or may not have been a man in a non-English-speaking part of the world, obviously. There was a message waiting from "her."

Heyyyy cuteman! How am schools is goooood?

Would've deleted and blocked her weeks ago, but that slight sliver of doubt told me to wait until I was absolutely positive. "She" wasn't who I was after, though. I had no time for imposters. DarthGray needed iNRuEnS66 to share in his righteous fury.

DUDE, I pounded into Ruben's inbox.

The response came within seconds.

YO

I hit the keys like it was their fault.

GEORGIE FUCKIN BOOKER

i know man messed up not cool, he replied, not nearly as upset as he should've been.

HE PUT A DOG SHIT IN MY BAG

wat??? when?

"Seriously, Ruben?"

when he was fuckin w/ us!!!!

His fingers worked fast, responding in a block of Emoticons to express his rage and disgust in equal measure. A legion of cartoon faces scowling or on the verge of vomiting. I couldn't agree more. I sent back a platoon of angry yellow faces, steam shooting out of their ears.

did u see wat brittany m posted?

He changed the subject so fast I can still feel the whiplash. Brittany Munser. One of three Brittanys in our class. One of five in the school. One of a thousand in town, probably. The only reason Ruben ever begged and negotiated for yearbook money from his parents was for the pictures of her. We didn't see it, frankly! Her bleach blonde hair and novice-level caking of makeup reminded us of the McDonalds we passed twice a day. But the pubescent heart wants what the pubescent heart wants, I suppose. I didn't see how Hello Kitty jpegs or Mandy Moore lyrics were supposed to help, but I followed his thread.

nah?

`go check,` he urged.

Opening a new browser window, I navigated to MySpace. She wouldn't have added me in a million years after my Change, but I got in under the wire back while I was still considered "normal." A handful of the popular master race were counted amongst my friends list, they just didn't remember that. I did my best not to interact with them, lest they rediscover the vermin hiding amongst them.

Pixelated flames curled up the edges of my page, hard won in a battle with HTML copy-pasting. I clicked to my greater friends list and scrolled. There weren't that many to go through. My Top Eight was really only a Top Three, padded out with band pages and an account dedicated to Jack Skellington. People like Brittany M stood out like road flares on asphalt. Bright and bubbly islands in my sea of despair and doom. Ashley Simpson assaulted my ears the second I clicked on her profile. I slid the laptop's volume down so quickly it's a miracle I didn't snap the dial off.

Nothing immediately stood out. Other than the neon pink of her wall and the showering cascade of sparkles that violated my screen. BRITNI'S CANDI CANE WONDER DREAM blazoned across the top of the page. Her most recent wall update was a blog post ranking the top ten best "sushis," and a fresh set of pictures. At least a dozen different versions of the same picture, with minuscule changes that only Ruben could've possibly noticed. Standing in front of a dirty bathroom mirror in a lime green zebra print tank top, her french fry hair blown out, a digital camera in one hand, and a peace sign with the other. Of course that was what Ruben was getting at. Not the list that ended with "breadless fish sticks."

I double-checked anyway.

`pics?`

`scroll!` he insisted.

I kept going. She had been incredibly busy since she got home, apparently. Unless she drafted the fish list ahead of time, which I could see. It probably took her weeks to compile and test that data. Regardless, she had found the time to post three times since school let out.

Must be nice getting picked up.

The blog update, taking *and* uploading the proto-selfies, and a regular status update on her wall.

"Paaaaartay @ Georgyyyys!! shhhh don't tell ;))))"

A horrible, Grinchy idea percolated. I couldn't see it exactly, but the vague brush strokes were there. Jordan's instincts were right.

This aggression will not stand, man.

Saw that movie on cable once.

Something needed to be done. If he hadn't caught up to those dickheads, they probably would've ran my backpack clean through to the next county. Or at least until they got bored of it, ditching it somewhere, *and then* filling it with shit. The Georgies of the world never stop, never fuck off, never even consider it. They had an idea of what they were going to be in high school, unaware that everyone starts over again at the bottom.

Where would that put us?

Their hierarchy would continue to rise all the same, if its tenuous balance wasn't shaken up, its ladder of dominance disrupted. A retaliatory strike was needed to show them that the lower class was not be trifled with, as only they could provide. A firm line in the sand. That's what Ruben was getting at, wasn't it? He saw it too? I was full of just enough stupid, youthful idealism to dress it up however I needed. We were the Rebel Alliance, flying down the trench to a two-meter exhaust port. The BPRD riding out to save the world from occult Nazis. The last stand of Men and Elves, waiting at the Black Gates.

Let this be the hour we draw swords together

Théoden, King of Rohan, plucked on Ruben's heartstrings, tempting his newly developed sense of justice. He fired back immediately.

NOW FOR WRATH! AND FOR RUIN!

A devious smile curled my lips. Images of Upper Deckers and burning bags left on the porch, stuffed generously by every dog in town, danced through my head like that Russel Crowe math guy movie. They didn't feel big enough, though. Not enough of a mission statement or declaration of rebellion for the next four years. Punishments unworthy of the crime. And they probably would've just gotten our asses kicked even harder, in all honesty. Whatever we did demanded perfection with only three real requirements. Something to say "Hey! We're not taking your shit anymore!", and nothing that would get us arrested, grounded or laughed out of town. That's where having a solid brain trust came in handy.

Rally the troops!

Ruben sent back a block of thumbs-up Emoticons, ready to ride into battle. And then one more message.

Just gotta ask my mom

Right, of course.

I changed out of my school clothes and into my slightly different all black clothes. Baggy cargo shorts, since I didn't know what I'd need for this mission. The heavy chain for my empty wallet, since it looked cool. And a promotional shirt from *Batman Begins*, to embody his spirit of vengeance.

Thudding down the stairs as quickly as I could, I jumped the last two. The tile slid out from under me, but I was too fired up to care. I caught myself on the rail just before eating shit.

"The hell are ya doin'?" Dad's head popped around the corner of the kitchen, not concerned so much as mildly annoyed.

"Cool if I go meet up with everyone?" I asked hopefully, a little out of breath.

"Who's everyone?" Mom appeared in the kitchen doorway too, asking like the answer would ever change.

"Ruben and Alex and Jordan and them." There was no "and them", but I always included it just to make Mom feel like maybe I had friends outside of those three.

Her eyebrows creased together.

"You know I don't like that Jordan boy, Grady Burton."

A chill shot through me like I had licked a nine volt. The first *and* last name. Only a step above using the middle in terms of severity. Terror Alert Orange.

"He's barely gonna be there!" I argued innocently.

"Where is there?" Dad quizzed, turning back into the kitchen.

"Ruben's house," I shrugged.

Mom's eyes narrowed, smelling the lie.

"And what will you be doing at Ruben's house?"

"I don't know." I shrugged again. "Watch a movie. Play games or something."

Mom locked antlers with me, staring me down and waiting for the cracks to show. I stood my ground in shaky high-tops, hoping I wouldn't.

"Home by the streetlights," she finally allowed.

"Sweet!"

I charged for the garage, blowing through the living room and sliding across the laundry machines. A gray button on the wall, just inside the door, brought the house to life. The garage shuddered, a motor ground, and the big white roll-up door lurched up. Walking wouldn't do, no. I needed speed. Haste. Urgency. My black BMX bike, tucked into the corner. Glowing in the light of the retreating sun as the door rose. I asked for it two Christmases ago and had yet to learn how to do anything on it beyond putting my feet on the tubular front pegs jutting out of the wheel. But that wasn't the point! It was my war horse. My thundering Johnny Blaze chopper, trailing fire down the driveway. There was still a scar on my elbow from the time I crashed it into a trash can.

"Helmeeeeet!" Mom sang through the house, still clear enough to hear over the growls and squeals of the rising door.

It was draped over my handlebars, hanging from its strap, waiting to be forgotten again. I threw it on out of necessity. Every time I rode off on anything, bike, blades, skateboard, or scooter, Mom watched through the front window to make sure I didn't get hit by a car coming down to the end of the cul-de-sac. Not sure how that would've prevented anything, but it wasn't worth questioning.

I threaded the bike carefully around the towers of boxes and the Aztek's fragile plastic bumpers to the top of the driveway. Stuffing my earbuds in as far as they could go, I turned them up equally high. Guitars burst in rhythm, waiting for drums to join them with a splash. Staring out at my dominion, I saddled up my steed. Vocals came together to rage into the chorus, and I pushed off. Wind brushed my face as the bike shot down to the asphalt, rocketing into battle. The speech was already being drafted in my head.

Who threw your gym clothes in a urinal, Jordan? Who dropped a pudding cup down the back of your shirt, Alex? Who, Ruben, chucked a football at your face to see if it would make the puss explode?

Not Georgie, actually. But people who hung out with him, and would more than likely also be at his house. It was the principle of the thing!

The street rose up to meet my tires. My feet took over the pedals and I kicked like hell, flying down the block. As soon as I was clear of the house and Mom's view, I unbuckled the helmet and slipped it back onto my handlebars. A legion of butterflies raged in my stomach. Pure, unadulterated freedom whipped through my squashed porcupine hair. Home and school were their own things, but this? I was in the wild. On my own. Where no one could tell me how fucking stupid my decisions were.

The neighborhood blurred by as my cheeks turned crimson. I let the bike coast for a couple yards, enough speed built up to carry me before my breath gave out. Up and down the neighborhood, open garages slowly filled for a night of noisemaking. At the mailbox, I pulled the bike in toward the curb, careful to take the turn in a position that wouldn't get me flattened by a wayward work truck or minivan. I slowed just enough to consider the stop sign at the entrance to the neighborhood. Nothing was coming, so I barreled through, pedaling across the two-lane blacktop to the lot.

My wheels slowed like they were rolling through wet cement as they hit the loose sand and gravel. BMX, not exactly built for off-roading. The exact reason why I never dared to attempt Jordan's makeshift jumps and dips. Looking ahead at them in the middle of the lot, the temptation was always there, just not the desire to explain to Mom why I had a face full of burs, stickers, and thorns. Or where my helmet was when it happened. The bike skidded and slid to a stop next to the power box.

I dismounted, leaning it on its pegs against the big green cube. Testing the temperature, I tapped the metal cautiously. It had soaked up enough heat over its few hours in the sun to still be hot enough to sear as shadows grew out of the neighborhood. I paced in circles, carving out a moat around its perimeter, an instinctual eye out for lizards.

It was gonna take a minute. I had left maybe a bit too hastily. Alex was the one with the phone. Her parents gave it to her for emergencies, though it was almost never used for that. Ruben and I had to wait until the start of freshman year, and Jordan couldn't afford one. So the order would go like this: once Ruben got the okay from his parents, he'd go to Alex. Alex would call Jordan's home line, hoping it hadn't been disconnected again. If she got the nod from her parents, she and Ruben would head over together. The seconds stretched into minutes and again into a fucking millennium. Luckily, I had just enough righteous anger surging through me.

I started picturing the best possible scenarios. Rolling up to Georgie's house, interrupting what undoubtedly was going to be a mono super-spreader event with a garden hose. Or maybe using Alex's phone to call the cops and tell them there was a meth lab in the garage. His dad wouldn't be home. Dudes like him always took advantage of a parent that worked evenings and nights. From the stories we heard in the cafeteria on a weekly basis, tonight would be no different.

As soon as the best-case options played through my head, the worst took over. Georgie and his friends waiting for us. The entirely of the kids we knew, laying bait to trap us in something worse. Maybe Georgie's dad gave him permission, maybe he knew. Maybe he would be there. As unlikely as that felt, it was never out of the realm of possibility. In which case, anything we did, even showing up, would get us in mountains of trouble. The fear of it started to seep in as Jordan hauled ass on his bike through the unfinished drainage ditch.

Not too late to turn back, I tested myself. *Maybe just let it go and actually rent a video or something.*

Jordan raced across the lot, fire in his eyes. He knew already. Ruben must've spilled the details. His speed, weaving around tumbleweeds and dead bushes, brought me right back in. What was going to happen could never be undone.

To WAAAAAR!

He hit his brakes and glided through the dirt. Not quite enough, his front tire thudded into the power box. That fit mother fucker wasn't even remotely out of breath.

"Dude!" he howled at me. "Are you serious? A shit in your backpack?"

"A shit," I nodded. "In my backpack."

Jordan threw his bike to the ground as he climbed off.

"Who does that tub of fucking lard think he is?" he growled.

"He thinks he's better than us! They all do!"

Jordan kicked at the dirt, all he could do to vent his own anger. A rock went sailing across the lot. Alex and Ruben rounded the corner, walking. She had changed too, black fishnets running down her arms. Ruben was outside, in the view of the general public, so his hood was still pulled up high around his face. Neither of them came in with the same heat Jordan had. They stopped at the intersection, checking both ways before strolling to the power box.

"He's disgusting," Alex said to me, her eyes dripping with sympathy like her eyeliner on a sweaty day. "I'm sorry."

"Question is," Ruben started evenly, not a hint of emotion in his voice, "what can we do about it?"

"There it is!" Jordan jumped.

The speech I had scripted flew out the window. When the moment came, I couldn't remember a word.

"It's not just me!" I blurted. "It's all of us!"

"Yeah . . ." Alex prompted me to go on.

"We gotta do something," I pressed. "Stand up to them! Put our feet down. Say, 'Fuck you! This is the line!'"

"Exactly!" Jordan agreed. "I've waited too damn long to get to high school just for people like Georgie fucking Booker to ruin it!"

I'm sure Jordan had a certain vision of high school for himself. A girlfriend, maybe a couple bands, definitely not getting bullied by a guy two years younger than him. Those years counted for a lot. We were lucky to have him.

"Should've let me go after them," he fumed.

"No," I shook my head. "We gotta be smart. Nothing that's gonna get the parents or the cops involved,"

"What could we do that's not just gonna make it worse?" Alex quizzed, nowhere near sold.

"I could make a rotten butter bomb and hide it in his house!" Jordan's head was in the right place.

"Nah." Ruben tested the top of the power box, same as I did. It was too hot for him too.

"It's not like a bomb-bomb!" Jordan corrected. "Just something you break and it smells like shit."

He was getting warmer.

"I don't know," Alex rained on the parade. "Do we really wanna put ourselves on their radar any more than we already are?"

"Isn't that what Carrie White would do?" I hadn't read that one yet, but it sounded right.

"Don't you dare invoke her name!" Alex took offense like I was talking about her mother.

"Stand for nothing, fall for everything," Ruben kicked at the dirt.

"What he said!" Jordan pointed an excited finger at him.

"Hamilton said that," he corrected.

"Who?" Jordan asked.

"The guy on the ten," Alex informed him.

We could've stood there debating it until our shared outrage calmed and we ended up dropping it and doing something else entirely, but Ruben was right. I got them back on track.

"How bad do you think it's gonna be once those preppy pieces of shit start playing in the high school stadium? And their egos get even fucking bigger!"

"They can get bigger?" Alex rolled her eyes.

"They'll find a way," Ruben agreed.

"He'll get a letterman jacket," I hypothesized morbidly. "The girls will start cheerleading—"

"They'll start doin' it!" Jordan interjected.

"That too!"

"I'm not helping you with that!" Alex crossed her arms.

"That's not what I'm saying!" I rebounded. "They're just gonna become even bigger assholes!"

"And if this is what makes them that way?" She was the only rational one of us. I'm sure there's something in there about girls maturing faster than our dumb asses.

"C'mon!" Jordan scoffed. "It's gonna happen anyway."

"At least this way they'll know we're not always gonna take it."

It felt like I was pleading for the future. Not just my mine, but theirs as well. I was thirteen, for fuck's sake. It would've felt like that if I was trying to talk them into watching *Dream Warriors* over *New Nightmare*. Everything did. Jordan and I had solid points, though.

"What do we do then?" Alex asked, dipping a toe.

"You see Britanny M's post?" Ruben checked.

"Dude, her again?" Jordan cringed.

"Georgie's having a party tonight," I clarified.

"That's perfect!"

"For what?" Alex asked again.

"Vengeance!" I roared to the heavens. "Justice!"

"Something!" Jordan didn't even care what it was, as long as it actually happened.

"You were close with the butter thing," Ruben nodded to him.

"We need something that stops the whole party," I got down to business. "Kill everyone's boners."

"Gross," Alex rolled her eyes.

"No, he's right," Jordan shook his head. "There'll be boners."

"What if we, like, snuck in and clogged all the toilets?" Ruben pitched.

"See, I was thinking of kicking in the door with a garden hose."

"I can get my hands on a fire extinguisher!" Of course Jordan could.

His brother's room was an armory of weird shit like that. Like he was collecting for both a very specific apocalypse and every single one imaginable, all at the same time. Military MRE's, samurai swords, Bowie knives, hand-crank radios, ninja stars, nearly all the R-rated movies we had been exposed to, fire extinguisher, fire . . .

"Fireworks!" Jordan shouted. "He's got a whole milk crate of them in his closet!"

"Do what with them, though?" Ruben perked up.

"We sneak up on the party," Jordan plotted. "We each take a side of the house. Set them off at the same time, watch them shit their pants!"

"Dude, that's good!" It was better than good. I fucking loved it.

"Not *in* the house though, right?" Alex needed to be sure our idea wasn't any stupider than it already sounded.

"No, no, just at it. In the windows, in the doors," Jordan explained.

Ruben found the glaring hole in that plan.

"How will they know it's us?"

Not that Alex cared.

"I'm still not sure they should."

There was one more thing in Jordan's brother's room that could help us. He and I realized it at the same time. It would solve both problems, a happy middle ground to satisfy everyone. Give the enemy a good idea of who did it while hiding the actual proof and leaving them second guessing the next time they decided to turn on us. If they thought we were some kind of subhuman monsters, then subhuman monsters was exactly what we would become.

"Would he care if we took them?" I asked.

A new excitement crackled through Ruben. A small grin curled Alex's lips, finally fully onboard. Jordan rolled it over for a moment.

"He's already gonna be pissed about the fireworks. But if we get them back before he gets off shift, he won't even know we took them," he concluded.

That was all we needed to make the single worst decision any of us would ever make.

No more than ten minutes later, having to walk for Ruben and Alex's sake, we were stepping up Jordan's front yard. A plot of dirt surrounding a tree that hadn't sprouted leaves in any of our lifetimes. The one-story box was in desperate need of literally anything. Its paint was peeling, shingles were missing. The metal security screen on his front door was rusted through from top to bottom. A windowpane near it was taped over with cardboard. His brother couldn't afford to fix everything and still keep the lights on. And honestly, who could've asked him to? The garage was open, not because his parents hung out in there like some of the others, but because it never closed. It couldn't. The chain was snapped, and the track was bent beyond reason from the time his dad rammed their old, mismatched Plymouth into it. There was nothing worth stealing in there for anyone in his house to care anyway.

Jordan wheeled his bike up and into the garage. Cobwebs and dirt covered every available surface outside of the Exxon-sized oil puddle on the concrete floor. I parked mine next to his as Alex and Ruben followed us up.

"It's cool, no one's home," he waved us in through the unlocked door.

Jordan disappeared into the dark inside. The stink of sweat and stale cigarette smoke wafted out as he stepped in. For obvious reasons, he didn't like hanging out there. He didn't even really like being there in general. It was much easier, and much more comfortable, for him to flee when the opportunity presented itself, taking whatever he needed with him. This required all hands on deck, though.

Jordan led us through the house. An unease rippled up my spine, like we were somewhere we weren't supposed to be. And not just because I had been explicitly forbidden, on more than one occasion, from coming in. Mom and Dad knew more about Jordan's parents than I ever would, and refused to reveal their reasoning. They wanted me nowhere near them. But that wasn't an issue. Jordan's parents were rarely there; off somewhere on what I could only guess now was a never-ending bender that only occasionally blew in to that port of call. Every single time Jordan and his brother busted their asses to get the place up to snuff, their parents would show up out of nowhere and destroy it all over again. At a certain point, I'm sure it became like building a house of cards in a wind tunnel, an exercise in frustrating futility.

The house was dead silent. Perfectly still, like it had been abandoned some time ago. I filed in after him with Alex behind me and Ruben behind her. The garage door led directly into the kitchen. Its sink was piled high with dishes, the counters covered in clutter. Newspapers, empty beer cans, unopened cases, and ashtrays were just about everywhere. Each one packed beyond capacity and on the verge of a carcinogenic avalanche. The living room beyond it was two mismatched armchairs, pocked with holes and tears over faded, dull upholstery. A twenty-year-old TV dug into carpet peppered with burns and unidentified stains. If Buena Vista had social workers capable of welfare checks, they never would've let Jordan stay there.

"Don't touch anything," he warned us. A precaution for our own safety, more than anything else.

No lights were on inside as he led us down the hall to the bedrooms. A grimy back window looked out onto a yard full of weeds, leading the way. Rusty free weights and a workout bench sat in the sea of overgrowth. Jordan carried on past the door that never opened, what had to be his parents' room. Past the room covered in posters for the full gamut of black metal and hardcore bands. Past a bathroom, fit for one and serving four. At the end of the hall, near the window to the backyard, was where we were headed.

The door was closed, but that wasn't going to stop Jordan. I doubt it ever had. He kicked it in like he owned the place. A heavy sheet hung over the window, in place of expensive curtains. His brother's doomsday bunker bedroom, a spectacle we didn't get to see often. Boxes and milk crates full of supplies, towers of CDs and movies, both in VHS and DVD. Unorganized boxes of comic books jutted out from under the twin mattress tucked into the corner. A massive stereo took up the entire wall under his window, flanked by subwoofers nearly as tall as me. And just as wide. It was like breaking into Scrooge McDuck's vault. Everything in it was pure gold.

The crown jewel, half of what we came to borrow, was up above us. Wrapping around the room, on all four walls from front to back were DIY wooden shelves. Boarded slats held up by anchor joints, lined with the heads and faces of horror's greats, cast in rubber, latex, and plastic. Jason's hockey mask, Freddy's deep-fried smirk, Leatherface's leather face, the Hanniger Miner's dark respirator, Max Schreck's rodent bloodsucker, Tim Curry's killer clown, and just as many that I couldn't recognize yet. Each on a crumbly Styrofoam display head, glaring down at us from every side.

"Start thinking about who you want." Jordan nodded up to them as he crossed to the closet.

The door was long gone, and a chin-up bar had been installed in its frame. Polyester work shirts hung on hangers, but everything else was piled on the floor. Jeans, Dockers, boxers, socks, T-shirts, all flowed out and into the room like an invasive species, slowly taking over the matted carpet. Jordan dove in, digging through the pile to what he knew was buried in the back.

Alex, Ruben, and I stood in the center of the room, the safest place, and perused our options. On some weird subconscious, telepathic level, they spoke to us. Each demanding their time to shine. Each requiring careful consideration like there was a chance we'd inherit their powers after putting them on. Or at least that's what I was hoping for.

Jordan emerged from the closet, dragging splintery crates through the clothes. Filled well past capacity, stuffed to the brim with every kind of firework the town council had deemed illegal. Bottle rockets, Roman candles, firecrackers, mortars, there was even a few road flares in there for some reason. He dragged the crates out and presented them with a game show flourish.

"Lady and gentlemen," he said. "Choose your weapons."

By the time we were locked and loaded, the sun was nearly gone, retreating into the desert to leave the streets to fend for themselves. Finding a way to inconspicuously carry a full bombardment's worth of fireworks took longer than actually acquiring them. We worked with what we had. Jordan dumped out his school pack and refilled it. Alex opted for an old plastic grocery bag she found in the kitchen. Ruben went with an unused gym duffle, forgotten in the corner of the living room. I filled the pillowcase Jordan's brother wasn't using. It felt the least intrusive.

To avoid suspicion, we tucked our chosen faces into the bags, waiting until the opportune moment to don them. Slinking back through the garage like the bugs and critters nesting in its shadows, we hit the driveway with our payload in hand. On foot was the smart option, silent and stealthy. We'd come in out of the night like wraiths, ready to feast on their Preppy, Sporty souls. The time it would take Ruben to go get his scooter and for Alex to get her skates was something we couldn't afford. It would only make it all take longer, be more obvious, give us more to manage when the time came to use the lighters we scavenged from around Jordan's house. It probably would've given us ample time to rethink it all too, maybe even change our minds.

Jordan and I led the way down to the sidewalk. Nervous energy picked up all four of us as we left the house behind. The clock was already ticking. The streetlights were already—

"Oh shit!" I yelled, not even to the next house yet.

"What?" Jordan stopped, expecting calamity.

"Can I use your phone?" I asked Alex.

"Your mom?" She handed it to me.

"I totally forgot." The whole endeavor could've ended right there and then.

I dialed the home phone and waited. And waited. And waited. It was a number they didn't recognize. Of course they weren't gonna answer right away. I had a walkie-talkie for just such occasions, a placeholder for the phone I was supposed to get next year. But the batteries had been dead for forever and I had no fucking clue where the thing was. Plus, it had a range of like twenty feet, so what use was it?

"Hello?" Dad answered suspiciously, like Al-Qaeda somehow found our home phone number.

My request came out in a rolling flow of panicked verbal diarrhea.

"Hey it's me I'm using Alex's phone I totally didn't notice the streetlights we're watching a movie is it cool if I stay a little longer?"

"Who?" Dad asked.

"Me!"

"Me who?"

"Grady!"

"Oh!" It clicked. "You better be on your way home. Your mother's about to call the National Guard."

He wasn't exaggerating that badly.

"We're watching a movie, can I have another . . ." I made a show of it, hoping he'd think I was checking the runtime or something. "Like hour?"

"Twenty minutes," Dad countered.

"Please!"

"Fifteen minutes."

"Forty-five! Please!"

"Twenty-five."

"There's like forty left in the movie, and I still have to ride home!"

The line went silent. He loved making me sweat in moments like this.

"I guess!" Dad sighed, relenting. "Forty! Don't stay for the credits."

"Thank you!" I didn't realize I had been holding my breath. "Be back then!"

I checked the time before handing Alex her phone back. We were gonna have to move quicker than I was used to.

"All good?" she asked.

"Let's go." My eyes narrowed, trying to regain some composure.

We jammed our earbuds in, hoisted our bags, and took off down the street, just below a jog. Georgie's house wasn't far. Just far enough to make the timing a little close for comfort. We needed to be quick, precise, a surgical strike. And hope nobody questioned what we were doing. Alex's bag was incredibly obvious. The tips of brightly colored recreational explosives poked out and through the thin brown plastic, just waiting for someone to ask about them. Garages were already occupied, music and nonsense TV spewing from their open doors. A hundred different dinners being made at once clouded the air around us, and yet all of them still smelled like some form of beef. Parents were home, but did they know where their kids were? Probably not, but we did.

We flew through the neighborhoods, moving in silence, our respective devices supplying motivation in the form of power chords. Down one street and up another, around corners and through intersections, cutting through backstreets and across empty lots where we could. Hopping some of the block walls dividing the neighborhoods up would've been the easy route, but Jordan was the only one of us who could clear one without having to put his payload down. Alex would've at least tried, but Ruben and I knew better. It'd take us longer to get up and over than it would to just walk around.

Every block gained, every street cleared, the temperature dropped by two degrees. The heat of the day died quickly, the spray of sweat on our foreheads chilled us like raw meat. The closer we got, the more real it became. For better or worse, there was no stopping it. Let it be known far and wide! The Weird Kids weren't about to take abuse or injustice lying down! The idea of it kept me locked in, when I should've turned back.

The last corner rounded spat us into the neighborhood directly behind Georgie's. Everyone knew where he lived, he wasn't hard to find. Everyone knew where everyone lived, nobody was. Horribly obnoxious pop-rap floated over the tops of the houses in front of his. Songs that said shit like "right hur" and "over thur". Add offending our ears to the list of crimes Georgie and his ilk were responsible for. Their standards were impossibly low. If it was on the radio, then it had to be good! How that didn't raise red flags and piss off his neighbors, I will never understand.

A small square of dirt separated the two blocks. Dead trees stood uselessly around the lot, dehydrated out of existence. The makings of some kind of rudimentary clubhouse sat in ruins at the base of one on the far side. Fencing off the neighborhood, a dividing wall crumbled in the middle where the builders had flat out given up. Rebar and jagged cinder block stabbed out of the unfinished edges. Georgie's neighborhood was tucked on the other side of it like an afterthought. Two and one-story houses mixed into a bizarro blend of my block and Jordan's. It had hopes at one point, dreams of being fit for human occupation, but its occupants didn't care to hear them. The last house in the cul-de-sac, right on the edge of the abandoned attempt at a wall, was the one we were after. A Gadsden flag flapped over the garage, broadcasting the fact that its owner never finished high school. Something the owner's son was just as unlikely to do. Jordan stopped, taking a knee and pulling us down to the dirt.

"Only hand signals from here on out," he coached, waving his hands around like he had seen in Navy Seal movies. It looked like a cross between American Sign Language and shadow puppets. We had no fucking clue what he was getting at.

"Got it," Ruben confirmed anyway.

I appreciated the effort.

"What's the plan?" Alex asked, down to business.

I surveyed the other side of the unfinished wall. From here, peering through its opening, I could see at least a half dozen bikes cluttering the otherwise empty driveway. A net meant for catching footballs stood in the dying lawn. Upstairs was completely dead and dark. The ground floor was where the action was. Every light was on, the bass from the music shook through the dirt like foreshocks. The house hugged close to its most-of-a-wall, leaving little room to move between them. Plenty of room on the other side, though, next to the neighboring house.

"Okay," I finally said. "You two go around the left." Alex and Jordan. "Jordan, take the backyard. Alex, stay on the side. Ruben?"

"Yessir!"

"Take the right side, and I'll hit the front. Find a window and set everything up. Try to get their attention, but, like, be creepy about it. Light everything up, and we'll meet back at the hole in the wall."

"Best we got?" Alex checked.

No. But nobody had any better ideas.

Jordan reached into his pack and pulled out the Miner's dark lenses and gas mask. It was chosen almost arbitrarily. He just reached up and grabbed it on the way out. I chose to believe it was more than that. The Miner, after all, was another symbol of vengeance and foreboding. Pretty sure he chose it just because of how cool it looked, though. He tugged and jerked it into place over his head and I'd never envied another human being more.

Jordan looked fucking awesome.

"Ready," he nodded. His voice muffled through the rubber and plastic.

We each donned our masks in turn. Pennywise for Alex, Orlok for Ruben, and Jason for me, our eyes lost behind theirs.

"Good luck and Godspeed," I mumbled through the hockey mask.

"God's not here tonight," Ruben added devilishly.

We scurried for the wall, bent over at the waist to avoid being seen. Not that there was anyone around to see us, but still. As we crossed through the gap, we split up. My head swam with a rush of nerves as Alex and Jordan peeled off to the narrow gap between the house and the wall, disappeared into the dark. Ruben darted across the lawn to the right, vanishing around the other side. And I cut straight up the driveway, keeping low and out of view of the front window and its bright strips of light.

I dropped the pillowcase under the wide pane of glass. Heavy curtains hung over it from the inside, not pulled close enough to block out nearly everything Georgie would've needed them to. His music vibrated up my legs as I crouched down to the bottom of the frame. I was absolutely right about the party. That living room was a teenage Saturnalia. Dozens of kids from across the cliques, the entirety of our class, it seemed, coupled off and locked in moist embraces. With all the tongues flying and wagging, trying to find homes in mouths other than their own, Georgie really should've laid out tarps. Or given everyone ponchos. The couch, the leather recliner in the corner, the floors, the base of the nearby stairs, it was all a splash zone. It reminded me of something out of a Romero flick. Legions of the brainless undead, feasting on faces.

Across the room, I could see into the kitchen. Cans of soda, bags of snacks, and even a couple of questionable bottles littered the counters. A sliding glass door led into his backyard. Through it, a dark form worked low to the ground, just out of its damning light. I repositioned, trying to get a better view. There had to be other windows somewhere, places for Alex and Ruben to also appear. Through Jason's eyeholes and the gaps in the curtains, it was impossible to tell for sure. I had to trust they were in position and getting ready to go. I had to assume Ruben was seeing what I was.

The party's host and leader, the ravenous hunger in charge, was wedged in the middle of the couch. Flanked by Sporty Boys, each with a Preppy girl in their arms. Her back was turned, but the outfit matched. Brittany M straddled Georgie's lap awkwardly, doing her best to duplicate things she'd only seen in movies or music videos and looking more like a chimpanzee trying to wrestle a panda bear.

I turned the pillowcase over. A half dozen mortars spilled out in a pile with long strands of cherry red firecrackers and just as many bottle rockets. Over me, the roof hung down the exact right amount. If I set the fireworks up directly under the window, they would explode no more than a few feet above it. So that's exactly what I did. Standing the mortars up across the length of the window with bottle rockets spaced in between them. The firecrackers were for the front door. I had that planned out in my head the second I saw them. Each strand got stretched out and laid flat right at its edge, ready for anyone who might run outside in the coming confusion.

Back across the living room, in the sliding glass door on the other side of the house, Jordan was in position. He stood ominously in the light of the kitchen, the Miner's mask darkening his face and reflecting just enough to look exactly how I hoped he would. If he had been standing there the way he was when Georgie's dad was home, there's no conceivable way he wouldn't have been shot on sight.

Jordan took a step closer to the door, waiting for someone to notice him. No one did. There wasn't even anybody on his side of the house, as far as I could tell. They were too busy being ground to death by their zippers, drowning in spit, choking on tongues. I stood up, ready to reveal myself. Jason's mask filled the space between the curtains, perfectly framed by them for maximum impact.

Not a single person saw me, except for Jordan. He shrugged across the house. Neither of us had any idea where Ruben and Alex ended up. Quality recon, that's what this expedition needed. Quality recon, and maybe that fire extinguisher he had pitched.

Jordan knocked on the door. Three knuckle-raps died in the music, unheard and unnoticed. I did the same on the window, practically punching it, only to get the same result. Judging by the vibrations rattling the hell out of the walls of the house, I was closer to the stereo than he was. There was no way we were gonna get their attention without help.

"Dude!" Alex cried as she came around the side of the garage, holding her mask halfway up her face. "There's no one in there!"

"In where?" I asked, full volume, no need to whisper.

"I don't know, it looked like a dining room or something. I couldn't see shit!"

"They're over here," I grumbled back.

She slid into the window next to me and gagged violently the second she saw the carnal spectacle inside.

"What the fuck is wrong with people?" she heaved.

"Dude!" Ruben spat through his mask as he stepped out onto the lawn. "Where is everybody? Think I was looking at a bathroom."

I pointed to the window. He looked in and his blood combusted like jet fuel.

"Him! *Seriously?*"

"Sorry, man," I offered.

"She can do so much better!"

"Can she, though?" Alex argued, revolted.

Jordan was gone, no longer in the back door. Part of me hoped he was about to reappear inside the house, skulking out of a closet or from the hall, ready to strike. Instead, he followed Alex's path back around to us.

"Okay, what the hell? Was there a gas leak or something?"

"They can't hear us," I explained.

"What do we do?" Ruben pressed urgently. "We gotta do *something*!"

Brittany M was his final, final straw.

I pivoted the best I could.

"Go get your shit," I told them. "We'll set it all up here and go for the door."

"Ohhhh that's good!" Jordan agreed. "One big bang instead of four small ones!"

He raced off first, back to retrieve his fireworks. Alex pulled her mask down and chased after him while Ruben stomped off to the other side of the house. Jordan's shape darted into the backyard, hunched over to collect what he needed. I took a step back and surveyed my explosive distribution. It was perfectly even under the window, but there was room to grow. We could go back into the yard, over to the corner Ruben turned behind, across to the door. It was a blessing in disguise. This plan was better. Make them think the whole front of the house was about to come down. Noise and light, and nothing more.

Jordan and Alex came running back, their bags hastily reloaded in their arms.

"Alright, let's spread them out here," I waved at all the empty space around my setup as Ruben returned with his repurposed gym bag.

"On it," he nodded.

They went to work redistributing their supplies in rows behind mine, stretching from the door clear to the corner. More mortars. More bottle rockets. Enough firecrackers to blow the door off. Jordan handed Alex his lighter.

"I'll get the door," he hissed as he slunk off to it, stepping carefully around the piles and lines.

"Last chance," I said. "We doing this?"

It only felt right to give them one last out. Cleaning it all up again felt like a bigger pain in the ass than lighting them all, but the offer was there, regardless. Ruben responded by flicking his flame to life and kneeling to the fuses.

"Hell yeah!" I beamed under my mask.

One by one, we lit them, except for Alex, who lit two at a time. A sizzling, crackling inferno flared to life in front of Georgie's house. Their sour stink flooded our noses and stung our eyes, even through the masks.

BOOM! BOOM! BOOM!

Jordan pounded on the door.

"POLICE!" he roared through it, dropping his voice as low as he could. "POLICE! COME OUT NOW!"

BOOM! BOOM! BOOM!

The music inside stopped as we retreated to the edge of the lawn and held our collective breath. A hushed murmur of excited, scared voices replaced it as bodies scrambled. I can't say for the others, but under my mask, I was grinning ear to ear. The door creaked open as the fuses crept toward home. Georgie's big, stupid face poked out. When there was no badge and gun to greet him, he threw open the door in a huff and stormed out.

A vampire, a miner, a clown, and a goalie stood on the sidewalk, middle fingers raised high.

"What the fuck?" Georgie puzzled, confused as all hell.

The sounds and smells smacked him across his jelly doughnut face. He gasped in sheer terror at the amount of fireworks assembled in front of his house. A high-pitched squeak of a noise like the exhale of a dog toy. If I could've lived in that moment for the rest of the summer, I would've been perfectly happy. If we could've stayed right there, the four of us united and watching his mind melt at the villains waiting for him and the small blaze they set, seeing him scramble to try and stomp them out, yowling like a cat in heat, absolutely nothing else would've mattered. We would've had nowhere to go but up.

It was a simple plan.

But simple plans are so rarely perfect.

The firecrackers went first, exploding around Georgie's feet. He danced around them and fell back into the house while paper and powder popped and flashed after him. The bottle rockets went next, adding their whistles to the chorus of blasts. They veered in every direction imaginable. Flying up into the overhanging roof, into the open front door, and across the lawn at us. We scattered as they detonated, laughing maniacally in the mayhem we had created on the lawn, in the street, in the house. Screams bellowed out from inside as a smoke screen started to fill the cul-de-sac, and everything went sideways.

Namely, the mortars.

They started to tip as rockets and crackers popped around them. More than a few fell directly onto their sides. The chorus deepened as they launched themselves. In retrospect, we probably should've done our due diligence and figured out what exactly those mortars would launch. Not a single one of us thought to check if they were the big ones. The massive, professional-grade sky flowers.

Georgie's house turned into a war zone. Thundering blasts shook the front of his house as sparks of green, blue, and red covered it. Some hit the roof and showered down, others veered off to the door, and the real unlucky ones rocketed straight into the front window. Deep, gut-punching concussions shattered the glass, blowing it back into the living room. My smile finally died. More fireworks followed in, exploding across Georgie's living room, bouncing off walls and the ceiling and landing on the couch. Bodies thumped down and tripped over each other as the screams only got worse. From somewhere inside, glass continued to break. The curtains caught first, heavy gusts of smoke rising out of them. Boners killed, their party truly shot to shit, Georgie and his guests retreated. They flooded out into the driveway like rats off a sinking ship as the couch cushions started to smolder.

"Run!" Jordan yelled.

He was already gone, sprinting for the break in the wall. In a panic, I darted after him, pumping my arms and pounding my feet as fast as I could. Alex flew up behind me with Ruben close on her heels. We ran back across the lot and into the next neighborhood, not looking back at the biggest fucking mistake of our lives.

I pulled Jason's mask off, tears distorting my eyes and vomit bubbling up my throat. Was that a fire truck I heard behind us? Or just my wheezing breath as I ran harder and faster than I ever had? No one chased us, not that I saw at least. The few times I was brave enough to look back, all I saw was Alex and Ruben. Masks off, their faces shining. We couldn't stop, couldn't look back, couldn't even slow. We ran like our lives depended on it.

Back the way we came, we retraced our steps in half the time. The garages full of adults, now well into their cases of beer and bottles of whatever they felt fit to supplement, stared at us curiously. None of them moved to investigate, though. Nothing to see here. Until phones started ringing, their rolling rattles and dancing chimes drifting out at us as we ran. I would've put the mask back on if there was any chance I could run and breathe through it at the same time. No idea how Jordan did it so easily, like he had been breathing through rubber since birth, occasionally looking back over his shoulder to make sure we were all still there. The curious eyes watching us quickly became accusatory, like they knew something about us they shouldn't have.

Up his driveway and through the garage, Jordan barreled through the door like SWAT was pulling up behind us. I caught it as soon as it touched the jamb and flew through. Ruben held it for Alex as they followed. My breath caught in my throat, coming through in ragged, panicked rasps. The house was as dark as we left it, his brother still not home, parents still MIA. Thank god for small favors.

Jordan dropped to his hands and knees in the living room, scampering to the broken window. His eyes were wild, but his breath was frustratingly even. He peeled back the cardboard and looked out. As we landed next to him, getting low to the floor too, I braced for impact. They had to be following us. There was no way they weren't. A mob was coming, helicopters and sirens would follow. The door would fly in, shattering into slivers against the wall. Georgie and his friends would drag us out, string us up from the dead tree in the yard, and beat us with sticks like the least colorful piñatas. All for an army of news cameras and a state's worth of police to revel in. Not to mention what Mom would do if I ever made it home. We rode out to strike, both preemptive and retaliatory. Now we were cornered, waiting for the enemy to devour us. Those shuffling Romero masses that had been all too content eating each other's faces until we disrupted them and turned their attention on us.

But no one came. No sirens, no mob, no Georgie. The only thing we heard was a house a few doors down, its garage occupants yelling at the TV and chucking beer bottles out into the street.

"Where are they?" Alex finally asked, after the ten or twelve most tense minutes of our lives.

"They're not coming." Jordan sighed as he stood, relieved.

"What if the whole house is burning down?" Ruben had to ask.

We were all thinking it.

"The whole house wouldn't burn down." Except Jordan, apparently. "There weren't nearly enough fireworks for that."

"Then—wait." It wasn't making sense to Ruben either. "The curtains. The couch!"

"They burned a little, yeah, but I don't think the whole thing would've gone up. It's not like a brush fire," Jordan said a little too calmly.

"What did we run all the way here for then?" I questioned, more aggravated that I had to than anything else.

"Did you wanna get your ass kicked?" Jordan chuckled, nervously. "There were a lot of fucking people there!"

It was a fair point.

"The window is our real problem," he added.

"Oh shit." My heart sputtered.

"We're so screwed," Alex moaned.

"All things considered, I'd still call that a pretty successful raid!" Jordan grinned.

"How?" I argued, maybe a little more forcefully than I meant to. "We were supposed to scare them, not blow the house up!"

"My dad's gonna lose his shit." Alex rubbed her eyes like a migraine she was too young for had set in, so hard that when she pulled her hand away, she had two black raccoon patches of eyeliner and mascara around them.

"I might actually get sent to Catholic school this time," Ruben resigned, his face aimed at the floor.

"Alright." Jordan started thinking. "Let's all just go home. Go home, act like nothing happened."

"How is that gonna help?" Alex bit.

"We were just hanging out," he explained. "Nothing else! You could say I wasn't even there if that helps!"

It probably would've helped, actually. He was well aware of what most parents thought of him, but without an alibi, the blame had the potential of falling solely on him. And that wasn't cool.

"No," I shook my head. "You were there. Just not the whole time, you showed up late."

Jordan nodded, accepting it.

"But not too late!" he pointed out.

"Right," I caught. "Not too late."

"And when Georgie's dad starts making calls?" Alex pressed. "You know he will."

"Georgie saw us, but he didn't really get a good look, did he?" Was there even time for our true identities to register before pandemonium descended? Probably. But I had to run with it.

Ruben shrugged.

"Don't think so," Alex shook her head.

"And nobody else saw us," Jordan hoped. "We got out of there before they could. He'll live in fear of us, but they've got nothing to prove we were there! Nobody knew my brother had those fireworks! Shit, I wasn't even supposed to."

"What are they gonna do, dust them for prints?" I asked for my own reassurance.

"And since when is owning a mask a crime?" Ruben started to soften. "They make hundreds of those things."

"Exactly!" Jordan turned away from us confidently. "They've got nothing on us!"

He started collecting the masks we dropped in our panic, before they could suffer any more than they already had. Show pieces that saw more action in the last half hour or so than they had since they were cast.

"Alright," I laid it out. "We were at Alex's house. We watched a couple movies, her mom ordered pizza or something, we went home, that's it."

"But what if someone asks my mom?" she drilled.

"Say we were at my place," Ruben suggested. "I'll just say we were in my room the whole time, and I made an oven pizza. My parents won't even know."

We had been to Ruben's house dozens of times, and not once had his parents even really said hello to us. I think they were under the impression that we were imaginary.

I sat with it for a second and nodded. "That'll work."

"Why does no one ever want to hang out here?" Jordan snarked as he returned with his arms full of rubber faces. "What movies did we watch?"

"Does it matter?" Alex rolled her eyes.

"For continuity's sake," Ruben suggested.

"Nothing with those characters in it!" I thrust a finger at the masks. I didn't think anyone would make the connection. It just felt safer not to tempt fate and invoke their names. Though they probably would've been a little proud of us.

"*Howl's Moving Castle,*" Alex poked.

"Fuck you," I cringed. "*Blade* one and two?"

"My brother just got *Hostel*!" Jordan argued

Ruben perked up.

"*Saw* one and two!"

"Those movies are gross." Alex was never a really fan of blood by the gallon. "Something old?"

"*American Werewolf* and *The Howling*?" Jordan suggested.

That sounded even cooler to me.

"Save those for the sixth!"

"Keanu *Dracula* and *Interview with a Vampire*," was Alex's counter.

"Do you want them to think we were fucking the whole time?" Jordan was right. Those movies were best watched independently. In our own rooms. In the middle of the night. With no one around. And the volume down low.

"Let's just go with the torture," I decided. "No one's gonna poke holes."

"*Fiiiiine*," Alex groaned. "If we must."

This felt good. A heist crew with a solid alibi, like there was a chance to get away with it if it all held together. A slim chance, practically microscopic even, but a chance all the same.

"Time, Alex?" I asked.

If I was late, it wouldn't matter what story we concocted or what we talked ourselves into. I would've been screwed, regardless. She checked her phone.

"You got like three minutes."

"Fuck!" I ran for the garage, charging through the door.

The shape of my bike wasn't hard to discern from Jordan's in the dark. The helmet on the handlebars gave it away every time. I threw my legs over and kicked through his garage, hitting the driveway in a burst of speed.

The asphalt was rougher in his neighborhood, rattling up my handlebars as I hauled ass for the drainage ditch. Cutting across the lot at night was an accident waiting to happen, an injury in every rock, snake hole, and dug out jump. For any of our lies to matter, though, I had to be home to tell them. Anything past my assigned time would only destroy whatever credibility I needed. Mom didn't fuck around.

"Trust takes a lifetime to build and a moment to ruin," she used to say.

No doubt something Mee-Moo had forced upon her every chance she got when Mom was my age. I needed all the Good Boy points I could get my hands on.

Pedaling like the devil himself was after me, I hit the dirt and sand. My tires slowed through it, and I eased down into the seat. Keeping my eyes focused and my legs moving, I wove around the lot's obstacle course, more or less just hoping for the best. Around sticker bushes. Over gravel and broken glass. Past rocks and wide around Jordan's jumps. Lizards and bugs scattered and fled ahead of me.

From the edge of the lot, I could see both ends of the street for a solid few yards. No headlights broke up its coarse black, so I didn't slow as I hit the street again. I stood in my seat and pedaled through the intersection, hitting the turn at speed. If a car had been coming at that exact moment, I would've gone clean through the windshield and into their backseat. But my luck held. The neighborhood was clear. More importantly, there were no cop cars at the end of the cul-de-sac, waiting with their cuffs at the ready. That felt like a small miracle all on its own. Maybe Jordan was right. Maybe they had no idea. It did nothing to ease the anxiety eating a hole through my chest.

I didn't stop pushing until I hit the bump up to my own driveway, coasting into the open garage. The automatic light kicked on as I rolled in and gripped the brakes for dear life. I dropped the kickstand and left the bike where I got it, taking a second I knew I didn't have to try and catch my breath. Work some of the abject terror from my head and heart. I hit the button to at least signal that I was back. They'd hear the garage door growl and clank from one end of the house to the other. Call off the search, Grady's home.

Nothing to see here.

I was covered in sweat, but that was nothing new. My shirt stuck to me, and a small swamp was growing between my Swedish Fish thighs as I grabbed the handle and opened the door into the laundry room. I spared a glance over to the cabinet as I went in. The final resting place of that shitty backpack. Jordan was right about another thing: If Georgie at all processed what he saw, made the connection between the four monsters in front of his house and the four kids he liked to use as playthings, he was gonna think twice before doing something like that again.

I stepped through into the living room to find Mom and Dad waiting on the couch. Whatever they were watching droned on at a low volume. He wasn't gonna want to mute it entirely, he'd have no idea what was happening when they jumped back in.

"Cutting it a little close, aren't we?" Mom smirked.

"Sorry," I panted. "The movie! There's another one coming out, so we were talking about rumors and theories and all that."

"What'd you watch?" Dad asked.

"*Saw,*" I gasped. "One and two."

Mom's nose bunched like a raw sewage line burst in the kitchen.

"I don't like those movies, Grady."

"I know," I said guiltily to the floor. "They're just movies."

Mom scanned me, studied me, searched for any sign of weakness or cracks in the facade. That gaze was too much to take sometimes, especially when I had actually done something wrong. It was last year's "Who put *Lusty Busty 2* on our Pay Per View?" debacle all over again. Her eyes narrowed on me, pinching into a suspicious squint. I flapped my arms in a pathetic shrug, like a penguin begging a dragon not to notice it shot fireworks into his classmate's house.

"Okay." Mom released me, sinking back into her seat and turning the volume up.

I fled for the stairs.

"You eat anything?" she threw after me.

"Oven!" I blurted as I started to climb.

"You ate an oven?" Dad asked, on the off-chance that was actually what I meant to say.

"Oven pizza!"

I hopped up the stairs, trying to keep my retreat casual but quick. When I hit the landing, I darted into my room. The light switch on the other side of the door would've woken up the thin black standing lamp buried in the far corner, but I couldn't be seen, didn't want to be. I wished for the billionth time that I owned some sort of billowy cloak to pull up around me and camouflage into the dark corners.

My laptop was left open and on, but it didn't care what I wanted it to do. It had powered down again. I dropped into my chair and held down the power button. I swear, it took even longer now that I needed it. Really milking its boot-up cycle to make me sweat. I pulled my iPod from my pocket and married it into the dock, its ghost-white screen spewing a square of light onto my desk as I let Shuffle pick for me.

The progress bar ticked along, trying to see just how fast it could make my foot tap and leg bounce. One block at a time, it marched across the screen. The TV called my name, but I couldn't do it. Not yet. I even turned the music down just a little bit lower than Dad would've requested. I couldn't have distractions. Trying to will the laptop to life required too much focus.

I've never been so glad to hear those welcome chimes. As soon as my desktop loaded, I attacked, mashing the trackpad buttons on the Messenger icon. Did iNRuEnS66 make it? What happened after I fled back home? Was the lie off and running on multiple fronts? Had he already broken and spilled his guts? I didn't think he would, but he also reminded Rainer that we had homework due once and no one ever really forgot about it.

He wasn't online yet.

My fingers flashed across the keyboard anyway.

Anything?

It felt like an eternity before the dot next to his name turned green. Long enough for me to ask every search engine I knew of how old you have to be to have a heart attack. When he finally responded, it took even longer. Like he was writing an essay on just how fucked we were. That his parents found out. That

Georgie called his dad and the two of them were on the war path, ready to scorch the rest of our lives to ash. Exactly how I imagined their curtains and cushions, despite what Jordan said. A few seconds of waiting stretched into a lifetime before his response finally came through.

    All good so far

KILLING LONELINESS
JUNE 2, 2006

"GRADY HENRY BURTON!" Mom's voice shook the foundations of the house, hitting every last syllable with explosive force.

I shot up from my bed the way I imagine firefighters probably do when the bell goes off. Breath left my chest like I had been kicked in the gut and my heartbeat redlined, all before 9AM. The middle name. Mom used the middle name. Something had gone horribly awry.

Footsteps rumbled up the stairs like a stampede. Dad was following her. They were coming to bury me, and I was still in my god damn Beetlejuice pajama pants. My head snapped to the door, eyes wide like a train was about to barrel through it. For the briefest moment, I contemplated diving through the window, landing with a roll in the backyard below, flying over the wall, hijacking a car, and driving until I hit the border.

They'll never find me down in Jalisco.

Who was I kidding? I could've fled to a different fucking planet and Mom still would've been there waiting for me.

The door flew in with gale force and the hurricane followed. Mom's eyes were as wild as mine, laced with glowing fury under arched eyebrows. She cut across the room in a single step, towering over me before I could give retreat another thought.

"Did you shoot fireworks at George Booker's house?" she snarled.

"What? No!"

We're fucked.

"Brittany Munser's mother said she called her crying last night because you and your friends shot fireworks at them and set George's living room on fire!"

The PTA phone tree was alive and well.

"We didn't!"

Keep it together.

"She said she saw you running away!"

"No, she didn't! We were wearing masks!"

God damn it, Grady.

In my defense, that look Mom had, that fiery Penance Stare, could've gotten Saddam himself to spill his secrets. And I had been awake for like thirty seconds! Cut me some slack. I went from the warm and tender embrace of a Kate Beckinsale dream, straight to Advanced Interrogation Tactics.

"So, you did!"

Dad sighed from the doorway, his day officially shot.

"Where did you even get fireworks?" He was focused on the important shit.

"We didn't have fireworks! We watched movies!" Too little, too late.

"You just said you wore masks!" Mom countered.

"We did! While we . . . watched . . . movies." Nailed it.

"You wore masks while watching movies?" She bought it as much as I did.

"Yeah! It's a thing we do. It's fun."

"And you didn't take them over to George Booker's house and shoot fireworks at it?"

I might as well have said we had Sasquatch and Jesus with us too. Mom might've believed that a little more than the shit I was spewing.

"No! Why would we do that?" I tried to play it off. "That's stupid."

"He put a shit in your backpack!" Dad scoffed.

Mom didn't correct the language. One of the rare times it was warranted in her eyes.

"He messed with your stuff so that little *Jordan* punk convinced you to burn his house down!" She said his name like it was some cardinal sin. The line had been crossed.

"Jordan's not a punk, and he didn't convince us to do anything!" I defended.

"Where else would he have gotten fireworks?" Dad rolled his eyes.

"That's exactly where he got them!" Mom decided like I wasn't there anymore. "Who knows what else he's given them or talked them into doing!"

She didn't have to say it, I knew her mind was running wild with doomsday debauchery. Every dreaded buzzword she had seen on the news or talked to Mee-Moo about. Rowdy nights full of MARIJUANA and ECSTASY and HEAVY PETTING, topped off with a little light TERRORISM for good measure.

"He didn't talk us into anything!"

Mom's attention snapped back to me.

"Lighting their house on fire was your idea then?"

"His house was on fire?" I asked nervously. Rather Mom was exaggerating, or that's what Georgie's dad had reported.

"Georgie's dad said their couch and curtains are completely ruined!" Mom snarled. "There's scorch marks all over his walls, and his front window is totally blown out!"

Nothing we didn't already know about or suspect then. Good.

"Okay," I reasoned. "But have you actually seen any of it? Maybe it's not that bad."

She knew. She always knew. Hell, she probably knew last night! Mom had an impeccable sixth sense about when I was doing something I shouldn't have been. It really was *Lusty Busty 2* all over again.

"You are such a liar, Grady Burton." She turned in a huff back to Dad. "Take his laptop! I don't want him talking to any of them."

"NO!" Have mercy! Take the boy's life before you take his computer!

"Alright," Dad sighed.

"And his remote! No TV either!"

Because I couldn't use the buttons next to the screen, I guess.

Dad scooped up the laptop and my remote from their resting place on my desk.

"And the video games!"

"Jesus Christ," Dad muttered under his breath. "Should we have brought the movers with us?"

Mom whipped her furious eyes at him.

"I got it, I got it!" Dad went for the PlayStation.

He wasn't sure how to disconnect the entire console, so instead he just unplugged the controller and added it to his growing pile of confiscated electronics.

"And you just sit here and think about what you did!" Mom ordered. "I'm going to have to spend the rest of my day sorting all this out! I hope it was worth it."

With that, the hurricane moved back into the hall. Dad followed, shooting me a little half smile on the way out. Somewhere between apologetic and understanding, as a parent, Dad couldn't give me the seal of approval for what we did, but that was close enough. He closed the door behind him, trying to juggle all the contraband in his arms. As it latched, I heard a thump from the other side that could've only been my controller hitting the carpet.

"Damn it," he barked, voice muffled.

Their combined footsteps rumbled back down the stairs. Cold, still silence took my room, oozing out of the walls and rising up from the carpet like a thick fog, freezing me to the bed. I had to pee, but that was gonna have to wait. Like a prisoner with an unlocked cell door, there's no way I was about to walk into the trap of stepping outside. Not so soon after I had been sealed in. Mom would hear my footsteps, hear the door, no matter how quietly I opened it. She could hear my heartbeat from two hundred yards if she wanted to.

I pulled my iPod from the dock and plugged my earbuds in. Clicking the wheel quickly, I chose the first album I could think of to fill the silence and adequately capture my fresh despair. I kept the volume low, just in case, and only one bud in. The one facing the wall as I laid back down and hid my music under the sheets, lest she storm back in and realize she forgot such a pivotal device.

We tried. Gotta give us credit there. There was an actual attempt to cover our asses. And at least Jordan was right, the house didn't burn down. My curiosity over what it actually looked like was overpowered by worry for the others. Were they okay? Or had they been incarcerated too?

Ruben wasn't exaggerating. The first time he came home with Sharpie on his fingernails, his parents threatened to send him to a Catholic school in Mexico for troubled youth. If they considered black nails troubling, I couldn't even imagine what they'd think of Georgie's disease-ridden couch. For that matter, did nobody bother wondering why so many kids were at his house in the first place? Did nobody stop for a second and notice the clear precursor to teen pregnancy happening on a residential street?

No.

No, they did not.

All they saw was the attempted arson, apparently.

Alex's dad would've seen it, though. Every time he looked at me, Jordan and Ruben it was like he could see all the uncouth things he suspected we were doing with his daughter. All the various ways we had corrupted her and turned her into what she was growing into. People weren't allowed to change. They had to be obsessed with *Lizzie McGuire* and *Powerpuff Girls* into their twenties, I guess.

The possibilities for Jordan were the darkest. Mom wasn't the only person in Buena Vista willing to believe he could talk us into something seriously criminal. Even if it wasn't. They just didn't know him like we did. They didn't understand, man! His own parents wouldn't have been much of an issue. His brother, on the other hand, would kick his ass up one side of their street and down the other. If he could keep the cops off of it first.

Like our house was built on a fault line, my entire world came crashing down on me. Cataclysmic. Apocalyptic. All because stupid, tubby, little Grady got an idea in his head and thought he could do something that never should've been attempted in the first place. Because he let his imagination run right the fuck away and take his only friends with it. I couldn't even message Ruben to check in and ease my worry. Have him ask Alex to put out a call and verify Jordan's status. The flipside possibility, of course, was that they were all totally fine. That our phone number was the only one Brittany's mom had, and I was the only one having the hammer brought down on them. But good luck trying to convince a thirteen-year-old the world isn't ending after every bump in the road. The great doom of our time was all I could see.

Halfway through *Dark Light*'s third full rotation, my bladder was fit to explode. And going out the window, as tempting as that idea was, was only gonna piss Mom off more than breaking containment. I could just barely make out her voice downstairs as I crept my door open. She was in the living room, no doubt. Her unofficial office and command center. She was on the phone, but even as I tiptoed out of the room and down the hall to my bathroom, I couldn't make out what was being said. The fury had left her tone, that much I could tell. She sounded . . . almost desperate? At the end of her rope? Backed into a corner. Heartbroken. Good job, Grady! That's on you too.

I tried to listen closely as I stood at the toilet, in my sunflower bathroom, but the rumble of the water drowned her out. The flush didn't help either. When I came back out, I checked to my right. No sound came from the office, and Dad's chair didn't shoot back into the open door. I stood there for a second just to make sure he wasn't there. As much as it felt like a Saturday, we were still in the working week for normal adults. Blame the school schedule. Took me a bit to realize that Dad wasn't home anymore. Whatever punishment was coming would have to wait until his day was done.

Great.

At the top of the stairs, I waited just another couple moments. I tracked the sad mumble of Mom's voice as it moved toward the kitchen.

"You should see his room, Mom."

Mee-Moo was getting the rundown. That meant everyone in the extended family, all the cousins and uncles I couldn't pick out of a lineup, would know how much of a fuck-up I was by the end of the day.

"I think that would help, yeah," she said faintly. "I'll talk to Hank when he gets home."

Her voice drifted off again as she wandered farther away, taking my fate with it. My head hung to the floor as I went back to solitary. I closed the door slowly, quietly, and waited for the inevitable.

I could've sat in bed, with the blinds drawn and the sheets pulled up around me, wallowing in my grief and guilt all god damn day if it was up to me. But it wasn't. Sometime in the afternoon, the sun high over the backyard, there was a knock on my door. I stashed the iPod, burying it and my earbuds under my pillow. The knock was gentle, yet firm enough to tell me she still wasn't happy. I opened the door like I expected a lone gunman on the other side.

Mom held out her hand expectantly.

"Reading list," she demanded.

"What?" I wasn't following. The reading list had nothing to do with anything.

"Your summer list. Give it to me."

Oh, right, that boring-ass collection of fun killers.

It was on my desk. Near where my laptop should've been, its charge cable laying sadly in the empty space. I slid it off and handed it to her like an olive branch. She snatched it out of my hand like contraband.

"You will read every last one of these. And to prove you did, you're going to write three paragraphs on each."

"I don't have my laptop." Ah *ha*! A loophole.

"Paper exists," Mom replied flatly.

She pulled a small plate from behind her back. A Hot Pocket and a handful of Doritos filled it, molten cheddar liquefying nacho dust. At least the inmate was getting fed.

"And don't you go thinking that's all! Your father and I are gonna have a talk with you when he gets home."

I took the plate with a weak smile, and she headed back for the stairs.

Hellboy stared down at me from over the bed as I closed the door, understanding better than anyone else on my walls. Locked up, kept in the BPRD's vaults to spare the world from ever having to see him. Just like me. Just like us. Technically speaking, Ed Scissorhands would've understood that too. But I was never gonna be that thin.

You and me, Red.

I closed my door and dropped the plate onto my desk. In a stack next to my TV, I carefully pulled his first collected paperback volume from the others sandwiching it in. Mom would've had a field day placing the blame on a comic called *Seed of Destruction*, but at least I could get it in one more time before the rest of my summer was hijacked by books without cool pictures of monsters in them. One last ride with the Right Hand of Doom. I sat at the desk with a sigh and cracked the book open, ready to devour the last choices I'd make for myself.

With the read done, I returned Hellboy to the stack reverently, like I knew I was putting him in his grave. The plate sat empty on my desk as I crawled across the bed, all the way back against the wall. No sooner had I pulled my iPod from its hiding place, the garage door howled through the house.

"Grady Henry!" Mom called from downstairs.

The sun had shifted, casting strips of yellow through the slats of my blinds. Late enough in the day for . . .

"Shit, he's home."

I lurched off the bed and shuffled for the door, imaginary shackles around my feet. It was time to walk the Green Mile. That stretch of carpet between my door and the stairs, down to my execution chamber and the shallow grave I imagined they dug in the backyard. *Here Lies Grady Burton, Blame Georgie Booker.*

Mom and Dad waited impatiently at the base of the stairs. Keys dangled from his hand as she folded the reading list and stowed it into the bulky purse on her shoulder.

"We're leaving," she said decisively. "Stay in that room. I'll know if you don't."

"Alright." I nodded, with zero intention of listening.

She didn't take her eyes off of me as they made for the garage. Even after I heard the door clunk closed, I could still feel them. A chill rattled up my spine as I listened to the big white door grind its way back down.

The silent fog of my room infected the rest of the house like an odor no air freshener could kill. My heart boomed through my chest like a double-pedal kick drum. There was no bookstore in town. Not a big reading community, unless you count Sports Illustrated, TV Guide, or The Buena Vista Penny Pincher. They were gonna have to go to the Borders in the mall. The mall, full of all its sickeningly not-grounded kids and shoppers.

That gave me at least forty minutes.

Dad didn't have the patience for long shopping trips. He would tell Mom to just "give the list to the lady". I saw him do that in Albertsons once. Didn't work out the way he wanted it to. Still, forty minutes was forty minutes. I went back to my bed to count down the first ten, too far for Dad to turn back.

Two songs were as long as I could take before convincing myself it was fine. It was that or sit there feeling like my skin was about to liquify. I shot up from the bed, ready to get it over with.

The hall was clear. Dad's office sat open, his computer unguarded. It would take a minute to connect to Messenger without its dedicated desktop platform, but maybe I'd get lucky and find Ruben or Alex on Myspace. I took one step out of my room. When no bear trap clamped around my ankle and no cenobite chains shot from the walls to hook me, I took another. Hugging close to the corner, I darted a look downstairs. No movement. No sound. They were gone. The house was empty. But then again, that's exactly what they'd want me to think. Entrapment at its finest! Paranoia at its worst. I dashed across the top of the stairs and pressed myself flat to the wall. One inch at a time, I pulled myself along.

The interior of Dad's office came into view. His mud brown filing cabinet, open and overstuffed. Certifications and licenses framed and hanging on the wall. His desk was empty. But there was a closet, wasn't there? What if he was hiding in it? What if he and Mom were just waiting to spring out and dole out even harsher punishments? Why the hell was I surprised when I was diagnosed with anxiety? Why was that such a big fucking shock?

I stepped into the office. The window out to the front yard glowed through the room. Before I sat at the desk, I made a point to peek my head out. When Mom and Dad weren't staring up at me from the driveway, I went for the computer. Sitting comfortably on the special desk Mom insisted he needed for it, the eggshell-colored cube of a monitor was nearly lost under mountains of invoices and technical manuals. Its bulky tower sat on a small ledge under the desk's surface, cold and powered down. I slid the keyboard tray out and clicked the mouse, just to be sure it wasn't resting. The monitor reflected my own dower face back at me. My eyes dark and vacant, like the ghost of Grady Burton was trying to get online. I leaned down and held the power button until the internal fan started to hum. But the monitor didn't crackle to life. The little red light in its corner glared back at me. Of course he turned that off too. I was surprised he didn't feel the need to also unplug it. I clicked the button next to the light and the progress bar took over the screen as it fizzled into view.

Only slightly faster than my laptop, Dad's computer eventually chimed at me. The same melody of bells welcomed me in. A fresh rush of adrenaline stood my hairs on end. Find Ruben. Find Alex. Inquire about the guy who had no digital footprint. That was the order of the day. But it never got off the ground. No sooner than the computer booted up, I was slapped in the face with a lockscreen, asking for a password I didn't have.

"*Fuuuuuuck!*"

I stared at the keyboard like it had the answers. If only I could've picked up his fingerprints on the letters and run them through an algorithm to tell me the most used and possible combinations. Maybe have Alfred bring me a scotch and prep the Batwing for takeoff while I was at it.

I went with the first most likely candidate: PASSWORD1234. The input shook, and an annoyingly loud CONK came through the speakers, wherever they were in all the clutter. PASSWORD4321 gave me the same result. Dad clearly put more thought into it than the five seconds I gave him credit for.

"It's gotta be here."

Careful but quick, I searched through the papers. Somewhere, there had to be a Post-it note with the password written down. Or maybe a notebook page. An old invoice. Something! Anything! How he ever found what he needed in that mess was an absolute mystery. One wrong pull of a page or shift of a book, and the entire thing would've come crashing down in a logistical landslide. Would've tried Mom's real name and her birthday, if for the life of me I could've remembered what or when that was. I usually relied on Dad handing me a card to sign for that kind of information.

It wasn't gonna happen. I sighed out my frustration, breathing steam through my nose, as I powered the computer down again. Finding them online was a dead end. Two other routes forked out ahead of me. I could spend the next thirty-three minutes and counting tearing apart the house, looking for wherever Mom had hidden my laptop. Or I could just ride to Alex's house and risk her father's wrath.

One of those sounded infinitely less complicated than the other.

As I ran down the stairs, it occurred to me that I was still in my Beetlejuice jammies. Changing would take time I didn't have. The world was just gonna have to deal with seeing me without my face on. I jumped the last two steps and landed squarely on the tile. Horrible time for the cold shock to remind me that I was still barefoot.

I flew across the living room and into the garage. The automatic light clicked on. Even without the Aztek taking up the whole middle, the garage was still mostly full. All those boxes didn't leave much breathing room. Mom had been busy, though. My bike, scooter, skateboard, even my roller blades, which could've more than easily been handled without socks on, were all gone.

"WHAT THE FUCK?"

That was a step beyond! She had never gone so far as to hide my only modes of transport. Where could she have even put them? Her hiding places changed literally every time she needed them. Finding Christmas presents early was a fool's errand. If Easter eggs weren't discovered on the day, then they never would be. The skateboard, blades, and scooter, sure, they could be stashed all over the place. But the bike? Where do you hide a bike without anyone noticing it? I would've heard if she brought it upstairs to hide in their closet. There's no way she could've done that without thumping the wheels on every last step. The answer came to me in a flash.

The backyard!

I ran across the living room to the back door and threw it open. A huge patch of sand took up most of it, where Dad had said we'd get an above-ground pool sooner or later. The unoccupied dog run, leading straight up to the side gate, was an obvious choice. Easy for Mom to access. But there were tire treads clearly imprinted in the sand. Leading straight to the rusty metal shed on the other side of the yard. The one we never used because they lost the key to the equally rusty Masterlock hanging from its plastic handles. Or so I was fucking told! They had the key, it seemed. And now my wheels were locked in there. Along with whatever else they saw fit to hide from me.

"Liars," I growled at the shed like it was to blame.

As I stomped back inside, brooding and grumbling, I contemplated the distance. It wasn't a far walk. But more than I was willing to do. The bike was quick. Seconds would become minutes without it, and exposure would go from a calculated risk to an outright threat. Nobody walks away from a prison break. Not if they want to succeed anyway.

I double checked the carpet for footprints as I made my way back up to my room. Just because I couldn't see them didn't mean Mom's eagle eyes wouldn't.

"Get down here, Grady!" Dad shouted as they came back in through the garage.

It had been closer to an hour and a half. Every minute after the first forty was spent kicking myself in the ass. I could've gone. I totally could've. But how was I to know? After their clock ran out, it became a matter of "any second now." Long, agonizing ones, spent waiting for the blade to fall.

Sighs and whispers fluttered out from the living room as I came down the stairs, really taking my time, hoping to overhear a preview of whatever was coming my way. Trying to prolong it, more than anything.

"Did you not get dressed today?" Dad scowled as I stepped up to the couches, still wearing his standard work shorts and white polo.

I shook my head, embarrassed, but not really.

"Sit," he ordered. "Vacation's over."

They took up the couch against the wall, so I took the bend, lowering myself gingerly like I thought the whole room might explode if I moved too quickly. Or that my Tiger Mom might finally pounce.

"Your dad and I have been talking," she said through an exhale.

I think, even now, those might be my least favorite words in the English language.

"Okay," I accepted.

"We're worried about you," he added. "That's all."

"You're at a pivotal point in your life, Gray." Mom only used the nickname to soften the blow. "Where you get to decide the kind of person you want to be. We see all that"—she gestured up to my room—"Hellguy, the blood and guts, the evil music, the comic books about serial killers."

I did my best not to flinch at that. Technically, *Johnny the Homicidal Maniac* was Ruben's. And it needed to get back to him at some point.

"We don't want to see you go down a path you can't come back from."

"I'm not!" I defended pointlessly.

"Dave Booker's living room might argue that," Dad scoffed.

That's his dad's name?

"You don't know how many calls I made today!" Mom jumped back in. "How much it took to keep him from calling the cops. But I think we found a solution to everyone's problems."

"I don't have—"

"Oh, yes you do!" Dad cut me off. "You have some major problems, kid. Your mother worked her ass off to figure them all out."

"We're paying for the window," she said gravely. "Out of pocket! And it's not cheap."

"Not even remotely!" he added. "Lucky for us, Alex's dad is paying for the couch. And Ruben's parents said they'd handle the walls and the curtains."

"I haven't heard back from Jordan's parents," she shook her head in knowing frustration. "So we can only assume they're unwilling to help."

I wasn't about to tell them that they needed to call his brother. If they hadn't talked to anyone in Jordan's house, then he might've escaped that shitshow altogether.

"You will work with your dad," Mom laid out the terms, "every school break until the end of freshman year to pay us back."

I nodded, a lump forming in my throat as she leaned forward, ready to swing the axe.

"And you are *not* to associate with each other anymore."

"What?" I gasped, tears swelling.

"We're gonna look into a different high school for you," Dad explained.

"NO!" I shot up from the couch. "You can't!"

"Sit back down," he instructed calmly, trying to smooth it over.

"You don't really get a say here," Mom shot back. "This is the decision I was just talking about! These upcoming years, high school, they're going to determine a lot of your future. We're not stupid, we know you're gonna find a way to see them or talk to them anyway. But we can at least keep you from having to go to school with them."

"I don't *have* to go to school with them! I want to!"

"We know," Mom nodded. "And that's the problem. They're a terrible influence! You weren't all doom and gloom before you started hanging out with them!" The timing was questionable, yeah, but it was in no way their fault. "And now the group of you are running around town trying to burn houses down just because the other kids were mean to you. Do you want to end up like those Columbine boys?"

Those particular Boogeymen were a catch-all, left over from the time before Osama and anthrax. Talk back to the teacher? That's what those Columbine boys did! Skip PE? I bet those Columbine boys did that! Cut in line at lunch? That's just like the Columbine boys! It didn't matter. Their minds were set in stone.

"It wasn't like that!" I argued through an angry sob.

"It won't be now." Mom put her foot down. "You're going to take these." I hadn't noticed the overstuffed bag on the floor next to her, until she thrust it at me. The reading list in full. "And pack some clothes."

"What?" I choked. "Why?"

"I spoke to your Mee-Moo today."

No shit.

Wait . . .

The lump in my throat suddenly tasted like acid and Hot Pocket.

"Oh god," I groaned. "No. Please."

"She thinks some time away will help you, and I agree. So, Dad will drive you up to them first thing in the morning tomorrow and come pick you up again before school starts. Pop-Pop could use your help around the house with some things, so that's what you'll do. Read and do whatever he asks of you. Consider it a reset on your teenage years! The time away from everything will be good for you." She could sugar coat it six ways to Sunday, but it still tasted rotten. "You'll see! It's gonna show you that all of this really isn't you!"

"What do you know about who I am?" I bit back, my cheeks soaked.

"*My* son would never talk to me that," Mom seethed, eyes smoldering. "But whoever *they've* turned him into will apparently."

"They haven't turned me into anything!"

"You need to think long and hard about that! Is this the person you want to be—"

"Yes!"

"Do you really want to be—

"YES!"

"Stop." Dad raised a hand to signal me, bringing the whole thing to a halt.

I dropped back to the couch. Mom took a moment to settle herself, collect her thoughts.

"Some distance from those bad apples is gonna show you that they weren't really your friends in the first place, Grady."

"They're my only friends!"

"You'll make new ones next year," Dad said, no big deal.

"A real friend would've said no to the fireworks," Mom piled on.

"It wasn't their idea!" I blurted desperately, spit and tears flying from my face. "I wanted to get back at Georgie! I said we needed to do something! I didn't think the fireworks would trash the house! I just thought it would scare them!"

They weren't expecting that. All the expression and color melted from Mom's face. Dad's head dropped to his feet, sighing out an even deeper disappointment.

"Well," Mom said firmly, steely eyes locked on me. "It's worse than we thought then. And it certainly sounds like we made the right call anyway."

"She's not wrong, you know," Dad added a bit reluctantly. "If they were your friends, they wouldn't have gone along. They would've put a stop to it."

I refused to believe that. I couldn't. I wouldn't! There was nothing they could say to quench the burning coals in my chest, and nothing I could say to change their minds. Still, I tried.

"You can't do this!" I wailed. "*Please!*"

"We already did." Mom dropped the axe. "They're expecting you."

BRING ME TO LIFE
JUNE 3, 2006

When Mom said, "First thing in the morning," she fucking meant it. The sun wasn't even up when Dad burst through my door and kicked the light on.

"Come on, I got other things to do today," he rushed while my eyes were still blurry and half closed.

At least I'm pretty sure it was Dad. There was a moment while I laid there clawing toward consciousness where I questioned if the day before really even happened. Any hope of a stress-induced nightmare shattered like Georgie's window when I saw the forest green rolling suitcase standing at the foot of my bed. One of Mom's, packed full of shirts and shorts, and everything else I'd need to survive weeks at Mee-Moo and Pop-Pop's.

She hovered over me for an hour the night before while I packed, making sure none of the shirts I chose were too outwardly offensive. Not like any of them had "fuck" or "pussy" blazed across front of them, but some of the artwork and characters were apparently too much for their retirement community. Only a few that I actually liked survived the culling. The rest were chosen by her. "You look so nice in this one!" and "This one's really cute on you!" Bright colors and Disney characters. I doubted they'd even fit, given how old they were. But if bringing those meant the few I actually liked survived, then so be it. Mom swore up and down that Mee-Moo could do my laundry, but I wasn't taking any chances. Anything purchased from a Hot Topic, when washed or dried incorrectly, would shrink to the size of a washcloth. Speaking generally, of course. I have no idea why they did that or if it happened to anything Ruben, Alex or Jordan ever scored, but I wasn't gonna risk my *Three Cheers for Sweet Revenge* or *Corpse Bride* shirts becoming crop tops.

My backpack she packed herself, after a healthy spray of disinfectant and Febreze. A blank notebook, a stash of pencils (no pens in case the vandal's itch struck me again), and the summer reading list were crammed inside. The only one that even remotely caught my interest was *Lord of the Flies.* The title sounded enough like Tolkien that it might be cool, and I had heard there was some light cannibalism or something like that.

She wasn't thirty seconds behind Dad after he woke me up.

"You heard him, come on, get moving!"

I swung my legs over the side of the bed, still not fully aware of what was going on as she hurried in and checked my bags for contraband one final time. The sole reason why I chose to forgo earbuds while I slept, a habit I couldn't break no matter how many warnings about hearing damage Mom issued. I waited up for my iPod to hit a full charge, wrapped the earbud wire around it, and stashed it under my pillow where she wouldn't think to look. It and its separate charge cable waited to be smuggled. The only things I was willing to risk the attempt for.

"I'll be going through this mess of a room while you're gone, too, Grady Henry," she snarled at the DVDs without really looking at them. "We're going to have a talk about some of this stuff."

"Don't get rid of anything, please," I groaned, groggy.

"Oh, I'll be getting rid of things!"

"No, Mom, please. Not all of it's mine."

99.9% of it was. But I knew there was at least a movie or two that needed to find their way back to Jordan's brother, and a few old games and a couple of books that needed to go home to Ruben. She didn't know which was which, though. Her trash bags would fill all the same.

"Well, then you can explain to their parents why they're not getting them back," Mom replied unsympathetically. With my luggage to her liking, she turned for the door. "Up! C'mon! Don't keep Dad waiting!"

As soon as she was gone, I attacked the backpack. Slowly, quietly, I unzipped it and buried my iPod under the pencils. I wasn't about to go spend an unending amount of weeks at their house, with only local news channels and Mee-Moo's old country music bumpkins whining about their horses and alcoholism. No, if I was gonna survive, I needed weird skinny dudes whining about death and pill addiction. *Huge* difference!

"Today, Grady!" Dad yelled from downstairs, rattling his keys to signify that the two minutes I had taken to get out of bed were two minutes too long.

I threw on the first pair of shorts I could find on the floor, a T-shirt that didn't smell too ripe, and grabbed the bags. By the time I got down to the garage, Dad was already in the Aztek. Its engine didn't sound any happier than I was, or he looked. Exhaust billowed up to the big white door like the garage was on fire. Mom stood behind me, watching the prisoner transfer like there was a chance I was gonna bolt out of the garage, hop the wall, and hitch a ride to Nova Scotia.

That's not a bad idea . . .

With my head down, avoiding eye contact with either of them, I stowed my bags in the back seat. Dad had the radio going already, the morning show he liked on the old man rock station. The hosts were in the middle of talking to a guy over the phone who swore his dog could bark the Pledge of Allegiance. Mom cut me off as I closed the door and made my way around to the front passenger seat.

"I know it sucks," she said, coaxing immediate tears from my eyes. "But we only want the best for you. I promise."

I nodded, swallowing the hard pill.

"You're gonna get out of this whatever you put in," she reaffirmed. "Remember that! Listen to your Mee-Moo and Pop-Pop, do what they say, *read your books*, and we'll see you in a few weeks, okay?"

"Okay," I croaked, still looking away, my bottom lip quivering like a current ran through it.

Mom pulled me in for a hug. I bit my tongue to keep from turning into a blubbering mess and begging for a stay of execution I knew wouldn't be granted. She rubbed my shoulders as I pulled away like she thought she could scrub the mood from me. Like it could've been that easy. I forced a smile, its corners wobbling and wavering, and opened the passenger door. Dad had the car rolling down to the street before my seatbelt was even buckled. Mom stood in the door to the laundry room, watching with the same sad smile I had like she was sending me off to Iraq, immediately after signing my enlistment papers. When we hit the bottom of the driveway, she threw out a solemn wave and pressed the button on the wall. The door shuddered, closing its jaws and the garage, shutting me out from any other hope of staying.

Dad kicked it into gear and pulled away from the house. The fastest way to the freeway was the route that passed by Alex's house, then took the corner, threaded through Ruben's neighborhood, and out the other side. He decided to take the long way. We turned at the intersection facing our lot before I even got a glimpse of their houses, or a chance for an overly emotional internal goodbye. Something like Gandalf at the end of *Return of the King* would've been appropriate.

Farewell, brave hobbits.

"It's only gonna make it worse," Dad said under his breath, reading my mind.

"Probably," I gulped.

He turned up the radio as we passed the lot, enough talking for one drive. A glimpse of Jordan's neighborhood through the drainage ditch was all I got before Dad pulled through the stoplight on the corner and wrapped us around the other side of our cul-de-sac. I itched for my iPod, but there was fuck all I could do to scratch it. The song stuck in my head was probably better, anyway. Less depressing than what I would've chosen to supplement the black hole in my chest.

I scowled out the window the whole drive through the town, trying not to notice the school I went to or the school I was supposed to start at. It just would've raised questions about where I was actually gonna end up. And let's be real, some of the blame was on BVJH here too. There were more schools closer to the mall. Different schools, other kids. The people who looked down on Buena Vistians as subhuman trailer trash. An entire town of Jordans from their perspective. When we'd descend on the mall like a mongrel horde, no one ever owned up to where they lived, no matter their social status. I couldn't see Dad wanting to drive me twenty minutes out of his way every morning and back again at night. I shuddered at the thought of learning the bus schedule.

The sun crested the desert around us, erupting golden and white over the dirt and tumbleweeds. Through intersections and lights, we left everything familiar behind on our way to the freeway. The McDonald's Hub, not yet ready for the breakfast crowd. The little shopping plaza with the comic book store, and a place we never ventured into with a canvas sign over its door that read simply BEEF + MORE. The Blockbuster that Jordan convinced he was actually eighteen. The Hollywood Video that didn't even let us in anymore. The furniture store where every mattress in town had been purchased at one point or another. The coffee shop Dad said was "too fancy" because they blended Folgers and ice. A handful of chain restaurants, all situated on the same block, where literally everyone and their mothers went for any kind of special occasion. Walmart, with its parking lot already filling up with bargain hunters. No one my age was up and moving yet. Youth didn't take to the street much before ten. And why should they have? They could enjoy their summers. They weren't me.

Dad hit the onramp, wrapping around in a full 180 past the site we were all promised would one day be a Costco, the freeway racing along beside it. He gunned it as the sharp curve straightened and floated us over to the far lane. Dead brown hills rose up ahead, ready to cut off any hope of retreat. Beyond them, mountains set a hard fortifying line. Nothing in or out without their say-so. Like every kid my age, I dreamt incessantly about the day I finally got to cross them for good, never looking back. But this wasn't nearly as sweet as I imagined that was supposed to be, as the movies and songs made it sound.

Maybe the real thing will be better.

Ten miles past the Welcome sign, the hills moved in to engulf us. Civilization, if it could even be called that, vanished on the other side of them. Dad slid down in his seat, settling in for the long haul. We fled the rising sun, keeping it square in the back window as we chugged along. The path through the hills was relatively straight, slicing between them like they were nothing more than a slight hindrance. Once we were clear of them, though, the road twisted and turned through flat stretches of rock and brush. Like the people who built it went, "Well, shit, it was straight for a while, let's make up for it here and put in a bunch of turns that go nowhere." They did nothing, other than bring us around the smaller hills and larger rock formations, always spitting us out in the direction we were headed in the first place. I always wondered if it was just to make the drive take longer than it needed to. A punishment for anyone who dared to leave.

The radio hosts droned on, trying their hardest to be energetic and engaging at such an ungodly hour. Auditory coffee for the people like Dad who listened to them every single day. A pick-me-up on the way to something less fun. I tuned them out, choosing instead to focus on the soft hum of the engine. The dash clock told me that we were only twenty minutes into a drive that would take for-fucking-ever without headphones, or anything cool to read. Instead, I quizzed myself on the movie lines we all knew by heart, seeing if I could get the scenes to play in my head. For all I knew, it was the closest I was gonna get to watching any of them again until college. If they hadn't been forced out of my system by then, lost in the greater library of my head the same as my friends. The early hour crept up on me while I tried to conjure the jukebox scene from *Shaun of the Dead.*

Don't! Stop me nooooow! I'm havin' such a good time. . .

It bit me firm on the ass, dragging me back down to sleep.

A puddle of drool soaked into my shoulder when I woke up again, a web of it connecting to my mouth. An entirely different planet sat outside my window, exploding into view around me like guitars into a chorus. Gone were the shades of beige and brown surrounding Buena Vista, replaced by green as far as I could see. Trees! Actual trees, not the ugly-ass dead things that infested Buena Vista.

Lush, towering pines standing guard for even taller redwoods. Short kids in front, bigger boys in back.

Dad had to have changed freeways at least twice since I faded off. That much was obvious by the veins pressing out from his neck like they were trying to escape. His knuckles were pearly white around the wheel and the relaxed slouch he adopted during the easy chunk of the drive was gone. He wanted it to be done just as much as I did not.

We cut through the trees down an off-ramp, and hints of humans began to emerge. A gas station without a name brand over it. A diner older than I was, and twice as colorful. We banked hard past them, and the tops of hidden houses and buildings appeared. No tract neighborhoods or chain stores. No Applebee's or Walmart. What I know now are the warning signs of a different economic class altogether, what I thought of then as simply "nicer".

Dad slowed us to a stop at the end of the ramp. Cars whizzed by ahead of us, cutting across at blinding speed. Too fast to make out any significant detail of them, but I didn't have to. They sounded vastly more expensive than ours. A two-lane highway intersected the road, tempting us with death on the other side of its stop sign. Dad growled at the other cars, waiting for the right moment to jump in between them.

"Slow down, people!"

When a sufficient gap appeared, he took it. The Aztek's tires squealed as he hit the gas a little too hard and hung to the right, straight toward a tunnel.

Oh yeah.

I had seen it all before but never remembered any of it. For as much as Mom talked to her, we didn't visit Mee-Moo and Pop-Pop often. When Thanksgiving or Christmas rolled around, they came to us. In the extremely rare instances where Dad couldn't think of a good enough reason not to, we did this same drive. I sucked in a heavy breath as we entered the tunnel and held it.

Wish this won't suck. Wish I'll still have friends when I come back. Wish I won't have to change schools.

We barreled toward the light at the end. In a blinding flash, the tunnel opened again. A rock wall hugged close to my window, and a steep drop looked down out of Dad's. A solid bed of sapphire was perfectly set at the bottom, brushing softly against paper white sand. Dad refused to look over. Not even a glance, and I can't say I blame him. The tall pines on my side could've been ripped from the ground, dropped over the edge and impaled like arrows in the sand below. They wouldn't have come close to cresting the road.

The two-lane blacktop continued into a switchback, and the trees took over. Towering over us, they flanked both sides of the car. Ripples of water shined beyond Dad's window, glimpses through the dense woods. The road banked and weaved as a canopy of branches and leaves closed in over us. Nothing like our freeway, and far more perilous to navigate. Every car that blurred by in the opposite direction looked like they were only inches from impact. Knuckles pearly, teeth gnashed tight, Dad hugged as close to my side of the lane as he could without clipping a rock or root.

The grade changed, and the Aztek climbed, winding up even higher from the beach. Evidence of life scattered around us. Beach houses stood on stilts a million miles below. Sprawling estates peppered the hills so far out that they looked like Micro Machines or Polly Pockets. Seasonal properties waiting for the true start of summer. They vanished behind us as the road evened out again and a straight shot through deeper, darker woods led us further away from the world.

The tops of a town peeked out, hiding amongst the trees. If I hadn't known any better, I would've assumed it was abandoned as we slowed to the lone stoplight on its edge, dangling high on a wire over the road. A white wooden oval, big enough to smash the car flat if it chose to, stood on thick legs at the edge of the woods. Raised letters painted in icy blue read WELCOME TO SEA BREEZE - WE APPRECIATE YOUR VISIT.

Dad's eyes snapped back and forth between the light and the rearview mirror, making absolutely sure no one was flying up behind us with little intention of stopping. The light switched to green, and we rolled forward again.

Curving to the right around the sign, the town developed in front of us. Tucked into a small valley, set back in its trees, a collection of tourist traps waited in two neat rows. A thin layer of marine fog hugged their feet. Rolling emerald hills surrounded Sea Breeze on all sides, waiting for the opportune moment to push it into the ocean in one definitive sweep.

Small shops and restaurants ran straight back on either side of the street. Surf and beach supply stores. Bike repair. Guided fishing tours. Places with names like Surfside Grill, Catch 'O' the Day, and Sandy Attire. A hardware store that had probably been run by the same family, the same two people, since the dawn of man. A grocery store fit to serve a small contingent of full-time residents was nestled in a field of grass, a miniature parking lot in front of it with space to hold no more than a dozen cars at a time. A single mail truck waited at the curb in front of a post office only a little bigger than my last classroom. An honest to fucking god white-steepled church with a bell at the top sat on a hill in the back.

The farther we got from the cliff and the suicide drop down to the water, true signs of life started to materialize. Lights kicked on behind perfectly polished glass, like they were waiting for us to arrive before revealing themselves. Cars pulled up to the curbs, blue handicap placards hanging from each and every rearview mirror. A two-thousand-year-old couple inched their way out of the post office, him leaning on a cane and her hobbling with a walker. Dad hung a left at the end of the block, the only other direction we could've gone, and the matching rows followed us through the bend.

It all made me fucking sick.

Nothing but cheesy, hokey, forced charm and an overdosing level of postcard quaintness. It reminded me of the time I was flipping through channels and accidentally saw exactly three seconds of *Gilmore Girls*, a fate I wouldn't wish on my worst enemy. A large white bandstand sat atop a wide roundabout, complete with a coned roof and carved railing that looked too finely shaped to be mass produced. The other side of it spat us out onto a road that rose sharply into the hills boxing Sea Breeze in.

Dad gripped the wheel tighter as we climbed. And climbed. And climbed. Winding through sharp curves and dramatic banks. Trees reached up above us on one side, solid rock blocked us in on the other. Aluminum guardrails wound up with us, their dull gray smeared with skids from tires and bumpers that dared to get too close. Pockets of fog and mist waited at every turn, until the town was a tabletop miniature below us.

The sun emerged, bright and hot, on the horizon behind an unnecessarily tall rod iron gate. Our approach was cut off, unless Dad felt like some off-roading. Its polished bars and regally rounded bulbs reflected like a warning to approaching boats or aircraft flying a little lower than normal. In a fine script, metal twisted to form a single word: BLUFFS. The framework of a spider web stretched across the peaks of the U.

A callbox stood up out of the dirt on our side of the enclosure. Dad slowed to it as his window dropped. With a groan, he leaned out. A small, printed directory didn't offer much help. Encased in glass on the front of the box, condensation clouded its view.

"God damn it." Dad leaned even further, wiping the directory clean.

He searched for the number he needed, down the list of at least a hundred. It occurred to me as I sat there, staring up at the gate, that I had no idea how long it had been since we had been there last. Years was my best guess. Had to have been. Sometime back when I was too young to recognize the Bluffs' fortifications as the perfect thing to keep zombies out. The whole town could've served as a solid place to ride out the end times, or been the perfect location for a coven of vampires to embrace their eternal retirement. Those fantasies hadn't filled my head the last time we pulled up to that gate, as far from my natural environment as we could get while still technically being in the same state. All of which would've been preferable.

The callbox buzzed. Once, twice, three times. Dad drummed on his door impatiently. He checked the time on the dash with a long, exasperated sigh.

"Hello?" A voice laced with static and age finally picked up.

"It's Hank, can you let us in?

"Who?"

"Hank. And Grady."

A moment of silence while Mee-Moo pondered his response.

"Who?" She couldn't hear us.

"Hank Burton!" he shouted, his voice echoing out into the trees. "And Grady! Your grandson!"

Nerves crackled up my spine and my palms dampened. This was it. The great edge of oblivion, with no chance of escape.

"Oh," Mee-Moo answered coldly, like Dad said he was there to deliver a court summons or a late notice. "Alright, then."

He shook his head, jaw clenched tight. "Unbelievable."

The line clicked dead and a moment later, the gate lurched in. Mechanical arms swung back up the road until the way was clear. Dad hit the gas, and the Aztek jumped through. We rose sharply for another few yards before the road evened out flat. The trees spread out and the Bluffs appeared out of thin air.

A cheap imitation of the Trevi Fountain crowded our entry. SEA BREEZE BLUFFS RETIREMENT COMMUNITY was laid in bronze at its base. Beyond it, concentric circles of houses surrounded a pool and clubhouse like a bullseye. Three wide rings of meticulously arranged and delicately maintained mini-mansions, each spaced apart by a single lane blacktop. A split straight up the middle opened onto the steepest cliff face we had yet to see. A shelf of rock jutting out over an endless drop, carrying the entirety of the neighborhood on its stiff shoulders. The houses stopped dead like they were afraid to get too close to the edge.

This, I remembered clearly from the years before. Every time I saw their neighborhood, their community, fear drowned out my higher brain function. And this time was no exception. When I was younger and we'd pull into the Sea Breeze Bluffs, I always asked Mom the same thing I was currently wondering.

What keeps it all from falling into the ocean?

All it would take was one bad quake to snap the ledge off and take the entire neighborhood with it.

6-6-06

Dad coasted past the fountain. From there, we didn't have far. I sank into my seat, kinda hoping I'd fuse to it and they wouldn't be able to get me out.

Sorry, can't stay! I'm part of the car now.

The pool shined with the kind of clarity that only biweekly professionals could provide, fenced in and surrounded by umbrellas, loungers, and picnic tables. Long windows looked into the perfectly rectangular clubhouse. The lights were on, but no one was inside. A ping-pong table was folded against the wall, a small lectern stood at the head of the room. The lawns were manicured within an inch of their lives, each spread out from identical gardens that stretched along the front of their houses and down to a hard line at the sidewalk. Walls were pearly white, reaching high into the sky, but kept simple in what I could only guess was a futile attempt at modesty. Every house had a two-car garage and the same covered porch. Doors with identical brass knockers sealed them.

Old people. Old people everywhere. As far as the eye could see. Sitting on porch swings. Shuffling newspapers with their morning cups of Metamucil. Power-walking up and down the connecting streets. Staring out windows and through doors, they all watched the new arrivals with suspicious interest, cloudy eyes and crusty crap in the corners of their mouths. As much as they would've had the outside world believe it, it wasn't some scenic retirement village. At best, it was a mausoleum with a view. Sea Breeze Bluffs' population was just waiting for their sun to set and had the money to ride out the clock in comfort. And if God moved too slowly, all it would take is a step in the right direction to go straight to the source to file a complaint.

Dad rolled up the driveway of the house numbered nineteen discreetly on its face. I assumed they were labeled in order, working their way around. Three windows looked down from the upper level, and one ostentatiously large one twinkled behind the swing on the covered porch. A short concrete ramp led up to it from the driveway. The only real difference I could see was in the garden. Where the others were in full bloom, Mee-Moo and Pop-Pop's was an empty patch of dried soil.

The car drifted to a stop, and a shrill voice assaulted us.

"No parking in the driveways!" An old lady stormed out of the garage next door, wagging her finger with an annoying urgency over her mane of granite curls and glasses so thick they could stop a bullet. "No parking! Lines! It leaves lines! No parking!"

"Oh, Jesus," Dad muttered under his breath as he kicked it into reverse and rolled back down.

He spun it around and pulled up to the curb instead, but the old lady remained.

"No cars on the curbs!" she banshee shrieked. The line between order and chaos clearly rested in where we chose to park. "No cars! No cars on the curb!"

Dad killed the engine and threw open his door.

"Where the hell am I supposed to park then?" he bit back, zero patience for her ancient declarations.

"In the garage! Only in the garage!"

"I'm not staying, lady!"

"Visitor! Visitor parking!" Her skeletal finger waved toward a long maintenance shed on the far edge of the neighborhood, back the way we came.

Dad took one look and laughed.

"No." He rolled his eyes. "I'll be here thirty seconds."

"Visitor parking!" she cried to the heavens, her voice trembling with righteous discipline.

Dad looked back in at me, still hoping I'd fuse with the upholstery.

"Enjoy this," he said with a smirk. "Come on. Get your stuff."

I pushed off against my seat. To my absolute dismay and frustration, I hadn't become part of it. No excuse now. This was happening and nothing was going to stop it. Didn't mean I was gonna move with any kind of speed, though. I milked my last few moments before the transfer was complete, opening the door slowly and getting out one leg at a time. The eponymous sea breeze wafted in, caressing my face in a chill that reeked of low tide and pine. I stared up at the house as the memory of it slowly trickled back to me. The couches wrapped in plastic. The TV no one could ever figure out. The long wooden dining room table meant for holiday meals and nothing more, same as ours. The strict No Shoes policy that extended past the front door. A never-ending sting of cleaning chemicals in the air at all times.

"Today, Grady," Dad moaned, not daring to cross any further than the sidewalk.

I opened the back door and shouldered my two-ton backpack. The rolling suitcase hadn't even made contact with the concrete when the front door of the house flung open. Mee-Moo and Pop-Pop stood waiting on the porch. A soft smile wrinkling his face, a deep scowl creasing her's.

"There he is!" Pop-Pop waved excitedly to me.

"Hank," Mee-Moo sneered at Dad.

A rail-thin skeleton of a woman, her makeup was tattooed on, head encased in a wig that was already out of fashion when she bought it before I was born. Her lips were pursed tightly, like even the air around us wasn't good enough for her. Wrinkles carved her face like arrows pointing to her disdain. That scowl never let up. Not once. Permanently sagging her inked brows and darkening eyes that were beginning to grow fuzzy.

To be entirely honest, I don't remember if she was always so miserable, or if my memory has just been severely tainted by everything that followed. I'm sure there's good in there somewhere. There has to be, in my even-younger years, buried deep under everything else. It's like a drop of poison in an apple pie, though. It only takes one bite to ruin the whole thing forever. For now, I can't recall a time when Mee-Moo wasn't absolutely oozing with venom. Particularly toward Dad. Never got that explanation.

No fucking clue how Pop-Pop stayed with her as long as he did. Convenience, maybe? Comfortability? On the day he retired, he stopped cutting his hair. A shock white ponytail dangled carelessly at the back of his head, retreating from a nonexistent hairline and tickling his neck. A few days of snowy scruff bristled his face, and a pot belly stuck out from under a bright Hawaiian shirt.

When he came back from the Western Front, way before Mom was even an idea, he got himself a real cherry gig as a civil engineer. Designing bridges and tunnels and all kinds of things that actually helped people. He laid down his guns for good, and Mee-Moo, it seemed, picked them right back up. Retirement and pension kept them both in comfort while they raced to the eternal finish line.

"Welp!" Dad patted me on the back. "See you in a few weeks. Do what your mom said."

Before I could turn back to him, he was in the car and pulling away. Mee-Moo watched him go, her eyes disappearing into squinted lids like she expected Dad to steal something on his way out. I watched him too, using all my mental powers to will him to come back. But it wasn't enough. Mee-Moo turned her attention to me, looking me up and down without moving an inch, burning with judgment and discontent. With an eye roll and a scoff, she went back inside without so much as a hello.

Pop-Pop waddled down the lawn to me, a smile from ear to ear, his flip-flops flip-flopping with every awkward step.

"Let's get you settled in, bud."

BLOOD RED SUMMER
JUNE 3, 2006

"There will be rules!" Mee-Moo barked as soon as the door was closed.

Pop-Pop gave me that look that said, "I know, just go with it."

"Your mother told me exactly what you did," she continued fiercely, her bony chest rattling. "This isn't going to be a vacation for you, so get that idea out of your head this instant."

With a curling Reaper finger, she beckoned me deeper into the house. Apparently, there was more to it than the front sitting room with its (I called it) shrink-wrapped couches that looked like something that once belonged to the Duchess of Bad Taste or the Lord of Grandiose Overkill. Golden yellow tassels would've hung from their red velvet arms, if they hadn't been smashed flat and packed in to preserve the freshness.

For a house that sat so perfectly in the sun, it was awfully dark. Every window was heavily curtained, greedily draining away any light that had the nerve to venture in. The interior walls were surgically white, and the stink of bleach fried my nose hairs down to nothing. The staircase rose up next to us from the entry way, an ivory rail leading to the switchback landing halfway up. Pop-Pop took my bags, his smile constant, and took off to the upper level. Smart man! He knew when to evacuate.

A shoe tree organized obsessively by style and color sat under a long oval mirror on the wall next to the door. Which worked for me, because I got to see the shock on my face when Mee-Moo yelled, "SHOES!" as I took a step forward after her. Like someone fired a gun next to my head, I jumped and turned a sick shade of white. Even better, I got to see just how much I stood out in their house. I had no business being surrounded by decorative vases, porcelain figurines, and framed bible verses. I looked like the portly poltergeist that haunted them.

My high-tops took a second to unlace, but I did it as quickly as my fingers would move. With no room on the shoe tree, I placed them gently on the marbled floor next to it. Mee-Moo stood in the hallway next to the stairs, watching like she expected cloven hooves instead of feet. I would've paid good money, if I had any, to do literally anything else in the world. But I followed her down.

The hall dropped into an open floor plan halfway across the house. Pictures of Mom dating back to her infant years lined the stretch from end to end. A few of me. Even more of Mee-Moo and Pop-Pop from various points in time. Their wedding, what looked like a Naval Ball, Mom's birth, vacations, his retirement party. And zero pictures of Dad.

A living room appeared at the end of the hall, separated from the chrome chef's kitchen by a high-countered bar top. A leather section wrapped around the space, in front of a flatscreen that was light years too advanced for them. On one side, a set of French doors led into an office with a desktop and a long drafting table. Another short hall ran away from it to what I vaguely remembered, and mostly assumed, was the garage. Pop-Pop's computer called my name like a siren on a rocky cove. The open doors begged to be crossed.

Noted.

On the other side of the living room were two massive glass doors leading out into the backyard. The curtains over them were as heavy and sprawling as a theatre's.

"You will report down here at exactly 6AM, every morning." She pointed to the bar that had no chairs. "You will eat breakfast; fruit, or whole grains only! None of that processed sugar mess. After, you will wait for your Pop-Pop to come down and give you the day's instructions. Understand?"

"Yeah," I nodded.

"I'm sorry?" Mee-Moo raised an offended eyebrow.

"Yes," I corrected.

"Thank you. We speak properly in this house."

Who in the fuck was she kidding? The resentment broiling in my gut was instant. When I look back at the holidays spent at our house, I remember Mom always cleaning like her life depended on it, going over every detail with a magnifying glass and a white glove. Maybe Mee-Moo was warmer when I was little, and not in trouble. Or maybe this was why Mom's level of anxiety and stress could be felt through the entire house before every visit. That might explain why she dove for the phone every time it rang. I was old enough to get the real deal now, not the happy grandmother facade.

She disappeared behind the counter, too short to crest its top.

"I'm over here now," she called.

I shuffled along after her.

"After every meal, you will help me clear, clean, and load the dishwasher."

And what time do the first-class passengers like to be served?

"When you're done with whatever Pop-Pop wants you to do, you are to read and write your reports for the rest of the day."

"Ok," Pop-Pop said as he stepped in, putting an end to it. "He's got a whole summer's worth of punishment to get through, let's not dole it all out on the first day, huh?"

He shot me a wink that I've clung to ever since.

"He needs to know," Mee-Moo insisted.

"I'm pretty sure he does," he said innocently. "Let's let him get settled."

Mee-Moo softened a degree as she looked at me, doing her best to reset.

"We're glad you're here." Didn't believe that for a god damn second. "But you're here for a reason."

"You're darn right he is!" Pop-Pop put a hand on my shoulder. "I'll show him to his cell."

He turned me around and angled me back to the hall.

"March!" he commanded playfully.

I did as I was told, making a show of stomping my way back to the stairs. As soon as we were out of earshot, which at Mee-Moo's age should've been around three feet, Pop-Pop gave me a nudge.

"Hey," he whispered. "Don't worry about her."

"You think?"

"I know, bud! Her bark is worse than her bite on this one."

We started up the stairs, Pop-Pop leading me.

"Your mom's just a little freaked out, so she feels like she needs to put the heels to ya," he added.

"Freaked out?" Mad I could understand, but actually scared?

"She's afraid you're gonna end up like one of those murdering Satan boys Mee-Moo tells her about." He waved his hand to dismiss it.

"Murdering Satan boys," I poked as we curled around the landing. "Good name for a band."

"I'll write it down." Pop-Pop chuckled before shifting gears. "She was right, though, there are gonna be rules."

"Okay." I was much more willing to accept them this way. Someone had to have passed that tip along, and I don't think it was Dad.

"No computer, no phone. Your mom was really big on those," he explained. Of course she was. "No TV too. You gotta finish all those books you got, write your stuff, and I got some chores I could use a hand with. But it's not like we're tearin' down the Berlin Wall, right?"

I wasn't sure what that meant, but I smiled back anyway.

"Just make sure to mind your Ps and Qs around Mee-Moo," he suggested as we hit the top. "I'll work on her. She'll ease up."

"Thanks, Pop-Pop."

"Hey, no skin off my back!" He grinned. "It'll be nice having another set of hands around here! That's punishment enough, in my book."

Two tall doors were dead ahead, closed against each other to hide their bedroom.

"There's more, I guess," he sighed as we moved past them, down a hall that never seemed to end. "But you'll learn those tonight."

"What's tonight?"

Even more doors dotted the walls around us. Linen closets and a pearly tiled bathroom. A small study for Mee-Moo, filled to the brim with crocheting supplies, and two guest bedrooms at the far end.

"The HOA meeting," he said with a grimace as he led me to the farthest room.

"The what?"

"The Homeowners Association meeting," he informed me like it was a cancer diagnosis. "They're every two weeks, gotta go."

"Alright." No idea what that had to do with me, but cool.

Pop-Pop led the way into the last guest room and stepped up next to the queen bed in the center of it. I was just glad it wasn't a cot on the floor or a blanket in the corner with a bucket. From what I recall, this was my room every time we stayed with them. After weeks spent on that seldom-used mattress and its still fresh springs, going back to my lumpy half-a-bunk would be the real punishment. Plush pillows laid at the head of the bed, and a quilted floral comforter as thick as my arm was tucked with military precision. The rest of the room was as bare as bones could be. A tall dresser was tucked next to the window, my bags stationed in front of it. A small closet retreated into the wall to the right of the bed, its sliding doors open and empty except for a solitary metal hanger on the crossbar. There was a TV stand in the corner next to the window, but it was as deserted as the closet. The cable box was depressing, with nothing for it to plug into. A curled mess of cables without a home. Its clock blinked like an SOS.

"Had to take that out." He pointed to it. "But the rest of the room is yours to get comfy in, of course."

"Thanks." I tried to sound grateful. At least I had an idea of where the outlets were, and a place to hide the iPod and charger I smuggled out in the pocket of my shorts.

"How long you think it's been?" Pop-Pop asked.

"Huh?"

"Since you guys were here last," he clarified.

"Oh." I hadn't really done the math. "I dunno. Few years, I think."

"Wow!" Pop-Pop wiped his brow, the fact making him sweat a little. "You're, what, twelve now? Thirteen?"

"Fourteen in August!" I said a little too proudly.

He laughed deep, his belly quivering.

"Practically a man! Wow!" He settled as he stepped back to the door. "I'll be sure to treat you like one."

He was trying, but the worry hadn't quite come off me yet.

"We really are happy to have you here," he added with a smile as he crossed into the hall. "Even if your Mee-Moo refuses to act like it!"

Pop-Pop left me alone in the room, standing there wondering what the hell I was supposed to do next. Unpacking the bags sounded like a start, though I wasn't sure if it was entirely necessary. There was still a nanoscale hope Dad would turn back. It shrank with every mile he gained toward the freeway. And probably should've died completely as soon as he crossed through the gate without me. I decided to start with the books.

I stepped around the bed to the dresser and the window. The blinds were closed tight, but after a few seconds of struggling to figure out the pull cords, I got them raised. Light blasted onto my chest, threatening to boil me down to a puddle of angsty nothing. The view wasn't bad, looking out onto the pool and its adjacent clubhouse. The sun hit the chlorinated water just right, turning the surface into a mirror of blinding silver. Ancient trees fenced us in, clawing at the sky like they were ready to pull out of the earth and drift away to some wonderful, magical realm not overrun by old people. If I pressed my face flat against the window and craned my head all the way to one side, I could just barely make out the cliff and the glassy ocean beyond it. I pulled away from the window to close the blinds, and there she was.

Down on the street, just at the edge of the clubhouse, standing on the curb, staring up at the house like it wasn't supposed to be there. An old woman, a little more on the ball than the others I had the pleasure of interacting with so far. Her long silver hair was tied into a rock hard bun on top of her head. A tweed blazer did its best to conceal her visibly sinewed frame. Her eyes were shielded under bifocals, but even from that distance, it was obvious. She was looking up and into my window with a scowl that rivaled Mee-Moo's. Pure, unfiltered, unearned hatred twisted her lined face. Scum and villainy had found its way into her quiet little graveyard.

I grabbed the cords and tugged, trying to bring the blinds again. Anything to get away from that stare. Hell, if the blinds hadn't fallen when they did, I was prepared to drop to the floor and stay there until I couldn't feel her eyes on me anymore. As it turned out, I did that anyway. The blinds rolled down and clunked hard against the windowsill.

A jet-black spider the size of my thumb fell with them. Like it had been waiting up in the blinds' housing, disturbed by the sudden action.

I jumped back, the edge of the bed catching my legs and toppling me over. The weirdest looking little fucker I had ever seen landed on the carpet. I could've spent years trying to identify it and never would've gotten it right. And really, who would've wanted to? Its legs were Daddy Long, thin jointed wisps holding up a disgustingly plump frame. Its thorax looked like it belonged to something venomous, bulbously rounded and ending in a sharply pointed spinneret like some species of Widow. Its abdomen and head came from a different family altogether, a long body ending in sharp pincers under shining eyes.

It reared up on its legs, waving its front two defensively at me as I sat on the floor in front of it. I scurried up onto the bed, naturally. And the spider rose with me. Crawling up with sickening speed, it scaled the side of the dresser, claiming the high ground. Its legs popped up again, kicking through the air while its pincers widened. If I were at home, I would've fled the room and called for Dad, like any sane person would. But I had a hard time seeing Mee-Moo care, or Pop-Pop get to it before it hid again. Then it would only be a matter of patience on its part, waiting for me to fall asleep.

I reached a foot toward my backpack and hooked the strap around my toe. With a couple of kicks and tugs, I pulled it toward me. The spider bit at the air, a final warning. I yanked the pack onto the bed and unzipped it. *Great Expectations* and *Catcher in the Rye* both felt heavy enough to help. I rose from the bed slowly, like I was hunting a T. rex. The spider's soulless black eyes fixed on me. Its legs twitched and quivered as I kept my distance. I tossed the Dickens up in the air as the spider settled down on its haunches. The book came down with a flat spin and a heavy *THUNK*, crushing it like a pneumatic press. As thick as it was, I wouldn't take chances. I dropped the Salinger on top too, pressing my weight down into it. I felt it give and slide, pulverizing the spider under hard covers and mountains of pages. No such thing as overkill, I repeated that process with every book in my backpack, bringing them down hard until a neat little tower stood on top of what was left of the eight-legged monstrosity

"What's going on in here, troublemaker?" Mee-Moo asked from bedroom door.

I spun around, out of breath.

"Nothing, Mee-Moo!" I played dumb. She could deal with the spider guts after I left. "Just unloading my books."

Her eyes narrowed on me.

"Good! That's what I like to see. Get a head start on them before we have to leave."

"I can read in here?" I asked, expecting her to say I had to do it at her feet.

"Your Pop-Pop seems to think you can." She turned to leave. "Prove him right."

I unpacked my clothes next, stuffing them away in the dresser along with any lingering, dwindling hopes I had left. Were it up to me, I would've left it all in the suitcase, regardless. Unpacking on trips never made sense to me. Like, who uses the dressers in hotels? What, are people moving in? I figured it'd earn me some points, though. I stored my empty bags in the corner of the closet. Swear I could hear them begging me not to forget them as I slid the door closed.

If I crawled under the bed a couple feet, I knew I'd find an outlet there. The perfect place to plug in and hide my iPod. Listening to it during the day, while they were up and mobile, only would've invited disaster. There's no way

Mee-Moo would've known it for what it was. She probably would've assumed an MP3 player was how I communicated with the rest of my homegrown terror cell. It was going to have to sit there until the house had powered down for the night. A silver lining if I've ever seen one, I couldn't imagine they would stay up nearly as late as Mom and Dad. Watching their shows and games in the living room well after the sun had set, relocating upstairs to wrap the day up with a movie they could both fall asleep to. Those countless nights I'd lie under Big Red, waiting for the sound to fade from the other side of the wall before doing anything I didn't wanna risk being caught in the act of.

I resigned myself with a sigh as I sat on the bed, propped up against the wall with pillows, staring at the unopened window. Too afraid to open it again on the off chance that old lady was still standing there, or more bugs were hiding in its mechanisms. Instead, I screamed their names in my head, hoping they'd somehow telepathically hear me.

RUUUUBEEEEEEN!

ALLLLLLEEEEEEX!

JOOOOOORDAAAAAAN!

Nothing came back to me. No one mentally screamed my name in return. I tried to picture them. Jordan, on the lam from a state-wide manhunt. Alex, sent to a convent and robbed of her fishnets and colored clip-ins. Ruben, struggling to remember the Spanish his parents never taught him, at a boy's school in a country he'd never been to. It was easier than wondering what they were doing without me.

In my defense, I gave it a fair shot. I had done what Mee-Moo said and started working on my books. I grabbed the first from the stack, the notebook Mom supplied, a mechanical pencil, and went to work. Only to find that a title like *White Fang* did not in any way guarantee the presence of monsters. Just dogs. Like I was reading a fucking Clifford book.

All I had managed to write for Mom was, "Is this what that *Snow Dogs* movie was based on?" The rest of the page was full of attempts at sketching the werewolves that book promised but was so sorely missing.

Sometime in the afternoon—I had no watch or clock anywhere near me so I couldn't say exactly—Mee-Moo wailed up the stairs.

"Lunch!"

I didn't hesitate. I tossed the book back onto the dresser, flew off the bed, and straight down to the kitchen.

It took the peanut butter sandwich and handful of grapes she left on the counter for me to realize that I had been rushed out the door without breakfast. I inhaled the whole thing in a few ravenous bites as she watched me from the other side of the kitchen, her nose curling like I hadn't showered in months.

"Hubby!" she called when I was done. "What do you got for the troublemaker?"

Pop-Pop hemmed and hawed as he slowly got out of the chair in his office.

"Nothing right now!" He shrugged from the open doors.

The look she shot him had one clear meaning: find something and find it now.

"I'll need you later, though," he corrected. "Before the meeting. Why don't you keep workin' on your books until then?"

"Alright," I accepted with zero intention of returning to Alaska and its non-werewolves.

Mee-Moo watched me like she expected me to run off with the good china or one of her weird-ass cherub figurines as I made my way back upstairs.

I did my best not to fall asleep while working on the next book in my stack. Moving them too much, shifting them to find something more interesting, felt like a bad idea. The spider's squashed entrails didn't deserve any wiggle room. The spines gave me nothing to go on, and with no computer to look them up with, that was all I had to work with. Some I knew of from their movie adaptations, others I was totally clueless about. Their titles didn't exactly lure me in. Who the hell was Jane Eyre, and why was I supposed to care? Did she hunt vampires? Have some degree of demon lineage? Was she trapped in a snowbound hotel with a bunch of pissed off ghosts and her telepathic son, perhaps? No? That was a pass for me, then. For that matter, how hard could it possibly have been to kill a mockingbird? And if I wanted a story about an old man and the sea, all I had to do was look outside.

Luckily, from what I had been told, the next book in the stack did have monsters in it. I put the dog book back on top and pulled *The Odyssey* free, settling back on the bed with my notebook and pencil. Ready to fall into a mythical quest of guys in sandals and funny-looking helmets, with names I'd have to do my best at pronouncing, fighting a host of creatures from a time long forgotten. I knew I had been misled halfway through the first page. Like the time Ruben swore up and down that I would love *The Silmarillion* because I liked the other Middle Earth stuff, only to find a collection of paragraphs that had no Frodo and just as little clarity.

I fell asleep almost immediately. With the book on my face and the notebook empty next to me, a fresh page unmarked by any thoughts or critiques. My mechanical pencil rolled off the bed and landed somewhere on the floor while I fogged hot breath into the pages. I got more use out of them masking my definite sounds of sleep than I ever would reading them. The TV mumbled from downstairs, lulling me even deeper like Mom and Dad were watching in the living room. The day crept on outside, marching along at its elderly pace.

I honestly think I forgot where I was.

Thankfully, it was Pop-Pop who came to get me when the time came.

"Let's roll out, inmate!" he chimed from the door.

I shot up like I was caught with my hand down my pants. The book went flying to the floor.

"Is he giving you any trouble up there?" Mee-Moo called, hovering from the bottom of the stairs.

"Loads! I'm gonna have to take the hose to him!"

I clamored up and out of the bed, acclimating to their house all over again.

"Sorry," I mumbled. "Woke up super early."

"Better get used to that, bud! We're early risers around here."

"Cool." It wasn't.

I picked up the book and dropped it on top of my stack.

"How far did you get?" He was actually interested.

I couldn't tell him the truth. It wouldn't have been a satisfying answer.

"Couple of chapters," I lied as I made for the door.

"Can't wait to hear your thoughts," Pop-Pop chuckled as he led me down the hall. "Meeting's not for a bit still, but your Mee-Moo likes to get there early to set up."

"Okay."

"Which means you and I gotta set up while she tells us what we're doing wrong!"

"Wouldn't have it any other way." I was hoping I had slept clean through to dinner. Apparently, I was only out long enough to recharge for work.

"That's what I like to hear!"

Mee-Moo was already out the door, standing on the porch with the duffle bag she called a purse slung over her shoulder. She had changed from her normal, nothing special "house" clothes to a retina-searing bright floral sundress that dropped down to her blue veined ankles. Her good "going out" clothes. Pop-Pop slipped into his flops while I took a knee and retied my high-tops.

"He needs faster shoes," she complained.

"One fire at a time," he said as I stood up again, ready to go.

I followed Pop-Pop out and waited for him to lock the door. A force of habit, I'm sure, there was nothing to secure the house against at the tip top of the world. Still, it was safer to stick close to him than to follow Mee-Moo. She shuffled down the ramp and started across the lawn without us. When Pop-Pop was satisfied no other senior could get through his deadbolt, we followed her. It didn't take much to catch up. She wasn't exactly spry. Even with his stiff waddle and me slowing to keep his pace, we landed next to her in only a few short steps. If she could've moved any faster, she still wouldn't have. We were on Mee-Moo's time, a message she sent loud and clear.

Up the curb, through the pool gate, and across the smooth concrete deck, we stepped up to the clubhouse's flat white door, bleached near platinum by the sun and salt air. A carved wooden sign hung over it, MEET ME AT THE BLUFFS. In smaller letters below the main message, A RETIREMENT COMMUNITY was etched in, just in case anyone could possibly forget. Pop-Pop shifted through his keys, looking for the right one. Its jagged silver teeth slid into the lock on the handle, and the door popped in. Frosty, sub-arctic air barreled out. Fluorescent lights buzzed in the low ceiling. Mee-Moo shoved her way in ahead of him, but he didn't seem to care. A gentleman, Pop-Pop held the door for me as I followed.

Cobwebs hung from the ping-pong table. The finish on it looked so new that it was easy to assume it was delivered, assembled, and then left in its exact spot against the wall, where it remained untouched for who-the-hell-knows how long. Sets of brightly colored paddles and a rack of balls hung next to it, a layer of dust clinging to their curves.

The gray carpet was worn in a very specific pattern. A wide trail was pressed and darkened from the door to a large flat square in the middle of the room. Circles dotted the pressed patch in precise rows. Mee-Moo stood in the center of it, turning and studying the floor like it was a puzzle she was intent on solving. The lectern waited at the head of it all. SB HOA was scrawled across its dark oak face in flowing golden cursive. Stacks of metal folding chairs were lined up next to the long curtail window.

"Hmmm," Mee-Moo made a point of contemplating loud enough for us to hear as she stared at them.

Pop-Pop crossed to the chairs and nodded for me to follow.

"I usually gotta do this part on my own," he offered, happy for the extra set of hands. "Takes forever that way!"

We followed the divots in the carpet, placing a chair leg in each set of four. All the way across the flat patch, we filled the rows one at a time. He wasn't confident he could carry more than one, and I didn't really want to either. Mee-Moo shambled off to the lectern, watching us with a warden's eye and barking pointless commands when she saw fit.

"Wipe that off first!"

"Make sure they're even!"

"No, put the good ones closer to the front!"

"Leave room for the scooters!"

The sun was starting to dip below the cliff by the time we were done. I'm sure it looked spectacular, sliding down into the ocean, casting the water in shades of gold and orange. But I didn't see it. With at least one chair for every house in the Bluffs, Mee-Moo took up her spot in the front row. Directly in front of the lectern like she was there to see Bush speak. Yet, even her smile looked angry. Like her face muscles weren't sure how to form the expression and rebelled against her instead.

So, is dinner out the window or . . .?

Had I not seen it, I never would've believed that was the entire plan. Set up the chairs and then just . . . sit there. Stuck in between them, I leaned over to Pop-Pop. I had to ask.

"When does the meeting—"

"Shhhh!" Mee-Moo cut me off like I was interrupting something only she could hear.

Pop-Pop patted my knee, telling me to settle in for the long haul.

Shadows stretched across the streets, and lamps started to burn behind windows. There were no street lights to speak of, but the Bluffs didn't really need them. Every single garage around the three rings was equipped with a uniform floodlight, filling the driveways with LED white and arcing out to the sidewalk. I watched them power on, since there was fuck-all else to do. Whatever they were doing, however hard their parents came down on them, there's no way my friends were as soul-crushingly bored as I was. The stack of books looked great by comparison.

Once every house had a small spotlight shining out of it and the sun sank into the water, the others started to emerge. Like a horde of ghouls, they shuffled and shambled out into the street. The old Parking Enforcement lady made a point to check the curb as she wandered out. She stared at it, not convinced, like she suspected the Aztek was now invisible and Dad had his bare ass pressed to the window. Scooters and mobility chairs whined as they rolled through the streets. Greetings were exchanged in transit, and the legion of near-undead descended on the clubhouse.

Pop-Pop pushed himself up with a winded grunt. He wobbled over to the door and pulled it open. A rubber stopper was tucked against the dusty baseboards.

"Go help!" Mee-Moo hissed.

I jumped out of my chair, just to see if my legs still worked. Pop-Pop waved at the stopper on the floor, fanning his hand like he was trying to reach it but couldn't.

"I got it," I said helpfully.

"Good man!"

Jamming it in was the only way I could see to help. What else was there? Standing and smiling awkwardly at every nonagenarian as they crept in and took their seats? I took a step back to my chair, and Pop-Pop snagged my sleeve. He shook his head discreetly and pointed to the floor. No, we wait here.

I lost count of how many times I said, "Nice to meet you," after Pop-Pop gleefully announced, "and this is my grandson, Grady!" Every last resident filed in. Two dozen canes, just as many walkers, a lady in a Rascal whose feet didn't reach the bottom, and a man in a scooter who looked like it was growing out of him. A power chair covered in a heavy cocoon of blankets, a shriveled face peering out. A woman bent over at a perfect ninety-degree angle, her arms tucked at her side and hands dangling from her wrists like an elderly tyrannosaur. The men all wore some variant of Pop-Pop's Hawaiian shirt. From muted polos to standard silk button-downs, they were festooned in colorful floral designs. He was a trend setter, apparently, which meant Mee-Moo was too. The women all wore identical styles of long beachy sun dresses, really jamming their coastal aesthetic down my throat.

Is that something that happens when you get old? You start dressing like that?

Pop-Pop was the most popular man in the Bluffs. Every old lady lit up at his perfectly pleasant smile, and every old man shook his hand as firmly as arthritis would allow. I definitely heard more than a few joints creak and pop. They all looked at me with a perplexed interest as we greeted them, like there must have been a circus nearby that nobody bothered warning them about. Until they made their way to Mee-Moo. If he was the Senior Prom King, then she was clearly the Queen. They stopped to give her hugs or friendly waves, pausing only long enough for her to tell them something she probably shouldn't have. Before they broke off to their seats, they turned and looked back at me with spite filling their wrinkles and folds. Even the scooter-cyborg did a quick five-point turn to look back at me and scowl.

With everyone seated, we returned to our station in the front row. An excitable murmur covered the assembled masses, coupled with constant deep sniffling and a chorus of hacking coughs. I didn't realize she was missing until the old lady from the street stepped in. Those who could stand at attention, did. Slowly, of course, with a great degree of difficulty and a cacophony of grunts, groans, moans, wheezes, and rasps. But they got it done. Her critical gaze was worse than Mee-Moo's as it scanned the room, scrutinizing her rickety troops. It fell directly on me as she crossed to the lectern, surveying me from top to bottom like we were to draw pistols at ten paces.

Three men filed in behind her, like secret service agents old enough to have failed Lincoln. The first wore a snowy flattop, so perfectly level I could've rested a plate on it. Deep canyons carved across his jagged complexion. He took a spot on her right shoulder, staring out at the others from a position of guarded prominence. Racking in next to him was a grumpy boulder of an old man, a bottle brush mustache drooping down over his mouth like Wilford Brimley was the height of fashion. A lanky skeleton in a bow tie with a head of salt and pepper wool brought up the rear, flanking the left side. Once assembled, they clasped their wrists, hands secured officially in front of them, and glared at the one thing in the room that wasn't like the others.

Pop-Pop nudged my arm and jerked his head to the side. I took the cue and stood with them, in a quarter of the time. Pretty sure some in the back were still working on it.

"Sitting President Elaine Rubenfeld," Mee-Moo announced, her voice dripping with a level of pride and admiration I doubt Mom ever received.

"Thank you, Under Secretary Graham," she nodded slowly to her, her voice steady and frigid.

Oh yeah, Mom had a different last name before Dad.

"Be seated," she added.

It took a minute again, but they did. I waited until Pop-Pop was back down to follow him, not wanting to be rude.

Elaine produced a gavel from inside the lectern. Three sharp cracks split through the room and rattled my fillings.

"This meeting of the Sea Breeze Bluffs Homeowners Association is hereby called to order."

She put down the gavel and held out an expectant hand, her knuckles curled into a claw. The flattop behind her stepped forward. He reached into his back pocket and pulled out a small black leather-bound journal, the edges of its pages shining and golden. Elaine snatched it out of his hand, and he retreated to his designated position. She laid it flat in front of her and adjusted her bifocals.

"First, the old," she began, almost mechanically. "A motion was put forth last we met to repaint the curb numbers from sea foam green to sea spray green. Motion was previously denied." She looked to the room, searching for any objectors. There were none. "Denial stands. Arnold Finkle proposed that the postal carrier be given his own dedicated gate remote so that he no longer has to request access to deliver. It has been taken under advisement, but I, for one, would not feel safe giving an outsider unrestricted access to the neighborhood at this juncture. What would stop him from delivering our mail in the afternoon and coming back for our patio furniture at night?" A hint of outrage picked up her voice, like she actually believed that was a possibility. "All in agreement?"

Every hand raised except for mine, and the long white beard I could only assume was Arnold Finkle. Pop-Pop nudged me with his elbow, his other arm up high. I timidly joined the yea-sayers.

"All opposed?"

The forest of wrinkled hands retracted. One shot up indignantly, the nails yellowed and crispy.

"Arnold, you will remain his point of contact. It shall continue to be your responsibility to let him in every afternoon. Failure to do so will, of course, result in fines." She consulted the journal before continuing, her eyes darkened with the gravest severity. "The raccoon is back."

A wave of concerned mumbles crested the room.

Where is it supposed to go? It's the woods.

Elaine raised a hand, demanding silence. It fell immediately.

"Pat Smith has volunteered to deal with it for us."

"I'll get that sumbitch if it's the last thing I do!" a man somewhere between Walter Matthau and Peter Boyle howled viciously from the middle of the crowd, thick globs of bloodthirsty slobber flying from his meaty jowls.

Grateful applause broke out around the room. Pop-Pop shot him a thumbs-up over his shoulder.

BANG! BANG! BANG!

All attention obediently snapped back to Elaine.

"Have you made any progress?" she drilled, annoyed at another momentary lapse in focus.

"Naaaah, he's a slippery lil' bastard! But I'll get 'em."

"See that you do," she commanded before returning to the book. "Lastly, a reminder that our summer potluck will be happening this coming Tuesday, as previously approved by myself and the board." The men behind her nodded. "Right here in the community room."

Thunderous claps and wheezing cheers erupted from the assembly, vibrating through the windows of the clubhouse. The community room, I guess. Whatever lipstick they wanted to put on it.

I didn't have to do the math to know what day that was. It felt like a perversion of a perfectly good idea. A day that would come only once in a hundred years, baring the Mark of the Beast, and I was gonna have to spend it eating jello and rice pudding with people old enough to have seen the last one. Unless they were actually in a convent, a boys' school, or the Buena Vista Correctional Facility, there was no way my friends could be any worse off.

BANG!

She slammed the gavel and silenced the room.

"The proper preparations are underway," Elaine pressed on. "Are your assigned responsibilities understood?"

Nobody objected. Nobody said anything, in fact. They all only nodded, solemn and stern.

"Very well then. The summer potluck proceeds as planned. Moving on to new business." She leaned on her elbows across the lectern like she was about to share an extra special secret with us all. "If it pleases the Association, I would like to first put forth a question to the Under Secretary and her husband." Her steely eyes drifted to me like a cat cornering a mouse. "Is this the young man we've heard so much about?"

A bony claw reached forward, pointing to my chest like anybody else in the room could've possibly been misconstrued as a "young" man. Mee-Moo pushed off the back of the chair and rose to her feet. Pop-Pop gestured for me to follow as he stood too.

"Everyone," Mee-Moo explained, for Elaine's benefit alone. "This is my grandson, Grady."

"Hello." I waved nervously. A hundred wrinkled eyes locked onto the interloper.

"He'll be spending the summer with us!" Pop-Pop threw an arm around me and pulled me into a half-hug.

"He's a troublemaker." Mee-Moo dropped the bomb, straight to Elaine and Elaine alone. "He set another boy's house on fire."

The corpse in charge leaned back warily, but she didn't look away. Her fingers wrapped around the gavel, and for a second, I'm not entirely sure she wasn't about to throw it at my head.

"No, I didn't!" I said, desperately defensive and breaking away from Pop-Pop. "It was just fireworks!"

"It was just a bit of foolin' that didn't go his way," he added, trying to ease the rising tension in his neighbors.

Elaine's predatory stare shifted to him, outraged.

"It wasn't that serious, is all I'm saying," he chuckled.

"Well, young man." Elaine leaned forward again. "Can we expect any trouble out of you while you're here?"

"No!" I shook my head and raised my hands to my chest like they had guns trained on me.

"Keep an eye out for him!" Mee-Moo added to the others. "If he steps a single toe out of line, you let us know!"

It takes a village to tar and feather a convict. They nodded and mumbled their agreement, already building a stockade for me in their heads. Pop-Pop smiled sympathetically and gave me the nod to sit back down. We did, Mee-Moo easing herself back down after us.

"And I'll trust you'll discuss the dress code with him, Under Secretary," Elaine added, glaring at my clothes like I was wearing nothing at all.

My nudity might've been less offensive, based on the rumble of disgust that came out of the others. Mom's pickiness over my wardrobe started to make more sense, beyond the fact that I knew I wouldn't be coming home to a lot of my favorites. I looked around the room. The dresses and the shirts. More color than I had worn since I was old enough to pick out my clothes.

"We'll fix it," Mee-Moo said like it was a genuine problem.

6-6-06

Kill me now. For the love of God.

"Yes, you will," Elaine leered. "Otherwise, you will have to be fined on his behalf."

Mee-Moo nodded quickly, like she planned on burning the clothes I brought with me the second we got back to their house.

"And while we're on the subject," the President continued firmly, borderline forcefully. "Your house is the last to complete its summer-ization. Rectify that no later than the potluck."

"That's what I got him for!" Pop-Pop added happily, jostling my spikes and sending a blizzard of gel crust flurrying down my shoulders.

No one else was as enthused as he was.

When his brother came home with a bootleg copy of the *Dawn of the Dead* remake, Jordan went on for days about how cool the ending would've been in real life. That final moment played out over the credits where Ving Rhames and his friends, fleeing on a boat, stumble upon an island expecting salvation and finding nothing but hungry corpses.

"No, you don't get it!" he argued with us. "It's a place where there'd be nothing but you and a bunch of zombies!"

I didn't see much difference between the end of that movie and the community room. And I could already confirm that it wasn't anywhere near as cool as he thought it was.

Time lost any sense of meaning as Elaine and her elderly dependents shifted gears and rambled on about sprinkler maintenance, the pool schedule and God only knows what else. My brain shut down, presumably to protect itself, wondering just how far I'd make it if I dove off the cliff and swam for freedom. If I'd eventually wash up on an island off the coast full of creatures only slightly less alive than the ones I was stuck with.

Their dull words floated around me, but their eyes didn't shift. Hers especially. Elaine glanced at me every chance she got, whenever someone wasn't speaking directly to her or when her responses to them had finished. They scrutinized every inch of me and darted away again, like they had no choice but to, as they bounced between her people and the notes in her book. Following the leader, the others did the same. Like there was a chance I was going to vanish, gone in a puff of smoke to raid their homes and burn the village. The fact that I didn't seemed to only annoy and perplex them further.

Not Elaine, though. I had seen her look on teachers' and principals' faces more times than I would've liked. Not directed at me, but the kids in our classes who were perpetually in trouble. The real problem children. The ones that snuck lighters into school to burn the field's yellow grass, or the ones constantly equipped with Sharpies to scrawl their names on anything that would stay still long enough. The kids they had no choice but to keep watch over at all times. Elaine wasn't expecting me to disappear. She knew I'd stay right where she could see me, and she wouldn't have had it any other way.

At the meeting's end, she banged her gavel so hard against the lectern that I expected the whole thing to shatter.

"Adjourned!" she declared, closing her journal and holding it close to her liver-spotted chest.

Her posse advanced to the door ahead of her, waiting in a line beside it. She led them out and into the night while its temperature slowly dropped. Just to shake things up a little, I watched her. Elaine and the Board cut across the pool deck to a second gate on the opposite end. They crossed through and slunk into the street on the far side of the inner ring. The moon, crawling its way over the treetops, cut the bright white of the garage lights with gentle blue-gray. She made her way up the driveway of one of the other identical houses, her minions waiting in the street like good chaperones and escorts. When her front door closed, the Board broke off. The man with the mustache and the guy in the bow tie took to the houses at her sides, while the flattop remainder kept going to the row behind. Two flanking, and one to cover the rear.

The rest of the Bluffs shambled and wheeled from the room and out into the streets. The odd mix of light filled their wrinkles with shadow, darkening the lines, crevices, valleys, and gaps into warpaint. Their eyes sunk into deep pools of black. Like gold-cursed pirates, the moonlight revealed them for what they really were before they were washed to pale specters by the brighter seas rolling down their driveways.

Mee-Moo leaned against the lectern, sighing like the day had finally taken her last drops of energy. Can't say I was feeling any different, but there was work to be done. Pop-Pop and I folded the chairs, stacking them back in their spots on the wall in the same meticulous order we took them down. She watched again, but offered no coaching, corrections, or advice this time. Instead, she just kept groaning like she could've done it more efficiently. Every other load of chairs was encouraged with a long, exasperated exhale until we finally put the last two back on the stacks.

I stared at the asphalt as we walked back to the house, unable to look at either of them. I made the mistake of glancing up at Mee-Moo as we inched along next to her. Once was enough. The light played the same tricks on her face as it had the neighbors, deepening her scowl and the lines from her mouth into veins of black.

I didn't want to see Pop-Pop like that.

YOUR SWEET SIX-SIX-SIX
JUNE 3, 2006

"It's too late for dinner!" Mee-Moo declared when we finally got back inside the house. "I saw on my programs that eating too late is bad for you!"

Couldn't help but notice she was looking at my gut when she said that.

Pop-Pop saw it coming, at least. He came into the room and tossed me a granola bar before they packed it in for the night. No TV, no decompression of any kind. Their day was done, all the boxes checked, time to shut it down.

"Is it okay if I read for a little?" I asked as he stood in the doorway.

"Fine by me," he said as he left me alone. "Just not too late! We got an early day."

"Just another chapter or two," I lied.

"Have at it!" he allowed happily as he started to leave. "Night, bud."

"Night, Pop-Pop."

The door thunked softly against its frame and the knob inched back into place. Quiet hours had officially begun, best not to disturb the Warden. I listened carefully to the hall, stretching my ears as far as they could go. Pop-Pop's feet scuffed against the carpet all the way down to their door. It thudded into place and silence stole the air out of the Bluffs.

At home, I would've heard cars racing regardless of the time, dogs barking at anything that moved, neighbors whose time in the garages was reaching critical mass. Sea Breeze was supposed to be different. Crickets, owls, wind through the trees, nature shit! I heard nothing at all outside my window, like the woods and cliff worked together to form a perfect vacuum. My ears buzzed in the quiet, hungry for anything at all.

I knew what to feed them, but it also took time. Counting out the minutes, I waited the better part of an hour before I was willing to venture under the bed, once I was positive Mee-Moo and Pop-Pop were out for the night. With no signs of life in the house, I crept down to the floor. Lowering myself carefully to avoid any unseen creaks or groans the floor might make. In retrospect, I probably didn't have to do any of that. But midnight snack runs with Mom's canine hearing conditioned me.

My iPod dutifully waited against the molded baseboards. I snatched it out from the dark side of the bed and clutched it tight, my hand complete at last. It couldn't stay with me all night, though. I didn't want Pop-Pop to have to decide if it was against the rules or not when he came for me in the morning. If it was actually him who volunteered for that duty and not his less patient other half. A screen is a screen, right? It had to be back in its hiding spot before I went to bed, but that didn't mean I wasn't gonna get my time in. That I wasn't planning on keeping it glued to my palm until my eyes started to drop, until the very last second.

I buried the earbuds in deep and woke the iPod from its long slumber. I scrolled through my lists of artists and albums. Just about everybody sounded good, a real burden of heavy guitar-laden riches. We'd only been apart maybe eighteen hours in total, close and yet so far, but I'm pretty sure that was the longest we had gone since it landed under the Christmas tree two years prior. I hit Shuffle and let my shining black and red companion choose for me.

The first song the iPod landed on was one Alex had shown me. A band I wouldn't have known without her in the first place. To keep things equitable, I had traded her Claudio Sanchez for Ville Valo. The sci-fi epic of Coheed and Cambria for the dark sorrow of His Infernal Majesty. One of the proudest, most validating days of my young life was when she bought a Coheed sticker from the mall. I'm sure she felt the same when I picked up a Heartagram sweatband. One that I never had the chance to sweat into. There was no explaining to Mom and Dad that the band's symbol-logo hybrid wasn't the mark of the devil.

And let's be honest, this was always going to be where that first night was headed. As much as I argued it in my head, the second they closed their bedroom door, I knew I was gonna be headed downstairs at some point before the sun came up. I didn't need the extra motivation of Alex's ghost. What I needed was the balls to actually do it. If I was caught, the rationale was, it wouldn't be as bad tonight as it would be a week or two from now. I could already hear what they would say. Mee-Moo wrote the playbook Mom followed religiously. That prepared speech about trust, how hard it is to earn and how easy it is to *blah blah blah*. But wouldn't I rather have breathing room in the time remaining to work my deepening debt off? And not fumble closer to the finish line, just to have it follow me home. All assuming I'd get caught, obviously.

The excuses were just as easy to come up with as the increased punishments. I was getting a glass of water. I needed a new pencil, none of the ones I brought were good enough. I needed to look up something about the book I was reading. I wanted to check the time, and there were no other clocks in the house for some reason. I had the shits and didn't wanna wake them up. There were a million reasons why I could be downstairs that didn't involve Messenger or MySpace, and I was convinced they all sounded good.

My heartbeat kicked in time with the bass drum in my ears as I sat there, talking myself into it. Giving it a little more time felt safe and smart. If my snack runs taught me anything, it was that getting out of the room was only the tip of the iceberg. Steady focus would be needed all around.

Every song my iPod bounced to only fueled the fire. I took each and every track as a sign from some greater power. Linkin Park for Ruben. CKY for Jordan. Well, Jordan and Bam Margera. But I could at least ask about Jordan while Bam's fate would remain a mystery. And far less important. My iPod really did know what I needed, and it wasn't playing a fair game to push me toward it.

What were the odds that Pop-Pop had a password on his computer? What if he was like Dad and locked the whole thing down? He wasn't stupid by any means, but he was old. It was just as likely that elderly paranoia put up a million guard walls to his operating system, even if he struggled to figure out how to establish them.

What if he, like, locks the keyboard in a drawer? Or takes the power cord to bed with him?

Another hour was the best I could do. Middle of the night, on the later side of the midnight hour, was what I hoped for. But it wasn't gonna happen. Nerves don't mix well with being tired. They blended into a weird cocktail that shot my eyelids up every time they drifted down like they were tuned in to danger I couldn't see. Sleep was an easy out, but the excitement of teenage transgression filled me with pools of adrenaline that wouldn't allow it.

I took an earbud out and listened to the hall. There wasn't so much as the howl of air conditioning through the ducts. I took them out entirely, wrapping their cord around my iPod and powering it down to help the battery. This was going to be the end of my day, one way or the other, so I stashed it back in its hiding spot under the bed.

The trick, I had learned, was to make it look like nothing was out of place, out of the ordinary. I crossed to the wall and clicked the light switch, throwing the room into darkness. My natural environment. A round white face floating in a sea of black, I camouflaged into it as best I could. The door was cool, almost cold, as I leaned in. Gently, I eased myself against it to avoid any shifting thuds or creaks my weight might produce. I pressed my ear into the door and waited, listening.

No footsteps in the hall, no voices from behind their door. Only the persistent buzzsaw of Pop-Pop's snores down at the other end. They could've been coming from Mee-Moo, for all I cared. One of them was deep into their REM cycle, and the noise of it would help mask my approach. I saw them in my head, tucked into their king bed with the linen that hadn't been updated in decades, sleeping peacefully in perfect ignorance. That deep staccato rumble was all the signal I needed.

I gripped the knob and turned it with deliberate slow steadiness. The catch pulled free, and the door floated an inch toward my chest. Before letting it go, I listened again. The snores were louder with one layer of the filter broken. I opened it just enough to squeeze an eye through. No light from Mee-Moo's crochet cave or from the hall bathroom. I'm sure they had their own in the master suite, but bases needed to be covered. If, for any reason, one of them chose to venture out, I would've just said I was doing the same.

The coast was clear.

The knob turned slowly against my palm as I pulled it open just enough to thread myself through. For appearance's sake, I closed the door behind me as I stepped into the pitch black hall. The heavy curtains and blinds made perfect sense now. If those garage lights were on all night, and if the moon was as powerful as I had seen it on a regular basis, then blacking out the windows was a necessity.

I heard on the Discovery Channel once that closing your eyes in the dark is a good way to adjust them to it. Not sure how true that is, but it was a step I always repeated anyway. My eyes sealed tight as I counted down quickly from thirty. When they reopened, I stretched them open wide. Even if it hadn't actually helped, I could still see shapes. The bulk of the walls next to me, the shadowy cut-in of the door frames, the protrusion of knobs.

Like the Mystery Inc. gang sneaking through a haunted house, I took my first careful step forward. The floor stayed gratefully quiet as I made my way past the next guest room. Snores grew in ferocity from their door as I closed in on the crochet room. I paused at it, peering around its corner just in case Mee-Moo made better blankets and scarves in the dark. Nothing, just shelves upon shelves of endless spools and rolls of yarn. An empty easy chair sat in front of a table covered in what I could only assume were hooks and needles, glinting flecks of metal in the dark. I stepped across its entrance and to the guest bathroom, watching the other side of the hall like a hawk.

Unless Mee-Moo had a rich, deep baritone none of us ever knew about, they were definitely his snores shaking out of their door and through the linen closets. I could've hopped my way to the stairs and all the way down to the computer; nobody would've heard it. Hell, I probably could've shot a couple of oversized Samaritan rounds into the ceiling and neither of them would've noticed. Why take the chance, though? Every time I thought there was no way Mom and Dad could hear me, I always found one of them waiting at the top of the stairs when I snuck back out of the kitchen, arms loaded with chips and Mountain Dew. As loud as the snores were, Mee-Moo would've had to have been actually deaf to be able to sleep through them. I closed the bathroom door to sell the idea that maybe I had been there, and moved on.

The switchback landing was lost in the darkness. I stared down into the abyss, trying to remember how many steps separated us. Getting down was the real roulette, every step potentially rigged to blow. At home was easy, I knew those stairs, which one's creaked and popped, and where. Which sides to hug closer to and which to stay away from, which ones needed to be taken from the edge, and which needed to be stepped on closer to the rear. I hadn't been paying nearly enough attention to their house since arriving. Horrible time to realize I wasn't sure if they had an alarm system or not. I didn't remember hearing any beeps or chimes when we went in or out the front, and I definitely didn't hear anything arming itself before the house shut down. But that didn't mean much. Alarms were easy to slide past, if need be. I had gotten pretty good at commando crawling after ours was installed. I scanned the walls from the top of the stairs. Nothing immediately stood out as a motion sensor or even a keypad.

You wanted water, I reminded myself, just in case.

I took my first step down, easing my foot onto the first stair like I was afraid I'd fall through it. When it didn't creak or groan, I repeated the process with the other foot, all the way down to the landing. The flat stretch stayed silent as I hugged close to the rail and wrapped around to the second set of stairs. Whatever light managed to force its way in through the front windows bounced weakly off the tile. The random old person decorative crap Mee-Moo filled the house with became hulking, leering shapes in the dark. The figurines watched from their designated perches like they just couldn't wait for me to come down and keep them company. I tried not to make eye contact and focused on the floor as I snuck down.

At the bottom of the stairs, I paused for a moment. No alarm sounded, so I tempted fate and waved my arms like one of those used car lot inflatables just to be sure. The snores from above floated down after me like a landslide, but nothing else. I knew better than to relax, but my body didn't. My muscles unclenched, and my breath hissed out, relieved. The hard part was done.

I made my way into the hall, hunched low and stepping softly like I was trying to avoid booby traps. The glass of Pop-Pop's office door glowed through the darkness, reflecting the meager light and giving me a target to aim for. I stepped blindly down the hall, avoiding looking at the pictures of Mom on the walls on the off chance that they would rat me out. I could feel their eyes on me as if she were standing right there. They begged me to stop, to turn back and go to sleep like I should've been or read like I said I was. Thirteen-year-olds have the capacity to be good at a great many things, and masters of none. Listening fell into neither of those categories.

The French doors grew large and tempting. If there was a lock, I'd have to accept it and actually just grab a cup of water and go back to bed. But I was in luck. They weren't even closed all the way. A gentle push sent them floating into the room. I checked to the right, into the living room and kitchen. The bulbous back of the couch, the dark block of the counter, and the towering monolith of the fridge were the only witnesses.

Just do it. You've come this far. Be quick.

I dashed across the office in two big bounds. The rolling desk chair sat on one of those thick plastic carpet savers. The wheels growled softly over it as I pulled it back and sat. My breath picked up the second ass made contact with plush leather. Back before I had my own laptop, I had been told that such things could be found on the internet, so I snuck into Dad's office to Google "Lindsay Lohan boobs" in the middle of the night. This wasn't that, but the same rush of fear and excitement trembled through my hands. Now that I think about it, actually, that might've been when he set the password. I wasn't entirely sure I cleared the browser history, but it never came up.

Pop-Pop's keyboard and mouse sat in front of the monitor, newer than Dad's by at least a generation. A bulky tower crowded my feet under the desk, with nothing but the carpet saver to separate it from the floor. I grabbed the mouse and gave it a gentle click.

6-6-06

WHUUUUURRRR!

The tower kicked on like a jet engine climbing to speed. My head whipped over my shoulder to make sure no one was there. As the computer warmed up, I stood and closed the doors back over, just enough to still see out while absorbing any unwanted sounds. The monitor flickered to life as I sat back down, a blank screen shining a backlit spotlight onto my face. I pulled the chair in close and waited for it to fully wake up.

Oh shit!

I remembered Dad's welcome chimes, and panic hit me like a wet slap. Scrambling around the desk, I searched for anything resembling an external speaker. A stapler, a cup of pens, a box of brass brackets, a bone-dry, never-used coffee cup that declared IT'S 5 O'CLOCK SOMEWHERE. But no speaker. I went back to the monitor. Top, bottom, sides, its only button was the one that turned the whole thing on, already pressed in. My knee bounced a million miles a second as I looked back and forth between the monitor and the hall. Hall, monitor. Monitor, hall. Finally, the operating system came to life.

Silently.

In the corner of the screen, the little speaker icon had a cross slashed over it. Muted like he knew.

Good job, Pop-Pop.

I was in business. The desktop wasn't nearly as cluttered as my own, but the icons were just as seemingly random. Excel was the only actual tool. The rest were for slot machine games, a chess simulator, virtual blackjack, and a folder labeled FOR TAXES. In the bottom left, like an afterthought, a shortcut he didn't care enough about to put in a place of prominence, was Internet Explorer. The cursor rocketed across the screen.

It took three customer service calls, a technician request, and an entire afternoon on the phone with Mom and Dad to set up their Wi-Fi. Even if their router hadn't been so new and shiny, I'm sure it would've been just as intimidating.

"Just tell them to keep the damn dial-up if its that big of a deal!" Dad tried to throw in the towel sometime around hour two or three.

It was a good thing they didn't. The long process of connecting and the tortured robot screams that accompanied a phone line accessing the internet were a thing of the past.

The browser window opened, slowly loading its elements into place. I closed my eyes and tried to hear the house, to feel the Force around me, but nothing came back. Not even the snores could be heard that far from their source. Only the excited beating of my own heart responded.

If Ruben wasn't in Mexico, he'd be online. His parents could've taken the computer out of his room, thrown it into a wood chipper, and ground it into powder, and by the end of the day that kid would've figured out a way around it. Rather reassembling it speck by speck or hotwiring the mostly broken garage sale laptop he kept under his bed, plugged directly into their phone line. Warcraft was worth the effort in his eyes. And like a true creature of the night, he wouldn't sleep unless he absolutely had to. If guards weren't posted at his door, he'd be awake. 11:15 on a night with no school in sight? His evening would just be getting started.

I logged in to Messenger with MySpace in a separate window as a backup. He and Alex would both get messages, if need be. I'd give them each time to respond and if they didn't within a minute or two, I'd wipe the history and fuck off back upstairs, ready to check again the night after. Luckily, I didn't have to. iNRuEnS66 was present and accounted for.

DUDE, I typed gently. IS EVERYONE OK????

It took a couple minutes of pure agony for him to respond.

yea

That was something, having confirmation that the doomsday scenarios in my head hadn't come to pass.

where u ben? he added.

Mom flipped her shit. @ my grandparents house for the rest of the summer >:(

sucks! u gunna be here for 666?

Hold the fuck on.

nah. r u not grounded or anythin???

He typed for no more than a couple minutes to relay the fallout. It came in bursts and chunks, each punctuated by my sharply held breath.

not allowed out 4 a while

mom wuz mad as fuk but dad wuz kinda kewl

said georgey and his dad suck azz anyway

I liked Ruben's dad a little more. Just didn't wanna imagine whatever good ol' Dave Booker had done to warrant that kind of reaction from him. I'm sure it involved a few slurs I wasn't supposed to know existed.

Alex has to go to a purity ball? he added, not sure what that meant.

In her dad's head, us shooting fireworks at Georgie was clearly some kind of foreplay.

jordans chill. dude unplugd his phone.

Smart! Even when people were there to take calls regarding his crimes, they wouldn't get them. Wish I had thought of it.

gunna sneak out for 666 tho \m/\m/

They were in trouble, and Jordan was kinda in hiding, but the reality of it hit me in the face like a wet bag of garbage. Compared to me, they got off with a slap on the wrist.

dude, I sent, they wanna send me 2 a different skool.

That got Ruben's attention.

WAT NOOOOO!

I KNO!!!!! I fired back just as quickly.

Ruben pitched the single greatest idea in the history of human thought.

we can kidnap u!

I had to cover my mouth to stifle the laugh. As much as I wanted to say yes, just to see if they could for the sake of the sixth, Mom would've sent a team of bounty hunters on the trail. If she didn't already have my friends under surveillance to ensure they didn't try that exact thing.

`nah im stuck here :,(`

`u sur???` he prodded. `666!!`

I debated about it for a second, wanting more than anything to tell him to rally the troops and come immediately. I could slide past the gate, hike down the road, and meet them at the bottom before any of my elderly caretakers even knew I was gone. But still, I was in enough trouble for trying dumb shit like that.

`yea, i gotta stay`

He had to try to tempt me one last time. Not sure I would've respected anything less.

`ill b waiting!`

Still, I couldn't change my mind, as much as I probably should've. But it was good to know the support system was still intact. That's all I needed. My friends were okay for the most part. I hadn't dragged them down to the depths I had been sent to.

`later dude`

`lates!`

I killed Messenger and opened another window for clearing the history when I was done. A quick scan of MySpace and, in theory, I'd be good for the rest of my stay. One question remained, and I was dying for the answer. How pissed were our Hollister and Fubu overlords?

Snores blasted across the house, louder than ever, bellowing sharply like a backfiring motorcycle. I jumped in the chair, my heart jackhammering enough to give me pause. Their volume soared, roaring from the master suite like a caged beast in pain. If it didn't wake the whole damn neighborhood, then I didn't think much else would. I rolled the dice.

Real quick.

I clicked over to MySpace, tapped in my credentials, and held my breath while the page loaded. My foot bounced anxiously like I could pedal the Wi-Fi to a faster speed. The snores swelled again, booming through the house like they were amped. The screen turned black and blocky flames coiled up it. The cursor shot to my friends list the second it finished loading. I scrolled quickly through them, just a cursory search to see who still remained. Brittany M was no longer counted among them, but there were others. I knew for a fact that a couple of the boys I saw somewhere toward the epicenter of the slobber-soaked minefield were in my roster somewhere. Kids I was friendly with at the beginning of our time in BVJH, but was loathed by now. How loathed exactly was the question I needed answered.

Photos from that exact party had been posted to the Walls of the few spy accounts I still kept in my friends list, but not a single comment or post mentioned the fireworks or the masked monsters waiting in the street. All that, and we didn't even warrant an OMG. Disregarded and brushed off by the time they got the pictures uploaded.

I clicked the mouse a little harder than I probably meant to and killed the window. Gripping it tight, my teeth gnashed as my eyebrows furrowed into hard ridges. Like a bone stuck in my throat, I couldn't swallow the truth. I was having to sneak around a house in the Village of the Soon-to-be-Dead, my friends were in lockdown, and the few assholes that still lurked on my page had completely forgotten the reason why. In a night full of rug burns and wet spots, we weren't the most interesting part of their stories. Simple as that.

How is that fucking fair?

As much as I wanted to scream, and maybe throw up a little, the safest place to do either of those things was my room. I had lingered long enough. I forced myself to drop it for the time being and open the browser's history in my final window. A long string of HOW TO SCAN PHOTO and RETIREMENT INVESTMENT EASY and SAFE TO BUY ONLINE? scrolled down the page, mixed with the few odd websites Pop-Pop visited regularly. Weather and the news mostly, with ESPN and an engineering journal thrown in to really spice shit up. Mine stood out the same way I did with neighbors, clearly from another world altogether. I wiped them and shut down Internet Explorer.

The snores gurgled again over my shoulder.

Farther away this time, like they had thrown themselves down the hall. Like they had left the bedroom and were on the prowl.

I couldn't remember Mom ever saying anything about either of them sleepwalking, this might've been news to her for all I knew. I listened carefully to be sure I was hearing it correctly. The beast growled again to confirm, from deeper in the house. I got up and stood in the closed over door, my ear poking through to the hall. Their tone changed, deep and wet like a bullfrog's croak, from what had to be the other side of the second story.

Closer to my door.

My time downstairs had expired. Whatever the hell was going on above me, it was time to move. I rushed back to the computer and sat down to put it back to sleep. The cursor whipped to the Start menu and another snore exhaled through the house, raging down the stairs. In the glow of the monitor, a pair of legs crested the top of the screen.

Then another.

And a head.

A spider identical to the one smashed flat under my books crawled its way down and over the glowing glass. I pushed the chair back hard and fast, my eyes wide and pulse thundering. The chair slammed to a stop before even hitting the carpet. I leaped up from it and spun around.

Pop-Pop stood at the back of the chair, Michael Myers still, his fingers curled around the headrest, wearing nothing but a pair of plaid boxer shorts and a tattered white undershirt. Wet snores croaked softly from his open mouth without a trace of his usual dopey smile. His face hung blank and vacant from his skull. Black coals hid his eyes. A line of thick, glimmering silver drool ran out over his slack lip.

"What do you think you're doing down here, troublemaker?" he asked flatly, his mouth barely moving.

All the excuses left my brain just as quickly as I had formed them.

"There are rules."

"I—I know, Pop-Pop," I stammered, trying to remember any of the alibis I was so sure of before I made yet another stupid-ass decision. "I'm sorry, I—"

"No excuses!" his voice boomed. His mouth drooped further, lips twitching to form the syllables. "Upstairs!"

"Okay, Pop-Pop." I nodded quickly before trying one more time. "I just wanted to—"

"NOW!"

"Okay! Okay!" My tail tucked, and I made for the open door.

I rushed through and into the hall, but Pop-Pop didn't follow. Needing to make sure he was okay did me no favors. I tossed a look over my shoulder to see if he was coming. Silhouetted by the monitor's glow, he held out his hand as a platform for the spider. Its legs caressed his palm as it crawled gently down. My head snapped forward so quickly I thought it might loop all the way around.

Rounding the corner, I attacked the stairs. My feet thumped softly on the carpet as I struck a balance between fast and quiet. If she wasn't awake already, I wasn't about to tempt Mee-Moo and add to the freak show. Staggered footsteps charged down the hall behind me. I wrapped around the switchback, and Pop-Pop gripped the rail at the bottom, a cupped hand held close to his chest. A snore growled out of his limp face. I reached the top, and he crossed the landing. I banked down the hall to my room. He stopped at their open door, waiting, a perfect wall of undisturbed darkness beyond it. Cupped hand raised, he lowered his head down to it, whispering like he was having an intimate conversation with his fingertips, dark eyes glaring up at me.

I pushed through the door and closed it behind me with a soft click. Leaning against it, my breath was nowhere to be found. My palm greased the knob with sweat, and my knees quivered like they were about to give out entirely. On the other side, their door slammed shut, thundering through the house.

I don't know how long I stood there, waiting for fire and brimstone punishments to rage into my room. How many times I whispered, "What the fuck?", panting like I had just run a mile. Or how long it took to shake those images and filter out the adrenaline before I collapsed onto the bed.

The sky was turning purple by the time I finally fell asleep.

The sun had barely started its arc over the trees when Mee-Moo came barging through my door like a bull on a rampage.

"Up!" she shouted. "You've got a lot to do today!"

Still in my clothes, not under the starchy old quilt but on top of it, light attacked my eyes and burned clean through to the center of my brain as she raised the blinds.

"What did you do last night?" she drilled.

In the couple of short hours I was asleep, I had managed to wipe those details from my memory. They all came rushing back as I rubbed the crust from my eyes, my pulse pounding steadily against the walls of my skull. I wasn't sure how to answer her.

"I . . ." How much did she know?

"Did you leave this house?" she accused as she scanned the room for signs of malfeasance. Booze, drugs, a half-eaten goat, anything she could pin on me.

"No!" I defended through my haze.

"You're still dressed! We sleep in our street clothes now?"

"Oh." I looked at myself, my shirt damp with sweat. "No, I was . . . reading. Fell asleep."

Her eyes narrowed on me as she flung the closet open like she expected a gaggle of prostitutes and WMDs to spill out.

"What's in those bags?" She thrust a damning finger at them.

"Nothing," I sat up. "I unpacked them."

She wasn't buying it, but also wasn't going to press it any further either. There was no smoking gun for her to drop in my lap.

"I don't know how your mother runs things," she drew the line, "but in this house we don't dirty the beds with our street clothes."

With a righteous huff, she turned back for the door.

"Downstairs! Breakfast! Five minutes!"

The door was left open as she vanished into the hall. Pop-Pop and his little friend flashed through my head. I didn't want to get up, didn't want to go downstairs and face the scene of my crime and . . . whatever the hell it was that followed. But convicts don't get much autonomy. If judgment was coming my way, it was going to find me no matter what I did.

There was nowhere to hide.

I pulled on a fresh shirt, printed with the poster art for *Shaun of the Dead* and a not-musky pair of shorts, free of any chains, buckles, or decorative straps. Adding clean boxers and socks, I slid it all on out of view of the window. If Mee-Moo and Pop-Pop were up, then it stood to reason that the rest of the Bluffs were too. Scuffing and scooting around, doing whatever it was old people did before the sun had fully risen. Lawnmowers fired up all around the neighborhood, a small fleet converging on the back rings.

My head drifted uneasily, not quite up to speed with the rest of me. More than Pop-Pop, more than the computer, and even more than my friends, a single thought kept bouncing around inside it. Nagging at me, no matter how ridiculous it was.

The tower of forced culture stood on the dresser, waiting to be toppled. My higher brain function would've known better, but I was too fucking tired to listen to it. I shifted the stack of books, taking the top half of the stack off delicately, and placing them beside their counterparts. Wisps of legs stuck out from under *Great Expectations* like the Sharpie lines drawn on Jordan's desk. Still, I had to see it. Just in case the spider I crushed was like that guy who cut off his arm to escape the boulder he was trapped under.

I lifted the Dickens. The top of the dresser and the back cover of the book were smeared with arachnid viscera, like I smashed a rotten grape under the book. A thick, gooey smear of black exoskeleton and brown guts. Dead as dead could be, good enough for me. I put the books back and left the room before I could be summoned again.

Not that it did any good.

"Five minutes means five minutes, troublemaker!" Mee-Moo yelled as I took to the stairs.

"Coming!" I chirped back, trying to sound excited and failing miserably.

Dread slowed my steps, and I held the rail like I needed it. Down to the landing, I took it one step at a time, trying not to remember Pop-Pop coming up after me. The figurines and vases were less sinister, less gawking in the light of day. An optimistic prospect picked up my pace.

Maybe it wasn't actually that bad.

Maybe I overreacted. Wouldn't be the first time I thought something was scarier than it actually was. I once spent a night posted up in front of my bathroom door like one of those furry hat royal guards because I was positive there was a dead old lady in my bathtub, waiting for Nicholson to come put the moves on her. Turned out the shower head was just leaking onto the curtain. Mom warned me about the movies I loved most. A steady diet of that kind of imagery tends to play tricks on perception.

Right?

The pictures in the hallway weren't watching me, weren't judging, weren't begging me to stop. They were stuck behind their frames, frozen in time. The doors to Pop-Pop's office were still open, and the chair was right where I left it. The monitor was dark, powered down to sleep on its own good time. The smell of burnt toast filled that side of the house. That or I was having a stroke, it was hard to tell which.

Pop-Pop sat on the couch, in the bend around the room. His little smile had returned, his eyes were bright and alert in the new day's dawn. I would've sworn he was wearing the same shirt as the day before, if it hadn't been a different color entirely. A newspaper was open in his lap, a steaming cup of coffee on the armrest next to him.

"Good morning, sunshine!" He beamed at me.

"Morning," I muttered, confused as all hell.

"You alright?" He caught the look on my face.

"Took a while to fall asleep," I said, studying him, searching for any signs of the man that chased me up the stairs.

"Well, I hope you got some good rest!" he added pleasantly. "Got a big day ahead of us!"

"You didn't bring any other clothes, did you?" Mee-Moo asked from the kitchen.

"He's alright," Pop-Pop brushed her off. "We gotta go down the hill, anyway."

"Good. I'm not about to be fined because he's dressed for a funeral."

I'm not sure what funerals she had been to, but if the people there were dressed like I was then they must've been pretty cool.

She dropped a small plate on the counter in front of me like she couldn't wait to let go of it.

"Eat," she ordered.

It actually was burnt toast I was smelling. Charred to a crisp, soaked in a slab of butter and topped with a single tomato slice. I took it like there was a chance it was poisoned, my mind doing all kinds of acrobatics to try and force any of it to make sense. Not just the weird-ass breakfast, but the hard turns the three of us had made in the time since the HOA meeting. Sleepwalking still seemed like an obvious culprit, and my heavy movie filter probably didn't help me any.

Ash and buttered tomato coated my mouth as I bit into the toast, fighting the wince and cringe as they came. Mee-Moo watched me choke down every last chalky, squishy bite like she expected the weight to start melting off me immediately like candle wax. When it didn't, she just sighed and took the plate. It clattered into the sink, ready to face her discipline later.

"When you get back, and Pop-Pop's done with you," she went on, "you're gonna help me with all these dishes."

All these dishes?

How much of a mess could she have made burning the life out of toast?

6-6-06

I leaned over the counter to get a better view. Cutting boards, one coated in crumbs and smeared with butter, the other slathered red and dotted with seeds. Separate knives for each action. A dish with a mostly melted stick of butter already congealing to it. More plates than the three of us could've required. A frying pan and a spatula. I may not have been a culinary master—Mom occasionally trusted my skills enough to let me make microwave mac and cheese for myself—but even I knew all of that was absolute overkill. And my queasy gut told me it was intentional. A bigger mess than was necessary, so I'd have to work as hard as she wanted me to. Pop-Pop came around and added his empty coffee mug to the mix, the remnants of black grounds clinging to its sides.

"What happened to the things you used to wear?" Mee-Moo asked longingly. "You used to be such a cute little boy."

I became too aware of how messed up my hair currently was. Flat where I didn't want it to be and spiked where it shouldn't have been.

"Those little sweaters and polos you used to have," she kept remembering. "You had one with sailboats on it! I loved that one!"

Is she talking about the shit I wore when I was fucking six?

"Find him something like that while you're at it!" she commanded Pop-Pop.

He must've seen the disgust spreading over me, as much as I tried to contain it.

"You're a little old for those now, right, bud?" Pop-Pop jumped to my rescue.

"I think so," I agreed uneasily.

Mee-Moo grimaced, first to me and then to Pop-Pop. It wasn't a suggestion.

"Besides!" he added. "That's not the dress code."

I shrugged. What are ya gonna do? Rules are rules.

"Well," she begrudgingly said. "Anything's better than *that*."

"We'll figure it out! Won't we, bud?"

"Sure." I accepted it, trying not to take the offense she intended.

He yanked his keys out of his pocket and gave them a showy jingle.

"Let's get a move on then!"

I followed him back across the house, his flip-flops scuffing and snapping with his waddle. Mee-Moo crept after us, settling down on the couch with a sigh like she had done something other than make a giant mess. She snatched up the remote and turned the TV on. Her fear-mongering newscasters were waiting for her. Their voices boomed across the house and chased us out.

The open office taunted me as we passed it, like it remained how I left it just to fuck with me. Pop-Pop looked straight into it as he continued straight across, but I did my best not to. Down the small hall next to the office, and on the other side of the downstairs bathroom, the garage door waited. A collection of white tennis shoes and sandals sat ahead of it.

"Oh," I remembered, pointing back to the other side of the house. "My shoes."

"Got you covered!" Pop-Pop pointed to his collection. "You're gonna need some good work shoes."

"What size are they?" I asked dubiously.

"Close enough!" he shrugged.

A size and a half too big would've been the more useful answer. My feet swam in a striped pair of white New Balances as we stepped into the garage. Pop-Pop clicked a button on the wall. Clean white light burst down from above, bouncing and reflecting off the pristine epoxy floor. The rolling door lifted, rising with a quiet glide. In a sight I was in no way used to or expecting, the garage was nearly empty. On one side, a neatly arranged tool bench stood with its hanging pegboard filled with hammers, screwdrivers, and saws. An armory of gardening tools was arranged next to it. Rakes, trowels, gloves, shovels. No stacks of boxes, no bikes, skateboards, scooters, or rollerblades. And no Aztek. A four-door Cadillac gunship congested the heart of the garage, so old it still had ashtrays on either side of its leather bench seats. Burgundy paint on a cherry interior, like at some point in the late 70s Pop-Pop considered hanging a pair of fuzzy dice from the rearview mirror and becoming a fur coat pimp.

He slid in through the driver's door as I climbed into the passenger side. The interior was just as lovingly maintained as the rest of the car. For a vehicle made before either of my parents were old enough to drive it, it didn't show a minute of its age. The leather was slick and flawless, no cracks, creases, or tears. The wood of the wheel was polished, its deep browns and blacks untarnished by age. The dashboard console was as it was the day it rolled off the assembly line. A dial radio and cassette deck served his needs perfectly.

The Caddy rumbled to life, a cloud of exhaust puffing out of its ass. He hit play on the tape deck, and some old guy singing about a depressing hotel in California fought for my attention. Pop-Pop jerked the shift lever down and we barreled backward out of the garage, hitting the road with a hard bump.

"And away we go!" he sang, kicking it into drive.

We sped through the Bluffs, faster than he was probably supposed to or was allowed. A small army of hired gardeners in heavy boots and thick, SBB-branded jumpsuits wheeled mowers to and from the long shed on the edge of the neighborhood, tucked away toward the trees. An array of gardening and pool equipment waited for them inside its heavy wooden doors. Red metal gas cans lined the walls, surrounding a fleet of machines.

The fountain blurred by, and the trees zoomed past us, overtaking the Caddy as Pop-Pop shot toward the gate. We dropped down the road, in full free fall. I gripped the handle of my door, bracing for impact as it swelled ahead of us.

"Oop!" Like he forgot he had to stop. Like it was a god damn surprise to him that the gate was there!

Pop-Pop hit the brakes and the Caddy skidded to a halt, inches from smashing its shining front bumper through the expensive rod iron. I have no clue how that car wasn't absolutely covered in dings, scratches, and dents. A gray plastic rectangle sat on the visor above him, a long black button running over its center. He clicked it, the gate opened, and he let off the brake entirely. Didn't even ease it down the hill, just let it rocket to the first turn under its own gargantuan weight.

I braced against the dashboard involuntarily, still gripping the door handle for dear life as we wove tight to the edge of the first turn.

"I'm glad we're getting this time together today, just the two of us," he said genuinely.

"Me too, Pop-Pop," I grunted through gritted teeth and a locked jaw, my wide eyes watching our imminent doom with every curve of the road.

"Give us a chance to talk without your Mee-Moo standing over our shoulders."

"Yep."

"I shoulda warned you yesterday," he continued through a chuckle. "My sleeping meds can do some weird stuff to me."

My attention broke from the road. My neck creaked as I turned to look at him. His focus stayed on the road.

"Did I catch you using my computer last night, or did I dream that?"

"You dreamed I was at your computer?" I asked nervously. What color was left in my face drained away.

The guardrail came within glancing distance of my door. Trees and rock sloped sharply outside my window.

"Thought I did!" Pop-Pop laughed. "Weirdest damn thing."

"Super weird!" I tried to play it off.

"But you wouldn't do something silly like that, would you?"

He turned to look at me, eyes off the road, wheel turning on instinct alone.

"Of course not, Pop-Pop!" I was starting to sweat. And not just because every turn threatened to launch us out of existence.

"No, I didn't think you would. You know the rules, right?"

The tires squealed under us, weaving first too close to the edge, then uncomfortably toward the empty oncoming lane.

"Mm-hm!" I nodded as fast as I could.

"And you would never lie to your old Pop-Pop?" he asked playfully.

"Never!"

The front bumper teased at the edge of oblivion.

He smiled softly and satisfied.

"That's what I thought. Must've been my pills."

He turned back to the road.

"Oh, geez!" he gaped, startled by the dash and how far to the right the needle on the speedometer was.

The brakes eased down, and the Caddy slowed to a more responsible speed, taking the turns and corners reasonably.

"They can make me snore pretty bad sometimes too."

"I didn't hear anything," I played dumb and innocent.

"Okay, then." He grinned at me, ear to ear, happy as could be.

We continued down the hill, winding easily into the town, my heart trying to escape my chest. Pop-Pop hummed along to his songs until the road leveled out again, tapping out the drum beat with his thumbs against the wheel as we wrapped around the bandstand.

That's all it was. That was it. Sleeping pills! A stupid answer to a stupid problem. I had heard stories like that before. They had the capacity to induce all kinds of weird shit. Ruben said a guy down the street from him took more Tylenol PM than he was supposed to once and woke up in his backyard the next morning buck naked with a half-eaten bag of frozen shrimp in his lap. Last night had to have been on the same tree as that, projected through my cracked and bloody movie filter. I relaxed into my seat, content with that logic as we turned onto the great long street.

"One stop to make first, then we'll get you all squared away," he said. "Sound good?"

"Sounds good, Pop-Pop," I replied dutifully.

He pulled up to the curb down past the grocery store and the post office and killed the engine. On the other side of my window, tall white letters proclaimed TOOLS & LUMBER across a glass storefront. Pop-Pop was out and penguin stepping to the door before I registered that we had arrived. I climbed out and followed him, feet sliding through the too-big shoes.

"Hit the lock, would ya?" he threw back at me.

"Right."

I jumped back to the car, pulled open the door, and hit the manual lock on the inside. Tools & Lumber jingled as Pop-Pop went inside. I chased after him, the same bell overhead signaling me. Rows of overstuffed shelves were surrounded by piles of loose boards and beams. A snowy flattop and craggy alcoholic's complexion watched me from the counter, behind a register that still used mechanical keys.

"Mornin'," Pop-Pop nodded to him with zero response.

We recognized each other immediately. His bloodshot eyes narrowed on me, glaring like they had from his post behind Elaine, already planning what he was gonna say to the cops when he called to report the shoplifter. Pop-Pop was on his way to the back of the store. I pointed after him to remind the flattop who I was with.

Stepping fast, I caught up to Pop-Pop easily as he waddled past shelves of power tools and their accompanying paraphernalia. Across an assembly of metal paint cans, through a small collection of automotive needs, lug nuts, tire irons, motor oil and the like, around a standing rack covered top to bottom in pre-packaged screws. Leading us like a trench to a discreet back door labeled GARDEN in peeling sticker letters. We stepped through and were back outside again.

An open storage area bigger than their garage and just as square, originally meant for dumpsters and old boxes, had been converted to something resembling a tropical rainforest. Lush greenery, both domestic and imported, filled it. Saplings, bushes, thick leaves like something from the Jurassic period, all rose together, nothing over them but early blue sky. Tall brick walls surrounded us, broken by a chainlink fence ahead. A dirt access road waited on the other side. Bags of topsoil and tables of potted flowers crowded in the middle, and that's exactly where Pop-Pop headed.

"Alright!" He tried to drum up his own enthusiasm as he surveyed his options. "Summer-ize!"

I wasn't following, so he spelled it out for me.

"HOA's got a dress code for the houses too, bud. Not just the butts that live in them. Every season, I gotta rip out the plants I planted the last season and plant the plants for this season."

"They can't just stick with the same ones?"

"Apparently not! Winter is roses, spring is tulips. Summer, I think it's daisies, but I didn't check the handbook, so they're gonna get what they get, and they can fine me later if they want."

I smirked at his rebelliousness, a bit impressed. Pop-Pop, stickin' it to the Man. Well, the Woman technically.

"Can't grow them from seeds, of course," he went on, mostly to himself. "They'd never sprout in time. No! Gotta be full so we can rip up something perfectly good in a few months and throw it out."

"That's stupid," I couldn't help but scoff.

"It is! But, it's what your Mee-Moo wants. Who am I to argue?" He sighed deeply, like there was more he wanted to say, but couldn't. Not to me. He shook it off and perked back up. "Just gotta go along with it and hope for the best!"

He slapped his hand down on a stack of soil bags, almost as tall as I was.

"Think you can handle one of those?"

"Sure?" Fuck no I couldn't. But I doubted he could either.

"You grab one then, I'll get the flowers."

Pop-Pop broke off to the table of black plastic pots while I stared at the soil mountain, wondering how the hell I was supposed to manage it. He gave a very not-physical boy way more physical credit than he deserved. The 20LBS label on their shiny plastic bodies intimidated the hell out of me. But what else was I gonna do? Make him carry it? Tell the guy at the register we couldn't handle it, and be judged even harder than I already was? Absolutely not.

Starting at the top seemed as good a place as any. I tugged at the plastic bag, yanking it toward the edge of the stack. Faster than I would've liked, the whole thing slid down like it couldn't wait to land on my chest. It hit me like a shit-scented cannonball, nearly toppling me over.

"Hmmm," Pop-Pop pondered.

I looked back at him as I struggled to get a grip on the bag. He scratched his scruff as he surveyed the offered flowers, trying to remember which ones were closest to what he needed, paying no attention to his inept grandson, fighting not to die under a bag of dirt and manure. With a knee, I kicked the bag up into a better position and got my hands right. One under and one on the side to keep it from pushing me over. Couldn't see around it for shit, but I did my best to peer out from behind it as I made my way back to him.

"All set?" he asked.

"Yep," I groaned.

"We'll just make do with these, then."

Pop-Pop chose pots of what honestly looked like little yellow weeds, as many as he could fit into his hands and arms. He led the way back to the door, pots tucked into his elbows. Neither of us thought it through. His hands were full and so were mine. That door wasn't going anywhere.

"Can you?" he asked, nodding to it.

If the bag wasn't hiding as much of my face as it was, he definitely would've seen me scowl at that idea. Regardless, I stepped ahead of him. With my side-of-the-bag hand, I reached out, leaning to take the weight onto my back with the kind of disregard for injury only the youthful possess. I wrapped a couple of fingers around the handle and pulled. The door inched out. I caught it with my foot, kicked it open all the way, and held it for Pop-Pop. Like a fucking gentleman.

He shuffled through and back into the store. The door slammed behind me as I followed. The rows and shelves became a minefield with my vision blocked by soil. I could only see on one side, and even that was just barely. Pop-Pop's shoes were a wrong step away from becoming a tripping hazard. If I ate shit and knocked something over, ruined some display or damaged a piece of merchandise, I'm pretty sure the guy at the front would've fed me into a wood chipper. I inched after Pop-Pop, scuffing my way across the store in his giant shoes.

"And the bag, Terry," he said, pointing to me on my slow approach, pots cluttering the counter.

The flattop, Terry, looked at me like I was planning on taking that bag home to fuck it.

"Finally, summer-izing?" he asked dubiously.

"Yeah," Pop-Pop answered. "Been putting it off."

"Cost of livin' in the Bluffs," he said like it was something Pop-Pop should've known already.

"Oh!" Pop-Pop added as I reached him, leaning the bag against the counter. "This is my grandson, Grady!"

Terry knew that. But Pop-Pop might've done better introducing him to the bag of soil.

"Pleasure, Gary."

"Nice to meet you," I muttered back. I could've corrected him, but what did it matter? He had heard my name twice now and still didn't care to know it.

"What do I owe ya, friend?" Pop-Pop asked, his wallet at the ready.

"Fiddy," Terry burped without even touching the register. Pretty sure he just pulled a number out of thin air.

"You got it." Pop-Pop shifted through his bills to find the appropriate one.

He handed Terry a fifty. The grumpy old bastard snatched it out of his hand, hit a key to open the register, dropped the bill in, and turned his gaze out the door.

"Thanks for comin', thanks for shoppin'."

Pop-Pop scooped the flowers off the counter.

"Be seein' ya!" He smiled over their tops to him.

"Mm-hm."

Pop-Pop pushed his way through the glass door. He held it with his flip-flopped foot as I huffed and strained after him. We made quite a pair, heading back to the car. Flowers growing out his chest like his shirt had come to life, and the twenty-pound bag with legs shuffling its oversized feet after him.

"There we go," he said through a grunt as he rested the pots on top of the Caddy's trunk.

He dug in his pocket for his keys as I dropped the bag on the curb.

"I'm sorry if I seem a few drops short of regular, Grady."

I shook my head, playing dumb.

"There was just something I was hoping to talk to you about while we got ya out here, and I'm not quite sure how to put it."

Oh fuck.

"Yeah?"

"Yeah." He searched for the right words. "Think it's best I just come out with it. Did you know I went to the Front?"

The keys came out of his pocket and straight into the trunk lock, his eyes on them rather than me.

"Mom told me."

"Before I got sent over"—he kept going as he individually relocated the flower pots from the trunk to the asphalt—"I had never been in a fight in my whole life. Didn't really see the point of all that grief! Not for lack of interest, mind you. Plenty of guys always causing trouble in the school yard, stickin' their noses where they don't belong, trying to make sure people knew how tough they thought they were. None ever felt worth it, though, ya know? Most just fizzle out, barking in the dark before they become any kind of real problem. But when that German showed up and started makin' trouble for everyone, I knew." With all the pots down, he popped the trunk. "Sometimes, you just gotta! A fight comes along that you know you gotta jump into and not think twice because it's the right thing to do." Two-by-two, he lifted the pots into the trunk, talking to them more than me. "That one was mine. And when I came back, I coulda done a whole lotta different things. Knew I wanted to help put the world back together, though. I did my time! Served my country. There wasn't gonna be any more fights for me. None of them would measure up to the one I had just gotten through." He waited for the bag I forgot even existed, my attention solely on him. "Point is, you gotta know which ones to pick. What's gonna be worth it. You chase down every single bully, you'll go burning yourself out before the big one shows up. Nothing left in the tank for the fight that matters. Understand?"

I knew where this was going now, but I wanted to hear it anyway.

"I understand," I croaked, a lump swelling in my throat.

"This trouble you're in, back at home," he continued. "That boy and the thing with your book bag. Was that your fight? Was he worth it?"

I knew the answer, probably for longer than I realized or was willing to admit. Still, it wasn't easy to say.

"No." I shook my head, eyes locked to the sidewalk. "It wasn't."

"I'm not sayin' he didn't deserve it! And I'm all for you standing up for yourself. That's why I ain't mad at you the way Mee-Moo and your mom are! But you gotta know when to pick and choose, when to get dropped into Europe and when to stay the hell home! Imagine if I had picked some random squabble with a kid on my block and hadn't been able to enlist because I got hurt or locked up."

"I know," I mumbled to my feet like they were gonna let me off the hook.

"And these friends of yours . . ."

Please, no.

"Are they the ones to cover your rear when the shit hits the fan?" he asked, genuinely curious. "I know at your age it can feel like that, but I want you to really think about it. Are they really your friends, or are they kids you're gonna think are dorks in a couple years?"

I didn't have to think about that question either. They had already waged war with me. For *me*. Even if their consequences weren't as bad as mine, I knew the answer. And this one was considerably easier to say.

"They're my friends," I said, rock solid.

"Then that's all we can ask for, right?" he beamed proudly. "Good friends by our side when everything goes to hell and back. C'mon, bud," he changed the subject. "Let's get a move on before your Mee-Moo calls the coast guard."

I stepped to and lifted the bag into the trunk, smiling back at him as he waited. Without losing an ounce, it was lighter than it had been when I put it down.

Down near the one stoplight in town, nestled amongst the tourist traps with generic beachy names, there was a store. A boutique, if you will. One I hadn't paid much attention to on the way in.

Sandy Attire.

It exclusively sold bright Hawaiian shirts and flower dresses.

A forest of racks and shelves, each blindingly colorful, filled the space. Two floor-length mirrors hid in the back, flanking curtains into the doorless closets that had been reworked into dressing rooms. Warm fluorescents glowed in the ceiling, so as not to compete with the sun coming in through the big front window and thus fucking up the vibe. Near the front register, a more modern one than the hardware store, spindles full of seashell jewelry dangled. Earrings, necklaces, bracelets, anything a shell could be glued to or made to look like.

Pop-Pop stood behind me as I stared at myself in the tall mirror. Pride poured through his smile in our matching blue and white shirts. Shaun (*of the Dead*) begged for freedom under a shroud of synthetic silk. I wanted to kick my own ass, but I tried my hardest to hide it, to not ruin the moment for him.

Hovering near the counter, in our reflection, in between his shoulder and mine, Sandy Attire's sole proprietor watched us with vested interest.

Elaine.

Her icy eyes drilling holes in the back of my head.

"We'll take it!" he called happily to her.

"I'd say so," she said, thoroughly unimpressed as she stepped back behind the register. "It'll help you avoid *one* fine."

"Don't worry!" Pop-Pop replied as he crossed through the store. "Got everything for the summer-izing!"

I swear to God, if one more person says summer-ize *today . . .*

He was so happy about the stupid shirts that it took all the fun out of loathing them. Elaine didn't take her eyes off me, even as Pop-Pop stood in front of her with his wallet open. If she stared any harder, the shirt might've burst into flames. And I probably would've thanked her.

Pop-Pop handed her a stack of twenties as I dragged myself over to the door. Too many for what he was getting. A few buttons clicked and the register sprang open with a *DING*. She handed him back his change, too little for what she was giving him. I hovered at the exit. Not because I was super psyched for people to see my new look—black cargo shorts, royal blue Hawaiian shirt, gigantic clown shoes, and hair that desperately needed to be washed—but because Elaine's look made my skin feel like it was covered in crawling legs. I would've crashed Georgie's party wearing that exact outfit before I spent another second with her, eyes fixed on me like even her overpriced shirts weren't enough to make me fully human.

"See you at the potluck!" Pop-Pop waved as he stepped to the door.

"Will *he* be there?" she asked.

"Of course! He can't wait!"

I was already out, holding the door open and waiting for him. Pop-Pop shuffled through after me. I let it flap closed behind him as we walked together to the Caddy. I slowed to keep his pace, when all I wanted to do was run and hide, as he dug his keys out. It wasn't his fault the Bluffs were some kind of ancient money laundering scheme, built to fill the pockets of its residents.

"That was kinda weird," I said as we slid into place on the Caddy's leather bench.

"What was?" he asked, oblivious.

"The hardware store guy and the shirt lady." I pointed back to the boutique. "They're like your neighbors, right?"

"Oh!" Pop-Pop caught on as he started the car. "Well, yeah, bud."

He turned to me, his smile wide and eyes shining.

"It's just us out here."

Always and Never

June 4, 2006

"Oh, you two look so handsome!" Mee-Moo gushed the second we walked through the door.

With every step, I hoped and prayed the ceiling would collapse on my head.

"Doesn't that feel better?" she fawned over me. "You look like a proper young man now!"

No, I look like a proper old man.

"You think all the black and gloominess is cool now, but you're gonna look back at pictures of yourself when you're older and regret dressing like that. Just you wait and see!"

Still waiting, haven't seen.

We unloaded the trunk and stacked everything neatly in the corner of the garage, over by Pop-Pop's extensive workbench. I severely overestimated how brisk of a pace he'd want to work at. Used to Dad's tempo, I expected to hit the ground running and not stop until the job was done, rather to completion or until there nothing else we could do. But Dad was half his age and still had more miles left in his tank than he had traveled. With our score of flowers and bagged dirt stowed, Pop-Pop needed to sit. He returned to his post in the bend of the couch and took up his newspaper, shaking his head at just about every article he skimmed.

Mee-Moo took over from there. A pair of yellow rubber gloves were slapped into my hand with a huff, like she couldn't believe I hadn't brought my own. She hovered over my shoulder as I dove into the sink, scrubbing the cutting boards until the blue sponge she left for me started to pull apart.

She pointed out every last inch of them.

"Right there!"

"That spot!"

"You missed that!'

"Does your mother clean with her eyes closed too?"

Every snipe and comment brought me closer to hurling the soggy sponge and slimy gloves at her head to see if I could knock her wig off. For Pop-Pop's sake, I kept my cool as I moved through the rest of the pile, carefully rinsing the knives and running a fresh sponge over their blades. Boiling water pickled my hands, even through the thick gloves. She really had to dig to find flaws in the plates.

"Turn it over! Don't forget the bottom!"

"The edges! There's crumbs!"

"You got an eyelash on that one! Start over!"

It was entirely unnecessary. Every scrubbed and scorched dish, utensil, and implement ended up in the dishwasher anyway. When they were done, she loaded it with soap and let the machine run like I had never even touched them.

"Just to be sure they're *actually* clean," she said like I had left a myriad of diseases on them.

The fun didn't end there. As the afternoon labored on and Pop-Pop finished grumbling at his newspaper, she made lunch. Cheese and Saltines on a plate.

"Good calories" she declared, incorrectly, while staring at my gut.

For her insistence on whole foods, I had to fight the laugh shuddering up my throat as she unwrapped a half dozen Kraft singles, tore the slices to bits, and placed their chunks on the cardboard crackers. Just to keep things balanced, she dropped a small box of raisins onto my plate and a banana onto Pop-Pop's. No clue how he ever developed a belly eating like that. When she opened the closet pantry to get the crackers out, I got a good look inside. Every shelf, from floor to ceiling, was nothing but dry goods, cans of Chunky soup, loaves of bread, and shit to spread on them. The doomsday prep message boards all recommended a healthy stock of things like that for when the big day finally came, but I don't think that's what Mee-Moo had in mind. Mom wouldn't have been caught dead with a pantry stocked so lazily. Breakfast was cereal, lunch often came from the fridge or freezer, but dinner was her time to shine. She was prepared to make almost anything at the drop of a hat, whenever the muses took her. That apple fell pretty damn far from the tree, apparently.

When the "lunch" was gone, she made me clean the kitchen again. Top to bottom. Even the stove and microwave she never touched. Sprayed with cleaners and doused with caustic compounds I could only hope would ruin my new shirt while sparing the infinitely cooler one underneath. The rubber gloves went back on, and there they stayed for the rest of the afternoon.

"It's fine," Pop-Pop said, too agreeably. "We'll get to our stuff when it cools off a bit."

He hadn't been outside since we came back from our trip to the company stores. None of us had. It wasn't hot then and I suspected it wasn't hot now. He just wasn't in a rush to get to the backbreaking part of the day's program. Pop-Pop took up a new position on the couch, on the reclining end directly in front of the TV. He levered the footrest out, switched the TV to a more sensible news outlet, and promptly fell asleep.

Mee-Moo was all too happy to round out my day. With the kitchen to her ridiculous standards, wiped, sanitized, and mopped from end to end twice, we left Pop-Pop on his throne in the living room and moved out. The dining room needed to be dusted. The silver and china that hadn't seen action in years needed to be buffed and polished before meticulously returning them to their hutch. The long wooden table was sprayed down with Lysol. Every inch of its surface, legs included, was sterilized. Mee-Moo stood over me, arms folded and watching like I couldn't be trusted to operate a rag.

The vacuum was no better.

"Do you know how to use one of these?" she asked like I was still in diapers.

It was the kind of thing I had only seen in movies, set forty or fifty years in the past. A heavy, bulky contraption with a lone toggle switch on its square chrome base, a cold metal pole running up behind a puffed-out canvas collection bag. No attachments, no settings. Nothing developed in the current century.

"Yeah." I fought to keep my eyes from rolling, confident I could manage such a highly advanced piece of technology.

Her eyes widened like I had called her a moldy old bitch instead.

"Yes!" I corrected. "Yes, I do."

"We'll see about that, troublemaker."

Standing on the edge of the dining room, touching the room full of preserved couches and creepy-ass porcelain angel-babies, she left it in front of me like a test she didn't expect me to pass. I unrolled the cord and looked around for an outlet, but there was none to be seen.

"You need to plug it in," she condescended.

"I know, I can't find an outlet."

"By the stairs!" she barked.

How the hell was I supposed to know that? Did she think I had a schematic of the house?

I plugged the vacuum in and got to work. She stayed right on my heels the entire time.

"No, not like that."

"Diagonal patterns! Diagonal!"

"Careful of the couch!"

"Careful of the table!"

"I got that figurine in metropolitan Orlando! *Be careful!*"

It started to become clearer why Dad did everything in his power to avoid going there. I couldn't imagine she was ever any nicer to him in their private moments, when no juvenile eyes and ears were around.

I dragged that damn vacuum from one end of the house to the other. Every new locale meant finding a new outlet, which Mee-Moo pointed out with growing frustration. The unmitigated gall I must've had, not knowing their house backward and forward!

I found one halfway down the hall as she herded me toward the office, stopping only when I was made to dust the very not-dusty hanging photos.

"Don't forget the glass!"

"Show some respect! Those are your mother's baby photos!"

"You missed that one!"

"This one still has a speck! Do it again!"

I didn't miss any of them, and there were no specks.

I pushed the vacuum down to the garage door, and Mee-Moo cornered me against it.

"Make sure you get all the shoe dirt! The shoe dirt!"

We came back up to Pop-Pop's office. I made a point not to look at the computer, like our one-night stand hadn't happened, keeping my focus on the carpet. The one thing I actually agreed needed some tending to was the small gap between his desk and the wall. Cobwebs connected the two like a support structure. I shoved my dust rag in as far as I dared and flailed it around to break up the ones I could reach.

From there, it was up the stairs, and the vacuum's absurd weight finally showed itself. I lifted it up every step, paving a line across them. Mee-Moo stayed one behind, watching me and the vacuum in equal measure like we were conspiring against her. At the landing, she rolled her eyes and drummed her fingers over the rail. I was taking too long, apparently. But when I tried to pick up my speed, the scolding returned.

"Rushing only means you'll have to do it again, Grady Henry!"

She didn't have the authority to use the dogwhistle of my middle name, but I wasn't in a position to tell her that. Really, I should've been glad she used my name at all! Part of me suspected she had chosen not to up until then to avoid mistakenly calling me by my cousin's. I had gotten too many mislabeled birthday cards and Christmas presents over the years to rule that out.

At the top, she chased me down the hall, in and out of every room. There wasn't much space to work with in the bathroom, but I clunked the vacuum off the toilet and tub base collecting filth only she could see. In her crochet room, she shouted, "My yarns! Careful of my yarns!" so many damn times that I still hear it in my sleep. Among other things.

To be fair, the first guest room was actually dusty. It hadn't been occupied since the last time we were all there together, and it showed. Years of dust caked the headboard, dresser, and windowsill. All of that fell to me to deal with, and of course, none of it was good enough.

"Are you trying to do a bad job? Is that your plan? Do a bad job, so I'll take over?"

I had entered what I could only assume was a meditative state by this point. She might as well not have even been there, as I worked my way back out into the hall and down to my room.

"Don't forget under the bed!" she ordered, pointing like I couldn't find it on my own.

That was the most care I put into the whole futile exercise. If the monster machine sucked up my charge cable or earbud cord, I would've torn the damn thing to pieces to get them back. And then I just would've had to clean that up too. I pushed the vacuum under the bed, keeping a wide radius from where I knew my lifeline was hiding. Luckily, she didn't notice. Mee-Moo was too busy inspecting my books.

She took each one from the stack and shook the pages out like she expected a big bag of stink weed to drop out from between them. I killed the vacuum's incessant howl and watched her nervously.

"What?" she noticed. "Afraid I'll find something, troublemaker?"

Yes. The dead smear under *Great Expectations.*

"No, I just had bookmarks in some of those," I lied.

"Bookmarks, huh? And why wouldn't you want me to see them? Are they something inappropriate?" she drilled.

"Just don't wanna lose my place," I shrugged.

Halfway through the stack, she threw in the towel, slamming my books back in place. She could smell a lie on me, but couldn't place it.

"Get downstairs to Pop-Pop. Tomorrow we'll get going on the baseboards."

There was one room I had yet to touch. For a brief second, I contemplated not saying anything. I don't know if he had gotten the chance to talk to her about being nicer to me yet, but if he did, then he failed miserably. If I didn't mention the last untouched room of the house, it only invited further wrath when she finally remembered it.

"What about your room?" I asked, rolling the long cable back around the vacuum's handle.

"Not like that!" she snapped. "Tighter! And don't you worry about our room. You know better than to go in there."

I didn't. No one ever said that. It wasn't part of my introductory rules, but whatever. Any excuse to get out from under the thumb of the Dust Tyrant.

By the time the day's cleaning was done and all the tools were stowed away again, the sky had started to turn orange. Pop-Pop hadn't moved a muscle. Frozen in place, he slept with the remote on his chest and his mouth gaping open. Yet, he didn't make a single sound until Mee-Moo loomed over him and yelled, "Hubby!" like she was trying to wake the dead. He shot up faster than I had ever seen him move, snorting wildly like he hadn't been breathing at all.

"I'm awake!" he said like he had been the entire time.

"You're losing the light," she informed him grimly, throwing the blame at me from the corners of her eyes.

There was still a few hours to go before we really had to worry about that, but I got the feeling she was as sick of me as I was of her.

"Oh! Right. Yeah."

He pulled the footrest back in while I waited at the counter.

"Ready to get to it, bud?" he asked over his shoulder.

"When you are!" I answered, hoping Mee-Moo wouldn't feel the need to police that chore as well.

She traded places with him on the couch. As soon as he was up, she went down. Kicking the footrest back out and sighing deeply. Barking orders at a thirteen-year-old is hard work, I guess. My jaw unclenched, and the muscles in my neck eased their grip around my spine.

Thank fucking God.

"Alrighty!" Pop-Pop waved me toward the garage as he stepped out. "Let's get it done!"

A salty chill filled the garage as its rolling door whispered up the tracks. Pop-Pop embraced it, standing next to the Caddy and letting it wash over him like he wasn't sure when he'd get another chance to, hands planted comfortably on his hips. Even as the door came to a rest above us, he stood at the edge of the driveway looking contently out onto the neighborhood. Soft sunset beamed over the cliff, framing his face in shades of auburn. Lightening his scruff and trailing over his ponytail, each strand glowing twenty-four karat gold instead of platinum white.

"Can't complain," he finally said as he turned to where we had left all the new gardening supplies.

He took up the flower pots as I juggled the bag of soil back up to my chest. His giant shoes slapped at my feet as I followed him out onto the lawn and to the empty garden. We set everything in front of the long, brick-lined planter boxes, ready to go.

"I'll grab the other junk," Pop-Pop volunteered. He turned back to the garage for what I could only imagine were tools and gloves.

I looked out at the street, trying to see what he saw. Trying to see it the way he saw it. Absolutely none of it struck me the way it had him. The sun crept down to the cliff's edge, but it wasn't low enough to be awe-inspiring. It hit the water in a twinkling burst of yellow and white, but that wasn't really the direction he was looking. The Bluffs' maintenance crew had turned their attention to the pool, but I don't think Pop-Pop was happy and content watching an underpaid jumpsuit skim leaves from the surface. The community room hadn't been touched since the meeting. The chairs were right where we left them and nobody was inside. Mee-Moo would've had the time of her damn life making me dust and vacuum that whole building, but I doubt that's what he was thinking about.

Across the Bluffs, up and over the community room and the pool, two houses sat with their blinds rolled up. Two figures stared out, watching from their respective top floors. Nothing more than leering shapes, but it was them. In that collection of identical McMansions, I recognized the houses. On either side of the one Elaine had slithered off to. Faces and shapes distorted behind reflecting glass, dark surveilling forms that resembled something human, the direction of their shadowy heads unmistakable. Rather they too were staring lovingly at the pool, or they were watching to make sure we did what we were supposed to.

It took every bit of restraint my young body was capable of to not flip them off. The powerful need twitched through my fingers, but I kept them under control. Instead, I pointed to my shirt. Big and full of cartoony enthusiasm, I shot a big double thumbs up across the neighborhood. The forms turned in unison, their attention redirecting to the fountain. A white Lincoln rolled past it and hung over to their side of the ring. It bounced up into Elaine's driveway, and by the time I looked back to them, her Board members were gone. Their exposed windows were deserted. Front doors opened, the mustache emerged from one side while the bow tie came out of the other. Like flies on rotten fruit, they scurried to converge on Elaine's house as her garage door raised, following the Lincoln in. They waited dutifully for her to emerge as the garage slid closed again, and the HOA leadership disappeared into the dark of the house.

Pop-Pop playfully whacked a heavy pair of canvas gardening gloves into my chest, ripping my attention straight back to the matter at hand.

"Feel like some digging?"

We worked until we couldn't anymore. Not because the sun had finally plunged into the ocean, but because Pop-Pop's knees and back could only handle so much. No wonder he put it off as long as he had, the work brutalized his kindling bones. He winced with every bend and reach like he was kneeling on hot coals.

After the third or fourth time he pulled himself up along the front of the house, muttering and hissing, "Jesus H. Christ", trying to stretch out his tired body, I would've felt worse making him do anything at all. Pop-Pop patted torrents of sweat from his neck and face, soaking through his shirt as he coached me through the process. How to get the flowers and their clumps of dirt out of the plastic pots and back into the ground without damaging any of it. An easier, gentler experience than the unhelpful barbs Mee-Moo threw at me. Lucky for him, though, and even luckier for me, the work that he had scheduled for the rest of the week was done in a couple hours.

I led him back inside, letting him use my shoulder as a crutch. The flip-flops suddenly made a ton more sense. He didn't need to bend over to take them off. He stepped right out of them at the door, same as I did with his giant shoes, and I guided him back to the couch. I held his arms as he lowered himself down, wincing through his teeth but trying to hide it.

"I'm okay, I'm okay!" he kept saying like that would make it true.

"What did you do to him?" Mee-Moo spat at me from the kitchen, too deep in dinner prep for any greater concern.

"He got those flowers planted, is what he did!" Pop-Pop smiled through the pain. "Did a damn fine job too."

Her eyes narrowed suspiciously. "I'll be the judge of that."

They ate on the couch, standing TV trays in front of them. I stood at the counter, not trusted enough to even touch the leather sectional. All three of us crunched our way through salads she made from a bag. Not sure why that required three mixing spoons, two giant bowls, a strainer, a carving knife, and a heavy black cast iron skillet, but it did. As I ate, I glared at the mess, knowing what was coming next for me.

She stood right on my ass while I scrubbed the kitchen spotless.

Again.

When all was said and done, when night had fully fallen, we filed upstairs. I was given explicit instructions to read until I couldn't anymore. Which left a lot of wiggle room, in my opinion. More tired than I was used to being, even if those books weren't exactly *Pet Semetary*, I didn't feel like I'd get very far. Mom expected them to be done, but I don't think she expected them all to be by the second night. They were supposed to take *all* summer, right? There was time for me to be tired. And sore.

I ushered Pop-Pop to the stairs. Mee-Moo sulked behind us, bitterly staring holes into the back of my head because I didn't offer to take her arm the way I had his. He grabbed the rail when we got to it, and I stayed a step down, letting him push off my shoulder.

"No, I can do it!" Mee-Moo insisted as she stormed past me. "You don't know how!"

She took up a position a step ahead with her back turned to him. Not ready to support or touching him at all, but waiting for him to catch up.

"C'mon!" she snapped, as if all he needed was the right encouragement.

Pop-Pop nodded to me to let me know he was okay. He took the rail and pulled himself up as I followed behind. At the landing, she stopped and waited. But as soon as he came into the turn, she started up again. She was nearly to their door when we got to the top. Fastest I'd ever seen that woman move. He limped his way after her, walking like every step was on Lego.

"Night, bud," he said over his shoulder as they plunged into the dark of their room.

"Night, Pop-Pop."

Mee-Moo slammed the door shut without so much as a nod in my direction. *Whatever.*

I went to my room, hit the light, and closed the door. *The Odyssey* waited for me. I changed into the pajama pants I had yet to wear. SpongeBob, but who was looking? The blue Hawaiian shirt was peeled off and very carefully abandoned on the dresser. Balled up and thrown on top of the other books was the best I could do. A fair balance between keeping it for Pop-Pop and discarding it out of principle.

The mattress swallowed every one of my aching muscles. My legs and back were full of molten lead, like I had been on my blades for twelve hours straight. Even at rest, they twitched with phantom motion, too fired up to know when to stop. There was a difference between fun sore and work sore, I was learning. Summers with Dad, I'd be tired at the end of our business day, but not tired enough to pack it in and call it. I'd have energy left over for games and movies, and whatever my friends decided sounded fun. Work with Dad wasn't constant. There was the drive to and from accounts, for starters. But also the inevitable annoyed "It's fine, I'll do it!" when I underperformed. Mee-Moo wasn't so forgiving. My friends could've been waiting in the driveway at that very moment, Gameboys in hand and bikes parked on the grass, and I still wouldn't have had the energy to get up and join them. The window was open still, the only one in the house that I had seen actually let the outside in all day, but I couldn't even muster the enthusiasm to check and see if I had somehow willed them into existence.

Still, I had to get up again. Should've done it before I laid down—probably even before I changed—but the bed was infinitely more appealing. With the dull blue and bright white of the Bluffs radiating in, I was exposed. Elaine and her Board waited across the ring.

"Fucking hell," I groaned as I slung my legs to the floor begrudgingly.

Stepping to the window, I grabbed the cords and looked out. Not a single house I could see in our immediate vicinity showed any signs of life. No cars passing, no one navigating the sidewalks. Even the community room was dark. The pool next to it reflected the moon like a black mirror. Garage lights reached for the streets, but from the inside looking out, the Bluffs were completely dead.

I looked across to the houses in question. The handful I distrusted more than the rest. Their faces were as empty as all the others, powered down except for their garages, windows dark and drawn closed. Empty, but not lifeless. The blinds on Elaine's top floor fluttered and jerked. Caught in the act, peeping on the only person not in bed by 8PM. Movement struck the big front window to cover another retreat. Too dark to see anything more than that, but I didn't need to. I dropped my own blinds and fell back on the bed.

What's their problem?

They clearly had one!

"Is there a curfew around here or something?"

I dragged the book up to my chest as I leaned back against the wall and opened it, determined to let a story about a guy with a boat or whatever flush the HOA from my mind. Easier said than done. Elaine's judgmental glare was fixed in my head, staring at me even now like I had brought a previously undiscovered virus into her kingdom. And the silence of the Bluffs wasn't helping at all. Only a touch above intolerable, the same dome of soundlessness had fallen over the neighborhood. By the time I got back home, I feared I'd be adjusted to it. And the nocturnally noisy Buena Vista would be excruciating.

The one rule I was going to have to keep breaking waited under the bed, counting down the minutes the same as I was. My solution for every issue the night presented, even at home. I itched to silence the silence, same as I would with the nonsense my neighbors generated. A cure for all ailments, I knew for a fact my book would've been more interesting with heavy guitars to score its action. Even if its wording was a little rough to understand.

"Now Neptune had gone off to the Ethiopians," I recited quietly, hoping that would make it easier to understand. "Who are at the world's end and lie in two in halves."

I grabbed my notebook and jotted down my initial thoughts.

What the fuck is this guy talking about???

Mom was gonna see that. I scoured the eraser over it until the paper got hot.

"He had gone to accept a hecatomb of sheep and oxen, and was enjoying himself at his festival."

Another thought.

Look up HECATOMB.

"The other gods met in the house of Olympian Jove." Huh?

6-6-06

Who the hell is Olympian Jove?

Wasn't this book supposed to be the same thing as that movie with the claymation Kraken and all the skeletons with swords? That was the impression I was under. If I wanted gibberish poetry, I could've listened to Rainer's English lessons. Courtney W, one of two Courtneys in our class, recited an original work once titled "What'd I'd Do if I Was on The Bachelor." It read like Dr. Seuss if he ever became desperate for attention. And it made more sense than the god damn mother fucking stupid piece of shit *Odyssey*. I noted that down too before erasing all of it.

Enough was enough. Timing be damned, I slid under the bed and grabbed my iPod. Hell, I would've listened to Pop-Pop's Eagles cassette if it offered to make that book less boring. As I climbed back onto the bed, I stuffed my buds in and spun the click wheel until the volume could go no higher. Like a warm blanket in the snow, like coming up for air after a dive to the ocean floor, they hit me. Songs that were going to be stuck in my head indefinitely, taking the uncomfortable quiet of the Bluffs with them. My aches and pains faded. Elaine and her shriveled judgments dissolved away. Even that shirt started to look different. Worse, as a matter of fact! But if it kept the HOA and Mee-Moo off my back, then I could suck it up. A valiant sacrifice if I'd ever seen one.

I still had no clue what that damn book was talking about, though.

Super boring, really slow. Weird.

I tossed it onto the floor and stared up at the rest of the stack. Need be, I could find a way to stretch my five-word review into the paragraphs she wanted. Skimming would help with the rest, but that was as far as I was willing to go with it. As much of a try as I could give. None of the others looked practically appealing, so I flipped to the back few pages of my notebook and doodled.

Hellboy was too hard to draw from memory. My best approximation of his BPRD emblem was close, but not very. My Heartagrams were getting good, though. And those weird pointy S's everyone drew for some reason. Something I'm sure Mom would've flipped her shit about had she seen that page of the notebook.

The pencil wandered, floating aimlessly through whatever band related insignias my iPod felt inclined to jolt to the forefront. When that ran its course, my hand started following its own path. I let it go, let it mark and shade where it saw fit. A direct current to my head, graphite carved out what it wanted to as I drifted back toward home. We would've had our movie lineup locked down for the sixth by now, and plans would be in progress to determine the where and how of it all. What food we'd get, what games we'd play during. The page darkened in blobs and rivers as my thoughts came crashing back to Sea Breeze. I'd have to go to the potluck instead. I wasn't a proper resident or HOA member, obviously, but that wouldn't stop Pop-Pop from including me, and it wouldn't allow Mee-Moo to let me out of her sight. The pencil scribbled, filling in the shapes it had made. My stomach tightened and turned at the prospect of having to spend any extended period of time with their neighbors and their bitchy President. A whole night of stares and murmurs and suspicion, paired nicely with Jello molds, bread pudding, and whatever the hell else people their age ate.

The pencil stopped, its tip worn down to nothing, and I finally paid attention to what I was sketching. My eyebrows creased like I didn't understand what I was seeing, but it was recognizable enough. Basic, built of mostly circles and straight lines, a few banana curves and a long black cylinder. In no fine detail, but the shape was clear.

An oddly built spider, frozen on the page.

The end of one song began to fade out in my ears, lowering itself to silence as it finished. In the half second gap before the next one could boot up, a croaking snore roared through the house. One deep, angry inhale vibrated through the walls. How long that had been going on, I couldn't say. If it hadn't been for my iPod's lag, I might not have noticed it at all. But I had. And now I couldn't un-notice.

The snore kept going. No drop to the exhale, the aggressive intake swelled without breaking. My ear buds wrapped around the iPod as quickly as I could coil them and I tucked it underneath my pillow. On the off chance he came sleepwalking down the hall and barged through the door, his eyes dark and face limp.

You're being stupid.

It wasn't stopping. The snore refused to change directions, only growing louder.

It's just his meds. It's just his meds. It's just his meds. It's just his meds.

With how hobbled he was on the way to bed, my shiny new fear was that he was in the throes of some kind of nightmarish seizure. People his age are prone to those, right? In my head, I saw him convulsing and flailing, fighting for breath against his medication's hold while Mee-Moo slept peacefully next to him. I dropped the notebook on the pillow next to me, palms slicked with sweat, as it only got louder. Like a gorilla asserting its dominance, a howling roar echoed down the hall.

My whole body quaked like the temperature had dropped into the negative. Paranoia urged me to get up, to go check on him. Reality kept me in place. Thinking he was sick or dying was a safeguard I couldn't recognize. An attempt at denying that what I was hearing wasn't natural or medically induced. The snore changed in pitch, rising like a death metal guitar slowly dropping down its neck. Not even sure it could technically be called a snore at that point, but its the closest I can get.

Stop. Please.

When it didn't, I had to choke down the bile rocketing up my throat. My body filled with concrete, freezing me in place. Like a plug had been pulled, the snore stopped on a dime. Breath raked harshly through my nose. Still silence retook the house, the neighborhood, the whole fucking world. A constant whine rang through my ears like Mom had always warned me would happen if I kept listening to music as loudly as I did. My eyes didn't leave the door.

Until I felt something crawl up my arm.

"Shit!" I hissed like it was on fire.

A jet-black spider inched up to my elbow. I swatted at it, sending the little fucker rocketing across the bed. It landed expertly down by my feet, spinning around to raise its front legs and snap its pincers. I shot up, notebook in hand and ready to strike. In a scampering blur, it bolted after me. The notebook came down flat and wide, scooping it up and launching it across the room. I jumped up, standing on the bed like the floor was lava as the spider vanished behind the empty, freshly dusted TV stand.

My breath was gone, eyes wild and frantic, searching every inch of the floor for the counterattack. Just because I couldn't see the spider didn't mean it was gone. It lurked in the shadows, under the furniture, tucked beyond the reach of the overhead light, waiting to reveal itself when the time was right. I rolled the notebook into a club as it scurried up the wall, each leg moving independently. It zigged and zagged up from the corner and across to the door, slowing to a stop directly in front of me. I took an unsteady step across the mattress, raising my weapon high. Its pincers snipped at the air above it. I took another step. Its legs spread wide, settling down low. One more step.

And it jumped.

In the air, the spider was no more than a black spot, sailing too fast to be identified. On my chest, it was straight from the bowels of Hell. Pincers like meat hooks, a billion soulless eyes shining. Its legs pressed just enough to fire individual nerves on my chest as it crawled up for my face. I couldn't contain the small yelp I let out as I swiped the notebook down. It landed at my feet, and I leaped to the floor. Just in time for the snore to return.

My door flew open and crashed into the wall.

Pop-Pop stood in the dark of the hall, breath grinding out of his slack mouth, eyes seeing but not recognizing.

"What's going on in here?" he asked flatly, lips barely moving.

My mind wiped clear. Pop-Pop took a step forward. Light brushed his face, clammy and limp like the masks Jordan had access to.

"S—spider . . ." I lifted a trembling finger to the bed.

But it wasn't paying attention to me anymore.

The spider stared at Pop-Pop. Legs down, pincers closed. He stepped into the room as I retreated against the TV stand. His eyes were glued to me, but had no idea who I was. I inched over to the dresser. Pop-Pop put his hand out to the edge of the bed like a ramp. The spider dashed up it. He didn't look away from me as it crawled up his arm, over his plain white sleep shirt, and to his neck.

"Go to bed."

He turned and shuffled out of the room, paying no attention to the abomination clinging to his face. His crackling breath carried out into the hall with him, fading as it neared their bedroom door. Gently, it clicked closed and the house was quiet again. Like nothing ever happened.

I wouldn't sleep for the next two nights.

I was waiting on the edge of the bed when Mee-Moo came in. Every time my eyelids started to sag and the aches and pains forced me to lie back, phantom legs crawled over me. Over my pants, up my chest, across my face. Hairs bristled and skin rippled, feeling something they swore was there. I'd jump out of bed, rip the sheets and scratchy-ass comforter off, and shake it all, but nothing ever flew out. Nothing I could see anyway. The light stayed on all night, relegating whatever might've been lurking to the shadows. Keeping it at bay.

My nerves refused to believe I was alone.

The quiet of the house didn't help. My ears reached across it, trying to hear a hint of a footstep or the early rumbles of Pop-Pop's swelling snore, only to find perfect silence in return. My iPod said 2AM when I tried to block it all out, to get my mind right, but even my music couldn't solve the problem. Two earbuds became one when I convinced myself that shutting out the house and the hall to their bedroom would only set me up to be taken by surprise again. I even lowered my volume to a normal human level, but the rest of the night outside of my room stayed calm and still.

Around four in the morning, I opened the window. Slowly, to catch any eight-legged invaders that might've been waiting against the glass. Deep blue covered the Bluffs as the garage lights clicked off. The residents were already stirring. No wonder the community shut down so early, too many of them were up before the sun. Across the ring, on the other side of the pool, a car puffed its exhaust through the cold air as it backed out of its driveway. One of the Board minions, faceless in the near dark, drove for the gate. I ducked out of sight, only peeking an eye out of the corner of the window. Headlights passed the fountain and disappeared into the trees.

I left my iPod to charge under the bed and sat, staring out at the Bluffs as it slowly came to life. A few more cars pulled out and away, off into town. A herd of old ladies, over-equipped in jogging gear, visors, and hip-mounted water bottles, power-walked their way in from the far ring and to the pool. Porch swings were occupied with cups of coffee, shriveled faces waited impatiently over them as an old Toyota pulled through the gate and up around the fountain. Its driver window rolled down, and newspapers flung out.

The door flew in sometime after sunrise, clattering against the wall and sending me jumping through my skin. Mee-Moo charged in, ready to start the same song and dance she woke me up with yesterday. She was nearly standing on top of me by the time she realized I was already awake.

"Oh," she said, confused. "Good! You're getting into the routine."

"Yep," I replied, distant, still watching the spider crawl over Pop-Pop's face.

"Well, get dressed then! You and I have a lot to get done today and not a lot of time to do it!"

"Is he okay?" I asked.

"Who?"

Seriously?

I didn't even try to hide my disdain as I turned to look at her.

"Pop-Pop," I demanded.

"Why wouldn't he be?" She took every ounce of offense I intended.

"He wasn't walking too good."

"He's fine! I told him not to push himself too hard yesterday, but he never listens to me! And if he was hurting, then it was clearly *your* fault. You didn't do enough for him."

My fists curled around the corner of the mattress.

"His medication was messing with him again last night," I said, matching her glare.

"What medication?" She scoffed. "Pop-Pop doesn't take medication."

She might as well have said Pop-Pop didn't even exist.

"He said—"

"You need to drop the attitude, troublemaker." She beared down on me. "You're not the smartest person in the world, no matter how much I'm sure you think you are! Pop-Pop is fine. He needs the day to recover since you did such a lazy job with him yesterday. But you won't have any such luck with me! Now, get up! Put on some proper clothes. I'm giving you ten minutes to meet me downstairs before I call your mother and tell her what you did."

"Can I see him?" I asked, not budging.

"No! He doesn't need you bothering him!"

With that, Hurricane Mee-Moo changed course and blew back through the door. I waited until I heard her hit the stairs before I finally moved.

"Fucking bitch," I seethed under my breath.

She wasn't going to let me anywhere near that room. I tried to make sense of it, but my thoughts were lost in a tired fog. They floated to the surface, only to be dragged back down to the deeper recesses of my brain. As full of absolute high-grade bullshit as she was, I had no choice but to swallow it. Her filthy lies were law as far as she was concerned.

My legs were fried, eyes dry and cracked with crimson. I dressed with no real urgency, throwing the bright blue flowers over a Skellington T-shirt—one of the few Disney shirts where the Venn diagram of Mom's approval and my own intersected—and buttoning it closed. My hair had lost all its gelled luster, falling limply and defeated around my forehead. The bathroom supplies I packed were still tucked in the outside pocket of the rolling suitcase. It took digging them out to realize just how gross I had gotten over the last couple days. A shower was out of the question. As much as it would've helped bring me back to life, Mee-Moo wouldn't have the patience for a delay like that.

I watched Pop-Pop's door on my way down to the bathroom, hoping he'd pop out and tell me everything was okay. No need to worry, no spiders on his face. It wouldn't happen again, the pills went down the toilet. The temptation to knock got stronger the closer I got, practically daring me to defy her.

Steering into the bathroom, I flicked on the light and deposited my toiletries onto the small marble countertop. They bounced and rolled around the sink as I dispersed them. The untouched toilet sat to the right of it, wedged next to the shower-tub combo with a curtain covered in pastel butterflies. Toothpaste, toothbrush, deodorant, a tub of gel, and a black comb with thick, widely set teeth. I turned on the sink and dealt with my various smells first, brushing the grimy film from my teeth and rolling the musk out from under my arms.

I ran my hands under the water. There was a science to this operation, an art perfected through too much trial and error. Shaking out just enough water to leave my hands slick and damp, I raked them through my dry, dead hair. I unscrewed the cap on my gel tub and shoved a finger in. A sizable glob emerged, enough to plaster my hair in place for another couple days. I worked it around, rubbing it across my palms and fingers before forcing it over my scalp. When every follicle was sufficiently coated, I lifted them up. In a big clump with the comb first, then refined and shaped. Individual spikes formed as my sticky fingers and the heavy teeth worked in tandem to turn my head into a deadly weapon.

I took a lingering look at myself. This was as close as I was gonna get to Deryck Whibley in the "Fat Lip" video. Black peered out from under my flowery collar like a superhero suit hidden under the secret identity. That was a good way to get through the day, I decided. Try to be Good Boy Grady long enough to make her think it's who I was becoming. Let her send a positive report to Mom and maybe ease up on my newly imposed Pop-Pop embargo. Our post-Tools & Lumber conversation echoed through my murky mind. It seemed like a good time to try and put his advice into action. I took a deep breath, letting what spite I had stored cool off, bracing myself for whatever the hell Mee-Moo had planned for the day. Killing the light, I headed for the stairs.

Pop-Pop's door was still closed tight, the room behind it silent as a tomb. I took one last long look at it, hoping he'd poke his head out, but only if it remained spider-free. When he didn't, I rolled down the stairs as quickly and enthusiastically as I could. Really trying to sell the idea that I was psyched for our day together.

"Ready when you are, Mee-Moo!" I called, trying my hardest to sound pleasant.

Down the hallway, I wrapped around the kitchen, and Mee-Moo made that whole idea infinitely harder.

"Absolutely not!" She pointed to my hair like it was on fire.

She came around the counter, grabbed me by the collar, and dragged me to the bathroom next to the garage door like a puppy by the scruff of its neck.

"You will not look like some kind of skateboard hoodlum while you're under my roof!"

The gel hadn't even had time to dry. She forced my head under the faucet and rinsed it clean, scrubbing and pulling like she was trying to leave me bald spots. I gritted against the pain, the humiliation, trying to keep the vulgarities on the tip of my tongue from lashing out. For her compact frame, she was stronger than she looked. I figured I could've broken free if I needed to, but she held my collar firm with a mechanical grip. Water ran down my face and filled my nose. Laced with wasted gel, it stung at my eyes.

A medicine cabinet hung on the wall over the sink. She popped it open and pulled out a hairbrush that hadn't been used in decades. Dust congested its stiff bristles. She pulled me up from the sink and turned me to face her. I kept my eyes low and broken, hiding the fury brewing behind them. She took the brush to my head, ripping my hair to the sides until the nerdiest god damn part formed a perfect canyon down the center of my head.

"There we go!" she beamed, pleased with her work. "A proper little gentleman!"

"Thanks, Mee-Moo." I buried my fingernails into my palm.

"Excuse me?" she pressed.

"Thank you, Mee-Moo," I forced myself to correct.

"Well, look at that!" She took a step back, sizing me up with surprise on her permanently painted face. "Manners go a long way, troublemaker! Don't you forget that!"

Mee-Moo retrieved her massive purse from the kitchen counter and shooed me out the door. I pointed across the house, back to the collection of shoes at the front door and my abandoned high-tops. If the gardening was done, I didn't think I'd need gardening shoes. At least I could have that going for me.

"Can I get my—"

"No! It's a work day, you will wear your work shoes."

Pop-Pop's keys jingled in her hands as she used them to point to the grass-stained New Balances. I choked down my counter-argument as I stepped into his cavernous shoes and held the door for her. She inched toward the garage at a snail's pace, content to make me wait for her. Reveling it, even. When she was finally through, I half expected the sun to be on the other side of the neighborhood, finishing its trajectory for the day by the time she made it to out of the house. We split across the Caddy as the garage door rolled up, first light still cutting through the trees. I opened my door and was about to climb in when Mee-Moo cleared her throat.

"A gentleman opens a lady's door for her."

Her eyes bounced back and forth between me and the car expectantly.

I stifled the groan as I came around to the driver's side, but she didn't catch the sarcasm in the showy bow and wave I did as I opened it.

"Why, thank you!"

The door snapped back into place, and I went around to the other side. She started it up as I slid onto the bench seat.

"Seatbelt!" she snapped before my door was even closed.

I did as I was told, pulling it over me and clicking it into the buckle. Once the door was shut and she was satisfied, she jerked the shifter into reverse and pressed a single toe on the gas. She rolled us backward an inch at a time. We hit the grade of the driveway, and her foot slammed on the brake. The Caddy jerked to a halt and she eased up just enough for it to crawl all the way down, bumping softly into the street.

She cranked the gear, squinting at the dash like she wasn't sure what the D meant, and pulled away from the house. Mee-Moo waved at every walking skeleton and sack of loose flesh she saw creeping up and down the street like she was a candidate for Mayor of the Living Dead. The power-walkers, the porch swingers with their steaming mugs, even the late risers collecting their newspapers in barely closed terrycloth bathrobes all got the same big, forced smile and exaggerated wave. Couldn't help but notice that she didn't wave at the maintenance guys. They were out, wheeling equipment off to the second ring of houses and toward the pool, but apparently they didn't warrant the same warmth as her crusty, decrepit neighbors.

Once we were clear of the fountain, with a straight shot down the hill to the gate, I grabbed the door handle reflexively. Pop-Pop's driving left me a little scarred, but it was unnecessary with Mee-Moo at the wheel. Her speed didn't change. Not once. As we rolled up to the gate, she barely had to press the brake to stop. After it opened, we crawled through like we were trying to sneak up on the town. My only two options for getting down this hill, it seemed, were rather roller coaster fast or so slow I thought I was about to be spending my birthday in that fucking car. I think she could feel my frustration as we barely moved through the turns.

"You know," she said without looking away from the road, "I've actually been complimented on my driving before."

"You have?" I asked, doing my best to sound impressed.

"Yes!" she claimed. "I've even had police officers tell me that they'd rather people drive too slow than too fast!"

I looked over at the speedometer. The needle hovered somewhere between five and ten.

"That make sense," I agreed anyway.

"It's safer!" she insisted. "Would you rather get there late or in a hearse?"

At this point, it'll be both.

"Late," I answered.

"Good boy!"

She didn't hit the tape deck the way Pop-Pop did, so we rolled in silence for another few agonizing yards.

"You know, a lot of people think you might be a lost cause," she said out of fucking nowhere.

It hit me like a backpack to the balls.

"Like who?"

"Well, your mother for one!"

Low blow, Mee-Moo.

"She said that?" I quizzed, hiding disbelief behind curiosity.

"She didn't have to! Why else would she have sent you to me? I worked miracles with your uncles. I can work one with you too!"

My uncles. Dale, in and out of prison for "misunderstandings." And Jeff, who worked at Subway with my cousin, as his subordinate. The real miracle was that Mom turned out mostly normal, even if her punishments were a bit much.

"I don't think you're a lost cause, though," she added, an afterthought. "You just haven't had a firm enough hand."

I nearly bit into my tongue to subdue the laugh.

"These friends you have and the things you do together, the sooner you see that it was all a big mistake, the better off you'll be. You can rather regret it now or ten years from now when you're sharing a prison cell with them. That's the way I see it! Life doesn't give you do-overs often, but I can give you the best you'll ever get!"

If I ever had to share a prison cell with them, I'm positive Jordan would find a way out. Dude had seen *Shawshank Redemption* too many times.

"The way you've been acting is no way for a little boy to behave," she continued like I was actually listening, and not burning a line across the trees with my imaginary heat vision. "If they were really your friends, they'd see that! Friends don't let friends commit arson."

The argument bubbled up my throat. At the last second, as the words spilled over my tongue, I changed directions and broke away before her opinion of me could get any lower. If that was even possible.

"Is Pop-Pop gonna be okay?"

"Oh!" she gloated to the road. "Look who has a guilty conscience! Yes. He will be."

I had to test it, had to see if the answer would be the same.

"What about his sleeping meds?"

"That's a very rude question." She shook her head. "I don't know where you're getting your information from."

"He told me he was taking pills and that—"

"Don't put words in your Pop-Pop's mouth! He said nothing of the sort."

She was rather in denial, or extremely committed. Not sure which is worse. I took a breath to steady myself, to calm the urge to scream at her.

"I'm just worried about him," I explained slowly. "I think something might be, like, wrong with him."

"What? No! Absolutely not! He's perfectly fine!" She buried her head in the sand.

"I could just hear him the last couple nights, and then—"

"You can hear him?" She exploded into hysterical laughter. "That's why you're so concerned?"

"That's not all," I tried to say over her noise. "Last night he—"

"That's nothing!" Her laugh bounced off windows and ricocheted around the car like a stray bullet.

"Mee-Moo, last night there was a—"

"You can hear him?" She settled as she wiped her face. "Well, we can *all* hear you!"

That got my attention, freezing me to my seat. I didn't know what she meant by it, and I'm not sure I wanted to ask. Not like she was gonna give me a straight answer.

"No more talking!" As far as Mee-Moo was concerned, that was that. The matter was settled. Pressing it wasn't going to get me anywhere I wanted to be. And it definitely wasn't going to get me any further explanations. She leaned in close to the steering wheel, pressing herself against it. "I need to focus."

It took another fifteen minutes to get to the bottom of the hill.

Mee-Moo rolled us into Sea Breeze, only touching the gas when we had run out of residual coasting speed. I had no fucking clue where she was taking me. At best, it was to find a nice quiet place to shoot me in the head. At worst, it was to get more shirts. Every building we passed, she slowed even further, waving at whoever was inside. Even if they were nowhere near being able to see her.

Maybe a third of her waves were returned, and she made an excuse for the ones that weren't. The lone barber was a "nasty man." The patio furniture dealer was "always so rude." The mailman was one of "*those* types of people." The storefronts were as empty as the streets. Every business we passed was occupied solely by its proprietor. The danger of opening fuck-early for a highly specific clientele, I guess.

We inched our way to the grocery store's small parking lot. Only three spots out of the twelve spots were occupied, yet she still groaned like it was Black Friday. Mee-Moo pulled in as close to the front as she could get and killed the Caddy. She pulled her purse into her lap and started to dig.

"The lesson I want you to learn today," she said as she mined the satin depths, "is responsibility."

Is that something they have here, or is she about to sell me?

"Okay."

She pulled a piece of plain white paper from her never-ending bag, holding it up like I was supposed to know what it was.

"The potluck is tomorrow night. That's my responsibility, so *this*"—she thrust the paper at me—"is yours."

I turned it over and scanned it. A grocery list, filling the page from top to bottom in handwriting so large and loose it might as well have been done in crayon.

"Go in there," she instructed. "Get everything on the list. Tell them it's on our account. Come back. Any mistakes and you're walking home, understand?"

I wasn't sure if she was serious about that last part, but the rest of it, I took and ran. Anything to get out of that car.

"I'm on it, Mee-Moo." I forced a smile back at her.

"We'll see."

She pulled a book of crossword puzzles and a pen from her purse, easier to find than the list in the mayhem of her bag. I climbed out of the car and felt my tired body relax for the first time in too many hours. A rush of adrenaline flooded my muscles, like my bike had just hit the bottom of the driveway, something I had started to doubt I would ever feel again as I left Mee-Moo and the Caddy behind. Cold tidal air filled my nose as I crossed the small lot, finding the balance between rushing to get away and savoring the moment.

A concrete wheelchair ramp slanted up to automatic double doors. A frosty burst of air conditioning greeted me as they parted. Jimmy Buffett, or who I'm pretty sure was Jimmy Buffett, played softly over the loudspeakers in the store's tall ceiling. A small maze of aisles stretched from one side to the other, with a damp produce section and a meat counter bookending them. Two checkout counters waited just inside the door. A few wobbly metal carts and cracked plastic hand baskets were stacked in front of them. Each was manned by a plain red smock and a face I recognized. A gray-haired T. rex of a woman, bent over at a hard angle, and a man with a perfectly pleasant bow tie squared neatly under a salt and pepper crown.

Another neighbor. Another Board member.

They recognized me too. Their eyes darkened. Their whole demeanor, really, like the happy sunshiny morning they were having was ruined by the vagrant coming to raid their shelves and lick all the tomatoes.

"Morning," I mumbled as I walked between them.

"G'mornin'," Bow Tie grunted back.

"Mm-hm." She looked away.

What-the-fuck-ever.

I consulted Mee-Moo's list, trying to decide where to start. A cart would've been the smart call, but I was too far away from them and wasn't about to go back and be accused of trying to run off with one. I was missing the necessary people required to make a shopping cart worth the trouble, anyway. Jordan wasn't there to suggest some Knoxvillian Jackassery, and Alex wasn't around to tell us we were idiots. Two baskets would have to suffice. I pulled them from their stack, dropping the list into one and heading into the maze.

Each aisle was labeled at their ends, designating their contents in as much detail as they felt like sharing. I started with the one that simply read DRY. If that wasn't where I'd find boxed cake mix, then I didn't really care. She didn't give me a timeframe for how quickly I had to complete my supermarket sweep, and "box of cake mix" was as specific as her list got. This expedition was going to take as long as it needed, or as long as I wanted it to.

Moving down the aisle, I scanned its shelves on both sides. Pastas, seasonings, bread crumbs, rice. No cake mix. Dress shoes clunked against the floor behind me. Over my shoulder, Bow Tie was following me. When I turned to him, he jerked his attention to the shelves, like he was making sure they were adequately stocked. I rolled my eyes and continued down as he watched me from the corner of his own.

Freezer cases waited at the back of the store. They ran its entire length, packed with nothing but milk and eggs. Their flappy glass doors were stuffed to capacity with cartons of various shapes and sizes. Call me simple, but I was more used to the cases in the Buena Vista Albertson's, which were mostly beer and different types of sausages. Luckily, milk and eggs were on her list.

No quantity was given for either. Or type, for that matter. But I put my baskets down, regardless, and grabbed whatever seemed most appropriate. Didn't think in a million years that Mee-Moo would request skim and organic, so whole and jumbo went into the first basket. Bow Tie moved to the end of the aisle, peeking around the corner after me. As I turned back to continue down the neighboring row, I shot him a weak half-smile. His eyes narrowed on me like I had just shoved the gallon of milk down my pants or filled my clown shoes with eggs.

I ducked into the next aisle. Bags of flour told me that I was getting at least a little closer to the cake mix, but that wasn't what had my attention anymore. The T. rex stood at the other end, blocking off the exit, her head craned up from the floor, and her beady stare locked on. My eyes bounced between her and the shelves as I slowly approached. Thin boxes of Betty Crocker were arranged, only a few feet down from her. She folded her dinosaur arms and stood her ground like she was the last line of defense.

I stopped at the boxes, putting the baskets on the floor and making a point to keep my hands where she could see them. It was gonna take a wild shot in the dark to figure out what the hell Mee-Moo needed here. With everything from chocolate to carrot, angel food to devil's, the whole section was a guessing game. I was about to grab a box of plain sponge cake, the most general-looking one I could see, when Bow Tie appeared next to me. His dour face, like he had been sucking on a battery, ducked in alarmingly close to mine.

"Finding everything okay?" he asked.

"Oh!" I nearly jumped out of Pop-Pop's shoes. "Yeah, trying to."

"Good."

He didn't move a muscle. Just stood there, watching with the same pissy face. I dropped a box into my basket and fled with no real plan of where to go next. The T. rex didn't take a single step out of my way. I shuffled past her, working my baskets around the aisle's edge.

"'Scuse me," I muttered as I moved to cleared space.

"Mmm," she sneered.

The two of them came together as I crossed the store, trailing my every step. In the produce section, as I dropped a single bundle of raw broccoli into my steadily filling baskets, they watched from the edge of the misted bins of lettuce. Whispering to each other. When I turned back into the aisles, on a hunt for sea salt, they moved together after me. Pop-Pop's shoes rubbed at my heels as I rushed to the other end. A step slower than a run, I banked around the corner and shot down into the next row. They were waiting on the other side. Watching. Whispering. Conspiring.

My shadows followed me with frustrating persistence as I crossed the entirety of the store, collecting every ancillary item on Mee-Moo's nonsensical list. Maple syrup, cheese, toothpicks, sugar packets, one solitary orange, and nuts. Out of the seven billion different types, I went with unsalted peanuts. It wasn't lost on me as I perused the store that we were the only ones in it. The staff literally had nothing better to do. At least that's how I made myself feel better about their stalking and whatever secrets they were sharing between each other. At the meat counter, I found the owner of the third car in the lot.

The Wilford Brimley mustache appeared before he did. Two Board members for the price of one. He stepped through a flapping door, coming from the store's inner workings, to his cases and scales like he heard me coming. An apron stained with pink splotches hung around his neck.

"Help you?" He glared, the hairs curling into his mouth as it opened.

I checked my list.

"I need meat?"

"No shit. Wha' kind?"

Checked again, just to be sure.

"It literally only says meat."

I turned the list over and held it up to him.

"Potluck?"

"Yeah," I nodded.

"Meat," he parroted.

Out of all the choices, all the cuts from all the different animals, he went with ground beef. The Stache dropped handful after handful on his scale, slapping it down like that cow had done something to him personally. His eyes stayed on me the entire time, tiny slits in his furry face. Five and a half very angry pounds was what he determined I needed. He wrapped the beef in paper and tossed it over to me, leaning over the counter to watch me go.

When I turned around, the T. rex and Bow Tie were only a few feet behind me. They held a post between the registers and the door, waiting for me to run. I checked the list for the billionth time. Whatever she was making with all that, how any of it was supposed to come together to form something even remotely edible, was a puzzle I didn't care to solve. I'd be cleaning that kitchen soup to nuts regardless. It was all there, though, filling both of my baskets, every last ridiculously random request. I heaved them up and made for the checkout. Neither of them moved to take up a post, so I chose the closest one by default. They looked at each other, telepathically determining who would have the honor of ringing me up. The subordinate dinosaur shuffled forward begrudgingly. Bow Tie repositioned to the door, guarding it in case I got any fresh ideas.

I dropped my baskets on her counter and tried to fake a smile.

"Find everything okay?" she was obligated to ask.

You know damn well I didn't.

"Sure."

She didn't take anything out to scan. There wasn't a scanner to use if she wanted to. Instead, she sifted through everything, tapping numbers into her register. The machine whirred and crunched with every price. Bow Tie watched from the door, and Stache loomed over his counter. I tried not to look at any of them, gazing out the front of the store like the parking lot was surprisingly interesting.

"Eighty-six-seventy-nine," she finally said.

"Oh."

Mee-Moo and Pop-Pop weren't gonna be the names they knew them by. Really bad time to realize I didn't know what their real ones were. Mom's old name sprang to my head.

"Graham! It's on the Graham account?"

She groaned low in her throat, looking over my shoulder to her boss like she wasn't sure what to do.

"It's fine," he said. "Let him go."

I stepped back out into the lot with three overstuffed plastic bags squeezing the life from my fingers. My palms sweated against their handles as they threatened to pull free. I would've slowed my approach, enjoyed the last few moments of the closest I was gonna get to freedom, if it wasn't for their painful weight. Mee-Moo didn't look up from her crosswords as I got to the car. I set the bags down on top of the trunk and came around to my door. Of course, it was locked. In that hotbed of criminal activity, who wasn't waiting to carjack her? I rapped my knuckles gently on the window as I smiled in at her. The puzzle book went flying as she shrieked, jumping so high in her seat that her wig grazed the roof of the car.

"Don't sneak up on people!" she yelled through the glass.

"Sorry!" I wasn't. "I got everything."

"Oh, did you?" She didn't believe it any more than I did. There was no fucking way I translated her list correctly.

Mee-Moo lurched and shuffled her way out of the driver's seat. She came around to the back of the Caddy like I left a bomb on the trunk instead of my best uneducated guesses.

"That doesn't look like everything," she said on first glance.

I pulled the list, folded into a square, from my pocket. She snatched it away like a hundred dollar bill. Weighing it against the bags, she shook her head and clicked her tongue. Stupid, stupid boy.

"This isn't right at all." She tried to sound surprised.

"It wasn't very clear," I said earnestly.

"You are actually reading those books you brought with you, right? Not just looking for pictures or using the pages to smoke things?"

"I am!"

"Are you sure you can? Because anybody who can read wouldn't have a hard time following a simple list."

She pulled the ground beef out first.

"*This* isn't meat." Then the nuts. "Walnuts." The cake. "Devil's food. Why would I only want one orange? I don't know how much clearer it could've been."

How is that not meat?

"I'm sorry, Mee-Moo," I said anyway. "I can go back in and—"

"No!" She threw up a stopping hand. "It's fine. I'll make due."

"I tried." I shrugged.

"I'm sure you did!" she agreed with an unnecessary amount of snark. "Just put them in the trunk."

Mee-Moo inched around back to the driver's seat. I tossed the not-meat and its misfit companions back into the bags and pulled them clear. She scooted onto the bench and hit the trunk release. The back of the Caddy flung open and I stowed them inside, closer to the wheel well to keep them from shifting too much, like Dad had taught me. I pulled the trunk back down and slammed it closed. With a tired groan, I stepped around to my side of the Caddy. I don't know if it was being around all that food or if it was because Mee-Moo had yet to feed me my morning ration, but my stomach growled empty and hollow.

The door didn't budge when I pulled on it. Still locked.

"Nuh-uh!" Mee-Moo shouted through the window. "Shirking your responsibilities will always come with consequences! Don't you forget that!"

She wagged her finger as she started the car and drove off.

I must've stood there for at least ten minutes. Long enough for the Caddy to disappear down the street, show itself again around the bandstand, and vanish up the road to the Bluffs. My jaw slack and waiting for flies, eyes misting and rippling. I don't know how long it was before I finally accepted that she wasn't coming back. Isn't that a thing older people liked to do? Scare kids to teach them lessons? I needed that to be one of those times.

It wasn't.

She didn't come back.

When my feet started to hurt, I took a step forward. One at a time was all I could manage, telling myself it'd be okay as they came down on the pavement. Mee-Moo left, and the three in the grocery store watched me from the front door, vacantly, emotionlessly. I could feel their useless eyes drilling into my back, so I turned to confirm. They were huddled in the glass, watching, barely even blinking, but doing nothing to help. For a second, I considered asking to use their phone. Call Mom, ask her to pull me out of that particular circle of Hell. But I knew they wouldn't have allowed it. I jammed my hands in my pockets to keep from raising an angry finger as I made my way to the edge of the parking lot. It wasn't their fault. They were at best accomplices.

I hit the sidewalk, and the road stretched out in front of me. The right led to the turn and up to the Bluffs. The left, I knew, would eventually take me home. The lone traffic light hung over the intersection, controlling the flow of absolutely nothing. Thoughts of hitchhiking or getting my hands on a car *GTA*-style flashed through my head. The only thing stopping me was practicality. Two-plus hours from Buena Vista, there was no way to get back that wouldn't risk me being murdered or arrested. Both of those sounded better than going back to Mee-Moo, but I couldn't leave a man behind, and stalling was only gonna make it harder.

Just get it over with.

With a tired moan, I headed for the hill.

Through the town, with my head down low, I was sweating before I even reached the roundabout. My shirt clung to me everywhere it could. Pop-Pop's shoes ground against my heels and the soles of my feet in a way I knew wouldn't be good by the time I hit the bandstand. Mummified faces watched me from their windows, each with the same disinterested interest the grocery store people had. Not a god damn one of them tried to stop me. None of them so much as asked if I was okay or needed any help. They only watched as I passed their storefronts and crossed their neighbors.

Doors started to open. Wisps of gray hair and eyes with no light left peered out. I didn't dare look back. I knew they were there. Emerging from their commercial crypts, tracking the dreaded Troublemaker's movements as he took his morning stroll.

The road loomed over me dauntingly, taller than I remembered. I might as well have been asked to walk all the way up Olympus, to the ancient deities that always knew best. My heart pounded Xenomorphic blood through my veins, alive with furious acidity. I could've chased after Mee-Moo, she was definitely driving slow enough. But the old hag was jumpy, and I didn't wanna get blamed for making her crash. Hell, she probably would've run me over and dressed it up as a life lesson.

"This is why you don't try to get into a moving car!" I saw her shaking her head at me as I bled out in the street, all her neighbors watching like my death was a mild inconvenience.

Even as I trudged along the edge of town, part of me still expected her to turn around and come back. Once she had put enough fear in me to learn what she thought she was teaching. By the time I hit the incline, I could already feel the blisters forming. The heel of Pop-Pop's shoes were scraping me raw, not even a mile in yet. I stopped as the guard rails slithered up. And up. And up. The road to the vampire's castle, high in the Carpathians, waiting to feed on me more than it already had.

A few more moments was all my temper could stand. When I didn't see the Caddy inching back down, I started to climb. I hugged close to the inside of the road, with the direction of traffic heading to the Bluffs, if any were to come. No car passed me in either direction. It's not like they would've stopped to pick me up, anyway. They barely would've noticed if they hit me at speed and sent me sailing into the trees.

How could she do this?

Did she honestly expect me to translate her lunatic list? Could she not see how wildly unsafe and irresponsible this was? Or did she just not care? For my own sake, I wanted to believe that she did. But I knew better. It was exactly where the apple landed, how far it fell. Mom never would've done something like that. She wasn't a product of Mee-Moo, she was a response. I shuddered at the thought of what she must've endured at her mother's hands, how much worse she had it growing up. My stay was temporary, hers was permanent. Mom's undying loyalty to that creature had to have been born somewhere close to fear.

By the time I passed the one-mile marker, bolted tight to its post in the road, my feet were on fire. His shoes were full of hot coals, searing my skin everywhere they rubbed. At mile two, my socks were damp. I was afraid to check and see with what. The town shrank behind me, back to a tabletop model full of monstrous figurines.

The hill had seemed so benign driving up and down it, but I was making even slower progress than Mee-Moo did behind the wheel. Every curve and turn, I expected to see her pulled over and waiting. Every curve and turn, my temper only grew like a balloon fit to burst when she wasn't. Accepting that I had to walk was one thing, believing that she had actually abandoned me was another. And the incline wasn't getting any less steep.

By mile three, the trees had swallowed Sea Breeze, leaving me with nothing but the sun as it burned overhead. Sweat poured from every inch of me, my skin baking red. I had to stop. My legs were trembling, thighs chaffed raw. Every step felt like razorblades slicing between them. The white of Pop-Pop's shoes was starting to change. Splotches of red seeped through from the sole and stained them.

There was nowhere safe to wait on the road. My options were either the sheer rock face or the guardrail. Both prime positions to get run over. I hopped the rail and, like an animal looking for a quiet place to die, waded into the trees and brush. My legs and feet protested every step as I crossed the natural face of the climb, digging against loose dirt and rock. Another few yards were as far as they could go. Far enough for a canopy of shade and to be hidden from the road. I wasn't about to risk sitting down just to have a fresh corpse shamble its way over to me to gawk and point.

Shade cut the rising temperature, which only made my skin burn hotter as I collapsed under one of the shorter redwoods. Panting hard, sweat filled my eyes and nose with salt. I slid out of Pop-Pop's shoes and peeled back a sock. Soaked deep red, the fabric clung and pulled at my skin, glued in place with sticky plasma. My heel and sole looked as good as the ground beef she insisted wasn't meat. A chewed-up mess of open blisters and sores, leaking steadily with every thunder of my heart. I gingerly pulled the sock back down and tucked my feet into the bloody shoes.

Leaning back against the trunk of the tree, I spread my legs wide and rubbed the damage from my muscles. My eyes fluttered. Lack of sleep and physical exertion caught up to me like they couldn't wait to pull me down to their level. If I passed out right there and then, got eaten by a cougar or something while I slept, so be it. My eyes drifted shut, and salty air came through my nose in steady streams.

The lapping of waves, the breeze through the trees, birds hunting overhead and their prey scurrying through the brush, they were all missing. My eyes creaked open at the silence. No better than it was at night, I couldn't hear a damn thing. I snapped my fingers next to my ear, just to be sure I hadn't actually gone deaf. The clicks were there, right against my face, but nothing else was. For a moment, I wondered if I had died. If some car really had hit me, or if I had even left the grocery store at all. Maybe Stache was grinding me into not-meat, and this was what my brain felt like giving me in its final moments. That didn't feel right, though. If this was Heaven, then I wouldn't be starving. And if this was Hell, then it didn't look nearly as cool as I expected.

I faded out again before I could stop myself.

When I woke up, the sun had moved, losing some of the height it had gained while I was gone. I could've laid there against my tree into the night, if it wasn't for movement at my feet. A raccoon climbed its way down from a trunk across from me. It scurried down to the dirt and stood on its hind legs, sniffing my salty feet. Taking a wary step back, it cocked its furry little head like it didn't understand what I was doing there. Our eyes met, bringing me back to Pat Smith and his HOA-blessed vendetta. The two most unwanted creatures in the whole of Sea Breeze. The raccoon looked up the hill, a destination already in mind. It fell back on all fours and bolted up, stopping to see if I was coming or not.

When I didn't move, it kept on running. Darting around trees and rocks, to a ridge, and finally to the black shape of a maintenance shed high above.

The Bluffs weren't that far after all. Maybe another half mile up the hill. The gate was nowhere to be seen when I got off the road, hidden behind turns and trees, but the edge of the neighborhood had revealed itself. So close. So far. Every fiber of my being wanted to stay right there, in the dirt, under the tree, away from Mee-Moo and her bitchy neighbors. If it hadn't been for Pop-Pop, I just might have. My absence had been longer than I had anticipated. When I didn't miraculously teleport into the kitchen, she might've said something. The reasons behind it surely would've been omitted, or adjusted to fit what narrative she wanted to sell, but he would've worried, regardless.

And if there's one thing that aids physical recovery, it's worry.

I pulled myself up along the trunk of my tree to follow the raccoon. My legs and feet screamed in agony. The road, I knew, kept twisting and turning until it landed at the gate, but the woods offered a straight shot. Shorter, faster, but no easier. Every step sent waves of pain up to my waist as I pulled myself along on the trees, Pop-Pop's bloody shoes grinding and slapping at my mangled feet. I took it one yard at a time.

The raccoon waited a little past halfway up. My legs went numb, and my breath disappeared again. Loose earth shifted under me, dragging every wound over every pebble. I bit down and pressed on, telling myself that it was still better than the road, that it would take half the time in exchange for twice the effort. As I closed in on the little bandit, he dashed to the top.

Anger and resentment cooled into something heavier and darker, like an anvil sitting square on my shoulders. I lugged that weight all the way up, every agonizing step adding another pound. That was the exact moment when it happened. When I lost track of who she was versus who I remember. Any love or affection I had for that woman died on the walk back to the Bluffs. She knew how far it was. Counting the walk through town, I think it was sitting somewhere close to five miles, most of which was straight up. She knew what I was wearing. My high-tops weren't good enough. And she knew her list was asinine. I wasn't meant to figure it out. In her rotting, festering sore of a mind, it was all perfectly acceptable. If I knew her first name, I would've switched to it.

She was no Mee-Moo of mine. Not anymore.

The gate finally appeared, wedged between trees and rock below me. I came up and over the ridge. The raccoon contorted and squeezed through a gap in the shed's roof and was gone. The Bluffs circled out ahead of me like the lines of a blast radius. Limping, I made my way past the shed and into the third ring. Front doors opened as soon as I hit the sidewalk. They watched with stony faces, unquestionably disappointed in me on her behalf. She didn't have to tell them to be on the lookout for her missing grandson; they were already doing it, anyway. And he had just bypassed their grand security gate.

I left a trail of footprints, drops of blood mixing faintly with dirt, straight into the heart of the Bluffs. The neighbors filed in behind me as I trudged, leaving their doors and making their way slowly into the street as I cut up the spokes linking the rings. Walkers clanked, scooters whined, loafers shuffled. I didn't have the energy or the strength to try and keep ahead of them. Not that I would've needed to. Like a flow of magma down the side of a volcano, they pressed on after me. Constant and unrelenting.

I didn't care. I wouldn't be in their world much longer. As I turned down the correct street, I decided that enough was enough. They'd go to bed early, but I knew Mom and Dad would be up into the night. When the time came, I'd call her myself and tell her about today. Ask to come home. Beg if I had to, with the caveat that I'd try to keep in better contact with Pop-Pop after, even at the risk of having to talk to *her* too. If Mom still wanted me to change schools, fine. If she wanted me to never contact my friends again, I'm sure I'd find a way. If she wanted me to burn all my clothes, throw out all my books and movies and games . . . that would have to be a separate discussion. But anything she could throw at me had to be better than this. Another few weeks of it, and I'd be thinking real long and hard about taking a step off the cliff.

The neighbors followed as far as the community room, like it was a line in the sand they couldn't cross. A holy site by invitation only. I climbed up the lawn and to the porch, kicking Pop-Pop's shoes off. They bounced with a clunk off the door and scattered. I grabbed the knob, expecting to have to knock. It was unlocked. I took a deep breath and plunged in.

No one greeted me as I came inside and threw the door shut behind me. The manic ravings of her chosen news network echoed through the house. I grabbed my high-tops and held them tight in one hand, never to be separated again.

"Took you long enough!" she called from the living room.

Head down, fists clenched tight, my bloody feet left evidence all the way down the hall. I came around the corner, and whatever cool I had left to keep evaporated like water on a skillet. She was reclining on the far side of the couch, a cup of iced tea in her hand, not a care in the fucking world. I was gone for the better part of the morning and afternoon, and she never came to look for me. She wasn't even concerned. She was waiting.

"This is why you do things right the first time, troublemaker," she scolded from her fucking seat, sinking into its cushions like she was becoming one with them. "We have to go back first thing tomorrow!"

"Why?" I seethed.

"Well, all those groceries have been sitting in the car this whole time! And since you decided to take the scenic route home, apparently, they've probably gone bad by now!"

"You couldn't have done it?" The canvas of my high-tops folded as I squeezed them tighter.

"They were your responsibility!" she accused. "Not mine!"

Fire flooded through my nose as I tried to calm myself.

"Grab some paper towels and a few trash bags!" she ordered from her seat, wagging a finger toward the kitchen, her wrinkles pinching together. "You are going to clean that car inside and out. And I hope you remember how you got back, because if it's not right tomorrow, you know what will happen."

If she was trying to find my line, she succeeded.

"*Fuck! You!*"

"What did you just say to me?" She shot up from the couch, spry enough now that it was convenient.

If I was going to pick a moment to implement Pop-Pop's wisdom, I'd say this was it. Fight or stand down. Take it back and pretend I didn't say it, or double down.

"FUCK YOU!" The opening salvo in an all out war.

She blinked across the room and was on top of me with a speed I didn't think she was capable of, even in her younger years. My face seared as her open palm smashed into my cheek.

"How *dare* you talk to me that way! I am your grandmother!"

"Then act like it!" I shouted back. "I didn't shoot somebody, I *accidentally* broke a window! You treat me like I'm on death row!"

"You will be if you don't learn some respect!" Her body trembled, a splash of actual hate coursing through a heart that hadn't beat that fast in decades. "You're exactly what's wrong with the world and exactly what's killing it! Your whole generation thinks it's so cool to be a bunch of little degenerates! Elaine was right about you."

"The bitchy old HOA lady?" I scoffed.

BAM!

Another slap.

"You will not speak of her like that!" Mee-Moo shrieked. "Elaine Rubenfeld is what this world needs! Not ungrateful little brats like you!"

"She's conning you all! She's got you constantly buying shit from her Board people!"

BAM!

A third slap.

"You will not use that kind of language in my house!"

I couldn't help it.

"Shit! Shitty-shitty fuck-fuck cock bitch pussy!"

Mee-Moo turned the most sickly shade of white.

"I will call your mother!" Her voice shook.

"Good!" I yelled through a satisfying laugh. "Call her! Tell her how you made me hike up a fucking mountain in shoes that don't fit because I didn't know what 'meat' meant! You explain that to her! Tell her why those shoes are all bloody! Please!"

No matter what yarn of self-indulgent bullshit Mee-Moo would spin, Mom would see that enough was enough and that this whole idea was broken from the start. She was strict, not stupid. And definitely not cruel.

I turned and left Mee-Moo to shake and mumble to herself, content with my final word.

"Yeah!" she called after me as I neared the end of the hall. "You go to your room and do not leave until I tell you to!"

"Ohhh, nooo! Not my room!" I rolled my eyes as I mounted the stairs.

My proper shoes and I climbed up, bloody socks squishing into the carpet and soaking the steps red. At the top, I paused at Pop-Pop's door and thought about knocking. Thought about going in, but I couldn't face him. Not after that. I was still too mad to be ashamed. I continued to my room while Mee-Moo bellowed and moaned downstairs, already making her calls.

"You should hear what that troublemaker just said to me!" Her pity party was in full swing, over-the-top sobs wailing through her voice. "I could never bear to repeat it!"

I fumed into my room, slammed the door shut, dragged my bags from the closet, and started packing.

PRELUDE 12/21
JUNE 5, 2006

Mee-Moo continued on downstairs into the evening, calling just about everyone she knew to tell them the harrowing, heartbreaking saga of Grady Burton, Spawn of Satan. She switched back and forth between wailing like a Victorian child's ghost and spewing insults like she was scripting better responses than the ones she had given me. After the fifteenth time I heard her say, "He's just like his father," I had to drown her out.

Caution to the wind, no fucks left to give, I pulled my iPod from its hiding spot and plugged it into my ears. With all my clothes stuffed back into my suitcase, I was ready to go. Except for the books. The important shit was packed, and that's what mattered. As much as I wanted to hurl that fuck-ugly blue shirt out the window, I couldn't bring myself to. Pop-Pop had been so happy to see me in it. If I was going to take one souvenir from my few days in the Bluffs, I would've rather it been that than the crusty, crunchy socks I left on the dresser. Blood hardening them into plaster molds of my torn feet. Proof I would need when the accusations of me being a horrible lost cause of a child came flying back at me.

I changed into something more appropriate as I rolled the blue floral atrocity into a ball and stuffed it into my bag. A fresh black shirt, branded with the BPRD emblem in blazing red, and most importantly, wasn't rimmed in white dried sweat. I fed my earbuds up through it, pulling them out the neck hole and jamming them back in my ears. My shorts were covered in dirt. I could smell them before I even lifted them to my nose. Sour and musky like they always were on the days our PE coach was too lazy to have us do anything other than run around the field in the million-degree heat. The cargo shorts I arrived in felt more appropriate for my departure.

6-6-06

I sat on the bed against the wall with my music turned all the way up, waiting for the inevitable rage and flurry of punishment to follow. Staring at the door, bracing for the moment she stormed in to tell me Mom and Dad were on their way and how *very* angry they were. My feet throbbed against fresh socks, their clean fibers rubbing gently into my open wounds. A sunburn sizzled across my bright pink cheeks. My legs were reduced to jelly-covered bone. I didn't let myself fall asleep again, though, as easy as it would've been. Being startled awake by her self-righteousness sounded worse than just powering through. I could endure. Take the ride home and whatever lectures it came with, and sleep in my own damn bed. Surrounded by whatever Mom saw fit to leave in my room, if she had even gotten to that yet.

The Bluffs began to darken, and I was still waiting. When garage lights came in through my window, I started to doubt it would happen. I couldn't make out her voice anymore, but I could still hear cabinets and doors slamming through the sunset hours. Footsteps boomed up the stairs and into their bedroom, throwing the door closed behind them. I held my breath, waiting for my turn. But it didn't come. Their bedroom slammed again, and the steps boomed back down. Not in a hurry, not like anything was actually wrong. She just wanted us all to know her tantrum was still going strong.

It was the front door that finally got me up. It shuddered through the house, vibrating up the walls as it rocketed back into its frame. Despite my painful protests from the waist down, I shot up. My feet screamed as they touched down on the floor and took my weight. I could already see her rushing down the driveway, ready to recount the story to my parents one more time with eyes full of crocodile tears before she dumped me off on them for the rest of ever. But the Aztek wasn't there.

I looked down into the street, as deserted as it should've been. The lights in the community room glowed onto the pool. Driveways spilled their LEDs onto the pavement as the moon started to shine through the trees. Every house, as far as I could see, was alight and buzzing with more activity than I knew those people were capable of. Shadowy forms rushed across windows from room to room like they were preparing for the end times. Mee-Moo was hustling across the inner ring. Actually hustling! Like whatever business she was on was of the utmost urgency. She went wide around the pool gate and straight back to the far side of the inner ring.

Elaine was waiting in her open front door, arms folded impatiently. Her head wasn't angled to the street, though, toward the approaching hysterical woman waving and flailing like a bewildered Hanna Barbera character as she shouted her distant frustrations at her. It was aimed up to my window, locked on to me. In for a penny and sick to death of her shit, I flipped her off from behind the safety of my window. I could've stood there all night holding that defiant salute. Something about it eased the pain and strain on my lower half, or at least made it more worth while. Elaine shot a damning point over Mee-Moo, alerting her. She whipped around, and my other fingers expanded into a wave. I wasn't doin' nothin'! Just saying hello to the neighbors! The rude, leering, miserable old neighbors.

"Hey, bud," Pop-Pop said behind me with a rap on the doorframe.

I spun around, yanking my earbuds out.

"Pop-Pop!" I gasped.

His skin was ashen and spongy, tinted vaguely with the murkiest shade of pea soup green, like he had been stricken with a landlocked seasickness. His belly was horribly distended, bloated and sagging grotesquely down over his thighs. A sheen of sweat covered him.

"Are you okay?" I rushed to his side as he held onto the doorframe.

"Yeah, yeah, I'm good," he lied through a difficult smile. His voice was weak, like it was buried too deep in his chest to fully emerge.

"What's wrong? Is it your meds? I tried to talk to her but—"

"Sit down, Grady," he said softly.

"Okay?"

I sat on the edge of the bed. Using the wall, Pop-Pop pulled himself over and joined me. The scruff bristling his cheeks was denser, like a heavy dusting of salt over his face. Dark hairs flared from his ear like he'd aged another decade in the last twenty-four hours. His eyes vacantly shifted around the floor, unfocused and cloudy.

"Looks like this is it, huh? End of the road."

I wasn't sure if he was talking about my stay with them, or his life. From the looks of things, it could've gone either way.

"Just do me a favor," he said through a rattling breath, like he was full of loose screws and rusty bolts. "Don't forget about your Pop-Pop when all's said and done. We were pals, right?"

Terror gripped me by the throat and demanded I cry. I wrestled it down just enough to speak.

"What are you talking about, Pop-Pop? What's wrong?"

Another long, desperate wheeze, the exertion talking required stealing every ounce of his breath. He opened his mouth like he wanted to say something, but changed his mind at the last second.

"She told me about what happened today," he said instead.

"I'm going home, aren't I?"

"Don't know," he said vacantly.

"Then what's happening?" I pushed. "Why is this the end of the road?"

His bottom lip quivered as his whole jaw shook. Breath spilled out of his open mouth, reeking like rotting meat or expensive cheese. He pressed a knuckle against the outside of his ear, scratching at the hairs tickling him. Another wheeze shook through his torso.

"Did you think about what I said at all?"

"Of course." I think he was expecting me to say no.

"And this is your fight? This is your Western Front?"

"Pop-Pop," I pleaded, peeling off a sock. "Look."

His eyes glanced over to my foot and darted back to the floor, unable to stand the sight. The skin was ragged and red, ripped open and chapped by more blisters and sores than could be distinguished from each other.

"Not sayin' it was right, what she's done. In fact, it might be the cruelest thing I've seen her do." A vain of tears formed over his eye as he took another labored breath. "And who am I to let it all happen?"

"It's not your—"

He raised a trembling hand to silence me. The skin under his nails was a granite shade of gray.

"All I'm saying is, you're in it now. So you gotta choose if you wanna keep moving forward, or lay down and accept that"—a long wheeze cut him off—"what your Mee-Moo says goes."

I had thought about it. There was ample time while I sat ignoring her. My mind was made up already.

"It shouldn't be that way. It's not fair. It's not right!"

A proud smile tugged weakly at the corners of his mouth.

"No, no, it's not. But it's where we are. Just remember, bud . . ." His words drifted off, eyes widening like the horrors of Germany were rushing back. "There's always a bigger fish to fry."

"What do you mean?"

He stared at the floor like the bloody carpet fibers would give him the strength he needed, tears spilling past his milky eyes.

"I'm so sorry, Grady."

The dark wisps in his ear retracted, slinking back into his head.

Pop-Pop's face grew hollow and dark. His eyes blackened to coal. His jaw sagged open, and his breath took a hollow, grating turn.

That's not sleeping pills.

And those weren't hairs.

He pushed himself up from the bed like he couldn't wait to leave. I watched, unmoving, unable to.

"It's too late, troublemaker!" His voice hit me like a sonic boom.

He waddled to the door like a pregnant woman, holding his belly as he staggered off into the hall.

"Mind your own fucking business and stay out of our way!"

6-6-06

Like a deer caught in oncoming headlights, I watched him go, nursing my shock like I had touched a live wire. His footsteps shuffled back down to their room while my chest heaved like I had just run a mile.

A thought creeped into my head as I fumbled with my earbuds and stared into the dark of the hall. I know damn well it came through my movie filter, that I was connecting dots the likes of Raimi and Friedkin had left for me. I tried to fight it, tried to squash it down and tell myself I was being stupid. That it was just hair. That it was medication. But it wouldn't fuck off. The last few nights and days—how he was and how he became, the noises he made and the things I had seen—left me with a conclusion I didn't want to jump to. As constant and persistent as the neighbors following me, it buzzed through my head, repeating itself over and over and over again.

That's not Pop-Pop.

After I worked up the courage to close my door, I spent the better part of the night looking out the window. My feet couldn't handle standing for more than a few minutes at a time, so I sat on the edge of the bed, my suitcase at the ready, adrenaline pumping relentlessly. I waited for the headlights to come. For the Aztek to show up and rescue me. But as the hours pressed on and my songs looped around, a pit formed in my stomach. Mom and Dad weren't coming. Mee-Moo hadn't called them.

And she hadn't come home.

I was on my own, alone in the house with the thing that wasn't my Pop-Pop, or at least not entirely. Some kind of alarm, an early warning, was needed. In the event that I wasn't being stupid and this wasn't another leaky shower kind of situation. I kept one earbud out, dangling around my neck, and put my suitcase in front of the door. Any of the furniture in the room would've been too heavy, felt too dramatic on the off chance that I was wrong. Anxiety forced my hand, though. I grabbed my backpack and, one at a time, returned the heavy books to their resting place inside it. Spider guts were dried and plastered to the back cover of *Great Expectations* still. I scraped them off on the edge of the dresser and dropped the book in with a little more spite than I expected. My bags were never gonna be enough to stop that door from opening, if the person on the other side was motivated enough, but they'd let me know they were coming. A safety blanket, if I've ever seen one, laid carefully next to each other right at the door's edge. The only silver lining would be the story I hoped I'd get to share with my friends at some point.

Satisfied with it, I sat back down on the corner of the bed nearest to the window. If I craned my head to one side, I could catch any movement in the street. Turn it the other way, and I had a clear view of the door. Perfect for holding a post as the moon rose higher over the Bluffs.

Their bedtime came and went. 9PM became 10 and crept clear through eleven. I gave up the ghost waiting for the Aztek, but Mee-Moo was still off in the neighborhood. Still at Elaine's house, doing whatever it was they were doing in there. Visions of ritual sacrifice danced through my head. The entire community coming together in some sick plan to hurl me off the cliff to please their Old God. My iPod counted out the anxious beats of my heart, keeping time with the snare and bass.

As midnight came in hot and the day rolled over, she finally emerged. I didn't see the exact moment, but I caught her as she rushed her way back across the inner ring. Practically skipping her way toward home. My gut twisted into a mass of knots, squeezing tighter with every foot she gained. Shadows followed her out from Elaine's door. Terry Tools & Lumber, Bow Tie, and Stache took up positions at the end of the driveway, center stage in the garage light. The President herself slunk from the darkness of her house, stepping right down the lawn to the edge of the sidewalk. Doors all around the ring began to open. Their owners came out and down to the sidewalk. All of them watching in the glare of the LED spotlights.

The front door opened, and I started to sweat. Tiptoeing quickly across the room, I turned my one earbud down as I dashed over to my shoes. A soft thud rippled up from downstairs. I sat on the edge of the bed and pulled the high-tops delicately around my sensitive feet. My attention split between getting them tied and the bedroom door. Images of Deadites and demons unspooled in my head like a reel with no one to man it. Fuck getting yelled at, I didn't have the slightest idea what to expect when she got upstairs.

Footsteps landed at the top. A content, delighted little sigh joined them. I shot up from the bed and leaned against the door. My sunburnt ear cooled against the cold pressboard as I listened to the hall. Satisfied mumbles floated down to me. I couldn't make out what she was saying, but the tone was obvious. Mee-Moo was happy with her neighborly visit. Something had gone well for her, which could only mean something was about to go horribly for me.

The master bedroom opened, and she called out clear as day.

"It's time, hubby!"

Their doors slammed shut, and silence took the Bluffs. I sprang across to the window. The neighbors were still there. As far around as I could see, rather in front of their houses or coming up through the connecting streets. They infested the neighborhood, emerging from darkness and shadow, on a slow and steady path straight for the house. I flew back across to the light switch and killed it, their eyes crawling all over me in the exposed window. My breath started to shake as badly as my hands.

"What . . ." I stammered, utterly lost. "What the fuck?"

They're coming to get you, Barbara.

Fuck it. I flew to the empty TV stand, the only piece of furniture I was confident I could move, but that they might struggle with. With a groan, I grabbed the edges and hoisted it a few inches off the ground. I shuffled it around the edge of the bed, putting it down in front of my bags. They were just in the way at that point, so I pushed them to the side, slid the TV stand across the carpet, and pressed it against the door. For good measure, though, I piled the bags on top of it. No such thing as overkill. And even if it turned out I was just delusional, ruined by too many movies, I didn't think it hurt to be safe.

Explaining why I rearranged the room would've been better than whatever might come for my door.

I fell back, retreating into the closet, and dragging the door closed behind me. Pulling my knees to my chest, I tucked into the far corner. I had kicked the hornets' nest; all that was left was to wait for the sting. A sliver of light from the street, faded and diluted through my room, cut through the gap of the door, leaving just enough for me to see.

My iPod clicked as I turned it back up. Just a little, only two up from muted. Which I know sounds like a suicidal move, but I needed something. With one earbud still out, rising and falling quickly with my chest, it was the only thing that kept full blown panic at bay. It didn't matter what was playing. Might as well have been Pop-Pop's Eagles cassette. Hearing a band, even at a nearly inaudible volume, was like a hand on my shoulder, telling me I had someone watching my back from a distance. That I wasn't on my own. That there were others. Curled up in the closet, though, wishing for the billionth time that I wasn't so damn big, it was just me.

With an ear on the house, I sat shivering in the dark. If I was brave enough to go downstairs, I would've made a run for the phone. The Caddy too, for that matter. If I was anything like the characters scattered around my room at home, I would've plowed right out of there, never to look back. But I was no Bruce Campbell, certainly no Batman, and most definitely not Hellboy. As much as I wanted to be, as I sat in a ball, whimpering in time to my music, I was only Grady. And the Bluffs knew it. They had gotten the size of me, knew what they were dealing with.

They kept me waiting.

The house growled around me. Pop-Pop entered his deep sleep cycle, and with it came the roaring snores. They vibrated through the walls like they were breathing, alive. A deep, hollow inhale and a grating, shaking exhale. The soundtrack to me going slowly insane. I turned my music up just one more click, enough to give the lyrics a fighting chance and something more normal, less horrid for me to focus on.

If he was asleep, then there was a chance she was too. The computer, the phone, the Caddy, they would all be clear. But I was frozen to the floor of the closet, listening to Pop-Pop's snores howl down the hall. As they droned on into the night, they changed, becoming more distant like a pond full of angry bullfrogs, but no less loud. Steadily, they bled together until there was only one long croak, endlessly pummeling the house.

Adrenaline drained from my body, leaving my limbs to quiver like the closet was freezing over. My eyelids fluttered heavily like they each had a Dickens tied to the ends of them. Sleep teased me, daring me to follow it wherever it would lead. What dying resolve I had pushed back. It was a glaring issue with the movies, I realized. Whenever the hero was up against the wall, reduced to hiding for any hope of survival, they stayed alert, sharp, ready for battle at all fucking times. No one ever yawned while facing down the undead. None of the final girls ever said, "Hold on, let me grab a Rockstar or a Mountain Dew first." What was their secret?

And why don't I have it?

Hellboy wouldn't have hidden at all.

Every passing moment, every new song, became a challenge. I skipped the slower ones, obviously. Hoping something with a little more punch and a faster time signature could keep me going. None of it really mattered, though. I couldn't hear shit over the snores, and I wasn't about to turn it up any more than I already had or plug the other earbud in.

I started to wonder again.

Am I stupid?

Pop-Pop's scream exploded through the house like a hand grenade. I jumped out of my skin as it rocketed across the walls and filled my skull. It spilled out into the hall, barely masking the crash of their bedroom doors. A laugh joined in, fighting for dominance. Loud and cackling, rapturous and a little mad, Mee-Moo's good night had only better. Pop-Pop roared like he was on fire as he smashed through another door across the hall. Her laugh only grew as his absolute agony broke down into heavy, tormented sobs.

"Please! No!" he bawled desperately. "I don't want to!"

He's in trouble.

Against all better judgement, I pulled the closet open again.

"Yes!" she shrieked, elated. "Do it! Do it! DO IT FOR MEEEEE!"

Thumping bangs shook the house. Anguish and torment devolved into bellowing screams, his voice deep and groaning.

"IT BUUUUUURNS!"

That's not Pop-Pop.

A wet slap hit the floor, like the time Mom accidentally tipped over the spaghetti strainer.

He needs help!

Tremors climbed up the walls.

That's not Pop-Pop!

The argument tossed back and forth in my head while his screams shook the windows in their frames. Wild, triumphant cheers filled the street. Mee-Moo squealed with like a giddy little schoolgirl.

"They're here! They're here!"

I shot out and over to the window. Down below, the HOA filled the grass and driveway, flooding out into the street and swarming around the community room. Their voices crackled and rasped, excited but indistinguishable, more life than I had seen from them. Elaine and her Board led their ranks calmly, like cracked garden statues. She waved for them to calm down with a commanding hand. All attention snapped to my window.

I jumped back to the bedroom door, throwing my bags onto the bed. The TV stand dragged against the carpet as I cleared it just enough. The sounds only got worse the second I opened the door. Her laughs, his screams, wet splashes against tile, pounding on the walls, they blasted down the hall, drowning everything in their path. I was ready for that, just not the smells. Like the food she left in the car, rotting and rancid, it stung my nostrils. I stood frozen as Pop-Pop howled.

"KILLLLLL MEEEEEE!"

My feet took off without a command. He was right. I was in it now. If there had ever been a time to turn back, to avert disaster, it was long gone. Every action since the last firehouse bell of eighth grade led me right to the guest bathroom.

A trail of blood stretched from their bedroom, where her laughs were reaching a manic fever pitch, straight through to the broken bathroom door. In great dark pools, it soaked into the torn shower curtain on the floor, wriggling and alive. Handprints smeared the walls and mirror. Pop-Pop hung from the ceiling in the dark. Clinging to the corner above the shower like he belonged there, his loose skin rippled and crawled as bulbous masses shifted underneath it. His face was soaked crimson, eyes dead and black. Spiders consumed the bathroom. Crawling over the walls, swimming through his blood on the floor, hanging from the ceiling, scurrying across the sink and over the toilet, up his legs, over his chest, and out of his mouth. Thick, shining webs crisscrossed the room as they spun them, claiming it as their own.

Pop-Pop's mouth hung open, black skeletal legs curled out around his lips and over his teeth. His drooping belly twitched and quivered as convulsions seized him. His jaw opened wider as his screams hit a crescendo. And were immediately silenced.

A moment of calm took hold of the house, all too brief. Pop-Pop's black eyes drifted to me, but had no idea I was there. No recognition showed on his clammy face. He heaved once, and a tidal flood erupted from his mouth. Thousands of spiders and heavy webs poured out and broke onto the floor. They seized the bathroom, covering the walls and floor in a dense, squirming black. Webs shot out in every direction, coming together to ensnare Pop-Pop and seal him into his spot above the bathroom. His head lolled limp and lifeless on his shoulder as even more legs began poking their way out of his bellybutton. Mandibles snipped through his skin as those too impatient to wait in line bit their way free, slicing him open like surgical scissors. Webs buried him in a thick swath, staining red against the gore.

"Yes! Come to me! Come to me!" Mee-Moo beckoned from their room.

The floor squirmed around my feet. I jumped back from the river of spiders skittering across the hall, my mind melting to pudding. More legs than I ever would've been able to count raced through the bathroom's open door. Up my battered feet, over my shins, around my knees. Panicked back to life, I swatted them down like I was on fire, but the onslaught was relentless. I dove over their stream, crashing down with a roll on the other side of it, entrails splattering against my back. Their pincers clamped at my fingers and thighs, opening new trickles of blood between them.

As I scrambled back up, smacking my legs, I made the mistake of looking into the bedroom. On the bed, in the center of the cavernous room, Mee-Moo writhed. Her sagging, shriveled naked body squirmed and wriggled, her bald head shining in the moonlight flooding through their open window. Spiders crawled up the bed and over every inch of her. Spinning webs around her as they gathered.

"My . . . *children*," she moaned deeply.

My vocal cords disintegrated through a scream, and my eyes bulged from their sockets as veins pressed out of my neck. Any shred of sanity I had flowed out with the puddle of fresh piss running down my legs and pooling at my feet. It wasn't enough to deter the spiders. They scuttled up from the floor, attacking my legs. They jumped off the walls and up from the carpet, landing on my chest.

Flailing and swatting in every direction at once, I scrambled back. The floor fell out from beneath me as the stairs dropped. I rolled back, tumbling end over end down to the switchback. My head smashed a crater into the drywall as I landed, eyes spinning, brain thick and foggy. The spiders worked diligently, closing the second floor hall in a shimmer blockade of webs. Their numbers thinned as more diverted to their grim construction project, but the determined few raced their way down after me, leaping down the stairs and skittering over the walls and rail.

I pushed myself up and fled the rest of the way down the stairs. Spiders dangled from webs over me and crawled over the frozen faces of the collected figurines. The front door boomed like a tidal wave was breaking against it.

Voices called from the other side, chanting as loudly as they could in their creaking, shrill voices.

"Aranea! Oriri!"

The Caddy.

Ignoring the burn of my feet and the stinging bites all over me, I sprinted for the kitchen. Infant faces watched my flight through the hall, little baby Mom telling me to run faster. With a skid, I came around to the counter. Mee-Moo's purse sat on top of it.

"ARANEA!" echoed from the front of the house. "ORIRI!" burst through, hot on its heels from the back door.

I tipped the bag over and dumped it out. Candies, pens, puzzle books, cold medicine, a host of glasses she never wore, all spilled out across the counter. The keys landed amongst them with a sharp clatter. I tossed the bag back into the living room and snatched them up.

Of course, I had never driven a mile in my life. None of us had, except for Jordan. A learner's permit sat folded in his wallet at all times, on the off chance his parents ever left their car behind. But that wasn't about to stop me. No better time than the present, and no better conditions to learn under than absolute duress. I barreled through into the garage and smacked the button on the wall spitefully. The door hummed as it glided up. Dozens of feet and wheels waited on the other side.

"ARANEA! ORIRI! ARANEA! ORIRI!"

As the door climbed to the ceiling, the Sea Breeze Bluffs HOA stood waiting to block my exit. Their eyes fixed on me ravenously, faces dark and veined in black. Walkers jumped forward, scooters lurched, steps shuffled. The neighbors meticulously surrounded the car, cutting me off from it before I could make a move.

"ARANEA! ORIRI! ARANEA! ORIRI!"

"FUCK OFF!" I bellowed at them as they advanced on me. Tears flowed freely down my filthy cheeks.

I backed up against the door as the shuffling, scooting masses wormed their way in and across the garage. The tool bench! I looked over, hoping there'd be an ax or a chainsaw I never noticed, primed for emulation. Gardening tools, ratchets, and screwdrivers wouldn't get me as far, but that was all Pop-Pop had on hand. I fell back through the door and turned its lock as they swarmed after me.

Phone!

It struck me for the first time that I had no fucking clue where Mee-Moo kept it. I ran back to the kitchen, hoping she left the phone in relatively the same place Mom would've. Nestled in the corner, on the far side of the sink and out of its splash radius, the handset's cradle sat empty. I started panting again, struggling to keep a lid on the crushing dread.

BOOM!

Bodies slammed into the garage door.

BOOM!

Then the front.

BANG!

And the back.

All around the house, liver-spotted hands tried to force their way in.

Office!

I didn't remember seeing a phone in there, but that didn't mean there wasn't. I ran through the open French doors, my head on a swivel.

"ARANEA! ORIRI!"

His desk, the shelves, the drafting table, nothing. I was right. Not even a flip phone to be found. Dread got harder to suppress as I contemplated firing up the computer. The garage doorknob started to shake and rattle. Every ounce of me regretted leaving my hiding spot. But it only would've been a matter of time there too.

I flew to the kitchen, to the block of knives I knew were ridiculously clean. The sweat on my palms as I grabbed a handle and pulled told me they wouldn't stay that way. A backup plan for an eventuality, I resolved. A last resort, only to be used if they forced me to.

The banging and the chanting stopped suddenly, leaving the Bluffs to their unnatural, uneasy quiet. My heart blasted against my ribcage as I searched my immediate surroundings, looking for anywhere I could go. The bathroom was obvious, and the office was too exposed. I wouldn't fit in the pantry and upstairs was fucked six ways to my birthday. Backing out of the kitchen, I kept the knife raised as I stepped into the dining room.

"Sit, troublemaker," a horribly familiar voice ordered calmly out of the dark of the house.

With a barbaric yowl, I raised the blade high over my head as I spun around. The front door was wide open. Undamaged. But still, they waited. Like the neighbors hadn't been given permission to enter any further yet.

Elaine sat on a plastic-wrapped couch, a heavy key ring dangling and jingling from her bony fingers. The leather journal laid on the cushion next to her. Stache, Bow Tie, and Terry Tools & Lumber stood ready at her back, glaring under shadowed brows. She opened a hand to the couch across from her.

"This is your last chance."

"Wha—What?" I stammered, nowhere near comprehending. "What the fuck is going on?"

"Sit." She wasn't asking. "And watch your language."

"What did you do to them?"

"If you'd like me to explain," she offered as politely as her disdain for me would allow, "then you need to sit."

"What is this?"

"I won't ask again, troublemaker."

"No!" I raised the knife high, ready to strike.

"Sit!"

"Eat me, bitch!"

A certain level of freedom came with talking to a woman I was pretty sure was made of pure evil. As terrifying as that skin and sinew scarecrow had become, nothing she could do to me was worse than what I'd seen upstairs.

"Don't tempt me," Elaine said sternly.

The Board took a step forward behind her. I held my ground, gripping the knife tightly ahead of me like a spear.

"Is that really necessary?" She rolled her eyes.

"Yes!"

She snapped her fingers over her shoulders and the bodyguards deployed. They came down on me fast, darting around the couches and across the room before I could fall back. Like a cornered animal, I lashed out. Eyes wide as windows, sweat pouring down my face, I swiped the knife at them wildly.

And connected with nothing.

Stache's wrist fell on my own, snapping my weapon to the ground. His fingers clamped around my arm like a vice. Bow Tie was there to take the other.

Terry Tools came around the back. His calloused paw smashed into the back of my head, forcing it down for a painful view of my feet. With a feral cry, I exploded against them, pulling, tugging, thrashing, kicking. I even tried to bite one of them. But it made no difference. They jerked me forward and dragged me to the couch like I was being prepped for the guillotine. My face smashed into the plastic as they threw me down onto it and took up positions behind me.

"I just have one question," Elaine began like it was nothing at all, like they weren't at best in the middle of some serious child abuse. "Do you know what the purpose of a Homeowners Association is?"

"To be judgey assholes," I snarled under my breath.

"That's what I thought, you have no clue," she rolled her eyes. "The greater good. Its purpose is the greater good. To serve it, to protect it. To provide it to people when they don't even know they need it. That's what has happened here tonight. Your grandparents have given themselves over to something greater."

"What did you do to them?"

She ignored the question entirely.

"You've been given multiple chances! We let you into our community. We didn't have to do that."

"Nobody asked you to!" I spat back.

"Your grandmother did. She practically demanded it." The first hint of emotion I'd seen teased Elaine's face, a sick little smile as she sat forward. "So, I allowed it. Because she was someone important to this community and our purpose, believe it or not."

Was.

"You were told the rules," Elaine kept going like she too was disappointed in me. "You were told what would be expected of you. You fought it every step of the way."

"I wore the stupid shirt!"

"You did, but did you enjoy it?" she sneered. "Were you happy about it?"

I had had enough. My own questions fired in rapid demands.

"What is all this? What are you people doing? What'd you do to Pop-Pop?"

"Pop-Pop," she scoffed. "How cute."

I shot forward in my seat to tell her to go fuck herself. Bow Tie yanked me right back.

"Nothing was done to them that they didn't want," Elaine added, like it was supposed to be a reassurance. Her claws curled around the journal.

"What's that supposed to mean?"

"It means they're serving the greater—"

"What do you do to them?" I screamed. "What the fuck is going on?"

"You just refuse to behave, don't you?" Elain's voice rose to match mine. "It is *very* rude to speak when an adult is speaking! Don't you know that? Were you raised by wolves? When an adult is talking, you *stay quiet*."

I flipped her off without raising my hand, just in case Bow Tie was feeling jumpy again.

"This is exactly what I'm talking about!" she seethed. "This attitude! So rude and disrespectful. It's exactly what's wrong with the world these days. You and all your kind think acting like little hoodlums is something to be proud of! You don't belong here, troublemaker. You don't belong anywhere! And that much is clear to me."

As much as I wanted to call her every horrible thing I could think of, I bit my tongue. I needed answers.

"So, I offer you one final chance," she continued. "Join us, fall in line."

"What . . ." My mind spun desperately, hopelessly, searching for the smallest shred of understanding and coming up dry. "What are you even talking about, lady?"

She snapped her fingers again at the goons behind me.

"Take him up."

Shriveled hands grabbed on to my shoulders.

"Wait! Hey!" I bucked and flailed. "Let me go!"

Elaine rose from her seat. She followed as Bow Tie and Stache pulled me to the stairs. I kicked and thrashed, trying to break from their clutches, and only succeeded at knocking over vases and figurines. Terry Tools brought up the rear, gesturing for literally everybody else to follow. They forced me to the top, shoving, yanking, and pushing while I snarled and flailed like a lunatic in a straitjacket. A legion of Bluff retirees filed into the house after us. Wheels and walkers stayed down below, while the more capable took to the stairs.

They threw me to the floor at the top. I hit the ground with a grunt, all the wind forced from my chest. The carpet was clear at least, the spiders were gone. A glistening wall of web sealed the hallway, stretching between the master bedroom and the bathroom across from it. Twitching and rippling, alive under the surface. Fear doused my senses in kerosene and struck a match. My throat clenched as bile rushed up it. Pop-Pop was in there somewhere.

Elaine took up a position at the banister as I stared a hole clean through the back of her stupid fucking head. Her constituents clogged every artery of the house as far as I could see. Packing in tightly and oozing up the stairs, stopping a step down from their President as she waited to address them. She rapped her knuckles on the banister as loudly as she could, like firecrackers through the house.

"I hereby declare this meeting of the Sea Breeze Bluffs Homeowners Association to order." She looked back at the bedroom, waiting for an introduction that wasn't coming. "Oh, well. Sitting President Elaine Rubenfeld, presiding."

She opened the journal, reading from the page like it was just another update on the mailman or lawn standards.

"First, the old. As discussed in previous meetings, the Age of Aranea is imminent."

Applause barreled through the house as the nearly-dead masses showed signs of life. Jubilant and proud. Elaine banged on the banister. Obedient stillness took them.

"The Under Secretary and her husband," she informed them plainly, "have fulfilled their obligations as per our established agreements and assignments."

"What obligations?" I shouted from the floor. "WHAT DID YOU DO TO THEM?"

Terry Tools was just waiting for the excuse. He hauled off and kicked me square in the stomach. Stars shot across my eyes as his foot rammed into my guts. New tears rolled down my cheeks as I clutched my midsection and rolled on the floor.

The neighbors responded with wild cheers and shouts of approval.

BANG! BANG!

"Please!" she called them to order with a raised hand. "We have a lot to get through and not much time."

They settled, and she returned to her journal.

"The necessary preparations have been made, and at the community potluck later today, we will welcome her." She paused, making sure there were no further interruptions. Other than my pained groans, none came. "And so, we shall proceed to the next item on our agenda. The last step before we welcome Aranea, as outlined in her commands, we must first embrace her. All opposed?"

None. Not even a murmur.

"All in favor?"

Thunderous, rabid support.

I looked to the web wall as my vision started to clear. Breath returned slowly to my lungs, but the pain remained a persistent throb, like his foot was still stuck in my organs. The Board surrounded me, staring down with malicious eyes.

"Form an orderly line," Elaine instructed them. "We'll do this on the basis of first come, first served. Those of you who can't make it up the stairs will be tended to separately. I assure you, though"—she turned back to me, her cold glare locking on—"there's plenty to go around."

"I'm ready, Madame President," Terry volunteered. "I'd like to break the seal."

"Yes, of course." She glanced at him before declaring to her assembled, "The Board recognizes Rite of First Selection!"

Elaine turned to her goon. Their eyes met fiercely, determined. From my vantage on the floor, I could see his hands shaking like the fatal seizure had finally come. Stache grabbed a handful of my sweaty, greasy hair and ripped my head back.

"Pay attention, troublemaker," he growled down at me.

I latched onto his wrist, clawing for freedom with no success.

"Don't be afraid, Treasurer Chapman," she whispered softly to Terry. "She is our salvation."

"'Course," he nodded.

Elaine took him by the hand and led him to the web wall. It quivered upon his arrival, pulsing excitedly and impatient. Slowly, she lifted his palm to its shimmering face and pressed it in. Flesh began to sizzle like strips of bacon. With a deep groan, he bit down as wisps of smoke snaked between his fingers. She pulled it away. A perfect handprint was left in the web, its lines and patterns etched into his skin.

A spider crawled out through the handprint.

Bigger. Heavier. Closer to the size of my full hand than just my thumb. Thick, armored legs were knuckled at the joints. Two at the center of its long thorax, while the other six spread out over its bulbous abdomen. Snow-white hairs bristled its pitch black body. Pincers like garden shears snapped and clacked while it sized Terry up. He raised his burned hand and laid it flat. The spider's heavy legs lumbered forward, each moving independently of the others, yet still in synch. Onto his hand, up his arm, to his shoulder. It climbed confidently up his neck. As much as I wanted to look away, Stache made sure I didn't. I tried to twist my head free, but he only snapped it right back.

"You need to see this," Elaine caught me. "This is what you're here for."

Its front legs teased at the side of Terry's face, caressing it as he stared into the web wall. Black eyes began to shine within it. Dozens of them, hundreds, moving closer to the surface for a better view. Pincers bit through, opening fresh viewports.

"For Aranea," he whispered breathlessly.

The spider lunged, slicing its powerful mandibles through the cartridge of Terry's ear with ease. He choked down a scream as blood spilled down his neck.

The spider bit and gnashed, chewing his ear into a mangled mass of ribbons. Grunting and moaning, his mouth trembled while chunks of flesh tumbled off his shoulder. The spider raised its front legs, inspecting and testing the diameter of the hole it had made. Terry took a deep, steadying breath as it lifted itself up along his face, and plunged its head inside.

His cries punched through my chest like a shotgun blast as the spider burrowed deep. He dropped to his knees and grabbed his mangled ear. Wet crunches and snaps took the spider's thick legs deeper and out of sight, disappearing entirely into the dark of his skull. He collapsed onto his back, his skin becoming as dull and lifeless as Pop-Pop's had been. His eyes shifted, turning as black as the sky outside. Endlessly deep, set into hollow sockets. A stream of thick white webs spewed from his mouth and splattered onto the carpet next to him. Streams of smoke rose out from under them. With one last heavy bite, the spider settled. And so did Terry Tools. His screams died in his throat as he stilled. His chest no longer rose to take in breath.

All at once, in one seamless motion, he flew to his feet. His jaw hung loosely from his head, lips cracked and bleeding, his voice as deep and grating as Pop-Pop's croaking snore.

"Aranea Oriri," he belched, mouth unmoving.

The others cheered triumphantly all through the house, their faces soaked in proud tears.

"This is the chance I've left for you, troublemaker." Elaine leered at me without a hint of emotion, like I should've had any clue what I was seeing. "Do you want to be a filthy little degenerate your whole life? Or do you want to be *greater*?"

It was no choice. Even if being more like them didn't require a fucked up spider eating its way into my brain, there was no way in hell I would've gone that route. But Pop-Pop—and to a lesser extent, Mee-Moo—were in that mess somewhere. And while all signs pointed to it, I needed confirmation.

"Are they dead?" I had to ask.

6-6-06

Legs worked their way free of the webs, stabbing out at the air, flooding the hole left by Terry's hand. Sparkling diamonds grew dark, crawling with creeping black. Elaine looked at me like I had just asked if the sky was blue.

"I know this may be hard for you to understand," she exaggerated slowly, "but change requires sacrifice."

She turned back to the wall, eyes brimming with pride.

"They did exactly what was asked of them. For us. For *her*."

There's always a bigger fish.

"Who?" I demanded.

"Aranea," Elaine grinned. "The Cleanser."

The webs began to break down, crackling and burning. A cloud of smoke gathered at the ceiling as legs and jaws emerged. Almost instinctively, I felt for the earbuds still dangling from the neck of my shirt. I jammed them back into my ears and in one foul swoop, the wall collapsed, crashing to the ground in a hale of revoltingly furry bodies. The evolved spiders hit the floor with enough weight to generate a unified and sickening *THUMP*. Stache's grip on my hair loosened as he watched, awestruck.

They took over the house, erupting out in all directions. Up the walls, over the carpet, jumping straight for faces and ears with their legs spread wide like dark, disembodied hands. A spider landed on Stache's chest. He let go completely and stumbled back, leaving me to my fate. I slapped my hands against my earbuds, driving them in deeper as I shot up, eyes streaming and chest heaving. Pandemonium devoured the house.

Bow Tie was already screaming, blood flowing down his neck. The closest few at the top of the steps fell back as they clawed at their ears. Elaine smiled softly, untouched and proud. The journal was clutched firmly in her bony grip. Spiders flew at my face and raced up my legs, but I wouldn't let go of my ears. I ducked and dodged where I could, kicking wildly at the crawling sea at my feet. In the outside pocket of my shorts, something light clunked against my knee with every strike. It dawned on me when I wore those shorts last.

Stache dropped, flat on his back as legs slipped into his ear. Anguished cries filled the lower level as more found their way home. Blood soaked into the carpet up and down the stairs as the neighbors began to topple and writhe.

"Accept it, troublemaker," Elaine called to me over her symphony, barely audible over the nightmares and the music still playing defiantly in my ears. "Join us. Let us fix you."

I weighed my options, looking first to the tangle of shrieking bodies on the stairs. Tackling my way through the spider-people was a doomed idea. Too many in too tight of a space. Down the hall, my room had a window out to the front yard. Jumping out, dropping down to the porch awning, and rolling to the grass was a move I thought literally only Indiana Jones could pull off.

I looked to the President, standing amongst her carnage, supremely pleased with herself, the journal held closely to her side. She held her other hand out to me as a spider crawled down to her waiting palm.

There it is.

A way forward through her, an idea that would only work if life lined up with the movies in this one particular instance.

I took a step toward her.

"Excellent choice!"

Then another, my entire body shaking. I lowered my hands from my ears but left the buds in place. The spider waited in her hand, front legs up, pincers snapping, eyes glistening. She spoke softly, but I didn't hear her. All that was in my head was AFI, and the screams of the severely old as the creatures set up shop in their skulls. I stopped no more than a foot in front of her, my young heart ready to explode into mist. Her crease of a mouth moved in a way I could clearly read. She wanted me to take the earbuds out. One hand inched forward at my waist, reaching blindly as I held her gaze. The other stayed low, close to my pocket.

Down on the stairs, the rest of her people started to stand. Wrinkles and cracks darkened their deathly pallor, eyes like coal, mouths wide open and unmoving. The Board stepped up behind me to block any attempt at retreat.

6-6-06

The Necronomicon, right? Tom Riddle's diary? Indy's dad's grail thing?

In every movie I had ever seen that was even remotely similar to what I was stuck in the middle of, the book was always important. I didn't know what was in that journal, but I knew that she was pretty damn attached to it. And I didn't want her to have it anymore.

The second my fingers touched leather, they attacked. I ripped the journal out of Elaine's hand while I dug in my pocket. Recovered from the laundry strewn around my floor, dirty clothes meant for the wash at some point or another, I knew exactly which shorts those were. Worn last on the infamous Night of a Thousand Fireworks.

With her journal in one hand, I pulled Jordan's lighter from my pocket and flicked the flame to life.

"Back off!" I tried to sound as tough as I could, rolling the dice as I raised flame to paper. "All of you! Back the fuck off! I'll burn it!"

The Board froze around me, waiting for instructions. I held the journal and the lighter high over my head for all to see. Elaine started to laugh. More amused than she should've been, she doubled over as the spider clung to her hand. The others took their cue, joining in with their mouths stuck open like broken ventriloquist dummies.

"You want to steal our meeting minutes?" she howled. "Go ahead! Burn it! I have copies!"

My cheeks turned scarlet, practically boiling the sweat and tears soaking my face. My temper flared even darker than it already was. Being laughed at by people my own age was always a kick to the nuts, one I was pretty used to. But when it was people roughly ten times older than me doing it, that kick might as well have come from a Clydesdale. For a moment, copies or not, that journal almost didn't make it out of the house. The flame curled toward its soft leather like it was under my command. Fuming, I killed it and stashed the lighter back in my pocket.

The Board moved in, and I switched to my fallback. Tucking into my shoulders, journal tight to my chest, I lowered my head like I had seen in the football movies Dad made me watch, and charged straight ahead. Elaine collided off of me, flying back into the wall as I sprinted to my room. Her lieutenants raced after me, an army of feet pounding up the stairs and down the hall behind them.

Flying through my door, I slammed it closed and dragged the TV stand back in place. I grabbed my backpack and threw it onto the half-assed barricade for good measure. The door pushed back as I ran for the window. The stand tore across the carpet, and the Board flooded inside, faster than they should've been, stronger than age should've allowed.

No intention of waiting around, I shoved the window open and hoisted myself through to the roof overhang. They crossed the room fast, as quickly as they could fill it. Angling my steps, I inched toward the edge of the roof. The porch cover sat squarely below. Shriveled hands gripped the window frame, and Bow Tie pulled himself through. I lowered myself down and slung my knees over the edge, trying to do it as safely as possible. Even more joined Bow Tie as the rest of the Board followed. The window shattered into shards as he stepped calmly toward me and the HOA forced their way out. People crawled across the house like the spiders in their heads. On all fours, sticking to the walls, their heads and necks twisted unnaturally over their backs.

I held my breath and pushed off the roof. Coming down at an angle, I hit the top of the porch, and my feet shot out from under me. Bone popped in my ankle like a Roman candle as I tumbled over the ledge. Pain shot through me clear to the top of my head in a blinding bolt. My back slammed into the ground while the journal fluttered down next to me.

Gasping like a fish on a boat deck, unable to breathe, unable to scream, I'd get no reprieve. They spilled out in every direction, marching through the front door, crawling over the face of the house, dropping down from the second level. Calling her bluff, I grabbed the journal as I pushed myself to my feet, and fell right back down again. The pain in my ankle flared with even the slightest bit of weight. But I was gonna have to suck up. Spiders joined their two-legged brethren, scrambling all over the house as Bow Tie bared down on me. I forced myself back up again, cramming my earbuds in, though the music had stopped. My face drenched, wheezing with every step, I hobbled my way toward the garage.

Fumbling to dig the keys from my pocket, I limped to the Caddy. Mee-Moo drove it last, so of course the fucking thing was locked while parked in a perfectly secure garage in a gated neighborhood. The door into the house dangled from a single hinge. Leading a secondary wave, Arnold Finkle ripped it off the frame completely, his wizard's beard soaked red. Through violently shaking hands, I jammed the key in the driver side handle as I landed against it. Finkle reached for me as I popped it open and fell onto the seat, tossing the journal down next to me.

Gray hands and black nails clawed at the door, pulling it back. Bodies began to surround the car, coming out from the house and around the driveway. I lunged for the door handle. Leaning with all my weight, clear across to the passenger side. Fingers curled around the edge of the window and frame like spider legs.

"Leave! Me! ALONE!" I sobbed.

With one big pull, the door slammed shut, crunching and snapping Finkle's digits like kindling. His face stayed a blank mask of loose skin, showing no signs of pain. A heavy glob of web and bile shot from his mouth like a cat with a hairball. It splattered against the glass, burning itself in and melting through. I jammed the key in the ignition the same way I had seen Pop-Pop do. The Caddy rumbled to life, belching exhaust in a cloud around the elderly. I jerked the gear lever down and stomped on the gas.

It shot forward, crashing into the wall.

"Shit!"

D for Drive.

Blood sprayed up the windshield. Crushed bodies persisted on the hood. Pinned between the Caddy and the wall, the grocery store T. rex clawed forward like it was nothing more than a minor inconvenience. Jerking the lever back up a couple notches to R, I tried again. The Caddy lurched back, knocking clear anyone stupid enough to still be standing behind it. I flew all the way down the driveway, bumping over neighbors and crushing spiders, into the street, up the curb, and crashed to a stop against the pool gate. Broken glass burst into the backseat as the metal fence bent and crumpled around the car.

The legion of neighbors flowed from the house. Out the front door and through the garage, ignoring their broken kin dragging themselves along the ground. Scooters and chairs weaved drunkenly through the mayhem until their operators decided to abandon them, scurrying on their hands and feet instead. Spiders spilled out around them. Elaine came through the front and rejoined her Board. As a unit, they marched ahead, trails of furry legs and pincers following them like a living shadow.

"Bring him BACK!" she roared to them, lifting a finger to the Caddy.

I ripped the lever back down to Drive and gunned it. Tires squealed and I rocketed forward. The wheel whipped and the Caddy curved as it bounced back up the curb and onto Pop-Pop's perfect lawn. Grass and soil splattered as I leaned against the door. In a deep arc, I came back down the curb and hit the street. The trunk fishtailed out from behind me, and I swerved all over the damn place. One drastic overcorrection after another, I spun the wheel to one side and then the other, serpentining down street in a flurry of screeches and near misses.

Keeping the car straight wasn't as easy as the racing games I'd played made it look and feel. I might've done better with joysticks or directional buttons. I started to get the hang of it as I neared the edge of the inner ring, the wheels steadying under my desperate control. With the pedal smashed to the floor, I looked back over my shoulder. Behind me, the HOA charged, unrelenting. Running and skittering through the street, jumping across the fronts of their houses. Elaine and the Board walked calmly down the sidewalk, content to watch and wait. Spiders consumed the front of the only house I gave a shit about, turning its white surface entirely black. Garage lights flickered as they rampaged over them. One by one, the bulbs in their path went out, leaving the inner ring to the light of the moon as it crossed overhead.

I forgot about the fountain.

6-6-06

The Caddy barreled straight through it, coming to a sudden, violent stop in an explosion of plaster, tile, and water. The windshield imploded in a blast of tempered glass. The hood crumbled and caved. My head snapped forward, cracking into the solid wood of the steering wheel. The earbuds shot out, held desperately by my shirt. Rubble flew across the road as a cloud of dust and smoke plumed from the wreck.

Clinging to consciousness, my head swam as I lifted it from the steering wheel. Honestly, without the seatbelt I didn't have time to buckle, I was just grateful I didn't go flying over the dash and into the trees. The engine spewed from under the broken hood, vaporizing the fountain's water and whatever fluids were leaking from its lines. A constant drip trickled somewhere under me. The back tires spun uselessly, propped off the ground by the fountain's basin, my foot still glued to the pedal. My eyebrow was split at its point of impact, blood running down to sting and blind.

Croaks wailed through the neighborhood behind me. A hundred broken voices crying out in furious, hungry agreement. The rearview mirror filled with sagging faces and limbs that longed to be arachnid as the HOA started to close the gap between us. A singular vision in their infested minds. I grabbed the journal and the gate clicker. The door squealed as I flung it open and fell out of the car, into the basin. Enough water remained to soak my shoes in a harsh snap of cold. I tucked the journal into my pocket and stumbled out of the fountain. The lead I had on them was dying by the step. Every foot I staggered was a yard they gained down the road to the gate.

Out of the corner of my eye, I caught movement. Smaller, less significant than the flood of gray hair and death behind me, but quick all the same. The raccoon dropped down from the roof of its maintenance shed, standing in front of the door like it was gonna hold it open for me. Behind me, they were too close. Making a break for the shed would've only meant dying with the lawnmowers. I pressed on forward with something far more complicated and painful in mind.

Contorted limbs and twisted bodies crawled over the Caddy as they swarmed around the ruined fountain. Elaine and her bodyguards sauntered like they knew I was done, just too stupid to realize it. They stopped to investigate the damage, confident in their horde's ability. The road sloped, and the gate appeared, nothing more than thick black lines across the trees in the dark. My ankle roared as I dragged myself down, every nerve ending crying out in torment. Dull aches ground through my back. My head throbbed like my brain was outgrowing its shell. Blood poured down my face and into my eye.

As I neared the gate, I clicked the button. The two halves started their inward arc, and I veered off the road. Plunging deep into the woods, hustling as fast as pain would allow around the bushes and through the trees. Sticking close to the trunks and their shadows, I worked my way along the hill and out of sight. Footsteps began to crunch behind me. On the road, the spider-people came down.

THUMP!

A pair of human hands and feet stuck high on a pine at the road's edge. Then another. And another. Dark masses amongst the middle branches that barely looked human anymore. I ducked behind a tree and pressed myself flat to its bark, keeping my back to them and wishing myself thinner. The rest ran down through the open gate, taking the bait before it started to close again.

THUMP! THUMP!

Two of them peeled off the trees. One leaping forward through them and the other dropping to the road.

Thump.

The third moved in, following me deeper into the woods. Its voice bounced off the trunks and branches, floating around me like embers on a breeze, gravely and low like a broken garbage disposal.

"Trooooublemaaaaaker . . ."

I clapped a hand over my mouth to muffle my breath and catch my whimper.

Thump.

The voice came closer. I creaked my head around the side of my tree. Halfway between me and the road, it clung to the wide body of a redwood. Shivering, I watched it as it settled down low on its joints and rocketed forward again.

Thump.

I flinched as it landed even closer, sticking to the bark like it was meant to. Its head craned slowly around, neck bones crunching and popping like the twigs under me, until it was staring over its own back. The face I recognized as it came around into the light. The lady at the meeting that was more blanket than person, now more spider than anything else. Her head continued to swivel, scanning around for a line on me in perfectly sickening circles. I ducked back behind the tree and held what breath I had.

Thump.

She moved off.

"Trooooooublemaaaaaker . . ."

I shuffled around the tree, keeping her behind me.

Thump.

Farther along down the road.

Thump.

Following the others toward town.

I allowed myself a slow exhale as I eased off the tree. The shed was still a ways off, across the hill and back up. Scanning the woods, I checked to make sure I was alone.

Acidic webs shot out of the darkness.

I ducked a half second before they splattered onto my face. They hit the bark instead, sizzling and smoking into it. Terry Tools erupted from the shadows like he was made of them, his jaw down to his sternum. Another blast of webs flew at me, flying out of his mouth in a ball and stretching out to cover my head. I dropped to the ground as they sailed over me, smacking against the tree. He reached down with a steely, cold hand and wrapped it around my throat. Raising me off the ground, he lifted me to his face as I kicked and squirmed.

"Don't fight it." His voice came through his open mouth like grinding gears. "Embrace."

That close, the finer details burned themselves into my memory. His eyes, glassy and black, were reshaped, broken up into hundreds of geometric panels like the Epcot dome. I reflected in their miniature mirrors, dozens of tiny Grady faces, bleeding and weeping, eyes bulging from their sockets. Webs formed in his gaping maw, and a lump like a golf ball swelled larger in his throat. His lips and chin were singed, blistered, and peeling from the strays still clinging to him. His hand curled around my windpipe with robotic strength and the woods grew darker. Slowly from the edges of my vision, they began to fade out around me.

"Embrace."

In a last ditch, I ripped Jordan's lighter from my pocket. I sparked it and raised the flame to his face. Smoke curled into the air as a black streak charred up the side of his cheek. But he didn't react. Didn't even notice it. I raised it higher, burying its light in his insect eye. Fluid crackled and popped as it burned, but he still didn't stop. The ball forming in his mouth only grew.

In it, I saw Buena Vista. All the things I hated developed a sudden and inexplicable allure. I would've happily answered questions about why I don't like football or what I found appealing about the alien things I liked if it meant leaving Sea Breeze. Hell, I would've let Mom clear out my entire room if Terry went with it. Even Georgie Booker and his rabble of followers would've been preferable, mocking us from their posts in Rainer's class while she droned on about god knows what. My friends never felt farther. I could see them sitting in class beside me, one of the final times before the year ended and life collapsed. Alex took notes. Ruben hid his Gameboy under his desk. Jordan pretended to give a shit about his textbook, an issue of Fangoria tucked between its pages. Rainer rambled on, half a thermos in, staring at her teacher's science text like it was written in glyphs.

The metal of the lighter stung my fingers, heated orange, and ripped me back to the problem at hand. It leaped from my palm and fell to the dirt. His eye was burnt to a crisp, a cracked ball of ashy cornea. Thick black legs curled out from behind it, hooking around his socket like they didn't understand what happened. His head cocked back, ready to fire. I closed my eyes and braced for impact.

Snarling with rabid fury, the raccoon landed on the back of Terry's head, lashing out with claws and teeth. His grip released, and I fell to the dirt, coughing and cradling my crushed windpipe. He reached for the raccoon as it slashed at his face, racing over his head in every direction at once, pulling strips of flesh with it. Terry fired blindly. A massive wad of web flew over my head in a sizzling arc and smacked down into the dirt. He reached up, trying to get a grip on his attacker, but it was too quick, too agile.

I watched as the raccoon found its target. The ruined eye. Spider legs kicked from behind it, determined to defend their new home. The raccoon began to dig. Tiny hands plunged into the socket, ripping chunks of blackened eye and muscle out as it chittered and hissed madly. Terry Tools fell back, and the raccoon took the ride. They crashed to the ground like a falling tree in a plume of dust. He clawed at the critter, grabbing at its fur but unable to pull it free. His legs kicked trails under him as bursts of web shot from his mouth, raining back down around us. The raccoon sank its claws deep and gripped his head. It plunged its snout into his face, snarling and growling like it hadn't eaten in years. Its bushy tail waved as it rooted and chewed.

When its black masked muzzle rose, fur matted with gore, the spider hung from its razor jaws. Legs kicked and pincers sliced at the air as it tried to fight back. The raccoon's fangs snapped down, crunching the spider in half. Legs rooted with pieces of abdomen fell to the dirt, and their host went limp. Terry's arms dropped, and his legs slid to a stop. The raccoon turned and looked at me. Perfectly pleasant, if not a little pleased, despite its bloody face from snout to ear. Bug guts stuck in its teeth like strands of caramel.

The sound rolled out of my throat, somewhere between a relieved laugh and a caught scream. Tears cut through the blood on my cheek. The raccoon turned away, scanning the woods while still sitting on Terry's lifeless chest. The quiet vacuum sealed over the Bluffs. In a flash, the scourge of Sea Breeze sprinted up the hill, back to the shed. I recovered the lighter from the dirt and jammed it into my pocket as the raccoon stopped, looking back to make sure I was still there, waiting for me to catch up. Climbing to my feet along the body of the tree, I followed it up.

OVER MY HEAD (BETTER OFF DEAD)
JUNE 6, 2006

A salty haze settled around the neighborhood. At the top of the hill, I paused, ducking low at the pavement's edge. The crumpled Caddy sat on the smashed fountain, as abandoned and ignored as the houses around them. The quiet should've been a comfort, an indicator that their search had moved off. But it wasn't. It sat over the Bluffs like a deep breath before a long plunge. Elaine and her fucking HOA were nowhere to be seen, her house just as dark as the others. My skin rippled regardless as I started to doubt I'd ever shake the feeling of their eyes on me.

The raccoon bounded up to the roof of the shed, squeezing its way in through a gap barely big enough for it. Since that wasn't an option for me, I took my final exposing steps up into the moonlight and came around the shed's side. The door was cracked. Heavy, wooden and splintered, two halves sat an inch apart on a metal track. I leaned into one, and rusted wheels whined like sirens across the breathlessly quiet neighborhood. I spun around, looking and listening for any signs that my position had been discovered.

No one was coming.

I pushed the door open only as far as I needed to shuffle over the track and through. A foot of solid darkness, give or take an inch or two, formed inside it. The smell of oil and cut grass wafted out as I sucked it in and squeezed through.

A dome lamp hung in the center of the shed, wide enough to house six mowers, stacked by twos in three neat rows. You couldn't have paid me to turn it on, though. Red cans of gasoline and boxed pool chemicals cluttered metal shelves lining the walls, flanked by hanging racks of edgers, leaf blowers, and electric trimmers. Sea Breeze Bluffs jumpsuits hung on a hook by the door, reeking of sweat and grass. In the rear, a long tool bench was covered in greasy wrenches, detached wheels, and cannibalized mower parts. The raccoon waited on top of it, staring at me like I had taken way too long to join the party. I pulled the door over again. The two halves met, and the raccoon dropped to the floor. It scampered under the bench, blending into the dark of the back corner.

Aren't you supposed to go numb at a certain point?

I sure as shit wasn't! My ankle was swollen so badly I thought my high-top was going to rip open like I was turning into the Hulk. My throat stung like it was lined with broken glass. My foot felt like it was on the verge of falling off, like the broken bone had hacked through enough muscle to test my leg's willingness to stay whole.

A splint.

It's what Les Stroud or Bear Grylls would've done. Before I could even think about sitting, I needed to figure out how to fashion one. Something to use as a crutch didn't sound like a bad idea either. Careful to keep my finger away from the metal this time, I sparked the lighter and started to plan.

Absolutely nothing in the soft orange of the flame immediately stood out as either a splint or a crutch. For a second, I wondered if it'd be worth it to figure out how to ride a push mower. If I could get far with any kind of speed before spiders infested my skull, or their vessels melted my face like I opened the Ark of the Covenant. Instead, I took the lighter to the standing metal shelves, holding on to them for support. With the flame clear of the gas cans, I inventoried them. Rags, motor oil, broken pool skimmers, assorted plastic containers of nuts, bolts, nails, and duct tape. I grabbed a roll greedily, clutching it like it was my magic bullet, and moved on.

The raccoon watched from an improvised nest under the bench as I crossed to it. A collection of heavy gardening gloves, grimy rags, and a couple of muddy work boots were gathered to form its safe space. It sat at attention and on guard, watching the door like a sentry. I fell against the bench and waved the lighter over it. Scraps of metal with no hope for identification, tools I couldn't imagine the purpose of, and a few thin pieces of metal piping. Retired or reclaimed arms of lawnmowers. A long push broom and a rake leaned against the wall. Their handles could've easily been cut to splint size.

But cutting makes noise.

I went with a bit of metal pipe. Longer than I needed, when placed against my foot, it came up past my knee. I was in no position to be picky, though. The duct tape barked from its roll. With a wince, I looked to the door and held. The raccoon's ears perked, waiting for the residents to come tearing through. When they didn't, I got to work. The pipe hugged tightly as I secured it around the top of my shoe. Bare skin and duct tape don't really mix, but I had to do it. I wrapped it up the length of the pipe to my knee, striping my shin in shiny gray. Despite the sweat, blood, and mud covering me, it held firm.

Images of Gandalf and Mad-Eye Moody filled my head as I placed the tape gently on the bench and looked to the push broom. Who needs a crutch when you can carry a staff, right? Hobbling over stiffly, I stashed the lighter in my pocket and grabbed the broom from the corner. Its bristled head unscrewed easily enough from the splintery wooden handle. Flinging it forward, gripping with both hands, I pulled myself across the shed. It was shit at holding my weight, didn't do much to relieve the pain in my ankle as I stepped, but at least it looked kinda cool.

Be warned, spider-people! Grady Burton found a stick! Tremble at its might.

The laugh came out silently, filling me with delirious delight as I lowered myself down to the floor and sat back against the wall of the shed. My forehead throbbed, radiating out from the cut above my eyebrow. I rubbed my throat, its muscles tender and bruised. Every drop of adrenaline and strength I had left spilled out of my eyes as the noiseless laugh turned into breathless sobs. The shed, my makeshift splint, it all felt like a band-aid on a wound that really needed stitches. A hundred-something monsters lurked in the Bluffs, and all I had to back me up was a fucking raccoon. I could've waited for them to come back, clear the town, and make my escape. But how far down the hill could I realistically get with a bum leg? How far would they even allow me to get before dragging me back? The raccoon couldn't take them all.

As I sat there, waiting for what I could only assume was the end of days, it was Mom I really struggled with. It was almost involuntary to be furious with her, assume she knew what she getting me involved with. Mee-Moo called her every time so much as a blade of grass was out of place. She had to have known what was going on. On the other side of that scale, of course, was Mee-Moo and her effortless stream of bullshit. The pitch she gave to get me here had probably been dressed up in its best wig and made much less sinister than it actually was. Did I really wanna spend whatever time I had left being mad at Mom, for something she was most likely unaware of, and that I didn't even really understand? No. I wanted to see her again.

There was just no clear and present way to get that done.

The journal pushed uncomfortably in my pocket as I started to calm. Leaning over, I yanked it out. The soft leather was creased and folded, the pages crinkled. I wasn't even sure why I was still holding on to it, other than pure teenage spite. Still, if Elaine made notes in there, then I wanted to see them. If anything, to see just how severely fucked I was.

Soft yellow light danced over the leather as I held the lighter up to it. I folded back the cover, and a blank page greeted me. Several of them, in fact. Flipping through them desperately, there was nothing but white, unlined sheets of paper. I checked front and back, to be sure I wasn't missing something. Not a single line, note, or even a mindless doodle adorned any of them.

Until I got to the middle of the book.

One word, written over and over again in the exact same spot like the manic musings of a lunatic, centered on a single page.

ARANEA

My hand froze over the journal, like it knew I was looking at something I shouldn't have been, but had no choice but to keep going. I turned the page over, and Elaine revealed herself. Don't know what I expected. Detailed recordings of their meetings maybe, broken down by day and time. Individual assignments for the things the neighbors had volunteered for or agreed to. Plain, if not bureaucratically boring, English. What I found was none of that. Scribbles, frantically drawn figures, ran over in dark ink. Two entire pages of spiders, drawn in no greater detail than the way I had in my own notebook. Black blobs that formed hundreds of unmistakable shapes. Buried amongst them, I could make out a few words.

ORDER

GREATER

QUEEN

HARVEST

EMBRACE

CLEANSE

I turned the pages over and found a diagram. A hastily drawn moon over a sloppy sketch of the Bluffs. The shapes of houses were no clearer than if a five-year-old had drawn them. Inside it was the date in question, that once-in-a-century day of pure evil. Below it all, thick lines that could've only been legs hooked upward. My heart started to quicken as I turned the page again. Three more words, filling two pages, drops of blood freckling the paper.

GROW

FEED

GRAHAM

My stomach somersaulted. I had no idea what that was supposed to mean, but the intention wasn't hard to guess at. I threw the pages over before they could drag me down any further. More sketches and scribbles filled the next few. A shrieking, vaguely human face with an explosion of black lines shooting out the side of it. Crude flowers drawn by a hurried hand and **CONFORM** written more times around them than I could individually distinguish. The face of a raccoon and Pat Smith's name. More spiders, pages of them, growing in size with every turn until one finally took up both sides of the journal. Care and attention were put into it. Pincers and eyes, clearly defined as they stared out of the paper.

IN SILENCE SHE CALLS

IN DARKNESS SHE COMES

One more page was all I could take. In its center was something I'd never unsee. A clear list of requirements.

WISE IN MIND

STEADY IN HAND

YOUNG AT HEART

FOREVER

The ink was faded, like it was written months, if not years, before my arrival. Below it, written just one time, bigger and darker than the rest, was a name I had grown incredibly sick of hearing.

TROUBLEMAKER

The walls of the shed began to shrink, thinner than I remembered them being before I made the mistake of looking in her damn book of insane chicken scratch. The Bluffs closed in around me as I started to hyperventilate. Dozens more pages remained, but I couldn't look at them and still hope to cling to the microscopic sliver of sanity I had left. I closed the journal and tossed it into the shadows as my blood froze in place.

6-6-06

The raccoon stared at me curiously as the lighter burned out. Its flame shrunk back into the plastic housing, past the flint and glowing metal. I watched it die as the dark seeped in around me. Too hot to put back in my pocket, I dropped it to the dusty concrete floor, its purpose served. The raccoon left its nest, stepping carefully across to me. Clawed fingers scraped gently off the floor. Its wet nose rubbed against my duct taped leg as it sniffed. On edge, I couldn't stop from flinching. The raccoon retracted a step, waiting to see if I was gonna be cool.

"Sorry," I whispered.

A hairy mass of shadow at my feet, it took up a new position in front of me. Its eyes mirrored, shining with nocturnal white as it stared at the door.

"Yeah, I know," I sighed softly.

I couldn't stay. The shed was a relief, but no port. A place for me to catch my breath, not wait out the end times. There were too many eyes and legs in the Bluffs for me to linger in any one spot. I only knew of one option to call for rescue, maybe two, but I didn't have the nerve to do either of them. I doubted it would ever come at all.

My earbuds rested against my chest, still tucked into my shirt. I buried them back into my head, another layer of protection from the outside in every way they could be. Unplugged, their pointed metal jack dug in under me. Tugging it free, I pulled my iPod from my pocket. Still in one piece, thankfully, but its face was cracked all to hell and the click wheel wouldn't click. I pounded my thumb against the center button and on all its sides, but it wouldn't respond. One trick I could use, I pushed the Hold dial forward, then back. The screen woke up, still alive. I plugged the cable back into its port. Softly, forever stuck at the volume I had left it, the music continued.

With no way to see out other than the door I didn't want to go near, I could only guess at what was going on outside the shed. It wouldn't take Elaine and her minions nearly as long to get back from town as it did for me. Not if they could jump through the trees like a bunch of damn spider monkeys.

Do you go to work after something like that?

The forcibly quaint little village existed for one reason and one reason alone: to feed the machine the HOA had built and maintained. So close to their big day, I had a hard time seeing the lot of them clock in when the sun came up. They would all need to come back home at some point, to inspect every nook and crevice of the neighborhood and make sure I hadn't looted them blind. The clock ticked on.

The raccoon shot off deeper into the darkness of the shed, leaving its post with a pounce. Its paws scraped at the concrete as it dashed away. When it came to a stop, it hissed. Heavy, wet crunches gnawed softly from the floor as it chewed on something I didn't want to think about. I grabbed the broom handle and held it close.

Oh fuck . . .

The raccoon's jaws snapped and clicked as it started into another. Its growl grew deeper as it bit into a third. Dozens of legs skittered across the floor, tapping out their positions like nightmarish Morse code. I pulled myself up on my wizard staff as my hair stood at attention. Phantom legs worked their way over every exposed inch of my skin, curling up spine.

Another crunch, a feral screech.

I flicked the iPod's dial and shined the light of the screen under the bench. Spiders reared their legs to fight each other on top of the hodgepodge nest. They snapped at my glowing hand as the meager shine fell on them. Careful to keep my full weight off my injured side, I raised the broom handle to strike.

The raccoon yowled. The light whipped with my hand. Four more spiders wrestled with it between the mowers, biting chunks out of it where they could. Its claws flew wildly and its legs kicked as it rolled across the floor desperately. Something furry started up my leg. Before the screen timed out again, it caught a glimmer of bulging eyes working their way to my knee.

The broom handle cracked into my shin. Not enough to crush, but perfect to stun. The spider started to slide down. Pincers sank into my calf as it held on. I bit down on the scream and smacked at it again. Bright white bursts of pain shot across my eyes, and the spider fell to the ground. Before it could regroup, I raised my foot and brought it down hard like a piston. Like stepping on an apple, it crunched in the worst places and squished everywhere else, blasting juices out from the sides of my foot.

I flicked the Hold button again. Dim light fell on the raccoon as spiders overwhelmed it. An eight-legged cavalry came out of the literal woodwork, crawling up from under the walls and through the cracks, dropping from the ceiling. The raccoon screeched at me, hopelessly crazed eyes sending a clear message. Like or not, I needed to get the fuck out while I still could. I took its advice and limped to the door, throwing my staff out ahead of me.

With no clue what would be waiting on the other side, I pulled. It squealed on its track again, drowned out only by the raccoon's shrill cries as spiders descended on their big bad foe. Dozens of them, ripping out chunks of gray fur matted with blood. Too many of them for me to do anything about. Not without getting an earful. The raccoon thrashed wildly, banging off the mowers. I said a silent thank you as I closed the door again, letting the guilt of it pile onto everything else. It screeched in the dark as I turned to face whatever fresh hell was waiting in the neighborhood.

Fog was breaking into an opaque marine layer over the houses. Heavy clouds formed above to block the dying moon. Every garage light all around the three rings was down, rather ripped straight from their mounts or powered down prematurely. The Bluffs were left at the mercy of their residents, same as me. I held myself up on the broom handle, feeling more exposed than the first time I had to change out for PE. The streets were still empty, but I knew I wasn't alone. There wouldn't be another shot at what I had to do. There was nowhere else to go. I could've tried the first house I came across, spent time I didn't have searching for a phone to call Mom, the cops, and maybe the Navy Seals. But there was a computer in the center ring, and I had used it before. It was late, yeah—or early, whichever—but iNRuEnS was always online.

I took my first step forward, waiting for the darkness to strike back at me. When it didn't, I kept going. My hairs refused to stand down, feeling the pull of impending doom in every direction, even if I couldn't see it. My head stayed on a swivel, swinging in every direction with saucer eyes. The broken glass filling my ankle ground finer with every step.

The houses were perfect black monoliths all around the rings. Their porches were deep pools with no end in sight. No way to tell what was lurking within them. Sticking close to them felt like a terrible fucking idea, but it was still better than just walking up the center of the dark street like a gunslinger at high noon.

With my eyes on their back windows, I moved in on the rear ring. Heavy curtains shielded them, reflecting my own dark image in the street, watching as intently as their owners liked. But nothing moved within them. I hunched low as I crossed into the connecting spoke and along the lower ranking houses. Stopping at its edge, on the side of an empty house, I pulled an earbud an inch away from my face and listened. My eyes darted across the street ahead, left, right, above, and below. I told myself I was being careful, extra cautious, but the simple truth was that I was terrified. Every corner, every house, every yard, as uniformly revoltingly pleasant as they had been when I arrived, now looked like gruesome death. Traps with my name on every last one of them.

Hanging around was a great way to speed that process up, though. With a growl, I slammed the broom handle into the ground like I was staring down a Balrog and pulled myself forward. First a blistered foot, then the one wrapped in duct tape. My eyes narrowed on the next ring, and I limped forward.

Let them watch. Assholes.

Guitars chugged along quietly in my ears, subtle enough that I could still hear my heavy breath, picking up my pace as quickly as pain would allow. Sweat washed my face clean, burning into my open eyebrow. Another edge and the next street opened ahead of me. Not stopping to think about it, I pressed forward and across.

The inner ring came into view as I came up through it. More yards, more fences, more houses. More spiders. The center of the neighborhood was a fucking disaster. The street separating the houses from the pool was coated in mud from some idiot's panicked attempt at driving. The pool gate was folded over itself. Scooters, walkers, chairs, and canes were abandoned, littering the street and the sidewalks, waiting for operators who no longer needed them. Shards of glass and broken plastic twinkled in the lawns. While every garage light was out, the center ring took the brunt of their ferocity. The others might've been turned off—or deactivated, or unplugged, however Elaine pulled that off—but these were shattered. Ripped from the wall, knocked down and smashed into pieces. The front of the houses didn't fare much better. Dark red handprints smeared across them.

I stopped for only one second more. Just long enough to look over at Elaine's house. Like the others, it was nothing more than a dark box. I studied the windows carefully for any signs of movement. Expecting her gray face to peer out, but seeing nothing. The curtains didn't move, no shapes or figures filled the glass. I sneered at it like the house itself was the source of my problems, and continued on to the one that suffered the worst.

Twin black streaks of dragged rubber led up from the street and into the driveway. Shattered glass covered the front yard like jagged dewdrops. The grass was torn to shreds, not just from my attempt behind the wheel, but hundreds of feet and hands tearing across it. The flowers I so painstakingly planted were gone, smashed into oblivion or unrooted and cast aside. A scooter lay on its side on the porch. A walker cluttered the ramp. The garage light was nowhere to be seen. The front door was completely missing. Webs covered the house like a shining veil.

I pulled myself up the lawn to the porch. A shining screen held the front door's position, hinting at the interior beyond it, glinting with white corrosion. Didn't come that far to turn back, though. I raised one end of the broom handle like a probe and gently dropped it into the webs. Snaking wisps of smoke curled out of it, and the screen parted down the middle into stringy strands. Black chars crisscrossed the wood as I swiped the door clear.

A smell like old pennies wafted out. Inside, more walkers and a few canes were scattered over the floor. The entirety of Mee-Moo's collection of decorative nonsense was a minefield of broken porcelain and ceramics. Frames were torn from the walls, snapped to pieces. The dining room table was on its side. Her curio cabinet was face down. Blood pooled in the carpet. Prints marked their manic paths, hands and feet clear up to the ceiling and across it. Webs draped off every surface they could attach to. Chemical burns scored under them, cracking, bubbling, dripping. Bridging the rail up, filling the shoe tree, stretching across the plastic-wrapped couches, hanging from the ceiling, in the corners, across the walls, covering the tipped over table and connecting the cabinet back to the wall. Like the spiders were packing up the house they claimed dominion over. They squirmed and writhed under the surface. Armored legs and furry backs rolled over the house like flies on a corpse. A nest, if I'd ever seen one.

Nope!

I hobbled back down to the lawn and came around to the still open garage. The more direct, less infested path. The broken door sat in front of an abandoned scooter, parked where the car should've been. A Caddy-sized dent caved the wall. Dark splatters reached up and out from it. Shadows in the corners twitched and crawled. Webs draped over the empty door frame like a curtain. Lifting the broom handle, I swatted them down. Ribbons of hissing smoke trailed after it, charring the wood black.

I checked my earbuds, in as deep as they could go without punching through anything important. The burned broom handle led the way inside, taking me with it against my higher reasoning and anything even remotely resembling good judgment. An acrid fog sat in the house, singeing my nose and frying my eyes. A walker cluttered the short hall to the bathroom, its frame bent and twisted. The walls crawled around me, watching, as I nudged it gently out of the way. Shadowed pincers snipped hungrily as I crept past the bathroom. My jaws clenched and molars ground, on the verge of cracking.

The curtains were ripped from their rod over the back door. Its glass was cracked into pockets of ashen dust. The TV was a dead black window on the wall. The sectional was wrapped up tight from one end to the other, its leather cracked and burned, coated in creeping black and glistening white. Reaching forms dangled and twisted from the ceiling in the kitchen like acrobats.

The doors to the office were coated in web, and squirming with life.

"Fucking hell," I shuddered.

The hall to the stairs was coated in dense, shining white. Every picture was off its hook, torn and smashed on the ground. Mom looked up at me from the floor at the precipice, her spirits up despite the circumstances. If I hadn't been on the verge of pissing myself again, I would've been annoyed that I had to dust all of those. And vacuum that floor. A hulking shape toward the middle of the hall held my attention by the throat. Boxy and tall, its width nearly blocked the path through. A powerchair, with no one in it. Webs covered every inch of it, sealing it in a shrouding swath, warping and bending its shape. Tufts of foam rose out of the torn upholstery. A mass of legs wriggled in its burned seat, each fighting for position over the others.

No better options, I turned back to the office doors. I raised the already burnt end of my staff and batted at the dense seal. The wood hissed its way down as the webs fell with it, thick and sticky like burning rubber. I pushed against the bottom of the door and swung it in, breaking free from what was left and gliding into the office. Before I took a single god damn step, I looked across the expanse to the monitor. Pop-Pop's chair was right where it had been. The office was relatively untouched by the violence of the night, a risk I hadn't thought about or measured until I saw it in contrast with the carnage left behind in the rest of the house. Only relatively, though, it wasn't unscathed or unoccupied. Spiders lumbered over his shelves, across the walls, up his desk. But its power light was on. It was still functioning. After the phone went missing and the house went to shit, I wasn't sure if the computer was even going to be in one piece, let alone still powered on.

Spiders scuttled down the walls behind me as I slowly stepped inside. The chair was covered in webs, but none of them were moving. I waved the broom handle over it and caught them all. The end of it turned nearly completely black, individual patterns lost within each other. The chair growled softly against its plastic pad as I wheeled it to the desk. Webs branched from the monitor to the wall and tethered the tower to the desk, their plastic shells drooping and dripping.

I reached for the mouse. A pair of legs rose from the shadows in defense like I was stealing their child. Pincers lunged forward and clacked at my hand as it shot back to my chest. More than one way to skin a cat, though, I redirected to the keyboard without taking my eyes off the spider. Clicking the space bar twice, the screen's backlight kicked on. In front of the mouse, flanking the keyboard, lurking under the monitor's frame, spiders were spread across the desk. A small colony hellbent on making the computer their new home, they whipped around to face the monitor's glow. I eased myself down into the chair and leaned the broom handle against the desk while it held their interest.

The boot-up screen didn't load. Instead, the full desktop did. It hadn't been touched since I last used it. Pop-Pop didn't even bother killing my browser window. My previous internet history stared back at me, glowing white onto the eight-legged voyeurs around the office. They turned back to me, waiting for my next move. I tried to will my hand steady as I reached for the mouse. The spider guarding it took a step back, daring me to take command. Touching down on the cool plastic, I dragged the cursor slowly across the screen.

Messenger topped the browser history. I clicked the mouse over it gently—no sudden movements like I was defusing a bomb. Breath hissed slowly from my nose as my pulse quickened. More spiders crept in toward the keyboard as the page loaded. Pushing the cursor one pixel at a time across the screen to the login portal, legs fell on my hand. Locked in place, I glanced down as the spider started up me. I buried my teeth into my lip, sealing the shuddering moan in my throat. My other hand moved in on the keyboard as discreetly as I could force it to. Legs hooked over the letters, numbers, and commands. Hunting and pecking, I put in my username. The spiders slowly advanced as I clicked into the password field, taking the keyboard as their own. Webs fell out of their pointed spinnerets, melting into the keys. Legs tickled against my wrist. Pincers opened menacingly as my fingers moved to type. I wove delicately through legs and jaws, tapping in my password as the keys started to warp.

With a quiet click, the page refreshed. Its load time slowed to an eternity, like it wanted to see exactly how long it would take my nerves to shatter. Each second pushed me one step closer to the edge as spiders closed in around me. Legs tickled at my wrist, brushed at my ankles, and prodded softly against the chair. I was about to launch myself from the chair and run as fast as my bum leg would carry me straight down the hill when Messenger booted up in full. Ruben's chat log appeared, a little green dot next to his name.

Before I could feel any kind of relief, the spiders webbing up the keyboard diverted, and started up my arm. I bit down harder against the sting as webs blistered up my hands and over my wrist. My mouse hand lifted and came over to the keyboard. Legs crested my shoulders, coming up my back. Out of the corner of my eye, I could see them climbing to my summit. Up and over, down onto my chest, against my neck. The creatures on my arms kept pressing forward, their legs pressing gingerly against me while they left a trail of burns behind them. Any resolve I had pushed to its outer limits as I fought the painful shakes lighting up my body. The broom handle called to me, begging me to take it up and start whacking. Legs probed my earlobes, flicking it curiously, like they needed to be sure it was solid and real before moving in.

Another soft click and a message to Ruben opened. I barely pressed the keys as I typed, pushing them down only enough to evoke their responses without drawing too much noise or attention. We had been told once, when computers started to become more relevant in the educational process, that typing with one finger at a time was some kind of bad thing. Like we were a subspecies of caveman for not using all ten at once. But if any of our teachers could've seen the exact situation I'd need to slow it down for, they wouldn't have given me so much grief for it.

SOS SND HELP ASAP

Legs started up my face. I choked down my scream as I focused on the keyboard.

POP POP DEAD MEE MOO 2

It didn't matter that Ruben wasn't hip to their given names, the point was still made. White hair brushed my cheeks like overgrown stubble.

TRYIN 2 KILL ME

A tapping came against my earbuds, on both sides, inspecting them for weakness.

PLZ SND HELP! COPS! ARMY! GUNS!

SRS! DANGER! SEA BREEZE BLUFFS!

Spiders mounted my face, crawling up from my shoulders and under my chin. Legs hammered at the earbuds and fell against my lips. Tears streamed down my cheeks as they climbed and probed. Every inch of my skin begged to explode away from them.

SPIDERS IN THER HEADS

NO JOKE!!! DONT COME! SND HELP!

That was as much detail as I was willing to provide. I had no more time or patience to explain it any better. If I even could. Spiders made their way up the chair, onto my legs, my lap, my chest, my face. I hit send and hoped for the best. Pincers snapped at my ear lobe, and I shot up from the chair, blood spilling down my neck. The earbuds held, keeping them from getting any further. I grabbed a fistful of spider and launched it into the wall. With a thud, it bounced off and came down on the floor, barely concerned.

The office attacked. Spiders soared through the air and bit at my plugged ears. They sliced fresh nicks into my hands as I ripped them free and hurled them into the walls. Lashing out, I swung the broom like a baseball bat at the airborne attackers, making contact with nothing. In a tall arc, I brought the heft of it down on the floor, pounding into the ground infantry as they advanced. Exoskeletons crunched but didn't crush, like dozens of grotesque piñatas that refused to give up the goods. More came up my legs, skittering over my duct tape splint. Kicking where I could, they flew back across the office

One bolted from my shin to my face, faster than I could stop, climbing in every direction over my head in a furry flash. It came down on my ear from above, pounding its front legs against my earbud. I grabbed it by its bulbous ass and threw it to the ground. They wouldn't be deterred, though, not with blood in the air. The black and white tide on the floor continued to roll in. Outnumbered and outgunned, I fell back out of the office.

The doors swung back and I pressed them tight. Legs curled out from under like dark skeletal fingers and tore through the webs covering the broken glass panels. Stumbling back, I turned to the hall. The walls and their shadows gained autonomy, oozing across the surface to me. Spiders spilled down from the seat of the powerchair, breaking out of the webs, voracious and ready to feed.

"Shit!" I hissed.

I bolted for the kitchen as the couch came to life. Its shape shifted and sagged as more spiders rolled down to the floor. They dropped on webs from the ceiling, filled the sink, covered the counter, and scurried up from under the cabinets. Reaching, biting, running, gliding. With one hand on the broom handle and the other flailing to defend, I fought my way across to the dining room. My face stung from the burn of wayward strands. Holes formed all over my shirt, eating into the BPRD fist. Spiders bit at my ankles, scraping through the canvas of my shoes but getting no further. A pair landed on my shoulders, flanking my earbuds. Those little hunks of plastic, my third pair that year, served admirably. The spiders kicked at them, demanding entrance through locked doors. Their pincers moved in anyway. Before they could dice my ears any more than their buddy in the office already had, I grabbed one and chucked it into the sink. The basin thumped as it slammed into it. Then the other, launched back towards the office door as its brothers and sisters tore through it and cascaded down.

The knife block caught my attention. Stabbing individual spiders didn't even sound good on paper. Resting on a drying towel next to it, though, was the heavy black skillet Mee-Moo needed to make salad. That showed more promise. Heavily defended, the marbled counter was alive with arachnid abominations. But not undoable.

"Screw it."

I shot my hand across them and grabbed the skillet. Its cast iron body was barely touched by burns, despite the glistening webs covering it. They seared into my palm as I ripped it off the towel and started fucking swinging. With a stomach-turning crunch, the spiders unlucky enough to be in its path splattered into twitching bits and crushed guts.

It would do.

The broom handle supporting me in one hand, and the skillet waving in the other like the weirdest game of tennis, I stormed back out of the kitchen and toward the garage. The aerial attackers from above flew to the walls with a hard *CLUNK* against the heavy metal. I smashed marble from the bar and bits of stuffing from the couch, crushing any of them that dared to get too close. A reinforcement battalion surged out of the hall. My good foot came down hard, smashing as many as it could to muck under me.

"Fuck! Off! Assholes!" I grunted as I stomped and swung, at wits' end and well beyond my reserves of patience.

Pushing for the door, shambling on the broom handle, I struck wherever I could. Wherever I needed to. As I neared it, the open, empty Bluffs ahead of me and a trail of arachnid carnage behind me, the taste of furious victory died in my mouth, replaced by a bitter dryness.

Elaine circled back.

"Come out now, troublemaker!" she called to the neighborhood like we were playing hide and seek. "Don't make us come get you!"

She strode calmly through the street as I froze, trusting the dying darkness to hide me. Every second spent still emboldened the brood around me. They moved in on my legs, ready to avenge their fallen. I took a slow step back as she crossed in front of the wide open door. Her eyes, thankfully, were up. Looking at the house as a whole like it was just as much of a disappointment as I was. Like it wasn't destroyed by a mob of spider-people but by something even more avoidable and senseless.

"He couldn't have made it to the highway," she called over her shoulder. "Check your homes. Make sure he didn't take anything else."

I gripped the handle of the pan and inched backward. The surviving Board members came in to join her. The gap in their ranks would've only been more satisfying to see if I had caused it myself. All I saw were three people who wanted to jam otherworldly bugs in my head, and no raccoon to save me.

"Pity." Elaine shook her head at the house. "All that work."

Ducking around the counter, I limped back into the kitchen, swiping at the airborne division as they dangled from above and glided through the air. Sparing the wall crawlers, if only for the noise. Glass and porcelain crunched under my feet as I came into the dining room and around the upended table. From there, I had nowhere to go but up.

Through the tear in the web screen filling the front door, dark shapes began to gather. I pushed myself up the first few steps, webs sizzling the soles of my shoes. Panic picked up my pace, if only a little. I could hear them assembling out front. The pounding of their feet, the slapping of their hands on pavement, feral growls and snarls like a pack of coyotes. Pop-Pop's croak, amplified by a hundred slack mouths.

Their counterparts waited for me on the landing. The urge to take the frying pan to them pulled at my hand, but I tamped it down. I had no clear destination in mind once I got to the top, as long as I was out of their immediate sight. Somewhere less obvious and exposed before they dragged me out kicking and swinging. Pain tore through my leg as I climbed, more weight on it than I could stand.

The second floor wasn't in any better shape than the first. Coated in webs, crawling with unholy life. Like an autopilot I couldn't turn off, I started down the hall to my room and the window. A hiding place with a view of the street. My eyes to the carpet as I started into the hall, doing my best not to look into their bedroom if I didn't absolutely have to.

I'm good. Once was enough.

As much as I tried to ignore it, as much as I told myself to just keep looking forward, that there was no time for this, the bathroom screamed at me as I stepped past it. The door was still wide open, the light off. I couldn't pretend it wasn't there. I had to look. To know for sure. More than morbid curiosity, he deserved whatever fraction of a moment I had to spare, and whatever kind thoughts I had left. I slowed just enough to see.

In the corner above the tub, bones hung from the ceiling. Still intact, held together by the spiders' work. Empty eyes pressed against the webs. A bare jaw hung down, stuck in the agony of his last few moments. Picked almost perfectly clean except for odd lumps and chunks of flesh and muscle still clinging to his skull, his femurs, his ribs.

Pop-Pop.

All that was left of him.

Spiders still worked their way through and over his remains.

Weeping tears erupted from me before I could stop them. I folded my elbow over my mouth to silence it as I staggered in place. Fearing what had happened wasn't nearly as bad as seeing the evidence of it. Decorum told me I needed to go in there, to cover him. To say my goodbyes. Taking the frying pan to the bathroom would've given me some breathing room, but it also would've kicked up enough racket to bring his neighbors down on my head.

I couldn't.

I should've, but I couldn't.

"I'm sorry, Pop-Pop," I sobbed under my breath, barely above a whisper.

Rage mixed explosively with terror, forming something toxically vengeful in my veins, curling my knuckles tight and white. The wood of the broom handle creaked as I squeezed the life from it. The metal of the pan's handle dug into my tender, burned palm. Blisters popped and oozed down it. Against all better judgment, before I continued on, I looked back to their bedroom door. If she was like him, then there wouldn't be much left to curdle my stomach. I needed to know that she got what she fucking deserved.

There was nothing at all. Just a crimson smear on the sheets and an empty husk of webs burned into the mattress. Mom would've been pissed to see me. The tears started to slow and my breath evened out, raking through my nose in hot bursts as I turned to my room. She would've been even more pissed if she knew how vindicated I felt. His end was grisly; hers had been worse.

I hadn't paused for more than a few seconds, but it was already too much. Outside, they were only getting louder, spreading through the neighborhood again like a plague. Rolling croaks blanketed the Bluffs. I said a silent goodbye to Pop-Pop and pressed on to the end of the hall.

The bedroom was in pieces. The dresser had fallen against the bed. The TV stand was smashed to bits in a field of debris from the door to the window. My bags had been trampled. Clothes and pages were strewn from one corner to the other. Dark handprints and wet splatters smeared over every surface. The curtains lay in a torn pile on the floor. The spider count was surprisingly low, though. Like every one that came through this way decided to go out the window rather than stay to stake their claim to the territory.

I wasn't delirious enough to trust that. Even the webs were suspiciously few. With the end of the broom handle, I probed the open closet. The frying pan shot up over my head, ready to strike, but there was nothing to hit. Only carpet below the hanging bar, worn in the perfect outline of my ass and feet. I flipped over every broken book or stomped shirt. My head dipped low, and I looked in the space between the dresser and the bed. Under it too, while I was at it.

Nothing.

I wasn't gonna take chances any more chances than I already had. I collected whatever shirts and shorts were within arm's reach and closed the door softly. Lowering myself down on the broom handle, I jammed the clothes into the gap between the door and the floor. One access point was plugged, but I was still missing a window.

Pushing the broom handle out ahead of me, keeping the pan tight in my other hand, I crawled over to it. Careful to stay out of sight, my splinted foot dragged against the carpet until I landed at the wall. I peered my head up slowly, just enough to get a view of the street. The infestation overran the neighborhood. Up walls, through doors, over roofs, in the streets, they scoured for me across every ring. No doubt conducting an inventory of their valuables while they were at it. If they still retained their judgmental paranoia. The Board was hard at work, turning over the community room and checking every crevice for any sign of me.

Elaine held her position proudly in front of the house, her back turned to it. With her hands on the jutting shelves of bone she called hips, she watched her brood as they worked. Slowly, she turned back to my window, a look on her face like she couldn't believe how stupid I was as she stared directly into it.

I fell back against the bed, a rat in a trap. The broom handle and the skillet thumped to the floor next to me as terror dragged me down with them.

In the open closet behind me, up over the hangers, half of a hand emerged from the shadows. Fingers wrapped around the track and latched onto the ceiling, chewed down to bone and muscle.

What was left of Mee-Moo crawled out.

NUMB
JUNE 6, 2006

She was still fucking naked! Like their demon spider god— or whatever the hell Aranea was— looked at the situation and said, "How can we make this worse? How can we make sure this trauma never leaves him, no matter how hard he tries?" Half eaten and fully dead was the upgrade they decided on for Mee-Moo.

She looked like she had been through a wood chipper and somehow came out the other side still marginally intact and even more angry. Strips and shreds of sliced skin hung from her gnawed and gnashed frame, edged with blood drying brown. Her ears were completely gone, her eyes were black and compound. Ribs stabbed through the holes in her flesh. Her legs were flayed down to the muscle, arms revealing pearly bone in patches and fleshy craters. Her bald scalp was sliced to the skull, and her nose was an empty pit on her face. Her jaw hung, barely connected on one side. Pop-Pop's croak rumbled out of her throat as she crawled out and skittered over to me.

I grabbed the skillet and dove for the broom handle. A wad of webs shot out of her mouth as I grabbed it. Searing, sizzling goo slapped onto the bend of my shoulder and splashed my face. Hiding and discretion flew out the open window with my scream as her webs burned through my shirt and into my arm. Mee-Moo dropped to the bed as I rolled back against the wall with a thud. The mattress bounced as she came down on all fours, another heavy ball of web forming in her throat. Her jaw flopped lifelessly, dangling from her face.

If there was any slim chance of a hope that I'd remember that woman any other way, it died in that room. It would've been easy to write it all off as not her fault. That she was too enamored by whatever the hell she saw in Elaine Rubenfeld to do any better or avoid that fate, but I didn't see it. Like attracts Like, right? Two horrid minds melding around one macabre idea. Mee-Moo was right where she wanted to be.

A stink like chlorine and burnt beef wafted out of my shoulder. I growled through the pain and scraped it with the edge of the frying pan. As clear as I could get it under the circumstances, bubbled skin seeped through the charred hole in my shirt. Outside, croaks and snarls started to centralize, forming closer to my ruined hiding place.

Mee-Moo cocked her head and fired again. I dropped flat, ducking as the glob sailed into the wall with a hiss. The frying pan flew from my hand in response. Spinning through the air like a ninja star, it clocked her right above the eye with a loud crack and ricocheted clear to the other side of the bed. If she noticed at all, then she certainly didn't care.

Another ball started to grow in her throat. I stumbled to my feet with the broom handle in hand. Limping across the room, I could feel her dead bug eyes tracking me, lining up her shot. The smack of webs against the door cut me off. A smoking blob the size of my head ate through the particleboard. The hallway peeked in as the spot crumbled to bits.

Shifting on one foot, I turned back to face her. Mee-Moo raised herself to two feet, slowly, like she had been more comfortable with her hands in the mix. Behind her, the sun was waking up. Black clouds swallowed the early rays. Weak grey light radiated in around her. If I wasn't going to make it to the afternoon, then at least I could try to do what was right and take her with me.

"Fine!" I shouted at her unflinching, unfeeling face. "You win! Put me out of my misery! I'm over this shit!"

The second the webs left her mouth, I regretted saying that. I watched them as they unfurled in the air, reaching out like icy fingers. The broom handle shot up ahead of me as I jerked away from with a flinch. The webs hit high on the blackened wood, toward the middle of the shaft. With a howl of shocked victory and a dash of desperation, I struck back. One step closed the gap between us, but the next rolled my ankle and buckled my knee. In the fall, I swung as hard as I could. The broom handle hit against her open ribs and snapped in half.

Flat on my face, I hit the carpet. In the second it took me to roll over, I wondered if I'd ever be able to walk on that foot again. If I survived, would it ever heal right? Or if I didn't, would I be one of the spider-people out there with no other choice but to crawl around?

Mee-Moo wanted to find out. She sprang back up to the ceiling, positioning herself directly over me, her back to the floor. Her neck snapped, and her head spun around to me. Webs filled her twisted throat like the swirl of a cotton candy machine. I raised what was left of the broom handle like a shield, hoping that would work twice. Mee-Moo wasn't taking chances. She wouldn't miss again. She dropped like a comet down on top of me. Her arms and legs cracked around at their hinges to catch herself like joints and ligaments no longer mattered.

If it wasn't for the broom handle, our skulls would've collided. Instead, it caught her by the sternum. The cold leather of her skin pressed into my knuckles. Her breath wafted out like a cold breeze over a hot dumpster. My face reflected across her eyes. Hundreds of terrified, angry Gradys. The acrid ball of webs ballooned as she shifted her mouth directly over me, ready to vomit out her final strike and melt me to a puddle.

With a jerk, I pushed the charred hunk of wood, and Mee-Moo went with it. Roaring, I twisted her off me and into the wall. She hit with a thump as I shot up for the bed. Pushing myself on one foot, I climbed onto it. Her shot fired after me like a cannon. It thumped to the corner of the bed, burning into the mattress. Smoke floated up behind me as I scrambled to reclaim the cookware. Mee-Moo sprang back up onto the bed, her body twisting in every wrong direction. On the floor between the bed and the closet, my hand clapped down on the cast iron as she scurried after me. With a swing so hard I thought my arm might pop off and fly across the room, I came back up and clapped the pan across her face. She flew back to the dresser, crashing into it and rolling to the floor. Vibrations rocketed up my arm, stinging like angry hornets from my palm to my shoulder as the skillet fell to the mattress.

Thick, stinging smoke poured out of the foot end of the mattress, billowing up and floating through the window. It felt like my palm had shattered into a million pieces, but my hand still worked. I grabbed the skillet and tumbled off the bed. My leg threatened to erupt as I stood with my back to the open closet.

Mee-Moo thrashed and flailed for a moment like I had hit with her a blast of Raid. She snapped to quick attention, backwards hands and feet settling on the fallen dresser. Her head raised to me with an angry croak, ready to work out any lingering issues or grievances she had once and for all. Cracks and fractures ran along her exposed fields of skull. Her jaw dangled and spun, barely hanging by a thread of muscle. The open cavity of her throat filled. In both hands, I raised the skillet to my burned shoulder like a Jedi preparing to duel.

Mee-Moo charged. Her arms and legs stormed across the mattress as she howled. In an arc over my head, I brought the pan down. It cracked into the top of her skull and brought her crashing down on the edge of the bed. The rubber caps on the toes of my high-tops sizzled as her head slumped over the side and the contents of her throat spilled out onto the carpet. My hands went completely numb as tremors rang through my bones. She lifted her head like I had smacked her with a fly swatter, despite the dent in the dome of her skull. The pan shot up over me and came down again. And again. And again. And again. A volley of relentless hammering, a grunt for every swing that evolved into a long, remorseless scream.

"Fuck! You! Fuck! You! FUCK YOU!"

Unexpected tears flooded down my cheeks as I collapsed back into the closet. The skillet hit the floor with a dull thump. Like a cracked egg, Mee-Moo's head was split into pieces. At its epicenter, a spider clawed weakly at the air, twitching and convulsing as it powered down. I snatched up the cast iron in case it decided to pounce, my eyes as crazed and unsteady as my breath. The spider wasn't going anywhere, though. Most of its legs weren't even attached anymore. Its pincers bit at the air, jagged and broken, slowing until they stopped mid-snap.

Shivering as the early morning sun fought through the dark cloud cover, I melted into the floor, heaving like I was on the verge of cardiac arrest, covered in a mix of fluids and substances I'd rather not think about. My skin burned from top to bottom, reeking of chemicals and loose change. I'm not sure which movie Mom could blame it on, but it was safe to assume she'd never let me with a hundred miles of it ever again if she ever learned what had just happened. What I had just done. I only wish I could've thought of a good one-liner to throw out. Something detached and snarky to let the creature know how unimpressed I was with our battle. I rolled over, the closet's metal track digging into my side, and puked where my bags had once been, where I hid when that unending night began. A thought so obvious it surprised me flashed through my frazzled little mind.

I never made it back up the hill.

It had to be. I called it! For everything to have gone that sideways, that badly, I would've had to have been dead. In which case, Mee-Moo would've been locked up for child abuse instead of dripping onto the carpet and coating one of her own skillets. Pop-Pop would've been heartbroken, but at least he still would've had a heart to break. I was dead. And this was my punishment. Not sure what I ever did to deserve it, though! Surely *Lusty Busty 2* or my secret folder of jpegs couldn't have warranted that all on their own. Maybe it was compounding. Like all those times I'd watched those super special infomercials with the college girls and the steel drums had piled up and built a tab I'd spend an eternity paying down. I couldn't help but laugh. A small chuckle built layer by layer until it snowballed into hysterical cackling as I rolled in the closet door. It was so simple. So perfect. So stupid.

Too good to be true.

I wasn't alone, as much as I wanted to be. A great, collected roar shook the house. Every voice merged together into the soundtrack for psychosis, right outside my window. The skillet fumbled into my shaking hands as I sat up. I crawled out of the closet and to the end of the bed, leaving Mee-Moo in her resting place. With the corner of the mattress, I climbed up off the floor. Earbuds tapped against my chest as I stood. Dread mixed with my habits, and I stuffed them back in place. Their jack had come unplugged again, but that wasn't really the point anymore. The broom handle sat in two halves, one where I left it on the floor and the other clear across the room. Their ends were snapped into splintered barbs. I grabbed the closest piece as I limped along the edge of the bed. My leg quivered with every step, daring me to keep going.

Falling against the window, my makeshift weapons weren't gonna be enough. The entire HOA was assembled in front of the house. The roof of the community room crawled with reworked limbs and wrong-way necks. The street was thick with standing bodies, no less morbid in the forming light of day. Elaine waited at their head, flanked by her surviving Board and staring up into my window. Deep offense folded her face in on itself like I had said, "Fuck" in church. All at once, they surged forward.

"No!" she called them to a halt with a raised hand.

She turned to Bow Tie and Stache, cutting through the crowd and leaving them to their work. What she said to them I couldn't quite hear, but from where I stood, the way her tight mouth moved, it looked alarmingly like "not going anywhere". Maybe it was just anxiety, or the horrid realization that I was completely cornered. Hard to say. Either way, they had me right where they wanted me.

I looked to the tree line. Past the fountain and the Caddy, to the gate, toward the shed. Nothing stirred in the branches. Nothing scampered across the leaves and rocks. No four-legged rescue coming this time.

The two surviving Board members turned to the house, glaring up at me with limp faces. I took a hopping step back, trying to keep a lid on fresh panic. Every Romero or Kirkman siege defense I could think of were dead ends. The dresser would've fit perfectly in front of the door, but if I didn't think I could move it when I was in mint condition, there was no way I was going to do it after being torn from the package and kicked around the neighborhood. There was plenty I could use to board up the window, the smashed and strewn pieces of the TV stand, but nothing to nail them in with.

Bow Tie cocked his head back. A shrill cry like a broken siren shot out of his gaping mouth. It pierced through the walls, past my earbuds, and right through the center of my brain. He held the note well beyond the lung capacity of even the best vocalists I'd heard, or at least it felt that way. I clamped my hands over my ears as I staggered back, but nothing would stop it until he was ready. His head came back down, and the cry silenced like someone hit mute on him. The infested corpses watched the house, shifting with ravenous excitement. Webs drooled from their slack mouths like dogs waiting for a steak, melting their faces down to the bone.

The lower level of the house rumbled. My attention tore from the window. A hole big enough to stick my head through was burned into the door. With the wet skillet tight in my hand, I hobbled over to it as fast as I could. A rolling black and white carpet crested the landing, turning hard down the hall. Every spider from the lower level, thousands of armored legs and angry jaws, stampeded over each other and splashed against the walls, leaving smoldering trails of web in their wake.

Elaine's next wave.

My brain fired off commands before I could process them. I snatched up as many shirts as I could manage and stuffed them into the hole in the door. Legs tapped against the other side of it as they scurried up, but they didn't try to break through. Smoke swirled out of the clothes and scorched my nose as the spiders sealed them in place. I held the skillet high as I took a step back, waiting for literally anything else to happen.

The door began to crack, its particleboard crumbling in at me. The air turned sour and thick like the bile I left in the closet. A legion of legs worked diligently, in perfectly agitated unison, skittering and stamping across the other side. My shoulder tensed, ready to swing at any with the balls to come through. The hole widened, falling in chunks to the carpet. My shirts hung in place, suspended as the door collapsed around them. As the pieces fell, smoking and hissing, a solid plug of shimmering wet web filled the frame.

"Fuck!"

I stabbed the speared end of the broom handle in. It pierced through like a knife into tissue paper. My fingers stung at the edge of the webs as the speared hunk of wood started to jerk and shake. Heavy puffs of smoke shot out of the broken handle like an exhaust pipe, watering my eyes and charring my throat.

The creatures within fought hard to make sure I didn't keep it. The handle ripped from my palms, disappearing into the webs. A small hole no wider than a fifty-cent piece remained. A peephole barely big enough for me to see through. It was hard to tell where the web blockade ended and the hall began. An acidic haze fogged through them both as they glistened. Spiders rushed in to fill the gap, snapping their faces at me daringly. What was left of the door fell at my feet as I backed away. Thick, interlaced strands filled the empty frame from top to bottom, burning into the wall and rippling with unholy life. The shirts dissolved into burnt bits of fabric, reducing to atoms.

Bodies boomed against the outside walls. I stumbled back to the window, my head a flurry of static, unable to focus on one death sentence or the other. Stache and Bow Tie watched from the street as the entirety of their ranks swarmed the house. Unnaturally bent arms and legs scrambled up at me, evolving like the creatures in their heads. The degradation of their skin had gotten worse; graying where it remained over a network of black veins. Their jaws were fully exposed down to the bone and muscle, stripped raw by their own saliva. Long, ropey coils spilled out of their mouths in unending chains, sizzling into the house as they stuck. Wet growls, the thumping of feet, the thwack of hands, surrounded me on all sides. On the roof, up and down the walls, no spot was left untouched. They shot their heavy cables and spewed mounds like snowdrifts, swathing the house and their prey for later consumption.

In a panic, I grabbed a crumpled book from the floor—*To Kill a Mockingbird*, I think it was—and hurled it out the window at the closest spider-person. Though I'm not really sure "person" still qualified.

"LEAVE ME ALONE!"

The book clunked off what was left of Pat Smith's head and tumbled onto the lawn, as useful to me now as it had ever been. Just to be sure that was a pointless venture, and maybe make myself feel a little better, I reloaded, grabbing the next closet book and hurling it down. Its pages flapped and fluttered like wings that didn't know how to work properly, bouncing off a leathery back with no effect.

Heavy webs shot like vines over the window, narrowly missing my face. I jumped back with a yelp, nearly tripping over my own stupid foot. Sunlight blazed through the heavy webs as they locked me in completely. I looked to the skillet like it might have an answer for me as the window filled in one thread at a time, spinning in from every angle.

Smoke phased in through the walls, in between every crack and crevice, out of every socket, filling the room. The house started to creak and moan. All around it, bodies pushed off and came down on the street again like meteors as the neighbors descended. I stepped back to the middle of the room, watching the walls and ceiling with held breath. My eyes watered, the air reeking of burning bleach. The back of my throat was scorched raw, scratching like raccoon claws all the way down my neck.

The walls started to buckle and the ceiling sagged. I snatched up a shirt from the floor, paying absolutely no attention to how blue and floral it was, and tied it over my mouth. The improvised filter grew damp with my quick, shallow gasps. Creaks turned to cracks as the house fought to hold its shape. With a sickening crunch, the ceiling dropped a few more inches than it had any right to.

Smoke filled my lungs and seared them black. Hacking and wheezing, I doubled over. The stench of it was unbearable, the burn unyielding. Mee-Moo laid broken across the bed, none the wiser. I scrambled for pieces of an explanation as darkness settled in around me. All my brain could find was images of home. Of the friends who, at that rate, would be sending help too late. Of my parents, who would struggle to come to terms with what happened to me. And of Pop-Pop. Smiling in the mirror at our matching shirts. Standing contently in the garage. Sitting on the stiff quilted comforter at the edge of the bed with me, his eyes full of sorrow and fear.

An idea sparked through me. It was shit, don't get me wrong, but it was better than the alternative. Better than nothing. I had seen enough news clips and reports where people had done something like it to escape wildfires or burning buildings. It worked for them, so why not me?

Mostly hanging off the bed, I grabbed the comforter and tugged. The dresser held it firm, pinned against the floor. Limping over, I gave it a shove. Of course, it didn't move. It needed more torque than I thought I could produce. I gripped the edge of it and pushed. One hand held the top while the other braced against its side. My shoulder pressed in and the dresser tipped back. Not enough, but progress. I tried again, thrusting against it with a little more spite. With a jerk, it started to slide. I reached down and pulled the comforter while I leaned against the cheap QVC furniture. One handful at a time, I yanked it free. The dresser toppled over, crashing into the corner, and the quilt ripped out.

The ceiling drooped, bowing in at its center as bits of plaster and drywall flaked off. Grabbing the skillet, I squared up with the door. The heavy quilt flung over my head, falling around me like a scratchy cloak. Tucked into my fists, I pulled it tight around me, the skillet against my chest like an armor plate.

"This is so stupid," I wheezed as I sized up the approach.

But what else was there to do? Every weak breath lit my lungs and scraped them bloody. My vision reduced to pin pricks as the room was lost in a dense fog of smoke. Pops and groans sounded off all around me. I looked for Mee-Moo, to return her scowl one last time on my way out, but even she was lost to the smoke. Curling into the quilt, pulling it completely over my face, I charged ahead.

My leg raged and tottered as I hustled across to the door. Webs broke against me like a net, determined to keep me in place as I rammed my side through. Blinded by wool, I could feel the spiders pinching at me, snipping into the quilt. I held my breath as long as I could, smoke billowing out from me. The quilt crackled and burned as I powered through the door. With a death grip on the scratchy fabric, I kept it wrapped as tight as it would stay. The opposition used every tool at their disposal to take it from me. Webs yanked, mandibles clamped like grasping infant hands hellbent on keeping me there, tipped in razor nails. The skillet flew out from under me, and I started swinging. Like a machete through the brush, I plowed the rest of the way through, breaking out into the hall. My safety blanket clung to the doorway behind me as the spiders filled it back in, burning the coarse old thing to ash.

The same heavy fog filled the path to the stairs. Webs crisscrossed the hall like the laser grid in a bad heist movie. Studs were exposed through the walls, stripped of their flesh, giving out to corrosive strength. Sheets of ceiling crumbled on the floor. The house groaned, cracks and crunches ticking through it like the seconds on a clock. Spiders crawled into every opening, wrapping up the guts of the house.

I gripped the skillet, my breath short and careful through my shirt-mask. No choice left, I limped forward. My high-tops hissed, leaving drips of melting rubber in what was left of the carpet. The skillet cut through the air, slicing down webs. Fresh burns peppered me as they fell, eating into my arms and face as I fought my way down. Smoke came in heavy bursts from Mee-Moo's crochet room, all that feeble yarn evaporating without a struggle.

The banister and railing, thick with white and crawling black, collapsed as I came upon the stairs. My head started to swim, and darkness crept in around the edges of my vision. Heavy chemical smoke followed me as I stepped down, and waited for me at the landing. Behind me, something finally gave. A cataclysmic crash shook the floor at the other end of the hall. The impact blew through the air, swirling curls of smoke towards the stairs.

I kept going. The front door and windows glowed but were too opaque to see through, sealed up perfectly by the hand-and-foot soldiers outside. The lower level was nearly deserted, or at least it looked that way. In the walls, I could hear them. Infesting every square inch of the interior. A forest of webs dissolved the house bit by bit.

A scooter sat between me and the hall. I hobbled over to it, cutting down anything in my path like I was sneaking through some ancient tomb, full of traps and steeped in death. Outrunning them in my shit condition was never gonna happen. It probably wasn't gonna happen in a scooter either, to be fair. But at least it would've been delayed the inevitable a little longer. If the wheels hadn't been melted into flat puddles of metal and rubber. Webs hung from the sagging handlebars, ate through into the seat, and left the little basket on the front a dripping mess of flimsy plastic.

Back from the edge of the hallway, the abandoned powerchair sat a little lower than I remembered, lost in a framework of webs reaching across the walls. It leaned lazily to one side, on the way to falling over. Vapors rose from it as its molecules broke down to nothing. There was no shortage of other potential getaway mobility devices, thankfully, just a matter of finding one that wasn't totally useless. Preferably before I passed out or the roof came crashing through the second story any more than it already had.

There was no way in hell I was cutting through that hall, though. I was already a patchwork of burns and blisters, and the path back through the dining room wasn't nearly as congested. I swatted through the tangle as the skillet lost its shape. Already dented, its body started to warp and deform. It fought gallantly against whatever unnatural substances were working against it, but there was only so much it could do. It held out better than I did, honestly.

Every step into the kitchen came with a big fat question mark. The glass of the back door had sprouted even more cracks. Growing by the second, reaching out across the sliding panels as their surface was eaten away. My shoes stuck to the tile, pulling tendrils of rubber after them. The house swayed under me, rolling back and forth like I was lost at sea. The time had come. All systems power down, all stations abandon posts.

I came around the counter as my vision started to blur. Like balls of chalk set in my face, my eyes were dry and coarse. The brutal fog trapped in the house attacked them the same as my lungs. Every breath was like flaring embers in my chest, my throat torn to pulp.

The office doors had fallen, lying in broken, blackened bits in the room. Pop-Pop's monitor was dark. Its plastic oozed down over cracked glass. I'd hoped for a hint at whatever confirmation Ruben might've sent, or at worst, a screensaver lighting up the room. Either was asking too much, I guess.

6-6-06

The open garage waited ahead. A heavy cloud settled inside, glowing softly through the prism that replaced the big white roll-up door. Directly above, a furious *BOOM* shook through the house. The tide of spiders fought their way out of the walls. Hundreds of thousands of legs rushed in tight ranks down the stairs, through the hall, out of the kitchen, the living room, anywhere they could find an exit. They surged in every direction, breaking for the doors, burrowing through the web shields blocking them.

A full evacuation.

The house let out one long, desperate moan like a whale with a harpoon in its back as I hopped to the garage. It held out for as long as it could, but now it was ready to call it a day. My foot touched down on the smooth epoxy, and the second floor became the first. The ceiling gave out, and the house came down. I dove forward and fell hard to the floor. What air I had left was slammed from my lungs as I belly flopped. The skillet clanged like a misshapen church bell as it bounced away. A mountain of debris rained through the door, spiders scrambling to escape it. Like them, I reached a trembling hand out and dragged myself across the floor as I wheezed.

Pop-Pop was right. Anything the Georgie Bookers of the world could do to me seemed awfully inconsequential looking back. Add it to the list of things I'd scream in my dopey face if I could I go back. That stupid choices lead to stupid consequences. That it wouldn't matter what I did in retribution. Some people just suck down to their cores, and there's always worse ones waiting. It took the house caving in to get the point through my thick fucking skull. Some struggles aren't worth the effort. It just was a matter of figuring out which wars were worth waging.

Inching blindly across the floor, slowly suffocating in a house that was eating itself, I started to get it a little more. Survival would've been nice. It should've been the only real goal. But something stronger than vengeance or retaliation was tethering me to what vaguely resembled life. More than me, more than Pop-Pop, Elaine was worth the headache.

If I make it out of here . . .

My hand came down on rubber, and that's the last thing I remember for awhile.

96 QUITE BITTER BEINGS
JUNE 6, 2006

In my ears, the music was long gone, but in my head, it played on. Familiar chords and notes, on a constant loop, drawing me from one plane of existence to the next. Not down, but up. Like I was stuck at the bottom of the ocean, slowly floating toward a wailing siren at the surface. I kicked and thrashed but gained no ground, at the mercy of whatever current moved me. Heavy, persistent guitars cranked along a billion miles above me, pulling me toward the surface. My lungs clenched and collapsed, no air left to be found.

If I was already in Hell, what would happen if I died again?

Super Hell . . .

The guitars crept closer, swelling and clearing. Their melody was starting to make more sense, become more recognizable as I rose through the crushing darkness. Blazing over the surface as they grew louder, I wasn't rising to them. They were coming to me.

My eyelids listed lazily, working against the cement of crust gluing them shut with no real urgency. The stink was burned into my nose, frying the hairs down to the follicle. From head to toe, my body ached and stung like it was stuffed with gravel and discarded needles. My lungs were a vacuum, incapable of filling. With an involuntary, coppery cough, they released. But only a little. Only enough to wheeze a weak flow of oxygen back into them.

The music gained on me, closer and louder. Darkness broke, and my eyes cracked. Light assaulted them, shooting through my retinas and straight into my brain. With a moan and another cough, I dragged my hand to my face and rubbed them clear. The floor of the garage came into focus while the song kept on getting louder. Light beat from on high through the webs sealing the garage door, a wall of milky diamonds. It bounced off the perfectly polished floor and hit me like a second sun. I tried to blink it out as I forced myself to my knees.

My ankle screamed with every twitch of muscle. No matter how hard I tried to breathe, my lungs wouldn't open all the way. Their fibers were charred to a crisp. The garage wasn't in much better shape. Entire corners and stretches of ceiling had come down. But it still stood, even if it was sagging and sloping toward the tool bench. Wooden beams peeked through the holes above me, singed black and dripping with dried web. The hall back into the house was completely blocked by the second floor, packed solid with wreckage. I could see nothing of the house beyond it. A dark imprint of my face sat on the floor, tinted all the way through with splashes of crimson.

I was awake. I was alive. Everything hurt too fucking bad for that not to be the case. Every ache, every burn, sting, and angry flare sang out her name. I told myself the blood I was tasting was Elaine's in anticipation. Easier than accepting that it was actually my own, coating my throat and lungs.

Hacking, I spat onto the floor. A thick glob of mucus and blood splattered against the wheel of the scooter in front of me. Such a beautiful sight, I had no choice but to get choked up. Tears broke free as I tried to stifle my laugh. The scooter was whole. The handlebars were doused in their previous owner's blood, and the seat was dissolved into ridges of foam. Its fenders weren't even close to the right shape anymore, drooping and dotted with corrosion. Its bright red paint flaked to reveal metal underneath. But otherwise, it was in working order. In one piece, more or less.

The song got louder again, like my iPod had gained the sentience I'd hoped it would and was turning itself up slowly to a more acceptable volume. I definitely knew the melody. Episodes of *Jackass* and a whole host of skate videos had etched its signature riff into my mind forever. My earbuds were still in. I followed the cable back to the source and pulled it from my pocket. The iPod's dead black screen was a mess of cracks and bubbled glass. The metal backside was pocked and dented. Not even the Hold button trick could bring it back. Through the holes in my shirt, I could see it. Burned and broken, there wasn't much cable left. I pulled it through, just to be sure. Cut in half, whole inches of wire missing. Yet the song kept getting louder.

I took the buds out, but didn't move them very far away. My ears stretched through the fuzz and static filling my head. The song thundered through the air outside, heading straight for me. And a stampede was raging around the neighborhood. Hands and feet clapped against the pavement as they reassembled in the street. A hundred feral, angry croaks versus a band the only person I knew with a learner's permit had found before any of us.

"No . . ."

He got the damned thing earlier that year. We all thought it meant greater adventure awaited us, still a ways off from the proper age ourselves. There was talk of drives to the mall, around town, and the greater world beyond. We even talked about going to the annual Halloween film festival held an hour south. Halloween, both the holiday and the stabby franchise. But Jordan's brother never let his Miata out of his sight and his parents were never around enough to leave their multi-colored Plymouth lying around. Something must've gone horribly wrong for the stars to line up that way. And someone was bound to be pissed.

Panic lifted me from the floor as soon as I recognized it. My legs shook as I pushed myself up on to my good foot. 6-6-06, and my friends had come to get me like the movies had been picked and snacks had been procured. I should've been grateful, and in a way I absolutely was. If only Pop-Pop could've seen. The proof was in the crackle of a car stereo and the rattling hum of its engine. But they shouldn't have done it. I knew the odds of surviving to see the seventh were fucked sideways. They didn't. I should've known better than to use the word "Help" and allude to any kind of monsters.

I might as well have said I needed rescue from a coven of vampires or a pack of werewolves. Of course they jumped at the chance to channel the Frog Brothers over calling the cops or anyone else that might've had access to a proper armory. Not leaving alive was a concept I was coming to terms with. I idolized too many characters that had affinities for mythical last stands to not be at least a little enticed by the idea. But it wasn't even something they were aware of. To be fair, though, Jordan picked a hell of a jam for storming the literal gates.

Near the ruins of the tool bench, Pop-Pop's garden rake sat under a chunk of fallen plaster. I dragged myself over to it, my foot sliding uselessly across the smooth floor. Enough of the handle still stuck out that I could bend down and grab it. My head swam, nearly spinning me back down to the floor as I reached. Screws and nails stabbed out of the chunk of ceiling covering the rake, waiting for me to fall on to them and add tetanus to the growing list of things I needed to worry about. I grabbed the rake and pulled furiously. In a clattering crash of dust, it tore free.

The skillet waited dutifully for me on the other side of the garage, aching to do more damage than it already had. Why mess with a good thing when I could probably get a couple more solid whacks out of it before the handle started contemplating its hold to the rest of the cast iron? I grabbed it too.

The scooter's basket was lopsided and folding in on itself. I dropped the skillet in and took a seat on what was left of the vinyl and synthetic stuffing. The handlebars were sticky with blood, but the throttle still turned. I shoved it forward, and the scooter shot back. Wobbling and weaving, I flew back to the wall. The scooter slammed to a stop against it, nearly bucking me off. Cracks thick enough to stick my finger through widened and stretched. There was absolutely no reason for it to be that difficult. I looked at the scooter like it was doing it deliberately. Wouldn't have been surprised if it was. Its previous owner was charging towards my friends and had played some small role in trying to kill me a handful of times over the last day and change. I didn't have time to dick around with it, though.

The speed dial was already set to Rabbit. Dead center on the handlebars was a button with the imprint of a bike horn on it. On the other side was a dial that only shifted to two different positions. A left and right arrow. Set to right, I clicked it left and gently pulled down the throttle.

Because left and right mean forward and reverse now, apparently.

I positioned the rake on top of the handlebars like a battering ram. The music hadn't moved, waiting for the gate to open as the HOA descended in a frenzy. I took a breath, as deep as I could, steadying and bracing for the shit show I was about to stir up.

I cranked the throttle all the way forward. The scooter whined in compliance as it sped across the garage. With a savage cry, I shot to the wall of web boxing me in. At the moment of impact, I lifted the rake and swung it back down. It sliced valiantly through the webs, its prongs liquifying as it knocked them clear. I tucked myself tightly into the seat, trying to scrunch down into the smallest target a boy my size could've been. The rake barreled through, and the scooter did the rest, spitting me through the dense wall.

The sun was lost to angry black clouds above. Humidity blasted my face like an open oven door. A wave of heat in a world of gray as I rolled down the driveway. Fresh air washed mercifully over my face with a hint of salt and thunder. I let go of the throttle as my eyes adjusted, falling forward into the handlebars with a grunt at the driveway's edge. The house behind me was in ruins. Walls slanted and buckled. The porch was a crumbling heap of wood, its awning broken on the lawn. The roof was completely caved, webs blowing carelessly across it. The second floor was mostly gone, crushed under its weight. I couldn't see much in the first, but for whatever time I had left I was going to assume I made it to the only part of the house that actually survived. If it was left standing, then it was still covered in web, exposed down to the studs and that weird chickenwire-looking shit used inside of exterior walls.

The rest of the neighborhood was worse off than it had been. Doors were ripped clear, lying on the lawns. Windows were shattered, and glass was strewn all the way down to the street. Like the long-awaited looters had finally descended, the houses were turned thoroughly inside out in search of me. A significant effort was made in the community room. The ping-pong table had been set up in front of Elaine's lectern, but the hunk of wood with the Sea Breeze Bluffs seal on its front was gone. In its place, a new one had been constructed. Mounds of web reshaped like stalagmites, piled high to the ceiling in pointed spires, the carpet burned clear to the floorboards.

There was no time to relish in any of it; no time to ponder what the fuck it all meant. I cranked the throttle and shot down into the street with a hard bump. The motor whined like a hive of bees as the scooter hustled down the empty street. The HOA swarmed the fountain, marching and crawling to the gate. I like to think I looked something like Ghost Rider as I leaned into the handlebars and sped forward, raging toward my mission of vengeance. Or like Thèoden, riding out of Helm's Deep to meet his foe and decide the fate of his people. But it's impossible to look that cool when you're sitting on something with a horn that meeps like the damn Road Runner, armed with melted gardening equipment and cookware.

I laid on the horn as I angled what was left of the rake over the center of the handlebars. Its wide teeth were reduced to malformed hooks hanging out over the front wheel. The skillet bumped and rattled in the misshapen basket, there if I needed it. Meeps popped weakly from the horn, lost to the commotion of the ravenous corpses and railing of guitars coming from the gate.

"Hey!" I shouted. "I'm still alive!"

They paid no attention. The interlopers had their attention squarely fixed ahead.

MEEP! MEEP!

"Did you forget about me?" I taunted uselessly. "I'm right here!"

Scanning their backs, I couldn't see anybody I immediately recognized. No Bow Tie, no Stache, and no Elaine. I glanced over at her house as I closed in. The destruction of the neighborhood missed it entirely. Not a single blade of grass was out of place. Nothing moved in the windows. I gripped the rake with sweating palms like that Heath Ledger jousting movie. Come what may, I was ready.

"COME AND GET ME!"

They didn't even turn around to acknowledge me, just kept filing toward the gate like the welcoming party from Super Hell.

In the barely attached pocket of my tattered shorts, a hunk of plastic bumped against me through the hole to my raw and burned leg. An idea even stupider started to form. The road was too narrow. Jordan wouldn't be able to turn the car around before the HOA got over and around the gate. And backing down wasn't a choice I could leave for them. Couldn't imagine it being any safer than Pop-Pop going down forwards. With the added bonus of fleeing for their lives thrown in for shits and giggles.

I dug the gate clicker from my pocket before it could fall through and hit the pavement. Its plastic body hadn't done well. The corners were sagging, its gray body had tinted more black and brown and had taken the curve of my chunky thigh. I raised it toward the gate as I neared the fountain-Caddy hybrid and clicked the button with a defiant slam.

The whole thing shattered into pieces.

The button fell in, and the back broke away as the clicker crumbled in my hand. Naked electronics fell through my fingers like grains of sand into the basket and down to the street, crunching hopelessly under the wheels of the scooter.

The throttle slid out of my sweaty grip, and I smashed to a halt. The handlebars bit into my belly, knocking what wind I had out of me. The HOA slunk down the drop to the gate. I couldn't see the car from where I was, but I could definitely hear it. The music was so loud that even I thought it might've been a touch excessive. Its engine rattled and squealed like it had a dying bird stuck in it.

Absolutely not the Miata.

As I fought to catch my pathetic breath and formulate literally any other plan, the gate opened anyway. The visitors were granted the honor of access. Buried under every other noise assaulting the Bluffs, the motors turned and whined. The inhuman welcoming party's tone shifted to the unmistakable sound of pack hunters cornering their prey, posturing and menacing. I jammed the throttle forward and shot around the fountain. The HOA howled in collective defiance, and the car's engine roared as it barreled through the gate.

The smart ones jumped into the trees; dozens of spider-people fleeing like lice from a burning wig. The rest faced the Plymouth. Crashes and booms rocketed up the hill as I slammed to a stop. Screams burst from the car, over the music. Hungry roars croaked and crackled through the trees as the car shot up the hill, swerving at the last second before its rusted and bloody front fender could plow me down.

The windshield was a blind of splintered cracks, splattered in a wash of red. One green door, one blue, and a body that was dented just about everywhere even before it mowed through the HOA, Jordan slammed on the brakes. Twin streaks burned across the pavement as a cloud of smoke shot from the tires. The screams inside the car continued for another solid few seconds after it came to rest. The wiper blades kicked on, smearing gore across the glass.

I whipped the scooter around and zipped to the car. Jordan sat in the driver's seat, his hands in a white-knuckled death grip at ten and two, his eyes wide with what honestly looked like wonder. Alex rode shotgun, shivering with dark streaks of mascara already running down her wet cheeks. Ruben was in the back behind her, curled into a ball on the seat. For a moment, I was happy to see them. But only one. Down the hill, I could already hear the cracks and pops of rearranging limbs and the snarls of enraged monsters.

"What the fuck are you guys doing here?" I shouted into Jordan's window.

With another scream, his stupor broke.

"HOLY SHIT!" He jumped in his seat at the sight of me.

Alex flinched, bracing for further impact. Ruben retreated into the door on his side, tucking himself in tighter. They all looked at me, though they barely recognized me. It took a second for it to click in their heads.

"Grady?" Alex asked, still not totally convinced.

"Seriously, why are you here?" I pressed. But I knew the answer. Why watch movies on the Unholy Holy Day when you can charge headlong into something real?

Jordan turned down the music.

"We came to rescue you!" he answered, a mix of pride and immediate regret.

"Dude, I said don't come! *Send* help! Guys with bombs and helicopters and shit!"

At the gate and in the woods, they regrouped. Smashed faces and twisted bodies lurched their way up, pilots doing their best to operate heavily damaged vehicles. I grabbed the skillet and dropped the rake. Sliding from the scooter, I opened the back door of the Plymouth and landed behind Jordan.

"We gotta move," I urged him.

"Where?" he snapped back, adjusting to see through the bloody tint of the windshield.

"The whole thing's a big-ass circle! Just go!"

Jordan laid on the gas, and the car screeched down the outermost ring as the HOA flooded after us. We went flying, smashing into the doors and seatbelts as it started around the bend.

"I . . ." Ruben stammered. "I got your message."

"Dude, you look like shit," Alex threw back at me. "Are you okay?"

"Not really, no," I replied curtly. "You guys shouldn't be here."

"What are they?" Jordan asked, straight to the matter at hand as we came around the ring.

"Like demon . . . spider . . . guys?" I did my best. "I'm not really sure! They were grumpy-ass old people, and then a bunch of spiders ate Pop-Pop and they let them crawl into their brains, and now they're *that!*"

I pointed out the back window. They were coming. Of course they were. More of them skittered than not, through the street and over the houses, leaping over rooftops after us.

"We didn't kill them?" Ruben asked as he looked back.

"Gotta kill the spider, I think."

"So, they're like zombies," Jordan hypothesized.

"More like Deadites," I corrected.

"Deadites are possessed, though," he argued as we sped past the cliff, white caps raging below. "Demons! Not infected."

"Zombies don't do that." Ruben's eyes were stuck behind us, same as mine.

Unnaturally set limbs scuttled through the street and sprang from the roofs. Bone stabbed through skin, trails of blood and web spilled over the asphalt. None of their angles remotely made sense anymore. Hips facing the wrong way. Arms and legs bent in places they shouldn't have been, newly jointed and spread wide like the creatures operating them. Heads that curled and twisted against their necks and spines.

"Zack Snyder's zombies kinda do," Jordan pointed out.

"Not really!" Ruben countered. "They're fast but not like monstery!"

"GUYS!" Alex brought us back.

"They're not normal Earth spiders," I broke it to them.

"Aliens?" Jordan asked nervously, if not a little hopeful.

I shook my head.

"Don't think so. There was this book thing. I think they summoned them. And used my Pop-Pop to like grow them or feed them or both. It wasn't super clear!"

"So, what are we talkin' then?" Jordan asked as we came around the other side of the ring. "Invasion?"

"I don't know! I think they're trying to summon or conjure someone or something like that."

Elaine made her way out into the street. Walking with a calm patience that knew I wasn't going anywhere. For a moment, our eyes connected. Pure, rejuvenating hate crackled between us.

"And that old piece of shit!" I thrust a finger at her. "Needs to fucking die!"

"Is she in charge?" Jordan questioned.

"She is."

"Alright then! We have our marching orders."

"What?" Alex stepped in. "No, we do not. We came to get Grady, not fight demon bugs!"

"Is there a difference?" Ruben shrugged. "Do we have a choice?"

"Nope!" Jordan grinned.

The swarm kept their pace behind us, refusing to let us out of their sight.

"Yes, there is, and yes, you do!" I argued. "They're fucking dangerous! They spit, like, burning webs out of their faces!"

I pulled the hole in my shirt wider, exhibiting the bubbled, bleeding evidence Mee-Moo left on my shoulder. Ruben cringed into his hood. Alex gagged as her skin turned pale.

"Don't let them get you!" Jordan coached.

"Earbuds!" I blurted in a panic. "What are you doing? Put your earbuds in!"

"I'm kinda driving, dude," Jordan winced.

"They get in through your ears!"

"Are there any in here?" Alex pushed herself off her seat, checking the cab in a frenzy.

"They could be! They're sneaky little fuckers!"

The three of them scrambled to get them from their pockets. The Plymouth took a sharp swerve and filled with screams like it was about to go over the cliff as Jordan dug in his. He caught the wheel and righted it as his SportPlayer fell to the cupholder with a clunk. The car settled, but our pursuers didn't. As we came around past the fountain again, they started to catch on. Doubling back for us and cutting across the spokes.

"I'm stoked you guys came, really," I rushed to say as they plugged their ears, my attention on the mangled shapes cutting across the roofs. "But you gotta go."

"We're not leaving you here," Ruben looked to me.

"You have to!"

"No!" Alex put her foot down. "We're not going anywhere without you! We came all the way out here! What do you want us to do? Pull over and let you out?"

"You stay, we stay, man!" Jordan threw into the rearview mirror.

"That's not what I meant!" Alex shrieked. "You're driving, just get us the fuck out of here!"

As we came around to the cliff again, the HOA made their move. Bodies fell from the air and charged from the sides. They raced out into the street, blocking our path. Wet splats hit metal, and the clock started counting again. A sonic boom echoed through the car, and a body glanced off the hood on Alex's side. Jordan weaved around them as they leaped at the car, bouncing off it. The Plymouth exploded into a new chorus of screams, shaking the windows as my friends learned the new rules of the world. From every rooftop, out of every yard and from every curb, they pressed their attack. Webs hit the car with dull thuds on all sides. Smoke trailed after us as Jordan jerked the wheel from one side, cutting through to the heart of the Bluffs.

"This is what I'm talking about!" I yelled over their screams. "That shit will eat straight through the car!"

"Where do we go?" Jordan shot back at me. "You know this place!"

"The gate!" I hoped for the best. "Back into town!"

The tires spewed and squealed as Jordan wrapped around the center ring. Around the pool and the community room, past Elaine's house as she calmly climbed her driveway.

"We can't handle this!" Alex cried. "We're out of our fucking element!"

"I think I agree," Ruben seconded as webs burned into his door, smoke billowing just below the window.

"We're trained for this!" Jordan argued.

"We are not!" She pushed back. "We watch movies! That's not the same thing! Get us out of here!"

"Let me out!" I pleaded. "I need to—"

Alex's door fell from the car, clunking and grinding across the pavement, its metal eaten through, the hinges vaporized.

"Shut the fuck up, Grady!" she shrieked back at me. "You're coming home with us!"

If it got them out of the Bluffs, if it kept them alive, then I didn't have any more room to argue. Elaine and her homeowners had taken enough already, they couldn't have my friends too.

"Get us back into town, Jordan," I conceded. "We'll figure it out from there."

He whipped around the fountain, and the Plymouth bolted down the hill. Alex held on to her seatbelt so tightly that I'm surprised it didn't melt into her palms. Ruben braced himself against the roof of the car, his eyes wide with terror under his hood. Jordan's knuckles cracked around the wheel. We could all see it. But nobody wanted to say anything about it.

The gate was closed again.

Jordan stomped the gas all the way down. The engine howled in protest. Our screams crescendoed as the gate zoomed larger in front of us. Jordan let out a savage wail like he had practiced for the metalcore band he swore he was gonna start one day. In a shower of sparks, the car exploded through the gate. Alex folded into her seat, tightening into a careful little ball as the two halves dragged over us.

The wide front end of a pearly white Lincoln flew up on our back window. Its steel grill shined like bared fangs, growling with murderous intent. Its roaring engine gained fast on our bumper.

"Jordan?" Ruben asked politely.

"I see it!" he answered into the rearview mirror.

"It's her," I snarled.

Through the glare on her windshield, cut by shadows, Elaine leaned close into her steering wheel like she couldn't see over it otherwise. Jordan hit the brakes, squealing into the first turn, and she made contact. Her front end kissed our trunk, and the Plymouth started to spin. We bounced off the metal railing and swerved toward the rock. For someone who had barely ever used that learner's permit, Jordan was certainly at home. It's the sole reason why I swear racing games are some kind of helpful. Even if they weren't for me. He corrected our course and shot us down the hill a moment before the hood made contact. Elaine screeched through the turn after us, narrowly avoiding the rail herself.

"What's this lady's deal?" he spat furiously to the road.

"She doesn't like me very much," I panted.

"What'd you do?" Ruben assumed.

"Nothing! I existed!"

"Asshole!" Alex glared back in the rearview mirror.

The next curve approached just as fast. Jordan learned his lesson. Instead of the brakes, he lifted his foot completely from the gas. The Plymouth slowed enough for Elaine's front bumper to scrape against our back. He hugged the turn and cut in as it curved. Alex's eyes bulged as she let out a banshee shriek, and the rail inched closer to her again. She scrambled across the cupholders and gearshift like she would've been more comfortable sitting on Jordan's shoulder like a parrot. Ruben fell over to the middle seat while I pressed into my door. Elaine slammed into the railing. The wooden posts holding it over the road bowed out as she slid along the metal, spraying sparks back behind her like the Lincoln was about to burst into flames.

The next turn came too suddenly. Jordan had no choice but to lay on the brakes. Behind us, Elaine overcorrected back toward the rock wall. We nearly drifted through the turn as she bounced off stone, serpentining across the road. My throat was already a mass of raw hamburger meat, and all the extra screaming didn't help it any. My friends harmonized over one long, terrified note. I forced myself calm as the car righted, watching Elaine over my shoulder.

The trees behind us, all the way back to the top of the road, were alive with motion. Dark shapes darted through them, from top to top and trunk to trunk. Even in silhouette, I could see just how wrong their bodies had become. At that rate, the only shot in hell we had was getting back to the freeway. Leading them all the way down the hill, through the woods, over the bridge, and back to the tunnel, all without getting killed or cornered. And assuming the roads were any kind of passable.

Elaine started to slow. Guessing she realized her approach was just as likely to get her killed as it was us. The Lincoln started to shrink as we took each corner and turn right in the sweet spot between quick and careful. Her swarm persisted through the trees as we made our way down and Elaine's car faded from sight.

"Yeah!" Jordan cheered. "That's what I'm talking about! That's what you get when you mess with us!"

Alex eased back into her seat. Ruben looked to me, fearing the truth.

"She's not gonna stop," I broke it to them. "The only reason I'm alive, I think, is because they figured I died when the house collapsed."

"A house collapsed?" Jordan asked, stunned.

"You didn't see that?" Alex scoffed. "How could you miss it?"

"I had other shit to pay attention to!" He gestured to the road and the mess of the windshield.

"You were in there?" Ruben asked me nervously.

"Rather they thought I was dead, or they didn't think I'd get out. That fucking house is *full* of their spider buddies. They wrapped it all up and the whole thing came down on my ass!"

"Dude . . ." Gravity settled on Jordan. "Yeah, okay, let's go home."

"Thank you!" Alex sighed.

"You okay with that, Grady?" he double checked.

I wasn't. But maybe that was one of the finer points of what Pop-Pop was talking about. Better, more well-armed people could deal with Elaine and her horde. Surviving long enough to make the call was gonna have to be enough.

"Alex, do you have your phone?" I asked.

"Of course." She stuffed her hand down into the pocket of her pre-torn jeans and handed back her Razr.

If I made it home, Mom and Dad and I were going to need to have a serious talk about getting me one of my own. It would've solved a metric fuck-ton of issues. No matter how many the nightly news told Mom they'd create. The risk of overages was worth it if it meant something like this could've been avoided. But that's neither here nor there. I flipped the screen up and dialed 911. Three underage kids in a beaten and battered stolen car, what cop wouldn't want to come talk to us?

It rang against my ear, and Jordan laid on the gas. The road flattened out into the town as we came around the roundabout. Its bandstand was smashed to pieces, broken wood littering the road. Something about having a spider in their heads must've made doors harder to navigate, because all of them dangled from broken hinges or laid flat on the floor in the dark of the respective businesses. Windows were broken from the inside and out. The storefronts behind them were throughly turned, their merchandise or equipment tossed and scattered like there was a chance I had escaped into a rack of sweatpants or rode to freedom on the barber's chair. Behind us, the Lincoln reappeared up the hill. Jumping, inhuman shapes led it down.

For being an emergency service, I expected 911 to pick up immediately. But as we crossed in front of the ruined post office and the grocery store blurred by, the other end of the line was still ringing. I started to doubt it'd ever pick up as we sped toward the tourist traps, and the newly set limbs touched down on the roofs behind us. Elaine vanished again at the bottom of the hill, and an operator picked up.

"911, what's your emergency?" an almost robotic voice asked.

"Yes!" I blurted into the phone, my eyes still behind us. "I'm out in Sea Breeze Bluffs." For a second, I thought about telling the truth, just to see how far it would get me. "And I need to report a theft."

"What was stolen, sir?"

"Some kids just stole a car! They crashed it into a bunch of stuff and drove off!"

They snapped around to me. Jordan nearly swerved into the curb but caught himself, sending us flailing around the car. When we righted, I waved them off.

"I got this," I whispered.

"Your name, sir?" The operator asked.

"Grady . . . Graham." Don't know why I lied about that, it just felt like the smart thing to do.

"And where are you now?"

"Uh, in my room."

"How old are you, Grady?"

"Fourteen in August, please, come quick!" I really laid it on. "I think they hurt somebody!"

We barreled down the long drag toward the stoplight. Dark figures pounced over every roof behind us. Jordan pressed the pedal as far down as it could go, practically standing on it.

"Who was hurt, Grady?" the operator asked without really caring.

"I don't know, but there was blood on the car."

Their glare intensified like they were debating throwing me out it.

"Sea Breeze Bluffs? The retirement community?"

"Yeah, I'm staying with my grandparents. They're . . . out."

"Alright then," the operator sighed. "We'll get a unit out there as soon as we can."

The shapes behind us stopped jumping, perching on the roofs like gargoyles.

"Thank you, please hurry."

I clapped the phone closed and passed it back to Alex as she burned holes into my forehead.

"What?" I asked. "Like they would've believed the truth! How many movies are there where someone calls like 'oh, help, please, they're trying to kill me!' and the cops are like, 'yeah right, fuck you!' This way they'll actually come."

They sat with it for a second. A solution to satisfy everyone.

"That's fair," Ruben agreed. "Only reason we did is because we know shit."

"Exactly!"

The single stoplight appeared against the trees and water, jet-black under ominous clouds.

"What do we do about the car, though?" Jordan asked.

"Just get us closer to the highway," I suggested. "If they stop us or see us, we'll tell them how fucked it is up there so they can nuke the place."

Jordan started to chuckle.

"We're so screwed."

"Yeah, probably!" I smirked.

It might've been the burns, or it could've been the fact that I couldn't remember the last time I smiled, but my cheeks ached as they lifted the corners of my mouth.

Jordan slowed enough to take the turn, red light or not. We sped into the intersection, and a rocket exploded into the side of the Plymouth. We had come into it just enough to spare Alex and Ruben. Anything less and they would've been blasted to pieces. I can only blame the fire road behind Tools & Lumber. Its the only thing that made sense. Dust and dirt streaked off of Elaine's car as she rammed into our back corner.

The front end of her Lincoln crumpled and smashed as she slammed on the brakes. Smoke filled the intersection as we spun away, too stunned to scream. In a hale of broken glass and smashed metal, Jordan scrambled at the wheel, trying to paw it back under his control. Alex clutched her seatbelt, fighting the force threatening to rip her from the car and hurl her across the road. Ruben pushed against his door, bracing for the impact. With every spin, I tried to keep our attacker in sight, a lost cause through the swirling dust and smoke. One, two, three full rotations before it slid off the road, bursting through the legs of the Welcome sign and into the woods, coming to a rest only when the trunk of a tree caught the hood.

Fluids dripped into the dirt as a cloud of dust caught up to us, engulfing the car. Empty airbags hung limp from the dashboard. Alex shivered in the front seat, bleeding from her nose. Jordan gripped the wheel uselessly, a stain on his airbag matching the river pouring from a lip split wide. Ruben refused to let go of his door. My head spun like the car was still moving as the cloud swallowed us.

I blinked, and a lanky shape made its way through the dust. My eyes refused to focus, swirling and turning like I was stuck in a washing machine. Another blink and an army of others joined it, hunched down on reset limbs. A third blink and they descended. The remaining doors ripped open, clean off their hinges and flying back into the cloud surrounding us. Gnarled and mangled hands reached in, taking Jordan first. He kicked and screamed as they ripped him out of the car. Ruben was next. I reached for him as he vanished, desperate to catch his hand or maybe a foot, anything I could use to anchor him. Bony fingers clamped onto my neck like a bear trap, and Elaine dragged me from the car herself. Clones of her spun like a broken kaleidoscope as she raised me to meet her eyes. Her mouth full of blood, she bared her teeth in a vengeful snarl and hurled me to the ground at the trunk of the ruined car.

I blinked again, and a slate gray sky panned over me. The road marched along at my back. Or above my head. Hard to tell which, being upside down. Whiplash burned through my neck, and my eyes closed again.

When they reopened, trees surrounded us. The swarm filed in behind me as I floated over the road. A great herd of crawling ghouls, tucked low to the ground like their chosen arachnids. Their faces had degraded to the color of wet stone, compound eyes filled dark hollows. Jordan dragged across the asphalt, his battle vest taking the brunt of the scrapes and scuffs. Finkle carried him up the hill, one hand on his ankle, the other moving along the ground, burned and patchy beard scraping the road. Alex laid on Stache's chest, unconscious and facing up at the dark sky. His head was craned around to watch where he was going. Bow Tie, still upright, had Ruben clutched tightly over his shoulder, just as lifeless as the others. Elaine carried me by the waist of my shorts, staring down with a revolting grin. So confident and self-assured, it would've been enough for me to want her dead all on its own.

My eyes rolled in their sockets like they needed a peek at my brain. When they righted, the veiled sun was arcing over to the cliff, ready to get the fuck out of there while it still could. The smashed gate rested at the bottom of its slope. Jordan started to stir. Like a shot out of a cannon, he sprung to life. He kicked and punched and tugged at the dead hand around his ankle, but got nowhere. Every obscenity and threat he could think of flew from him in an endless string, lost to the murky fog filling my head. Three more scurried up their ranks to grab his limbs, holding them prone in their vice grips and lifting him completely from the ground.

We passed the fountain, and Ruben came back online. But he couldn't worm his way off of Bow Tie's shoulder, no matter how much he wriggled and flailed.

Mee-Moo and Pop-Pop's house passed at my side.

Their grave, I guess.

Alex's scream cut through just enough to get my attention. She jumped from Stache's chest and started to run, but he didn't let her get far. He scrambled after her, pouncing onto her back and tackling her to the ground. Another came to grab her legs, and together they hoisted her back into formation. Her desperate, raccoon eyes locked onto me.

"Grady, do something!" is what I'm pretty sure she was yelling at me. But I think I was way closer to dead than they were.

My eyes fluttered closed again, and in the darkness, I heard the high whine of a dented gate squealing on its hinges. They opened again, and blinding fluorescents cut through my skull. Like she was tossing a bag of trash into a dumpster, Elaine hurled me onto the ping-pong table. The others filed in and deposited my friends in the corner with the same callousness. A rank of guards took up positions around them. A half dozen spider-people caged them to the wall, blocking any path of escape.

The rest of the HOA filed in as Elaine took her rightful place at the head of the room, behind the web spires engulfing her lectern. Her remaining board filed in behind her, crawling up to new positions on the wall. Slowly, reverently, the others trickled in. Up across the ceiling, over the floor, along the walls, filling the room. Pop-Pop's croaking snore hit a final, inhuman evolution. Like their vocal cords had been melted down to nothing by the bile and phlegm in their throats.

Elaine raised her gavel high.

BANG! BANG! BANG!

The room fell dutifully silent, out of muscle memory if nothing else.

6-6-06

"Welcome, one and all"—she opened her arms wide in showy faux-grandeur—"to the Sea Breeze Bluffs Homeowners Association Summer Potluck!"

BEAST AND THE HARLOT

Crumpled, folded, and doused in what I had to figure was raccoon blood, Elaine pulled her journal from the lectern. She dug through the insane pages until she found whatever raving or contaminated scribble she needed. Calmly, she settled on her page and looked out to her constituents. Rabid excitement crackled through them as they covered every surface of the room.

"Before we get to it, just a few final matters of business require our attention."

She looked to the room, waiting for an objection they weren't going to give.

"Under Secretary Graham and her husband have dutifully fulfilled their end of the agreement, as this governing body sees fit."

The assembled growled and croaked in excitement.

"The juveniles were incubated to term, fed to maturity, and embraced with open arms."

More howls and hisses. Elaine banged her gavel and they settled in an instant.

"However!" she pressed on. "The Grahams have neglected to provide their pre-designated course for our little gathering. At least not in the agreed upon state."

She thrust her gavel toward my friends, trembling and covered with nervous sweat, locked into the corner on all sides.

"Does *that* meat look prepared to any of you?"

Oh fuck.

I sat up on my elbows, still fighting the spins and fog. The HOA changed their tone, angrier, darker. Hungrier. She banged her gavel once, twice, three times.

"No! It most certainly does not. Any changes to our evening's itinerary must be submitted for voting approval, so I would like to offer a resolution to all members."

She flipped through her pages again until she landed on whatever batshit crazy doodles were going to support her proposal. Her wording was careful and precise, even if her writing was not.

"The veil is weakening, and tonight our window will open. All other necessary steps have been taken. Aranea rises!"

"ARANEA ORIRI!" their mangled voices vomited around the room, barely functioning. If I hadn't heard it before, it would've sounded like garbled nonsense. But those words I remembered well enough to assume.

"Yes, yes, Aranea Oriri." She waved them down and continued. "In silence she called, and her arrival is upon us. Our mind is wise." She touched a reverent hand to her own chest. "Our hand is steady." She gestured to them. "And our heart is young." She glared down at me. "Even if he is unwilling. With this being the case, though, I would like to submit for your approval . . . the interlopers."

"Grady!" Alex yelled from the back of the room, panic knocking her brain around like a Koosh ball. "What do we do?"

I had no fucking idea. I wasn't even fully sure of what the next few minutes were going to look like! But I could guess.

"Young lady," Elaine warned, "it is incredibly rude to interrupt an adult while they're speaking!"

"They're big on that," I muttered over my shoulder.

"Eat shit and die!" Jordan spat.

"Yeah! Fuck you!" Ruben tagged.

Elaine brought the gavel down like she was trying to split stone, silencing all.

"As I was saying!" The annoyance in her tone would've only egged us on in different circumstances. "The troublemaker has provided us with a host of alternatives. Quite the bounty of riches, if you ask me. And seeing as he is no longer our only option, and each would require the proper preparations, I will now open the floor to recommendations."

The corpse holding Ruben to the wall threw him to the floor in front of the ping-pong table. He rolled across like a rag doll and came to a stop near the table's metal legs. That was all I needed. That got me up. I rolled off the table and came down with a crash, fire shooting up my leg.

"No!" I barked through the pain. "Leave them out of this!"

Jordan was thrown forward next. Then Alex. Each looking to me, on hands and knees, for an answer or a plan of action I didn't have. The HOA barked and croaked in debate, each pleading a case for their chosen without human words.

"We only need one!" Elaine reminded them, raising her voice sternly over their arguments.

When they didn't calm, she brought the gavel down.

"If I may! The Board and I would like to offer a recommendation that we feel will satisfy all demands of Aranea and the Homeowners Association. The troublemaker . . ." My stomach dropped as she spoke. "For all the senseless destruction and death caused on his behalf, should no longer receive this honor!"

They hissed and snarled in what I could only assume was agreement.

"The chance was offered to him several times, and each was met with the type of disrespectful dismissal that plagues his kind, so we must assume he is unwilling to fulfill our purposes at this time. His punishment must be fitting!"

I lifted myself up with the table's edge, turning back to Elaine and hoping this would be the moment my heat vision finally activated.

"And so, we would like to formally suggest that he be removed from contention." Her eyes landed on me again—judge, jury, and executioner. "He will, however, be made witness."

I limped to my friends as they slowly got up. In the middle of the room, we huddled around each other.

"One of them," Elaine announced, "will provide our young heart. While the troublemaker and his other rude little cohorts will serve admirably as the offering the Under Secretary failed to provide."

"What the fuck does any of that mean?" Jordan asked under his breath.

"I think they wanna put a spider in one of our heads," I whispered back, "and the rest of us get to hang around to get eaten."

"I'm good!" Ruben shook his head. "I don't wanna do that."

"The choice is not yours, young man," Elaine said to him like she was talking to an infant. "Aranea approaches whether you like it or not."

Alex caught the look in my eye. The tight creasing of my brow while my eyes darted around the floor.

"What are you thinking?" she asked hopefully.

I looked at my leg. The bit of pipe barely hung on to its tattered duct tape wrapping, ready to be used once my friends were clear.

As long as I take her *with me.*

"Do me a solid?" I asked the three of them.

"What's up?" Ruben leaned in.

"Don't stay here."

"Grady . . ." Jordan started.

I shook my head at him as I hobbled back toward the lectern, trying to muster whatever sincerity and earnestness I was capable of. The others watched, just as lost as I was.

"Madame President," I began, cashing in my Good Boy points. "I'm sorry."

"What was that?" She laughed incredulously.

"I'm sorry!" I raised my voice. "For the fountain. For Mee—the Under Secretary. For the gates. For everything. I'm sorry."

"Too little, too late, troublemaker."

"If it pleases the . . . congregation?" I didn't know what the fuck I was supposed to call them. "I'd like to offer a counterproposal. I was sent here to learn a lesson, and I think I finally have. My friends were just trying to help me. They don't need to be involved in any of this. It was my mistake dragging them into it in the first place. Let them go. Take me!"

"Hell no!" Jordan fought back.

"It's okay!" I spun back to him. "I've got this."

Elaine watched, amused, like we were nothing more than monkeys fighting over a banana.

"I'll do it!" I stood up a little straighter. "I'll do whatever you need me to. Give me one more chance. Please. I'm ready."

She sat with it for a moment. It was the best idea I had. It was the only idea I had, but who's counting?

Her eyes rolled as she scoffed.

"No! You need to learn the consequences of your actions." She thrust the gavel out. "The little whore! I vote we use her. What say you, voting members?"

Approval howled maddeningly around the room.

"So be it then!" She banged the gavel. "She will join us while the others will feed the Queen Mother Aranea!"

Ruben and Jordan closed ranks around Alex. Hands shot down from the ceiling and snatched her up anyway.

"No!" I screamed as they carried her overhead.

Alex thrashed and flailed, but couldn't break free. Her legs kicked like she was trying to run through the air.

"You should be thanking me, troublemaker," Elaine gloated. "I didn't need you alive for this. But now I'm *very* glad you are." She raised her eyes back to her assembly. "Let us begin!"

BANG! BANG! BANG!

She dropped the gavel, and the others got to work. The windows exploded in. Glass flew into the community room like arrows as the flood of spiders came spilling through. Hundreds of thousands of furry legs rippled down to the floor. They joined their kin, climbing and crawling over the HOA like long-lost children. Webs sprayed from mouths like fire extinguishers, covering the window and door. Alex fell to the ping-pong table with a crash, black running all over her wet face like she was leaking ink. Stache and Bow Tie launched from their positions as I reached for her. The grocery store manager hit me like a wrecking ball and pinned me to the floor. His jaw hung lazily in my face, teeth melted to nubs. His butcher came down on top of Alex, locking her to the table.

The titular mustache was patchy and burned, his lips mostly missing. Her legs kicked and arms pulled as she bucked and thrashed, screaming bloody murder.

Yet neither of them spat in our faces. I stared straight down the barrel of Bow Tie's throat. No webs pooled in the back of it, now that I had been demoted.

Jordan's booted foot flew over my head. It clunked off Bow Tie's skull and snapped his head back, not that he even noticed. Bone and tendons crackled and popped as his neck whipped, but Jordan might as well have been giving him a cute little peck on the cheek for all he felt of it. Ruben ran past him to the table with a roar I didn't know he was capable of. He grabbed Stache's arms and pulled with all his strength. Shaking and sliding, but they didn't break free.

Jordan gave Bow Tie one more good kick to the ribs. He popped up just enough for me to work with. His grip loosened, and I rolled him off.

"Go get her!" I yelled to Jordan. "And watch your ears!"

The earbud situation was fucked sideways. Long gone, they had to be rattling around somewhere between the community room and the stoplight. But that just meant extra caution was necessary. For once in their miserable existences though, the spiders didn't move to attack. They scuttled around the floor like it was the party they waited their entire lifecycles for. Excited, but not agitated. Fast, but not predatory.

Jordan wrapped the chain from his wallet around his knuckles and took off for the ping-pong table. From the side, he landed blow after blow into Stache's face as Ruben pulled. Bits of skin tore free, exposing grayed muscles underneath. Elaine stood over them from her position of prominence, her arms open wide and ready. In thick, dark streams across the dingy floor, the spiders made their way to her.

Bow Tie was ready to go again before I could get off my ass. Hollow metal clunked against my ankle as I tried to stand on shaky legs. He sprang from the floor and I braced for impact, but it didn't come. Instead, he sailed for the top of the ping-pong table. In one fluid move, mid-air before he landed, his hand clasped through Jordan's long hair and onto his skull. With a snap as he came down, he threw him back behind the lectern. Jordan crashed into the wall, caving it in against his back and crumpling to the floor. Bow Tie launched himself after him with a snarl, landing on top of his prey.

As I got to my feet, I grabbed my pipe-splint. Duct tape and I'm sure a little bit of skin ripped as I tore it free. Ruben froze, eyes wide and twinkling with tears as Stache whipped his attention to him. His hanging mouth gurgled and growled. Tendrils of web dripped over his bare jaw. Alex twisted her head in every direction it could go as they sagged down to her. With a bloodthirsty scream, I cocked the thin pipe over my shoulder and aimed. It cut through the air in an ashen streak, straight for the butcher's eye socket.

My ankle erupted as bony fingers clamped down on it with rigor mortis force. The pipe stopped midair. A roar of anguish tore through what threads of my throat were left. Under the table, the Parking Enforcement lady had me firm. Her face was mostly bare below the eyes, her nose barely hanging on.

With a jerk, she yanked me down to the ground. My head cracked into the exposed floorboards. Before I could register the pain, I was sliding back across the community room as the others began to converge.

"Grady!" Ruben shouted desperately after me.

"Go for the eyes!" I cried out as I disappeared into the swarm.

Ruben punched Stache straight in the eye. Over and over as hard as he could, like he was assaulting a mannequin or one of those animated Halloween yard decorations that none of our parents would ever let us get.

"GET THE FUCK OFF ME!" Alex wailed through the community room.

Off the walls and down from the ceiling, they came across to meet at the table. Clambering over and around me as Parking Enforcement dragged me back towards the door. Loose, cold flesh draped over me as I glided over the ruined floor. Putrid meat and a heavy dousing of chemical odors covered me, and I lost sight of the ping-pong table. Spiders flowed against us, racing to the head of the room. Her legs scuttled back as her fingertips pressed into my ruined ankle, like they were trying to finish the job and pull my foot off. With a breathless, broken howl, I buried a melted high-top into her jaw. The bone dislodged with a wet pop, drooping down to her neck. Offended rage hissed out of her as she stopped and scrambled up my body. I did exactly one more sit-up than I had ever done, bringing the pipe up with me to meet her. Aiming for the eye, I missed by only a couple of inches and speared it deep into her nose cavity. Bare fingers clawed at it as she fell back, but she couldn't get the purchase needed to pull it out. Thickly congealed blood oozed down it and spilled to the ground.

"Enough!" Elaine raged from the lectern.

I almost forgot she was even there. Through the dense forest of assembled arachnids, all attention shot to her. Spiders crawled all over her; her arms, legs, chest, across her sharp face, and through her hair. Trails of web carved a complicated roadmap of bubbling burns over her. Bow Tie stood at her side, Jordan held tightly to his chest. Dead arms wrapped around his throat like constrictors as he fought to stay conscious. Fresh blood leaked from his hairline, webs burning the shoulder of his vest as they slipped loose over bare bone. A determined spider crawled down Elaine's arm to the waiting platform of her hand.

"In light of this latest aggression, I move that we take what we can get. All opposed?"

None were, except for Jordan.

"KILL HER, GRADY!" he screamed through the pressure on his windpipe, eyes bulging from his skull. "FUCKING MURDER THIS OLD HAG!"

She raised her arm to his head as I forced myself up. My leg was mostly decorative at that point, but it could't stop me. I dragged it across the room, like trying to run with one foot stuck in mud. The spider teased Jordan's ear as he closed his eyes and waited for what came next.

Ruben dove forward, breaking from Stache and climbing up onto the table.

"Where are you going?" Alex called desperately as he flew past.

I could see right where he was going. And there was no way I was going to get there before he did.

"Good boy!" Elaine proclaimed as her brood crowded in tighter. "That's what we like to see! Initiative."

He dove from the table.

"Ruben, don't!" I tried to yell over the crowd.

Elaine caught him, snatching him out of the air like her morning paper. With one hand, she held him high by the throat. Ruben threw himself back, flailing against her grip, unable to break it. With the other, she placed the spider lovingly on his chest.

"Grady, do something!" Alex pleaded.

I rushed into the fray. Bodies waited rigidly, propping themselves around the table and rooting around the lectern. Stache released Alex, spinning around to watch Ruben kick and swing. She slid off the table and charged into the masses, shoving her way toward the lectern. Elaine watched with a smile like she was witnessing an infant's first feeble steps as the spider started up to Ruben's neck. Jordan thrashed against Bow Tie, but gained about as much ground as any of us. Like trying to break free from a statue sculpted around him. With a roar deep from his gut, he lowered on his haunches and flung himself back. Bow Tie went with him as he plummeted back to the floor.

Elaine ripped Ruben's hood down, exposing his face for all to see. Alex fought through the crowd, shouting his name the whole way ahead of me. I followed her through as best I could. Their hands didn't grab for me, their mouths didn't spit, but they were too tightly packed for me to work through with any kind of speed. What I imagine the pit at Warped Tour must've been like, if Mom and Dad had ever let me go.

"Your ears! Watch your ears!" I screamed to Ruben with everything I had left, lost in the noise of the crowd.

The spider crawled up his face, legs probing into his open mouth and over his bulging eyes. Alex closed in and Elaine's smile grew manic, curving farther toward her ears than should've been allowed. She tossed Ruben to the ping-pong table as easily as an empty grocery bag. Stache jumped clear as he drifted up over the lectern and slammed down to it, knocking its legs out and dropping to the floor. Spinning to face Alex, Elaine snatched a handful of her hair and ripped her down to the ground. Fake green highlights dissolved between her fingers.

6–6–06

Jordan bucked against Bow Tie as his face started to turn a grotesque gradient of blue and purple, windpipe collapsing under an unflinching grip. He threw elbows into his midsection, but all he was doing was burning up whatever oxygen he could get. Alex rolled on the floor at Elaine's feet, cradling the back of her head like it was the only way to hold it together, wisps of smoke rising from the webs stuck to her scalp. We needed more strength, more physical firepower than either of us could provide. But the only one of us who might've been able to help was pinned to the floor, stuck in some kind of monstrous demonic wrestling hold and slowly suffocating.

Trapped within their ranks, I shoved and pushed as terror sprang in streams from Ruben's eyes. He swatted and clawed at the spider as it raced around his face, biting with wild abandon, determined to find its cockpit, shredding his skin. His sobbing shrieks drowned out the rest of the room as I shouldered through the crowd, wishing I still had a pipe to whack their skulls with. Pincers found Ruben's ear, snipping it clean off at the seam. I forced my way to him, throwing elbows and shoulders like I had seen in all the moshing videos as he convulsed on the table, clawing at his shorn stump of an ear. I dropped to my knees at his side, lunging for his face.

Black legs disappeared into his skull.

Too late to do anything, I reached for them. But they were already too far in. Too far gone to be retrieved. It didn't stop me from trying.

"No, no, no, no, NO!" I bellowed as I dug at the disappearing legs.

Alex rose behind Elaine, seething, and ready to continue their cat fight. She grabbed the President by the scorched bun on the back of her head, an eye for an eye, a handful of hair for a handful of hair. She pulled as hard as she could, expecting to whip Elaine into the wall or down to the floor. All that came back with her hand was the bun. A shriveled patch of burnt skin held it in place. Alex doubled over, gagging as she tossed the clump of meat and hair away. If Elaine noticed, she didn't care. Her focus stayed on the ping-pong table.

Ruben looked up at me with eyes full of doubts and second thoughts as they rolled over in his head. His body calmed, and they turned jet-black. Like ink spreading through water. I pushed myself up, stumbling on my bad foot, and took a step back. Stammering and weeping, I muttered the only thing I could think to say over and over again, like it was going to make any difference at all.

"I'm sorry! I'm sorry! I'm sorry!"

I watched as the smooth surface of his eyeballs became rigid, as human inched closer to insect. His mouth stretched as wide as it could go as his back arched off the table, and a long croak howled out. It punched straight through my heart and shook the community room like a steam engine. Alex ducked away, hands clasped over her ears to shield against it.

BANG!

BANG!

BANG!

Elaine's gavel silenced room. The vacuum of quiet returned to the Bluffs.

"Meeting adjourned," she declared gleefully.

Webs flew in from every direction, whizzing over my head and splattering onto Ruben. The spiders left their mistress, dashing to the table to do their part. Long strands of acidic silk sparkled across Ruben. The HOA shoved past me, no longer even the least bit interested in what I did. In a mad scramble, they descended on Ruben. Alex backed into a corner, shaking as tears ran mascara down her cheeks. Jordan coughed harshly on the floor as Bow Tie finally left him. I limped away from the heap of bodies and webs forming in front of me.

Elaine stripped off what was left of her burned clothes as she came around to the table. Carefully, delicately, like she might need them for later, she peeled out of them, revealing a skeletal form wrapped tightly in burns both old and new across her parchment paper skin. I stared deep into her eyes, to avoid anymore fucked up details of naked old ladies, hoping she could feel the level of hate she had forced upon me. She stopped to meet me, in all her bare horror.

"I know we've been hard on you," she whispered softly, like she actually cared. "Run, if you'd like. If you can."

She turned back to the table, ready to take her place.

"She'll enjoy the chase."

6-6-06

The masses piled on until there was no more room, their roars and croaks and moans drowning us. Ruben was gone, lost under their numbers. They spewed their cables and piles all over each other. Webs rolled from their mouths, binding them to each other and breaking their bodies down. A writhing mass of flesh and web grew as they crawled together and took their places in the madness. Elaine climbed to the top, pulling their webs over her like a shawl. Skin bubbled and sizzled as their unending stream spewed and snared. The stink of melting bodies clouded the room and smoke choked the air. The floorboards under them cracked and curled.

Limping over to my only surviving friends, we couldn't help but watch. Alex sobbed breathlessly, tucked into her elbow to filter the fumes. Jordan's knuckles cracked and his fists clenched as he got up, a deep purple bruise ringing his neck. Bone stabbed through the fleshy mound as the HOA and their eight-legged kin melted into each other. A great mound of bodies, liquifying like candle wax.

Elaine basked in the glory of all she had created, sinking into their depths as web encased them. Limbs detached and rolled. Remainders of faces dripped and oozed. The legion of spiders scuttled over them, working as quickly as they could in harmony with the torrent of webs the former humans were leaking. Holes and patches filled in, hiding them all from view as a heavy dome formed over them. It surged against the floor, the shell of it puffing and expanding like the gases inside were inflating a nightmare balloon. Slowly, it reached up to the ceiling. Stopping only once it hit the lights, burning into the bulbs and shattering them to shards. The floorboards gave out and the dome of web sunk, eating into the earth. Rumbling and quaking, the entire mass retreated until only its top curvature was visible.

The community room calmed. Smoke hung heavily around us. The orb of web and bodies sat calmly in the center of the room, throbbing and pulsating like a beating heart. Its contents swirled and sloshed like turning cement. And somewhere in there, lost amongst the gore, was Ruben.

GOING UNDER

I don't know how long we stood there in silence, staring at the pulsing orb of web burned into the ground. A sick hum ran through it like a passing current, stirring the vile soup inside. The sheen of its hulking form slowly faded with the sun as it dipped below the cliff, drying to a hardened shell. The screen over the window and plug filling the door followed suit. Losing their luster, losing their life, hardening to the purely defensive.

Alex held it in as long as she could. She turned away from us and blasted puke all over the filthy floor.

"What the fuck?" Jordan hissed.

"Sorry," Alex groaned, a bit offended.

"No, not you," he said softly, eyes not breaking from the dome.

"Ruben." My skin went icy at the thought of what was happening to him in there.

The reality of it settled over us like an axe blade, the gap in our ranks apparent.

"What . . . what did they do to him?" Alex whimpered, shock wiping her thoughts clear.

We all knew a sacrifice when we saw one. Between the long list of Epic Last Stands and creatures that demanded blood payments, a "young heart" had only one clear meaning.

"He was trying to save me," Jordan choked.

"And me," she added guiltily.

"Because I couldn't," I seethed, tallying up Elaine's final tab.

No one spoke up in argument. We sat with it for a moment, festering in our shares of the blame.

"Dude, the fact that you're even still alive," Alex finally let me off the hook.

"Seriously!" Jordan shouted out of nowhere. "How are you not dead?"

His guess was as good as mine. There was only one thing I could honestly think to attribute it to.

"There was a raccoon, I guess."

"He's . . ." Alex pointed at the dome, needing to hear what she already knew.

"Yeah," I confirmed, my eyes darkening under a scowl.

Staring at the hardening, humming mass on the floor, its contents swirling and splashing under the surface, it became remarkably apparent that the perfect punching bag for every awful thing I was feeling and every terrible thing I was thinking was sitting right in front of me. Even if my friend was somewhere inside it.

"I don't think its gonna stay that way." I took off across the room, dragging my leg behind me.

"What do you mean?" Alex followed me.

"They weren't really that alive to begin with!"

"We're on the clock?" Jordan fell in behind us.

"They started small, and then they got *way* bigger," I explained.

The stacks of chairs were scattered around their corner and thoroughly mangled. I grabbed the first one I could get my hands on.

"What do we do?" Alex asked.

"She said she'd enjoy chasing us down," I growled grimly on my way back toward the lectern.

"And eating us," Jordan felt the need to add.

"I was choosing to forget about that," Alex winced.

"It's not gonna happen." I landed in front of the dome. "She doesn't get to take anything else."

I swung the chair up, its folded legs stabbing down like blunt daggers. With a roar, I swung it into the shell of webs. Metal clanged through my hands and the chair shot free like I was trying to chip through solid sidewalk. Its legs bent in and feet turned. Not to be deterred, and ignoring the pain stabbing through my palms, I picked it up and tried again. The flat back of the chair came down, glancing off the shell. Divots dug into the dried webs, shallow grooves of indifference to my attacks. I swung the chair back behind me and launched it across the room with a frustrated bark. It spun like a frisbee and bounced off the screen sealing the window, cutting a groove into it like drywall and ricocheting to the floor. Not as thick, not as hard, not as solid, if only by a little.

"That's one idea," Jordan surveyed the barely damaged dome as I went back behind the lectern.

Elaine's journal still sat open. The pages exposed were nothing I hadn't seen before, but there were just as many that I knew would be a surprise. I snatched the book up and handed it off to Alex as she caught up to me.

"You're smarter than me," I suggested hopefully.

"What am I looking for?" Her eyebrow cocked.

"Fuck if I know, dude! Anything useful."

Jordan crossed to the door as I shuffled back to the chairs. Perfectly encased in hardened web, the knob was melted flat. One final middle finger from the HOA on their way out.

"I gotta get back to the car," he said in a determined spark of inspiration.

"Would it even run still?" I asked as I grabbed another crumpled seat.

"Only one way to find out!"

"You guys go. Get back down the hill and find help."

As much as I didn't want to lose them too, they had just as much reason to stay as I did. Well, maybe not as much, but pretty close. I wasn't gonna try to talk them out of it any harder than that. The option was there, if they chose to take it. A clear emergency exit, should they need or want it.

"Fuck you!" Alex scoffed. "We're staying!"

"We didn't start this but we sure as *fuck* are gonna end it!" Jordan added.

I joined him at the door and handed him the chair.

"Start with this," I offered.

"Um . . ." He stared at the matte web dubiously.

"You're stronger than me," I shrugged.

We locked eyes as Alex came up next to us. In our shared looks, in our combined grief, something sparked. Fatal voltage crackled and arced between us. A moment of vengeful silence before we left him behind. We looked back at the dome one more time.

"We won't let him down," Jordan said.

"Damned if we do!" I had already come to terms with that possibility. The sooner they did, the better.

"No pressure," Alex sighed.

I shuffled over to the scattered and strewn chairs with my eyes on the window. Alex caught on and chased after me. We each took up a chair and went to work, hacking and swinging into the wall of web. Shallow gouges spilled dust at our feet. Fresh air refused to replace the stink of chemicals and burnt hair hazing the community room. The dome gurgled as we pounded away, like it had a drain in the bottom of it. Wide cracks spread out from it, shooting across the floor and venting smoke up into the air.

Jordan fit the pieces together into something only the MTV daredevils would've thought to try. He leveled the folded chair with his head, holding it up to himself like a cheap aluminum buckler. In a powerful sprint that would've broken the hearts of every football coach in Buena Vista, he let out one long, determined cry and barreled to the window. Diving over the frame, he pressed his shoulder into the chair and blasted through into the street like a wrecking ball. A storm of dust and dried webs crumbled to the floor around us.

Alex waved the air around her as she coughed. I stared through the broken window, waiting.

"I'm good!" he groaned as he waved from the ground.

"Oh, Jesus," she sighed, relieved.

Jordan sprang up from the ground like all he had done was eat shit on his dirt bike. Alex tossed her chair and stepped through, over the edge of the empty frame, careful to avoid the hunks of web or barbs of glass still hanging on. It wasn't gonna be that easy on my end. Getting my busted leg up and over the frame without falling through wasn't an option, and she could tell. Alex wrapped an arm over me from the other side as I swung my useless foot over. Holding me up, she held me steady as I got the other through and tucked under my arm for support.

"What'd you break?"

"What didn't I break?" I grunted. "Ankle, I think."

The Bluffs were prematurely dark, the plummeting sun fighting for life under heavy clouds. Alex half-carried me back into the street as Jordan stormed ahead. On edge, he checked every direction for attackers that weren't coming. Leering into the broken, empty windows, scanning every yard and dark corner. I pointed to the front yard of the collapsed house. Another scooter still sat on its side, sunken into the tire grooves the Caddy had left. Alex and I worked our way over to it as Jordan stood sentry in the street.

Once it was righted, I lowered myself down on the handlebars, making a point to check that the directional arrow was pointing the right way. Halfway to Rabbit, I dialed the speed all the way up and we started off again. Alex scanned the journal as I whipped myself down to the street, and our sad parade carried on.

At the fountain, Jordan broke off.

"I'll be—" He stopped himself from finishing the thought.

We knew what he was getting at, but I clenched all the same, hoping he wouldn't say it. Jordan's bloody forehead crumpled while he racked his brain looking for anything he could say that wouldn't tempt the Horror Gods.

"I'm gonna—" he tried again.

"Nuh-uh!" Alex jumped in. "Dude, hell no! I can think of at least a gillion movies where the person that says and does what you're thinking of saying and doing dies like thirty seconds later!"

"She's not wrong," I seconded.

"Yep," he conceded. "You're right. You're right!"

"Got a better idea." I pressed forward.

Jerking the handlebars all the way to the side, I shot for the shed as Alex chased after me, open journal in hand. Jordan fell in behind her, long-ass legs catching up in no time flat. The doors were open, pulled wide on their track. Darkness smothered the interior. Rolling the scooter right to the edge of the door, I clicked the little headlight switch and hoped for the best. A weak beam flickered through the melted and cracked plastic lens into the shed.

Inside, webs hung lazily from the lawnmowers and the ceiling. Blood smeared and scratched across the floor, littered with patches of fur and flesh. It would've been harrowing if it wasn't so damn depressing. Little guy fought like hell before the spiders cleared out, leaving only strands and gore in their wake. Every last one of them had to have joined the perverse dog pile in the community room. All hands, legs and pincers on deck.

The scooter wouldn't make it over the track, though I thought about trying. I pushed off of it with a groan and shuffled into the shed, careful not to step on any reminders of the cost that came with trying to help me. Jordan followed me in, but stayed back at the corner while I hobbled over to the metal shelves. Alex came around and through the door, moving to use the light to try and decipher the glyphs and ravings in the journal.

"Oh god," she gagged at the carnage on the floor.

"Shoulda seen him," I said reverently. "Little dude went out in a blaze of glory."

"Obviously!" Jordan added.

"Who?" she asked like she didn't really want the answer.

"The raccoon."

Neither of them knew what else to say to that any better than I would've. Alex stared at the floor, and Jordan took interest in the ceiling as their understanding of the world fell even further into question.

"You're not dead, by the way," I broke it to them as I started checking the inventory. "Trust me. Thought about that already."

I knew what I was after, but double-checking for anything else that might be useful or entertaining couldn't have hurt.

"I was starting to wonder," Alex choked. "None of this feels like I imagined it would."

"No." I shook my head. "It doesn't."

We'd pictured ourselves in these movies millions of times before. Put ourselves in the fight between good and evil and talked up our survival abilities. Alex hypothesized that Jason could be put down for good if he was soaked in a concrete block after death or dropped into an active volcano. Jordan had a working theory that vampiric mind control didn't work if you wore mirrored sunglasses. I had once looked up lucid dreaming in a quest to build an acceptable defense against the Dream Demon. And Ruben was the first to suggest that the mall or a Walmart would've been the worst place to try and hold up in the event of zombies, since everyone and their mothers would've had that same idea.

"They're gonna feel so fake now!" Jordan realized in shock and horror.

I hadn't thought of that.

"Oh god, you're right." I clunked my head against the shelf holding me up.

More than that, watching anything even remotely horrific was bound to evoke a host of memories I didn't want. And the ghost of the friend that could no longer watch with me.

I added it to Elaine's tab as I started pulling down the gas cans.

"What are we gonna do?" Alex asked.

"Barbecue," I said, tying my hardest to channel Bruce or Big Red.

"Hell yeah." Her spirits rose a fraction of an inch as she looked at the journal's plain covers. "You think there's something in here that might help?"

"The book is always important, right?"

"Holy shit, dude!" she lit up.

"That's what I'm saying!"

She looked down at the book with wide eyes and a shaking hand like she finally realized I had handed her a live grenade. Turning back to the scooter's pathetic light and taking a knee in it, she attacked the pages. She flipped through them as her brow tightened and eyes narrowed, giving it all the focus she had.

Jordan crossed to me and helped collect the cans. We pulled them down and clustered them together at the door. Four tall red metal cans, flanked by their smaller plastic counterparts. They felt mostly full, with the exception of a couple that sloshed around a little past half. If that wouldn't get the job done, then I wasn't sure what would. At the very least, it would burn the community room to coal. Anything beyond that was purely vengeful optimism. Even if it did nothing but the bare minimum, it was bound to make me feel a little better. Ending all of that with the crime it allegedly began with.

I pulled myself along to the tool bench as Jordan followed. Looking back at Alex, in the scooter's struggling headlight, I could see the impossible task I had given her. Frustration caved her face in on itself as she tried to decipher the purest of lunatic nonsense. Jordan broke off toward the abandoned nest as I leaned against the bench. Somewhere in the mess of tools and lawn mower parts, there was bound to be something else that could do even a minuscule amount of damage.

There was no situation I could foresee where I wouldn't want a sharp screwdriver in my pocket. I tucked a greasy crosshead into my belt while Jordan surveyed the offerings. Flipping through the parts and clutter, it was a relief to see him just as clueless as I was. He followed my lead and grabbed a flathead, tucking it into his belt, ready to strike if the situation arose or the mood struck.

Contemplating the height, I pressed my back against the bench and thought about hopping up onto it. How good it would feel to take all the weight off my battered leg. Getting up was one issue. Getting back down was something else entirely. If the option and space to lie down presented themselves, I don't know if I ever would've gotten back up again. Even as quiet rage surged through me, I still hadn't slept in fucking forever. Passing out on the garage floor didn't really count for much.

In the dark microsecond of every blink, Pop-Pop's face flashed in front of me. That soft smile of constant contentment that I didn't wanna lose to the decade's worth of therapy lurking in my memory. Ruben joined him. His eyes full of doubt and pain, looking to me like I had the explanation that would make it all okay as he bled onto the ping-pong table and the spider burrowed into his skull.

The wood of the bench creaked as I gripped it tighter. The collection of lawnmowers stared back at me, demanding to be used somewhere, somehow. If they were riding mowers, I would've been all over them. Pushing that many back across the rings to the community room was more than I could ask them to do, though, and definitely more than I was capable of. Six mowers, only two kids that were any kind of physically useful, it wasn't gonna happen. As much fun as it would've been running over the dome with them and then lighting the whole thing on fire.

"Jesus," Alex sighed.

"What now?" I shot up, on guard.

"Nothing! This is just like trying to read through one of the Courtneys' notebooks. It's all just half-sentences and fucking doodles! Like if there's a page in here about how great Chad Michael Murray's butt is, I wouldn't be surprised."

A soft laugh exhaled out of me, and Jordan rolled his eyes. A silver lining if I've ever seen one. Win or lose, the odds that any of us would have to deal with the Courtneys, Ambers, or Georgies ever again were remarkably low. In between blinks, another face joined the rotation. Jagged and burned, eyes wild but confidently deranged.

"She's no different from them," I mumbled.

"Who?" Alex wasn't following.

"Elaine!"

"The bitchy lady with the little hammer thing?" Jordan double-checked.

"Yes! She's the same as those assholes back home! She hates us on face value! Our existence is some big fucking offense to her!"

"Is that what she's after?" Alex angled the book to get more light on it, like that would help reveal its secrets.

"I don't think it's just us," I said, connecting the few dots we had.

Her eyes squinted at the pages.

"She kept talking about the greater good and the HOA's purpose and all that shit," I kept going. "I think she wants this to spread everywhere!"

"Cool!" Jordan snarked. "Can she start with my parents? They're gonna lose it when they find out about the car."

"She called her the Cleanser!" I remembered in a flash. "Aranea the Cleanser!"

"That makes sense!" Alex pointed to the page. "It sounds like Aranea is like some sorta demon or goddess. If you want to rule the world and make it do whatever you want . . ."

"You start an HOA," I confirmed grimly.

How long had Elaine been cooking this up? Sea Breeze Bluffs was a pyramid scheme, or a Ponzi, I don't really know the difference. But that had to have been her game plan for years before I got there. The free reverse mortgage generation were the exact type of suckers she would've needed. Mee-Moo included. Mee-Moo especially!

"Oh, here we go!" Alex proclaimed.

She turned the journal around so I could see what she found. Not far from where I had stopped was a crude drawing of what I'm guessing was meant to be Earth. A planet in space, with a giant spider perched on top of it. An arrow curved around and pointed to the spider, labeled ME, then hastily scribbled over and rebranded as ARANEA.

"Is there anything in there on how to kill her?" I prodded.

"What, like a spell or something?" Alex scoffed.

"I mean, yeah. Maybe! Or like a thermal exhaust port we could shoot."

"You want to shoot her thermal exhaust port?" Jordan chuckled.

"You know what I mean!"

"No." Alex shook her head firmly. "Nothing like that. Not that I can see."

"She said they needed a young heart," I hypothesized. "Is that a thing?"

Alex tossed the pages back and forth with a shrug.

"She wrote it a bunch." She closed the book and sat against the wall. "It's not like a grimoire, though. It's just like notes."

"Yeah, she wasn't that upset when I stole it."

"None of this feels like the movies, right?" Jordan added. "Why would it play by movie rules?"

"Fuck," I sighed.

"I think this Aranea thing was talking to her," Alex suggested. "And this is how she, like, transcribed it. Young at heart forever. It's all over the last few pages."

"Obsessed much?" Jordan scoffed.

"I think she's trying to say that if the spider lady rises," she continued morbidly, "there might not be any putting her back down again."

"Okay!" I shoved myself off the bench, patience dryer than it ever had been. "Enough dicking around. Let's do this shit before it gets any worse."

The BPRD emblem on my shirt started to feel a little more deliberate.

"Yeah, I've heard all I need to," Jordan agreed, following behind me.

Hobbling back through the lawnmowers, I thought about trying to ride them again. It was still too stupid to attempt, so I let it go as I dragged myself back to the gas cans.

"You sure?" Alex checked. "This doesn't really feel like a plan."

"We light it, and then we haul ass to the car," I pitched. "At the very least, we slow whatever's coming down."

"And if the car won't start?" She wasn't poking holes, just covering our asses.

"Then we see how far we can get," Jordan pushed.

Alex sat with it a moment.

"We don't have anything better, do we?"

"Sure don't!" I smiled at her weakly, nodding to the gas cans as I landed next to them. "Grab a couple?"

"Fuck yeah," she snarled.

We loaded the scooter with as much as we could. One of the smaller cans was balanced half in and half on the broken basket. A tall boy was laid flat across the footboard and another was wedged onto the back. I only needed one hand to steer, so the free one held another small can in my lap as I eased myself onto the seat, using the can at my feet to prop up my leg. Alex stashed the journal in her back pocket and took one of the remaining metal cans while Jordan took the other. I backed the scooter away from the shed, beeping like a teeny-tiny eighteen wheeler until I had enough room to come around. They followed me out, locked and loaded.

The scooter banked away from the shed, and I took off for the fountain, keeping an optimistic eye on the trees and the road. Nothing ran through them or came driving up to us. At the bottom, through the woods and past the curve, a sliver of the town sat under the blanketed sky. I tried to stretch my eyes, hoping for backup headlights and sirens to come drifting past the grocery store. As dark as I would've expected, as quiet as I had gotten used to, the town of Sea Breeze was completely dead. And nobody had the decency to bury it.

Alex and Jordan charged along after me, huffing but otherwise not letting the weight of the cans get to them. I should've slowed down, made it easier to keep my pace. The scooter's top speed wasn't blistering by any standards, but it was just a step faster than the average teenager could walk comfortably. Especially while carrying what I think was around five gallons of gas each. I couldn't do it, though. The very second the community room came back into my line of sight, I learned the definition of hell bent. The rest of the neighborhood blurred into the dark walls of tunnel vision. Mee-Moo and Pop-Pop's collapsed house, the others encircling it, even the cliff and the water shining like a metal plate, they all dissolved until the only thing left in the Bluffs was that god damn community room.

The scooter screeched to a halt in front of the broken window, looking in on the mass of web ahead of the lectern. Cracks in the floor had multiplied, spreading out to the walls and up them. Pulsing hums intensified, rising and falling, back and forth in a perfectly human rhythm.

"I think I'm gonna puke again," Alex moaned.

"Let's move," Jordan urged.

He flung his payload up and over the edge of the window. Alex dropped hers on the other side while I climbed off the scooter. Starting with the little cans, I tossed mine into the darkness, toward the moaning mound. They clunked and bounced across the floor as Jordan climbed in and Alex helped me over again. I dragged my ass over to the dome as they collected their cans.

"Just anywhere?" she asked, not sure where to start.

Jordan answered for her. He uncapped his first can and started dousing the floor. Gas splashed at his feet as I pulled my screwdriver and fell onto the dome. It came down hard as I swung, chipping into the hardened shell. Forcing myself up onto my good leg, I tried again. A flurry of frenzied stabs bit into its surface, digging a fraction deeper with each strike. Beneath me, the whole thing started to vibrate. A dull, deep rumble shook through my gut. With one last stab, sweat burning into my open eyebrow, the screwdriver broke through.

And the room went silent.

Jordan dropped his empty can and uncapped another, staring at the calm web shell as confused as the rest of us.

The ground started to tremble as proper darkness seeped through the Bluffs. Cracks in the floor hissed with escaping smoke like volcanic vents.

"Oh shit!" Alex cried.

They both switched from pouring to throwing. Puddles of gasoline spread across the room. I pressed myself up and pulled the screwdriver free, its metal shaft crumbling to dust. A smell like rotten eggs wafted from the dime-sized hole. I spun the cap off the first of my gas cans. Angling its mouth to the opening, I dumped the contents as close as I could get.

Gas sloshed and spilled down the curve, the puncture too small to accommodate much. Jordan and Alex dropped their cans, both empty, petrol pooling in the cracks at their feet. They darted to my side, Alex taking up the small can while Jordan grabbed the last tall boy. With reckless abandon and zero concern for just how wet our clothes were getting, we poured.

Tremors rattled out from the webs, spreading across the floor and up our legs. The community room shivered like the whole thing was bound for the waters below. We dropped the gas cans and staggered back, eyes glued to the dome. Shooting out of the screwdriver hole, a crack split down the middle.

Not a dome.

Not a mound.

Not a dog pile.

A cocoon.

An egg, ready to hatch.

"Run," I muttered.

Jordan swooped under me, practically lifting me off the ground as we ran back for the window. Alex fell through with a roll into the street. My foot glided across the soaked floor as he flung me through and leaped over himself. The neighborhood jumped and rattled, its houses shaking and swaying. Alex stared at the cliff, waves hammering below it. The fear in her eyes swelled into tears. The stability of the entire neighborhood was thrown into question in a matter of seconds.

"What do we do?" Jordan asked frantically.

I fell onto the scooter seat as Mee-Moo and Pop-Pop's house collapsed a second time. What was left of the interior blew out in a cloud of dirt and dust, crashing decisively to the ground. The walls of the community room buckled. Plaster and tile shingles shook free, raining down inside.

"Light it!" I finally answered.

Jordan reached into the pocket of his vest. Of course, there was a lighter tucked away in there. I never bothered asking when the whole fire idea occurred to me, but I didn't really have to. He flicked the flame to life as the ground pulled at itself. Looking into the community room and the small lake of gasoline soaking its floor, it was a solid way to flash-fry all the hair from his head and maybe char his eyeballs.

"With what?" he shot back.

Alex pulled the journal from her pocket. Rolling it tightly into a cone, she thrust it at him. He held the wider end of it to the flame like he was lighting the Olympic torch. Thin curls of smoke lifted out of the cover.

"Get on," I pressed Alex.

"Where?" Fair question. There was only one seat, and my lame ass was occupying it.

"Anywhere!"

"I'm not sitting on your lap, dude."

"Literally anywhere! Come on!"

Cracks barked out of the community room. The shell splintered, and the floor's crevices widened. Alex jumped out of her skin and landed on the back of the scooter, wedging her feet on its bulky body below the seat. The leather of the journal wasn't taking the flames, but the pages were. Their edges glowed cherry red as Jordan fanned the lighter against them.

The rumbling and shaking around the Bluffs stopped. All three of us looked in through the window, breath held, jaws clenched. The clock hit zero and time ran out.

A shape like a thick tree branch erupted through the shell. Leathery, lumpy with meat, pale as death, shards of dried web shot out around it. We instinctively ducked as they rocketed out the window and broke into dust in the street. The shape crunched and cracked as it bent at a hard angle and slammed down onto the ground. Tremors shot out of the community room, toppling Jordan. The journal stayed firm in his fist, but the lighter clattered and clacked to the curb. Another jointed stalk plowed through the shell, sending more of it flying out like shrapnel.

He clambered for the lighter, smoking journal in hand. I checked to make sure the scooter was still set to Rabbit, though it didn't feel like it would make much difference. Jordan clapped a hand down and brought the flame back up to the book.

"Just throw it!" Alex shouted.

"It's not fully lit!"

A deep moan like a herd of angry bulls rolled out of the floor. More of the shell shattered, and a face began to appear just under the surface. Eyes black as coal, faceted like disco balls, and just as fucking big, set into a head that had been reworked and stretched well out of proportion, like silly putty over a comic strip.

"We gotta go!" I screamed.

A lick of flame finally curled up the journal's edge. Good enough, Jordan tossed it inside. We watched as it spiraled into the dark of the community room. An orange glow trailed thin curls of smoke toward the massive form birthing itself out of the ground. The creature responded. A thick limb snapped up, batting the journal back at us. It hit right above the window frame as its weak flame broke into dying embers and fluttered back down to the floor.

"Oh god," Alex heaved.

"This ain't done yet." Jordan climbed on the back of the scooter next to her. "Get us to the car."

A scrap of burnt paper floated across the community room, its edges still glowing red. A third fleshy appendage shot out of the floor, bending sharply and coming down with a boom. Then a fourth. And a fifth. A sixth. The scrap touched down as the last of its light burned.

FWOOSH!

Unbearable heat belched out at us as a torrent of flames engulfed the community room. Good enough for me. The throttle cranked forward, and the scooter lurched with it. Their extra weight on the back whipped it into a wheelie as Alex screamed, holding on to the seat like it was the last lifeboat off the Titanic. I leaned forward and brought us back down. The scooter screeched, its motor straining under our collective weight as it took off down the street.

A heavy groan like a low bass note through a mountainous subwoofer spread across the Bluffs. It punched straight through our guts, reaching for the trees. I wasn't anywhere near brave enough to look back at what was causing it, but Jordan was.

"FASTER! FASTER! FASTER!" He thrust himself against the seat like that was gonna help.

Alex's tears dripped onto my shoulder as she leaned forward. Behind us, the community room blasted apart. Its ceiling and roof shot out over the neighborhood and into the pool, its walls knocked the gate into the street on either side like they were rigged to detonate, raining burning debris down. The fountain and the dead Caddy zoomed in ahead of us.

"Does that still run?" Jordan asked, pointing to the car propped up on the fountain like a display piece.

"We don't have time to find out!" I shot back over my shoulder.

"It's better than this!" Alex yelled at the scooter.

Not even the taillights were glowing off it anymore. Even if it did, by some miracle, start again, dislodging it from the fountain was only gonna burn up what few dwindling seconds we had. The Plymouth waiting for us on the edge of town wasn't any more promising, but the distance between us and the creature forming in the crackling ruins of the community room was.

As we closed in on the drop to the gate, I risked a look back. Over Jordan's shoulder, I could see her. In no great detail, but in shape and size. The dark silhouette of a mammoth spider, rising up through flame and smoke. In a flash, it launched itself up, high over the street, and came crashing back down with all the grace and savagery of a jet with no engines. A colossal boom sent debris and rubble flying as it smashed through what was left of Mee-Moo and Pop-Pop's house.

It's her . . .

"Aranea," I whispered breathlessly.

If I had any fluids left in me, I'm almost positive I would've released them down my leg. My internal temperature dropped into the negative. The handlebars quivered in my hands, zagging and wobbling the scooter across the road.

"Steady!" Alex cried.

"Do I need to drive?" Jordan asked, half-serious.

"Sorry!"

I gripped tighter, trying to will my hands to calm themselves as my heart jackhammered against my ribs, hoping they wouldn't make the same mistake I did.

The road dropped, and the scooter shot to the gate like a bullet. Wind stung at our faces as we flew down the hill. For the first time, I wondered if the scooter had any actual brakes, or if it was all in the throttle. Not the time to figure it out, I let it roll through the ruined fortification like a landslide. Alex and Jordan gripped the back of the seat, and the first bank came up faster than I would've liked.

Another furious boom echoed out of the neighborhood behind us, closer than the last. We leaned away from the turn as I cocked the handlebars as far to the side as they could go. Alex clung to the seat like a cat over water. Jordan threw his weight in the right direction and pulled us away from the rail.

Somewhere above us, closing in quick, houses exploded into pieces. And a voice followed it.

Tauntingly playful, deep and gravelly like the earth itself was calling. It filled the vacuum of the Bluffs, violating the air.

"Trooooublemaaaaker!"

ITS NOT A FASHION STATEMENT, ITS A DEATHWISH

The woods rippled like a parade of tanks was barreling through them. Some worse than others, they tilted from their roots and bent on their trunks. A stampede of earthquake shocks rolled down the hill with her scattered steps, like the Bluffs itself were coming after us. Rather than following the bends and curves of the road, Aranea took the express route and cut a straight line to the bottom.

Jordan looked back. Whatever lid he had on his terror flew clean off.

"HOLY FUCKING SHIT!"

Alex turned to see what managed to kick him in the balls so thoroughly. A piercing scream erupted out of her like the high note of an air raid siren. The bulldozer in the trees picked up its pace and a line of destruction banked in our direction.

"Stop! Guys! Shut up!" I snapped over my shoulder.

Easy for me to say, after everything else I had seen in the last couple days. Still, it felt a little dickish.

"Sorry!" I added as they quieted.

"What's the play here, man?" Jordan panted. "We're not gonna outrun it on this!"

He wasn't wrong. I was reminded of that with every branch or trunk that snapped or cracked.

"Working on it! Just try not to scream again!" I was asking the impossible, I know that, but we didn't need to broadcast our position so exactly.

Then again, maybe the situation demanded a little impossible.

We cut down to the roundabout, and the town rose up around us. The path the Plymouth took cut a clear line through a scattered debris field, but I veered the scooter over to the curb and up onto the sidewalk. Hugging close to the storefronts, broken glass crunched under our wheels as we started to slow. The landslide roared down the hill, ready to level the broken little village.

The corner neared, and a red light blinked on the handlebars. My heart dropped through my gut. Even with the throttle jammed all the way forward, the wheels started to slow. The battery finally gave out, and the scooter jolted to a stop, sending Alex and Jordan tumbling over my shoulders.

"Keep going," I pushed them forward as they climbed off me. "Go!"

Neither of them needed to be told twice. Jordan and Alex took off for the end of the block. I slid off the scooter with a groan and they paused, looking back to me while I shambled after them.

"I'll be fine!" I wouldn't.

And they knew it. They both came back, each taking a side and pulling me with them.

"We never leave a man behind!" Jordan tried his best to sound battle-hardened.

One final boom launched out of the hill. In the dim light of the rising moon, a shadow stretched from one side of the street to the other, filling it. Legs stretched and a swollen body descended as we wrapped around the corner. With a thundering crash, a plume of dust and wreckage flew from the remains of the roundabout.

Down the row, Tools & Lumber sat wide open, its door missing. One of many that didn't survive the flood of bodies that raged through Sea Breeze in pursuit of me.

"In there!" I urged.

Limping between them, I tried to keep up as they guided me down to the broken hardware store. The street shook as massive legs thundered across it. The inside of the store looked like it had been flipped upside down, then back again. Shelves were on their sides across the floor. Tools and their contraband covered every available inch around them. Broken lumber and splintered boards jutted out from the mess like defensive measures.

"The back door," I nodded to it. "I'll be good."

"You sure?" Alex checked.

"Right behind you."

The scooter flew down the street behind us. Tumbling and crashing into a mangled ball as it bounced past at a speed it never would've been able to achieve on its own. Steps pounded after us like incoming explosions. Alex and Jordan rushed around the clutter on the floor. My leg wobbled under me as I followed. Pins and needles shot through it and stabbed up my ankle like my foot had fallen asleep. I took a step, and it refused to pivot enough to lift. Dragging it after them, I think it caught on absolutely everything it possibly could, kicking hammers and sliding boxes and heavy plastic cases in my wake.

Jordan threw open the door and ran through as the steps rumbled closer. Alex followed him out. He sprinted across the garden section, lunging around piles of soil and standing pots, crashing into the back fence. Alex whipped around to me with horror hollowing her face. They could make it over, yeah. But I sure as shit wouldn't, even with their help.

"Under them!" I pointed to the tables of potted plants as I staggered to the door.

Alex dove under the side while Jordan slid in from the far end. They huddled together in the dark, balled up tightly. The walls of the store rocked as Aranea closed in. As softly and quietly as I could, I guided the door back as the hulking shape of a spider came into the open storefront. If it wasn't for the others, already hidden under the potted plants, shielded by flowers and hidden by supplies, I don't think I ever would've let go of the knob.

My fingers unstuck, greased in sweat and trembling violently. I turned my back to the door, and every nerve up and down my spine lit up like a circuit breaker, waiting for something to follow me through. Limping to the table, I tried to lower myself. No good with one working leg, I smacked down to the floor. My palms slapped softly against the ground. The entire building jolted, on the verge of total collapse as Aranea climbed up to the roof. Jordan held out a waiting hand. I scrambled to the table, and his wrist clamped down on mine, pulling me the rest of the way.

Thunder rumbled up and over the building. Her faint shadow fell into the open square, casting deeper darkness as she crept over the top, perched on the edge of the building. Against the sky, her body slunk, long and bloated as she scuttled around the side. Her voice hissed through the air, no less deep than it had been on the hill, but softer.

"Trooooooublemaaaaaker . . ." Like a secret she was sharing with the entirety of the Bluffs. "Where. Are. *You?*"

Alex clutched a hand over her mouth to snuff the whimper quivering her chin. Jordan shut his eyes tight and cocked his head away like he thought that'd make her go away. I stared up at the underside of the table, waiting for it to rip away from us or explode into splinters.

Aranea's steps came down with a heavy crash, raining down bits of the building. The roof groaned, straining to hold her up as she moved over and around us. The shadow passed as the back side of Tools & Lumber cracked under her. She held for a moment, staring out at the tree line beyond the fence, waiting for any sign of movement. When none presented themselves, she moved over, stretching across the gap and stalking down the row of stores.

Alex and Jordan looked to me, waiting for the signal to move again, the all-clear that the threat had moved far enough away. I waited longer than I needed to. An abundance of caution and absence of will. Seismic steps trailed off toward the stoplight. Like a true apex predator, she kept watch over every prospective path to freedom, three insignificant little insects caught in her web.

I tapped Jordan's shoulder and crawled out from the table. He and Alex followed, shuffling quietly across the floor. Pulling myself up on the door handle, I eased it open, and we slunk back into the ruins of the store.

"What do we do?" her voice cracked.

"How do we get past *that*?" Jordan stressed.

BOOM!

A small asteroid crashed down into the garden section behind us. The entire building jumped, and a blast of potting soil flew through the open door. Alex dove clear across the room, flying over to the register before I could stop her.

Jordan dropped to the floor for cover. Turning slowly, I braced for the worst. Pincers the size of my legs stabbed through the wall. With a snap like a bear trap, they ripped the door and its frame free, smashing them to shards.

Jordan shot back up, circular blades for a table saw in his hand like a collection of potentially lethal Frisbees. The shadowed form of the spider retreated a step, her head filling the broken doorway so that all I could see were those horrible, dark mirrored eyes. An uncomfortably human mouth was stretched wide beneath them, but it didn't move as she spoke.

"There you arrrrre . . ."

"DIIIIIIE!" Jordan roared.

The saw blades sailed from his hands like he knew what he was doing, like he had probably done it before. One at a time, they cut a perfect path through the air. The first embedded itself into what was left of the frame, hanging hopelessly in place. The next whizzed high and sailed into the garden section. The third hit its target, clacking uselessly against her disco ball eye.

I scanned the floor for anything useful, anything that might help. A hammer was the best I could come up with. The claw on its back side gave me an idea I really wish I could've resisted. Before I could stop myself, I charged.

"Grady!" Jordan barked.

"No!" Alex shouted.

Falling right into Aranea's waiting pincers, I raised the hammer high and brought it down with everything I had. My shoulder pulled on its socket as the clawed end cracked into her eye. The damage wasn't visible, but it must've done something. Before she could snap me in half, she stumbled back from the wall on thundering feet. A deep moan shot out of her like a shockwave over the remains of the store. Her leg shot through the door, on a mission to punch a hole through my chest. I dropped to the floor as it stabbed over me.

"Run!" I yelled, scrambling away from it.

Alex and Jordan bolted out as the leg probed and clawed into the store. Crawling out of its reach, I pushed myself up and limped after them, my dead leg working harder than I knew it could. Her head came back down into the door, pincers spread wide, as I rejoined my friends in the street. Alex refused to take her glistening saucer eyes off the back of the store as Aranea bit furiously through the wall.

I scanned the row, hammer in hand, for any place that looked like it might be a good idea. Each looked like a death sentence. Solid choices if we wanted to get cornered and probably eaten. Still, we couldn't stay in the street, and we were never in a million years going to make it to the car before she came down on our heads. I spun left, then right. Forward and back.

"Here." I limped off to Tools & Lumber's next door neighbor.

Jordan and Alex fell in behind me as I led the way through a shattered glass door, nothing but a metal frame in the wall. Porcelain crackled under our feet. I hadn't been in that particular store, hadn't even paid much attention to it on the drives and trek through town, but it was immediately apparent that the bulk of Mee-Moo's collection had come from it. Broken ceramic nonsense carpeted the floor.

Next door, a wrecking ball of pincers and rage plowed through the hardware store. I pulled them down to the floor as destruction and havoc shot into the street like a tornado was tearing through. We ducked against the wall, flanking the missing door, as Aranea skittered out into the street.

"*You can't hide.*" Both a warning and a command, it filled the air the same as our heads.

Alex pressed her palms into her ears. Jordan gritted his teeth like the words were driving a needle into his skull. I watched. And listened, hammer tight in my sweaty grip. Creeping and precise, her steps calmed, coming down slowly as she stalked the row of stores. Just as carefully, I ducked my head out to confirm her direction. As tall as the buildings she was skulking between, her bulging form strode confidently away from us, searching.

I ducked back in before she could change her mind and start looking our way. On the opposite side of the street, down toward the middle, I caught a glimpse of the worst fucking store in the whole of Sea Breeze.

"Idea," I whispered to my friends as it sparked.

"What do you got?" Jordan leaned in.

"Do you think you can hit that store"—I pointed Alex down to Sandy Attire—"with this?" The hammer.

She took it from me cautiously, looking at it like she wasn't even sure it really existed. Jordan stared at me, just as confused.

"We send her that way"—I pointed down the street—"and haul ass for the grocery store. From there, I think we can work our way around through the trees."

"Best we got?" she asked.

"Best I can do."

"I got jack shit," Jordan shrugged.

"You don't gotta hit it," I coached her. "Just get it in the ballpark."

"What do you know about ballparks?" She smirked playfully down at me as she stood.

Alex lined up the shot, peering around the corner of the door. She took a soft step out onto the open sidewalk, just enough to give her a better angle. The uneven booms of spider legs crept toward the post office. Her arm cocked low, pulling back behind her. A slow breath to calm and steady herself, Alex locked onto her target. The hammer launched out from under her and streaked up into the air. It flipped, handle over head, in a steady arc across the street. Tumbling effortlessly through the air, it came down not onto Sandy Attire, but something better. The store next to it still had glass in its window. Riddled with cracks, but intact for the most part. Perfect to shatter on contact. The hammer slowed, coming down on the bottom corner. Glass rained into the store, showering the floor and echoing down the street.

Alex darted back inside. Steps rampaged frantically down the row, blasting off like the town was under siege. First up onto the roofs, then across them. Plaster and stucco flurried like snow as Aranea ran overhead. The ceiling buckled and caved with every hammering impact. She came down into the street again in a sharp bank, closing the gap between her and the all-important boutique.

I drove them from our hiding spot the second she was clear of us. With her attention diverted, we snuck out into the street as she dove through the front of Sandy Attire. Her legs spread as she pounced, smashing clean through its face. Jordan ducked low and dashed across the street. Alex pulled me along as we followed, hunched over and hopefully invisible.

Aranea gutted the store from the inside out. Anything that wasn't smashed to atoms under her was kicked and thrown clear like she was trying to burrow through the racks and shelves on her way to our flesh. The block trembled as we landed across the street. Jordan pressed on, choking his sprint just enough to let us keep up. A roar like a wind tunnel bellowed through Sea Breeze. The colossal spider rocketed straight up through the roof, tantrum in full effect. The rest of the store came down with her, a cloud erupting from the ground at our backs as she landed.

The grocery store parking lot was close, but not close enough. There was a quick moment of that quiet stillness I had gotten used to out there. I don't know for sure what she was doing in the ruins of Elaine's personal piggy bank, but I could only imagine Aranea was taking a second to make sure she didn't crush us without realizing. Another crash broke the silence, echoing down the street as she moved on. Brick and wood blew out from the neighboring store, coming closer to us. Its roof sagged before rippling upward on her back. She tore clean through it once her brief inspection was complete, and on to the next, moving down the row, straight for us.

Jordan carried on ahead. I pushed myself into the red as I ran with Alex around me, her hot breath grazing my ear as it raked out. Sweat and tears poured from her face, cutting through the black smudges around her eyes and dripping onto my shoulder. I kept my sights locked on Jordan, following him like a beacon as he scrambled to the corner and the edge of the parking lot.

BOOM!

BOOM!

BOOM!

Rooftops rose and fell in sequence, one after another, her rage dialing up with every empty building she tunneled through. On a path straight for us, the town wavered and buckled. Behind her, buildings fell like a wave of dominoes as her scattered steps rolled after us. Her roar blasted out like a jet engine barreling toward the end of the row.

Jordan cleared it first, darting up the parking lot in an all-out sprint. Powered down, the glass doors weren't gonna open. Shattered, but not enough to step through. Shards and spears clung to their metal frame defiantly. Jordan curled his fingers between their edges and pulled with all his weight. They drifted apart, slowly, uncooperatively, as he strained. Pressing his back into one half, he forced them open and waved us up the parking lot. Collapsing buildings dogged at our heels, gaining too fast. The numbness in my leg spread through my calf like frost creeping up to my knee. Alex moved her arm down to my waist and pulled me across the lot.

As the doors clapped back together and we fell into the darkness of the grocery store, the last building in the row shattered into pieces. Blind with fury, the mass of the spider stormed through. A cry shrieked out of her, somewhere between mournful and bloodthirsty as she kicked her front legs at the sky. Without warning she pounced, launching herself high and coming down again like a meteor onto the post office. It flattened under her, and she was off again, plummeting down the street. Like a piston, she continued with mechanical precision, pulverizing every last structure. One side of the street, then the other, she bounded with no real pattern or plan. Shockwaves ruptured through the town as she rained down on every possible place we could've been hiding. A shadowed behemoth, flattening the HOA's nest egg like a hammer from God.

Trashed food greased the floors. All but a few resolute surviving shelves were knocked to their sides. The refrigerated cases in the back were shattered open, their contents defrosting and spoiling to rancid slime. With a single bound, Jordan hopped over Stache's meat counter and landed with his back to it. Alex followed him, swinging her legs over with ease. I tried, but there was no way I was gonna do it as fluidly as they did. Even able bodied, I still would've eaten shit. My belly dragged and snagged as I pulled myself up. Jordan grabbed my shoulders, pulling me over and down onto them with a grunt. Tangled amongst each other, they pushed as I rolled and collapsed to the floor.

My chest smoldered and burned as I stared up at the white tiled ceiling. The bombardment continued outside, like a sporadic countdown getting closer, then further, then closer again. Each smash and boom ticking off until the final impact. The panels above me trembled and rocked as she came down around the town.

"Where do we go?" Alex asked, her voice shuddering anxiously.

As well as I had acquainted myself with the store, it dawned on me that I had no idea how to get out from where we were. I let the moment sit, scrutinizing and second guessing every thought in my head rather than letting them move us to even deadlier pastures. It didn't sound like she had come down enough times to level what was left. She couldn't have been satisfied with her rampage. But before I could make any decisions, the town outside went quiet.

"Oh, for fuck's sake," I whined.

Tremors surged up the parking lot. Before we could stop him, Jordan was crawling over me to Stache's thin flappy door.

"Loading dock!" he hissed over his shoulder as he crawled through.

No choice but to follow, we scampered after him. On the other side, as Alex pulled me to my feet and the door closed gently behind us, the front of the store came in with atomic force. Glass and metal blasted in. Tree branch legs kicked the fallen shelves from one end of the store to the other and back as the spider continued her frantic search.

"I know you're here, trooooooublemaaaaaker . . ." her voice boomed across the store.

Jordan stood, scanning the dark storage room. Bloody smocks hung from hooks. On one side, a metal door hinted at a meat freezer. A hacked-up butcher's table sat in the middle. Knives sprouted out of its stained pink surface like the hunk of wood was their latest kill. Unlabeled boxes of god only knows what lined the walls. In the back, a steel door with a dead emergency exit sign sat square in the wall.

"Your brother?" I asked, quieter than a whisper under the devastation beyond the meat counter.

"That month he worked at Albertson's. Butchers always have a back delivery door." Jordan nodded to it. Exactly what I figured. "Keep doing what you're doing! I'm gonna go distract her."

"What?" Fresh horror slapped me in the face. "Dude, no!"

"You're gonna get yourself killed," Alex pleaded as she chased him to the door.

"That!" I pointed to her in desperate agreement.

"Nah, I'll be fine!" He grabbed a heavy cleaver from the table, the blade squeaking as it pulled free. "I'll sneak through the woods to the car. When she goes running, you guys haul ass."

I limped over to steal a blade for myself. The one I took from Mee-Moo's kitchen didn't do a whole hell of a lot of good, but holding another made me feel a little less fucked again.

"Shouldn't we go with you?" Alex argued. "Instead of waiting here to get eaten or crushed or whatever?"

Wood splintered and metal twisted as a shelf crashed against the meat counter.

"I'm only gonna slow you down." Wasn't gonna try and kid myself there. If it wasn't for me, they probably would've been long gone by now.

Though, if it wasn't for me, if I hadn't gotten dumbass ideas in my head, they never would've been there in the first place. Was kinda hoping they'd realize that on the mad sprint to the car and get the fuck out while they could.

"Glad you said it," he chuckled down at my leg.

"Come out, come out wherever you arrrrrre . . ."

"Be fast," I implored them both.

"Then what?" she asked Jordan. "You don't even know if the stupid car still runs!"

"It doesn't have to," he grinned.

"Why doesn't it?"

"Holy shit, you're right!" Alex smiled back at him just as deviously as she caught what he was throwing down.

"Why doesn't it have to run?" I know they didn't hear me the first time.

"That idea might not suck ass," she added, her eyes brightening.

I tried not to take offense.

"We'll see you in a minute!" Jordan said as he ran for the door with Alex in tow. "Don't die!"

"Wait, why doesn't—"

They were gone. And I wasn't. Smart on their end, horribly stupid on my own. I tucked back against the wall, next to the thin door and out of sight. My new knife felt heavier in my hand than Mee-Moo's had, but I'm pretty sure that only meant I was getting weaker. The deafening rampage through the fallen shelves and broken cases pressed on as the spider scoured every corner and crevice. There were only so many places outside she could flatten before realizing the obvious, and the same applied in the grocery store. There was a finite number of things to toss and spaces to trample before the backroom became embarrassingly apparent.

"Grady!" a chillingly familiar voice echoed from the other side of the wall. "Grady Henry, you get out here this instant!"

Mee-Moo.

"You better hope I don't find you, troublemaker! You'll be in even bigger trouble when I do!"

Another voice joined in.

"It's okay, bud! We're not mad."

My blood flash-boiled, and the knife in my hand started to twitch.

"Tell ya what," Pop-Pop coaxed sweetly, "come out and we'll let you play with your little friend."

"GRADY!" Ruben wailed. "IT BURNS, GRADY! IT FUCKING BURNS!"

Through my rage, tears began to bubble.

"Why would you let this happen to me?" he sobbed hysterically. "We're supposed to be friends!"

"Is that how you treat your friends?" Elaine jumped in. "I was right about you, wasn't I? Just another degenerate."

"What kind of a boy kills his own grandmother with a frying pan?" Mee-Moo added.

"You didn't even bother trying to save me!" Pop-Pop shouted, actual pain in his voice. "You just hid in the closet and let me die!"

"What was I supposed to do?" I whimpered to myself. "I didn't know."

"He let me die too!" Ruben howled. "I came to rescue him, and he let me die!"

"Look at what you did, troublemaker!" Mee-Moo piled on. "If you had been better, none of this would've ever happened!"

That's where they got me. I could blame myself for a whole host of horrible things, but Elaine would've been a vile, wretched excuse for human life, regardless. If it hadn't been me, they would've dragged somebody else's grandkid down into the muck with them. The HOA would've died for her greater good, taunting me from the other side of the grocery store, without me coming anywhere near them. There was plenty of fault to lay on my head, but not all of it. All that death, all that destruction and misery, it sat on Elaine and the spider like a steaming crown of shit. One hundred residents of the Bluffs, it could've been literally any of their young relatives staring down the monster they made.

But it wasn't. It was me.

I was there for a reason, and Pop-Pop paved the way to it. He knew I'd have only two choices.

Fight or lay down and accept it.

Perverting their voices was a blow too low. The burned emblem on my shirt hugged close to me, in case I needed the extra push. I wanted her dead, but now I needed it. Like an itch I couldn't scratch or a thirst I didn't know how to quench. As I poked an eyeball out again, I wondered just how far I'd get with the butcher's knife. How deep I could dig the blade into her before I got bitten in half or crushed like a cherry tomato. Aranea stood dead center in the wreckage, cocked on her back six legs while the front two teased at the tall ceiling.

"Everything will be okay, bud." Pop-Pop's voice filled the store with no definable source. "You can make it up to me."

Her front legs came pounding back down to the floor. The building rocked, and I fell back to the emergency exit.

"Come out, troublemaker!" Mee-Moo raged.

Another stomp, and the ceiling panels started to drop.

"Take it like a man, Grady!" Ruben sneered. "Don't be a bitch!"

Deep cracks ran through the walls like lightning bolts as she bucked and kicked.

"You can't run!" Elaine taunted.

Legs tore through the wall as I reached the door, punching clean through and whipping through the air. My knife hand landed on the metal latch handle as they ripped back into the store. Her attack raged, striking everything around her with no goal beyond demolition. The cold night swallowed me as I stumbled back outside, and the grocery store began to falter.

The rest of Sea Breeze was in ruins, for the most part. Like the footage they'd show on the news of the villages in Iraq after an indiscriminate carpet bombing. All but a few buildings sat crumpled and cratered to their foundations. Even the little church that I'm pretty sure was only there for appearance's sake was a hollowed hole of its former self.

I looked to the tree line as the ground quaked under me. Broccoli rained down as a produce case shot through the roof, crash landing in the grassy field behind the store. Limping quickly on my frozen foot, I raced over to the trees as the other cases joined it. The entire produce section, it seemed, was hurled through the failing walls. Followed by the checkout stands, ripped clean from the floor and sent sailing into the parking lot.

The walls came apart and the grocery store started to collapse as I snuck back into the woods, looking for the biggest tree I could hide behind. With a sonic boom, she shot herself up, blasting through what was left of the roof. Aranea came back down with a shock, and the grocery store caved around her, its broken walls folding and crumbling. I ducked with my back flat against one of the younger redwoods and held my breath. Waiting. Waiting. Waiting! Trying to will her to move on. The remains of the grocery store kicked and flew across the lot as she shook it all free, sifting through it like a starving dog in search of kibble. Chunks of wall sailed into the trees, disintegrating on impact.

Her roar blasted out behind me, shaking needles and leaves loose from above. Slowly, it died out as she regained her predatory composure. And the steps came closer. One crashing leg at a time, she crept to the tree line. My teeth rattled as I gripped the knife tight in my sweaty palm. No matter what, I wasn't gonna let her take me with nothing to show for it. Even if I had to slice and stab all the way down her gullet, she wasn't gonna get me unscathed. She had earned that much. The steps came right up to the edge of the trees, and the Bluffs started to explode.

High overhead, halfway up the hill, lights popped and fizzled. Trails of smoke hung in the air as fireworks burst. A second volley followed immediately. Higher up, closer to the neighborhood. Areana stomped back to the edge of the parking lot and paused. Facing up the road, she watched the hill as it popped again in bright flashes of blue, and green, and white. A growl rumbled low in her like the earth was about to split as even more detonated directly over her domain.

In a burst of speed and shocks, she dashed out over the town. Straight over the rubble of all that was left. The ground boomed as she launched herself up. Legs spread wide like a reaching hand, she smashed through the trees, clearing almost halfway up the hill with ease and carving out a landing zone on the way down. Her trail ran straight up in a mad sprint, the woods bending and flailing in her wake.

Like a starter pistol was fired over my head, I sprang for the road on the far side of the woods. Every rock and fucking pinecone threatened to roll my unresponsive foot out from under me as I ran in the general direction of where we left the Plymouth. My hopes began to rise, and my mouth salivated at the thought of what else Jordan might've stolen and stowed. As I pulled myself along the trees, I had manage my expectations. As much as I might've wanted it, as well as I could picture their applications and uses, there was no way he got his hands on a box of grenades or anything resembling the Samaritan. Then again . . .

His brother might know a guy.

Huffing and puffing, my breath turned to a dry wheeze as another long volley of fireworks ruptured over the hill. Through the trees, I could see their flashes as they ignited and rocketed up into the sky—the way they were supposed to when a house wasn't blocking their path. A perfect strip of moonlight broke through the clouds and radiated onto the road at the woods' edge. I charged toward the crumpled box of a car, and the two figures huddled beyond it.

"That's enough," Alex urged. "She's gone."

"We need to keep her ass up there!" Jordan argued.

"No, she's right," I panted as I staggered out from the trees.

"GRADY!" they shouted in unison.

Their voices rang out almost as loudly as the fireworks. I winced, my head retreating down into my shoulders like a turtle into its shell.

"Quiet!" I hissed as I landed next to the car. "She's not deaf."

I leaned against the side of the broken Plymouth, head hung between my arms, trying to suck in as much air as my fucked lungs could handle. Sweat dripped off me into the dirt, mingling and mixing with whatever fluids had leaked out of the car. The hood was folded back on itself. The windshield was gone. The back passenger corner was caved in, and the bumper sat on the opposite side of the road.

"We heard the store go down," Alex started as she came around to me.

"Yeah," I heaved. "I got out right before it did."

"Thank fucking god," Jordan sighed from the open trunk.

With one hand to stabilize me on the roof of the car, I limped my way over to them.

"How much did you bring?"

"Dude." Jordan smirked deviously.

He took a step back, gesturing to the open trunk like one of those game show ladies showing off a prize package as I came around. Inside it was the entirety of his brother's bedroom doomsday collection. The remaining fireworks, road flares, his machete, katana and Bowie knife, survival pack, military rations, and a plastic bag full of every lighter he could find in his house. Jordan packed like he was planning on storming the gates of Hell. Which I guess he kinda did.

"Holy shit." A bit of drool rolled out of my mouth as I stared at the smorgasbord he brought with him.

My mind was fixed. Centered darkly on a single solitary objective. I didn't care what happened to me, as long as it happened to her too.

"Stay here," I ordered as I grabbed the survival pack and started loading it up.

Any more blood on my hands and I probably would've lost track of who it came from.

"Are you out of your god damn mind?" Alex insisted as she came around to us.

"Seriously, last chance!" I told them gravely. "I need to do this. I know you guys wanna help, but— "

"I wanna watch that bitch choke on her own fucking blood!" Alex snarled.

"Holy shit," Jordan gawked at her before snapping back to me. "Deal with it, man. We gotta do this too."

"Fine," I grunted as I stuffed the pack. "I tried."

Firecrackers, bottle rockets, mortars, the road flares, as many and as much as his brother's bag could handle. A fresh lighter was dropped into the pocket. Jordan grabbed the katana. Alex took the Bowie knife, leaving the machete for me. I tossed the butcher blade to the side of the road and traded it out.

Under the pilfered collection, our masks sat flat on the carpeted floor of the trunk. Jason's dark, hollow eyes stared up at me, demanding retribution as badly as I wanted it. Orlok laid next to him, waiting for a host that wasn't coming. Without a second thought or even a hint of hesitation, I grabbed the hockey mask and pulled it down over my face.

"Hell yeah!" Jordan jumped, fist pumping. "We're doing this shit!"

He grabbed the Miner's reflective goggles and pulled them on. Alex stared at Pennywise, her face curled.

"Ugh, that thing smelled."

"I think that's just your face," Jordan poked.

"Fuck you, dude." She rolled her eyes as she snatched the mask up and pulled it on.

"Did you see if it still runs?" I nodded to the car. Ramming it up Aranea's giant ass seemed like a killer place to start.

Jordan went around to the driver's door as I slung the pack over my shoulders and gripped the machete.

"The headlights were on when we got here, but it wasn't making any sounds or nothin'."

In the distance, back on the hill, quakes raged. A howl of absolute betrayal echoed out from the top, shooting down to us and blowing through the trees like a hot breeze.

"Let's figure that out sooner rather than later," Alex stressed.

"Agreed," I seconded, taking a step back onto the road, a bloodthirsty eye on the hill.

The mortars and ashes of spent fireworks sat in a neat pile on the lane line. Alex followed me out as I crossed to them, and Jordan got into the car. With the door open, he gave it a try. The engine squealed and cranked but didn't roll over. The neighborhood rumbled above us. Through the trees surrounding it, a sliver of the spider flashed. A shadow zooming too quickly to discern as she ravaged the Bluffs.

Jordan tried again. The Plymouth coughed and sputtered, but still didn't start.

"God damn it!" he spit.

Thunder boomed from the top of the hill.

Jordan hit it one more time. Something under the hood rattled and jumped like the engine was trying to break free and end its revived suffering. A chill rippled up my back as I watched the hill. The engine whined and whistled.

Silence fell, and the neighborhood settled. I gripped the handle of the machete, greased with palm sweat. Heavier than the knife by a wide margin, it hung from my hand like it belonged there. Like it had sprouted from my arm, right when I needed it.

Trees started to lean and bend, cutting a fresh line down.

"Jordan?" Alex pleaded, not breaking her gaze on the hill.

The car sputtered and choked as he turned the key again. Headlights cut through the trees, but the engine dug its heels in. It kicked stubbornly, drowning in its own fluids.

A shockwave ruptured out from the hill, and a pale flash shot toward the clouds.

"Jordan!" I called as I followed her up. "We gotta—"

With a weak growl, the engine turned over. Black smoke burped from the tailpipe, but I think it would've done that, regardless.

"Hell yeah!" Jordan cheered from the driver's seat, pounding on the steering wheel. "That's what I'm talkin' about! Let's go get this—"

BOOM!

The sky fell and the car disappeared. Dirt kicked up and thick limbs flanked us as we ducked. Aranea laid where the Plymouth was seconds prior, spread out clear across the road and into the woods. Soulless, mirrored eyes locked directly with mine. Powerful legs dragged canyons into the asphalt as she pushed herself up, in all her grim glory. One hundred-something people melted down in an acidic bath, poured into a mold to create something worse than they ever could've hoped to be on their own. Something even older and even more evil, given form in repurposed human flesh. Elaine's face was stretched wide, out of proportion over the spider's head. As were the others. All over her grotesque form, faces screamed in warped and frozen agony. I didn't see Ruben through the fused quilt of skin, but then again, I really didn't want to. Stray hands and feet jutted from her legs, fingers and toes waggling like feelers. Her pincers glistened white in the moonlight, solid bone arcing out of her face.

A spatter of blood like a burst water balloon soaked out from the flattened metal under her. Its dark crimson filled my eyes as my knuckles popped around the trembling machete.

"J . . . Jo . . . Jor . . ." Alex mumbled to herself as hysteria set in, lifting her mask.

With a savage yell, I raised the blade and swung for the spider's front leg. She was too tall for me to hit her ugly fucking face, but it didn't matter. She just needed to hurt. The blade streaked through the air and stopped dead with a wet crunch. Black blood spurted from her leg, flowing down and spilling warmly out of the machete like a vain of burnt coffee. A deep moan bellowed out of her, but it wasn't enough. I ripped the machete free and hacked away like I was chopping through a log.

Alex took the cue, stabbing wildly with a bloodthirsty scream at the leg closest to her. Fuck the mask and fuck the repercussions, Pennywise flew off somewhere down the road as she attacked. Her face was splashed and soaked as the blade buried in and tore out. Our cries and attacks swelled, only a beat out of synch. Alex's eyes grew wild and vicious while my own narrowed, intent and unwavering.

When she had enough, Aranea struck back. Nowhere near cutting through them despite the holes and canyons punched through her legs, she kicked. Alex was there one second and gone the next, disappearing in the blink of an eye. Her scream carried high into the air. Dangling over me, she stuck face down to the spider's leg like she was made of flypaper and velcro. Fixed perfectly in place and gasping for the breath, she came back down with a slam.

I moved a second too late. Turning to limp to Alex, a bloody leg swung and caught me. The side of my face smacked into freezing cold skin and stuck. The machete was still clutched in my fist, but couldn't reach anything useful. Glued to her stalky leg like I was in the middle of hugging it, my head cocked toward Alex. Tears soaked her face, washing the dark blood clean, but there wasn't a trace of sorrow in them. She was fucking pissed. Frustrated. Maybe a little embarrassed.

Or maybe I was just projecting.

Wind howled over us, and marrow rattled from our bones as Aranea ran back through the town. The ruins and remains passed in dark, shapeless blurs. I tried to push against her with my chest and useful leg, but got nowhere. Even with the force of every impact, it wasn't enough to unstick me from her. Could only assume Alex was struggling just as hard. I caught a glimpse of her as the legs passed each other. It looked like she was trying to stab, but it was impossible to tell in the microseconds she was visible before we whipped by in opposite directions.

When she reached what I could only guess was the edge of town, we flew. Aranea leaped straight up into the air. Sea Breeze shrank into crushed miniatures like a toddler tore through a train set. The twinkling coastline sank as we soared, and the hill came up to meet us. I closed my eyes tight against the snapping branches and twigs shooting splintered shrapnel around us as we fell. Cratering into the earth, we landed amongst the trees. In the split second of stillness as Aranea absorbed the impact, I found Alex again. The knife fell from her hand as she jerked and pulled, thrashing like a fish on a hook.

Aranea took off through the trees. They glanced and cracked off her as she ran full bore up the hill, building up speed. In a flash, we flew up again, their tops stabbing at us like a pit waiting to impale. In a long arc, we cleared the top of the steep trek, and the neighborhood grew beneath us. Or what was left of it. She hadn't been any kinder to the retirement community than to the town that fed it. All around the three rings, the neighbors joined Mee-Moo and Pop-Pop, their houses a sampling that ranged from completely toppled to mostly gutted.

Except for one. Just beyond Alex's terrified face, like the time we convinced her that the Orbital Swing at the Buena Vista Fair wasn't *that* scary, Elaine's house sat untouched.

Aranea came in too hot as she landed, stumbling and bouncing up again almost as soon as she made contact with the pavement. Directly in front of the community room, a blast of heat raged out at us as she came down and took off. We didn't launch nearly as high, just enough power to land us at near the edge of the fucking cliff. Whatever hold her legs had released as they came down into the ground, and we fell clean off.

The machete tumbled across hard earth, coming to a rest with its handle teetering over the edge of oblivion as I landed flat on my back. The pack crunched underneath me. Jason's face ripped off at the straps, still stuck to Aranea's leg.

Alex, closer to the drop, scrambled on her palms and heels back to me. Her hair was as frazzled as her eyes, blown by the wind and battered by shock. Her hands landed on my stomach as she scuttled, which apparently scared the shit out of her. As soon as they came down, I grunted and she screamed, the veins in her neck bulging. She snapped her head around to see what she landed on.

"Oh fuck," she gasped when she saw it was just me.

But I was staring straight up.

Aranea hovered over us, pincers spread wide across her bulbous head. Alex exploded in a shriek so loud, so hard, so long that I expected her eyes to shoot from her head and bounce over the cliff like marbles.

I shoved her off me as the pincers came down. She rolled clear, and they crunched into the ground. Their points sliced into the dirt and rock, cutting deep at my sides. Alex crawled away, retreating to a safe distance through the spider's legs.

Elaine's frozen face came down to meet mine, her mouth stretched at odd angles. Bulging eyes reflected the ragged remains of the crimson emblem on my shirt like a dying coal fire. A song started playing in my head after what felt like a lifetime of hearing nothing but doom. As I'd always hoped he would be, Gerard was right there waiting for me, cheering for sweet revenge.

"Just relax, bud," Pop-Pop's voice came out of the beast like she had a direct line to him. "It'll all be over soon."

Elaine's face started to pull. Her mouth spread until its corners split, tearing clear across in a jagged smile from one pincer to the other. Deep black twitched underneath, unrolling and unfolding into long, hooked fangs as wide around as the Caddy's tires. Wriggling tendrils hung between them, quivering and waving, searching for flavor on the air. A final evolution forcing itself through where it could.

I refused to look away as her pincers closed around me and her heavy fangs fell on my shoulders. The tendrils whipped out at me, squirming and wriggling over my face like oversized, over-excited slugs. My face slathered in whatever slime they secreted as Aranea savored me.

With a deafening cry, she retreated, stumbling and limping. Her pincers released, fangs sprang up. She tottered and leaned, dropping down to just one front leg. The other, the one I had hacked into, lay broken and detached on the ground. Alex stood over it, machete held up to her shoulders like a softball bat.

"Let him go, you bitch," she growled.

Racing down to Aranea's back legs, the blade streaked through the air as Alex chopped and hacked. The spider writhed, a stream of black blood running out of her ruined leg. The severed half twitched and thumped on the ground, unaware that it wasn't attached to anything. Alex buried the blade into a back leg on the same side, showering the ground in a fine spray.

"WHY! WON'T! YOU! DIIIIIIE?" She swung furiously as her face grew a tiny bit deranged.

Aranea came around at her, pincers snapping. Faster and more able than me even on my best days, Alex jumped back as the spider lunged at her. The pointed dagger tips of her jaws clacked and gnashed at the air, her fangs high and ready to pierce. I sat up fast, unslinging the pack from my back. The sour scent of what I assumed was gunpowder puffed out as I unzipped it. Inside, the bigger fireworks had been smashed completely open. The mortars, the Roman candles, the bottle rockets, crushed cardboard leaked black sand into the pocket. Even the road flares had caved in on themselves and spilled whatever compounds they contained into the bag. The strands of firecrackers were too small to suffer, though. Folded and squashed, but still usable. Amongst the ridiculously flammable clutter of the pack, I dug the lighter out from somewhere toward the bottom.

Alex kept her distance, backing up to the cliff's edge as the spider limped after her. One leg down, and one on the way out, but still six others at her disposal. Alex countered with the machete, stabbing and swinging up at Aranea's face. Solid bone clacked off the blade as she continued to leap away, waving it in front of her like it would be enough. Gravel fell into the watery void as her heel ground against the cliff, and Alex saw her chance. Aranea raised her remaining front leg, primed to smash her down to the depths below. Alex ducked and dove through, sprinting under her and back to the hind leg she had been working on. Blood poured from it as it trembled under her mammoth weight. Before the spider could strike again, Alex swung wide. In a streak of silver, the blade sliced through, and the leg collapsed into convulsions.

Aranea let out another skull shattering cry as she dropped, rolling onto her back with her head over the edge. Her remaining legs kicked at the air like they were trying to escape the same fate. Alex sprinted to me, the machete dripping a gory trail behind her. If she had been the hero girl in one of our movies, she'd be the one we all ended up with posters and action figures of while Mom said shit like "why can't you like nice girls? What about that Lindsay Lohan?".

"God damn, dude!" I marveled.

"I wanna go home," she panted as she landed next to me.

"Me too."

I opened the pack to show her what we were working with. Aranea's legs continued to kick as revoltingly wet crunches popped out of them. Black nubs erupted from her stumps. Growing and stretching, they forced themselves out. Coarse white hair laid against them, slick with viscera.

The little baby spiders flashed through my head, then their bigger, angrier evolutions. Pop-Pop, Mee-Moo, the swath of webs they trapped them in, all that was left of them after. The buffet Elaine had prepared in the community room. The potluck that was left unfinished.

"She needs to eat," I muttered as Alex pulled me to my feet.

"Tell her to get in line."

"They started small! Then they ate Pop-Pop and got bigger!"

"Oh shit." Her face dropped into her hands like a headache was setting in. "Young at heart forever."

She had that. But was missing that one final tasty ingredient to kick her into high gear.

"She needs to die like *now.*" Before it could get any worse or any grosser.

Her new legs cracked and spurted as they birthed themselves, revealing glimpses of the final stage she was forcing herself to reach. No small consolation, judging by her tormented snarls and wailing howls, it sounded like a major pain in the ass for her.

"Let's do it, then!" Alex raised the machete over her head and lunged forward.

I grabbed her arm and yanked her back.

"Better idea!"

Or at least one that worked the last time I saw it in a movie.

I went to work on the pack. Pulling a strand of firecrackers out just enough to thread its stringy fuse through the zipper. The cherry red payload dangled inside as I locked it between the pack's metal teeth. Aranea's legs shot out with a splat, erect and ready to go. She flipped herself over with a single pounce, eyes locked on me as her fangs and pincers readied. Shaking with adrenaline and furious terror, I started across the cliff to her.

"What are you doing?" Alex shouted after me. "Grady, just throw it!"

It wasn't worth the risk, even if I wanted to. Couldn't take the chance of the pack being knocked down uselessly or kicked over the cliff. I had to make sure it found its mark, personally.

"Hey, ugly!" I yelled at the spider.

Her pincers clacked menacingly in response.

"I'm not a very good shot," I quoted Big Red, mostly to myself. "But the Samaritan here uses *really* big bullets."

"What?" Alex shouted after me. "What the hell are you talking about? What bullets?"

"So, what do you say we work this out nice and peaceful?"

"Grady, stop!"

She didn't get the reference. Which was fine. Just would've been nice to share that moment if it was gonna be the one I went out on. Transmitting the half-demon's calm indifference, I closed in.

Aranea lowered herself to me, pincers wide, fangs high.

"You killed my Pop-Pop," I growled so darkly I think even Georgie might've peed a little. "And my friends."

A sound came out of her like the engine of the Plymouth trying to turn over. Wasn't exactly anything a human could've or would've made, but I knew when I was being laughed at when I heard it. While her eyes were stuck on mine, I raised the lighter to the fuse. A burst of sparkling yellow and white spewed as it caught.

Not taking any chances this time either, her head shot down. I lifted the pack over me like an explosive umbrella and damp darkness took me. Her fangs clamped onto my back, digging in like angry hornet stings as they worked over me.

"Grady!" Alex shrieked.

In up to my chest and gritting through the pain, the thick stench of chemicals and rotten flesh filled her mouth as heavily as the fuse's smoke. My eyes closed tight, I didn't want to see where exactly I was. But curiosity got the better of me. I cracked a peek, just to be sure the pack wasn't about to blow next to my head. Crackling sparks lit the way to somewhere I never want to be again. Her throat pulsed hungrily, slimy and gray. Fresh bile filled my mouth. Not wanting to add any more awful smells to the collection already brewing inside her, I swallowed it back down.

I jammed the pack in as far down the chute as my arm could reach. Not much wiggle room, my payload was only a few inches from my face, burning into her throat. Aranea bucked and coughed, her throat jumping wildly. Muffled through her, I could hear Alex screaming and swinging, back to work with the machete. With my hands free, I dug my nails into the meat of the spider's throat. Deep ribbons tore free under them as she started to gag. The fuse dwindled, inching closer to the zipper and its target. The pack vanished under the cloud of smoke billowing in her long throat.

My feet left the ground as her fangs stabbed into my ass. Aranea lifted, flipping me upside down. The pack slid with me, taking its smoke down with it into regions beyond. Musty and humid, her pincers pushed me deeper as her fangs pressed into my thighs. With a flash like the rising sun and a boom like the broken sound barrier, the pack exploded. A flood of fluids rushed up her throat, and Aranea spat me out.

Covered in an oozing blend of bile and blood, I splashed down to the ground, inches from the cliff's edge. She hacked and spat as she stomped around me, rancid fluid streaming from her mouth in an unending torrent. Aranea swayed and lumbered, throat blasted clean open where it met her abdomen, gray vitals leaking onto the ground in wet mounds.

Alex backed away, machete still raised, a freshly severed spider leg in front of her. To one side, I had nothing but the ocean. On the other was whatever the hell was falling out of the dying spider. Webs like power lines shot from her underside in a wild, slithering tangle like she thought she could use them to patch the hole. Her mouth hung lax, pincers snapping lazily, fangs reaching for life as it flowed out of her. She slammed down on her bleeding belly as her legs fell out from beneath her, landing on the cliff's edge next to me, staring at me with the same vengeful hatred I was beaming into her.

Her weight rolled, and Aranea fell over the side.

On the way down, refusing to go out empty-handed, her newly formed front leg caught me in the gut. I came over the edge with her, and for one horrible second, I was weightless. Reaching and clawing, I grabbed onto the cliff, sharp rock pressing into my arms, on the verge of slicing. A jagged jaw of spiring stone waited at the bottom, stabbing up out of the water and waiting to feed. Aranea tumbled farther and faster, a long rope of web shooting from under her and after me. Missing by inches, it stuck right at my waist, connecting to the rock and holding solid. With a crash that rattled up to me and knocked stones free from the cliff, Aranea swung into the wall.

"Grady!" Alex called as she rushed to the cliff, eyes brimming with tears. "Hang on!"

I tried to pull myself up, but it was no good. Too heavy to do much else, I slid down onto the tips of my fingers. Aranea started to climb weakly, pulling herself up the web. She crept up after me, her legs slow and deliberate, guts trailing down to the water. Alex clamped onto my wrist, pulling as hard as she could but getting about as far as I did.

The thought of letting go crossed my mind. Of pushing off the wall and plummeting to meet her one last time, coming down on Aranea's face like a falling boulder and dropping us both to the water. But it would've been my luck that it wasn't enough, that she would just swallow me whole and keep on climbing. Alex threw herself back against my weight. The spider's pace quickened, if only enough to make me sweat, cutting the distance between us in half.

"Machete!" I yelled up to Alex.

"What?" she called back, confused.

"Give it to me!"

"Right!"

She let go and sprinted back to wherever she had dropped it. My grip on the cliff started to loosen. Below me, pincers clacked sharply. With blood on her tongue and a hollow in her gut only I could fill, Aranea closed in. Stained metal dangled over the edge and Alex returned, passing me the machete by the handle.

My hand darted from the cliff and my fingers wrapped around it. With the last cry my throat could handle, I swung it hard into the rock. A spark chipped off the blade as it cracked against it, and the web snapped.

Still clawing at the air ahead of her, Aranea tried to grab the cliff face she was falling too fast to reach. The stone spikes at the bottom rocketed up to meet her. They pierced straight through as she came down on them with all her seismic weight. Her legs broke out at odd angles, collapsing into the water. Her head splashed, and a pincer snapped off like it was nothing more than a weak branch. Smashed and broken, she quivered and lurched for a freedom that wouldn't come, writhing against the rocks impaling her. Black ink washed into the water. White waves hammered against her and crashed on the rocks. Around the cliff's teeth, at the joints of her legs, through the segments of her long body, she started to break apart. Dark sludge polluted the frothing sea.

For good measure, I dropped the machete. It plunged straight down to the water, splashing through what was left of the spider as the tide devoured her. I had to see it. I had to be sure. I watched, hanging off the cliff, until every last piece of her had been reclaimed. Elaine's grotesquely stretched and torn face sunk under the polluted surface, staring right back up at me like she couldn't believe I actually had the audacity to kill her.

Hands came down on my wrist again, pulling me back. With a heavy groan, I flung my arm up and grabbed the ledge. Alex gritted her teeth and dug in, pulling as hard as she could. She pressed herself on her knees as I curled myself up, arms trembling and ready to give. I pressed my good foot into the wall and pushed. She leaned as far back as she could until I started to rise. When my chest came up, she switched to what was left of my shirt. Hot coals filled my arms, dragging my gut up to the ledge, heart and head set to explode.

Alex clawed over me to the waist of my shorts and pulled me the rest of the way. We rolled over onto our backs a few feet from the drop, shaking and breathless. Any residual energy I had left burned away from me faster than soapy water on Mee-Moo's skillet. Alex exhaled long and slow, like her plug had been pulled and left her deflating, somewhere between laughing and weeping.

"Was that—" she panted. "Was that fucking *Hellboy*?"

"It was." I chuckled with a soft smile, the tatters of my shirt clinging proudly to my chest.

"That movie rules."

"Practical effects," we said at the same time.

In any movie it would've been the moment where we locked into each others' arms and, just so grateful to have survived together, kissed with more passion and tongue than two thirteen year olds should be able to produce as the camera pans up over the ocean and leaves the audience to wonder how much further we went. Our friends and Pop-Pop watching like Force Ghosts from the heavens above, avenged and finally able to rest. But Alex would've kicked my balls out through my throat, so I didn't even bother rolling over. Instead, we laid there staring off into the shifting sky, clouds breaking apart to a deep blue laced with silver stars.

The Bluffs were still, but far from silent. Crickets chirped from the edge of the neighborhood. Owls whooped and trilled in the trees. Wind gently jostled their needles and leaves. And somewhere down the hill, echoing over the flattened town, up through the woods, across the crushed houses and smoldering community room, the sirens finally came.

I spent my fourteenth birthday in the hospital. Exactly what every kid wants when the turn of that perpetual counter is that important. My leg took a couple of surgeries, and my lungs needed constant X-rays and scans. The burns wrinkling my skin needed fresh bandages every couple of hours. A patchwork of stitches held me together, and the scar forming over my eye wasn't going away any time soon. The handcuff linking me to the bed in that dreary-ass eggshell room only came off when the cops realized I couldn't exactly go anywhere in a hurry.

From the moment they showed up, to when they loaded me into an ambulance and Alex into the back of a squad car, to Mom signing the discharge papers and Dad wheeling me out to the Aztek, it had been a nonstop barrage of questions. Our story just didn't land with the uninitiated. In the gun-toting, closed minds of every officer, detective, and special prosecutor that descended upon us, it made perfect sense that a group of kids destroyed the Sea Breeze Bluffs Retirement Community and the town they diligently kept afloat. With no Elaine, no journal and no giant fucking spider corpse to back us up, they had to go with the most logical conclusion. No matter how stupid it was. The story, for them, went that Alex and I somehow managed to kill the entire neighborhood, decimate every house except fucking Elaine's, flatten the town, crush Jordan's parents' car with him inside it, and dispose of every last body all before the sun came up. Before any of it could even be verified, their half-baked logic was plastered across every news report and article in the state.

MURDEROUS SATANIC TEENAGE DEATH CULT
DESTROYS IDYLLIC VILLAGE

6-6-06

SATAN WORSHIPPING TEENAGERS SLAY
RETIREMENT COMMUNITY

My personal favorite was the headline the Buena Vista Herald produced. I still have it folded up somewhere.

"SANTA MADE ME DO IT!" LOCAL KIDS TURN
COLD BLOODED KILLER

The truth of our story didn't help our cause at all. I didn't see her once through that entire process, but I knew Alex had holes in her version of things. She was missing key days and events leading up to everything she saw with her own two eyes. If crime shows taught me one thing, the fact that I was asked to recount it all so many times that it felt like I never got a chance to stop meant they were trying to find the cracks in our presumed lies. The end of the story was the same for us, though, and that's what tripped them up.

Well, that and the fact that they never found anything to prove or disprove a single word we said. The entire town became a crime scene. Road barricades went up, and an army of forensic people swarmed its remains. The only thing they ever found was Mee-Moo, smashed to paste under her own roof. And a skeleton, ground to powder amongst the rubble. Mom was understandably upset. Every time she had to hear me tell the story of how I was attacked and nearly killed more ways and more times than most people would ever think of, she looked at me like she believed me less and less. Dad had no strong feelings one way or the other. All he said was, "Huh. Knew something was off with her."

I've got one thing to thank the HOA for, though, I guess. If it hadn't been for Aranea's path of destruction, the charges might've stuck. Even less than they believed evil spiders caused the whole thing, no one could figure out how we smashed every last building and house to splinters. The psych evaluations began shortly after that decision was made. And the entire ordeal was chalked up to some mild form of mass psychosis. That whatever really happened in the Bluffs was so horrible that our brains independently made up the same story to help us cope, projected through a lens tainted by movies we shouldn't have been watching and music too dark to be appropriate. Living proof of the imagined dangers our particular subculture produced.

Alex was released before me. She came to see me not too long after, as I laid there attached to more machines than was necessary, like I was being used as a battery for my robot overlords. While the official state accusations against us dropped, the court of public opinion had made up its mind.

Her dad already sold their house. At his urging and probably the advice of counsel, she couldn't tell me where they were going. But with no phone to speak of anymore and probably for the foreseeable future, she did promise to get MSN Messenger. All else fails, there was always MySpace.

Neither of us were allowed at Ruben's funeral. And Jordan's family chose to save the money and forgo it entirely. Can't really say I blame them, honestly. There wasn't much to bury. We avoided talking about them when she came to visit, but their names were on the tips of our tongues and bubbling in our eyes the entire time. When it was time to go, Alex came down to the bed and scooped me up into the first hug I had ever seen her give another person. We sobbed into each other's shoulders until her dad kicked in the door, yelling about how she didn't need to add an unplanned pregnancy to the mix. She kept her eyes on me as he dragged her out, the look lingering between us long after she had gone.

It was a week and change before Halloween when my time finally came. When the doctors said I was healed enough to not need to be stared at by people in scrubs twenty-four-seven. Dad pushed me down the sterile halls of the hospital. Mom followed at my side, carrying my fresh crutches and a bag of rattling prescriptions. But not making eye contact.

The ride home wasn't any different. Dad clicked on the radio once or twice, but she turned it off every time without saying a word. I caught her looking at me in the rearview mirror once, but it didn't last. She smiled at me softly, if not a bit terrified, and looked away again like the details of the Aztek were more interesting.

An hour later, we pulled off the freeway. The normal desolate beige of Buena Vista was exactly how I left it. Not sure what I expected, it had only been a few months since I saw it last. It wasn't like the town was gonna overhaul itself and get its collective shit together in that time. As much as I didn't relate to a single god damn thing in that desert before I left, it felt like I was looking at an entirely different race of humans when I came back. Every one of them, from the offramp to the Walmart parking lot, had malicious intent plastered across their faces. Even if they weren't looking at Grady Burton, the Big Bad Granny Killer, as we drove by I could see it on them. Smell it. Practically taste it. A general distaste toward everything that wasn't them and hatred for whatever dared to remind them of that.

They weren't my problem anymore.

Dad hadn't even killed the engine before Mom was out of the car and to the garage door. He shrugged at me in the rearview mirror, with no better explanation. He got my crutches out of the back as the big white roll-up door came down and held them out for me as I shuffled and scooted out of the car, my heavily booted foot clunking against it.

"Hey," he whispered to me with an uneasy smile as I took them. "Just give her time."

I doubted it. But at that age, what doesn't feel like the end of the world?

"If you say so."

Dad pulled me in, locking me to his chest.

"We're glad you're okay," he choked. "Really."

He pushed me back and gripped my shoulders.

"And I always knew there was something up with her!"

"She didn't like you very much either," I chuckled.

Dad grinned as he led me from the car.

"Then I must've been doing something right!"

He held the door open for me as I hopped through into the house. The smell of it alone nearly brought me to my knees. Mom was already in the kitchen, compiling the equipment and supplies she'd need to make dinner. The TV was already on, but it wasn't the regular news broadcast I expected to hear. A *Reba* rerun played instead. Twangy southern drawls yelled about god knows what through the living room. Mom didn't need to hear people talking about us anymore than she already had.

I clacked my way through and over to the stairs.

"We'll get started on Monday," she said as I mounted them, hopping on one foot.

"Yep," I grunted back as I thumped up and away.

My bedroom door was open and waiting at the top. Its walls and floor were completely bare. Mom had threatened to go through it all with a fine-toothed comb, but the investigators beat her to it. Damn near everything I owned sat piled in a precarious mountain on my bed, still sealed in their see-through plastic evidence bags. My desk was cluttered with books, every one of them new and stiff across their thick glossy spines. Algebra II, US History, Biology I, Advanced English. I changed schools, yeah, but they weren't going to have to take me any farther than that desk.

I let the crutches fall to my buried bed as I came down on my chair for the first time in forever. With a sigh, I habitually checked my crowded desk for an iPod that wasn't there. Even my backup earbuds were lost somewhere amongst the collected mess. I could turn my laptop speakers down a bit, though. If it meant hearing my bands outside of my head.

Lost in the pile, I dug my laptop out and tore open the plastic bag. A bright red tamper seal held the screen in place. It barked from the plastic as I ripped it off and rested the laptop on the untouched textbooks. I flipped the screen up and hit the power button, but nothing happened. Perfect black reflected a face I didn't really recognize anymore, my hair shaggy and lifeless against my forehead.

It should've made me queasy, thinking about strange adults going through my hard drive. But I couldn't care less how many of my secret folders they had uncovered. Fan art of Harley Quinn and the Penguin in very compromising positions was nothing compared to what they were hoping to find, and didn't.

Nobody had the decency to plug it into the charger in the time it was gone. More trouble than it was worth, I guess. I tipped the bag over, and the long black cord fell into my hand.

Booted foot out, I lowered myself under the desk in search of my power strip. It sat loose and unplugged in the far corner. Right below its socket, just inside the desk's edge. Not wanting to have to get up, I bent over and reached as best I could. The plug flicked and fumbled up into my hand, and I angled it for home. Spindly, wispy legs crept from the darkness beyond the desk. I dropped the plug, and a daddy long leg crawled out across the wall. Over the socket, it cut a winding path toward the desk's surface, stopping halfway up like it wanted to see what I would do.

Without hesitation, I curled my fist and punched it straight back to Hell.

HIDDEN BONUS TRACK

If you were attracted to this book, and stuck with it this long, some part of you probably recognized something in Grady, Alex, Ruben or Jordan. Dear god, I hope none of you saw yourselves in Mee-Moo or Elaine. A good amount of this book came from my current adult hatred of HOAs. And the rest was largely inspired by my childhood. A grandpa who was always pretty cool, a grandma I don't really have fond memories of. I was that pop culture obsessive weird little fat emo kid who had no friends beyond the other equally weird nerds he clung to like his life depended on it. Shit changes, though, obviously. And like Grady's, those friends are long gone.

My hope is that this book brought you back to that time. That you thought about Little You and your old friends once or twice while you were working your way through the spiders and grumpy old people. I hope the references stirred something, other than nostalgia. That you caught them and thought about revisiting some of those songs or books or movies. That you wondered about old bullies, and had a good laugh about how their lives turned out.

Growing up didn't suck that bad though, did it? We had some fun? Had some laughs? Despite all the bullshit? That's where the real open door of it all sits. If you were Grady or his friends, maybe its time to indulge them again. Maybe its time to embrace the shit you liked as unapologetically as you liked it back then. Don't lose your Grady, I guess is what I'm getting at. You're gonna need him.

Young at heart forever.

Alright! On to the gratitude.

My sisters had to deal with my grandparents for way longer than I did. They deserve a medal of fucking honor for that. Especially when the judgmental era rolled around and Grandma started saying shit like "Why can't you be more like your cousin?! He's 17, already has a kid, *and* a minimum wage job!" without a hint of irony in her voice. Sorry you guys didn't get characters here, but I had enough of them to try to juggle!

Blake, as always and forever, had to listen to the in's and out's of this book more than she would've liked to. But what else is new? She showed up to a first date with a guy who was trying to be a standup comedian, just for him to burn that bridge to coals and give in to a much older obsession. And she kept me around anyway! That's a keeper if I ever saw one. My romantasy fangirl, horror-averse better half sat with a smile while I said shit like "WHAT IF THERE'S SPIDERS THAT CRAWL INTO THEIR EAR HOLES?!" just to then have to contend with images that kept her up at night, but excited the living hell out of me. And for that, I'm grateful. Always.

Patrick is as solid a friend as I could've asked for, even if I never actually commit to any of the plans we try to make. Helps that he digs the same weird-ass things I do. Dude is my gauge for work like this, my target demo. If he thinks an idea is cool, nine times out of ten I run with it. And I floated a lot by him in the early stages of this one! So, if something in this book didn't work for you, blame him. He does improv comedy shows around the LA area, go find him. I can tell you where he works too if you want! Tell him I said "thanks for all the help" while you're at it.

I gotta thank the bands too. My Chemical Romance, HIM, Coheed and Cambria, Linkin Park (RIP Chester, you god damn legend), Sum 41, Evanescence, just as many that didn't end up in the TOC playlist. Each of the songs I picked had a specific purpose as it pertains to the story. Rather they were meant to score the action, or underline the more emotional shit Grady was dealing with. But each and every band referenced is one that meant something truly powerful to me when I was his age, and beyond. Hell, I still listen to My Chem incredibly regularly. So, thank you, boys! You shaped this book probably more than anything else.

Finally, to you, dear reader. Thank you for supporting independent books and independent horror. If you don't want a world totally overrun by whatever the fuck BookTok and the Corporate Overlords decide is cool that week, that's what you gotta do. If you want fresh stories and new voices, that's where you gotta look. Otherwise all we're gonna be left with is the same regurgitated Tropes List and dudes that claim horror-comedy but serve neither. Keep fighting the good fight, you god damn champion.

And fuck AI! You deserve better than that.

We all do.

Adam Cagley

January 2025

July 2025

www.ingramcontent.com/pod-product-compliance
Lightning Source LLC
Chambersburg PA
CBHW030548310726
48979CB00010B/2075/J